MINDFUL SELF DISCIPLINE

LIVING WITH **PURPOSE** AND ACHIEVING YOUR **GOALS** IN A WORLD OF DISTRACTIONS

GIOVANNI DIENSTMANN

Author of *Practical Meditation*

AMARYLLIS

AMARYLLIS

An imprint of Manjul Publishing House Pvt. Ltd.
• C-16, Sector 3, Noida, Uttar Pradesh 201 301 – India
Website: www.manjulindia.com

Registered Office:
• 2nd Floor, Usha Preet Complex, 42 Malviya Nagar, Bhopal 462 003 – India

Distribution Centres:
Ahmedabad, Bengaluru, Chennai, Hyderabad,
Kochi, Kolkata, Mumbai, Noida, Pune

This edition first published in 2025

ISBN 978-93-5543-534-7

Printed and bound in India by Repro India Limited.

CONTENTS

ACKNOWLEDGEMENTS

Special thanks and acknowledgements:

To my wife, Sepide Tajima, for all the support in this journey—from her insightful feedback on the early drafts to giving me advice on the book cover to taking great care of our little one so I could focus on this project for months.

To the several readers and meditation students who gave me feedback on the ideas, exercises and designs of this book.

To my coaching clients, who made me realize just how vital and transformational self-discipline really is.

To a publisher, who must remain unnamed, who contacted me in mid-2019 asking me to write a book on self-discipline for them. That project didn't happen, but the seed was planted in my mind.

To all my haters, doubters and critics, for reminding me to be a light unto myself and stand for what I believe.

To all the yogis and meditation masters, who inspired me to follow the highest and finest disciplines, and shaped who I am.

To my spiritual teacher, whose name I will keep private, for encouraging me in this process and assuring me of its success.

FOREWORD

ROY F. BAUMEISTER

Self-discipline is one of the most important and valuable traits to cultivate. In this wise and wonderful book, Giovanni Dienstmann brings together his extensive knowledge of ancient spiritual traditions with an impressive mastery of modern psychological research. If you recognize that your life would be better off if you improved your self-discipline—something that is true for the vast majority of us—here is a clear, well-written, well-informed guide to how to make that improvement happen.

Self-discipline is often used as a synonym for self-control, and other times it refers to a big part but not all of self-control. Regardless, the two are strongly connected. I bring this up because in the psychology research literature, there is much more discussion of self-control than self-discipline. Even so, much of that research is fairly recent.

To put the work in perspective, we can ask, what traits make for success in life? I started my career with a heavy interest in self-esteem. Like many colleagues, I thought that many people were held back by a lack of self-esteem. We hoped that raising people's self-esteem would lead to all sorts of benefits. Some people still believe that, but the accumulation of data was not kind. Self-esteem seems more a result than a cause, its benefits are few and small, and efforts to raise self-esteem did not produce broad improvements.

When I tried to size up what psychologists really found to be the most important traits, only two really had ample support: intelligence and self-control. Intelligent people are more successful in their careers than other people. And not just careers like being a professor or scientist. Intelligence seems to improve performance in just about every career that has been studied, including waiter/waitress, janitor, repair person, etc.

Self-control came along later, at least in the context of psychology research.

But in a short time it has amassed a truly impressive record of benefits. Many of these are documented in my book *Willpower: Rediscovering the Greatest Human Strength* (with John Tierney). People with good self-control are more successful than other people in school and at work. They earn more money. They have fewer psychological problems and are less prone to smoking, alcoholism, and other addictions. They commit fewer crimes and are less likely to be arrested. (Even convicted criminals with better self-control are less likely to be arrested again after they are released.) They have better physical health and better mental health. They are more popular with peers and teachers. They have stronger families and happier relationship partners. And they live longer.

Nor is self-discipline or self-control a matter of getting good results by slogging through a joyless routine of duties. My research group dubbed that the "Puritan hypothesis," in honor of those early American settlers who are widely stereotyped as serious, sober, fun-hating, duty-bound workers. On the contrary, we found that people with high levels of self-control were happier than other people. This is true in both ways that scientists measure happiness. Their overall, bird's-eye-view ratings indicated they were more satisfied with their lives. And if you track them over time, they have more frequent positive emotions and less frequent negative emotions.

Part of the joyful benefit of good self-discipline is that your life runs smoothly, with fewer problems. We found that people with poor self-control are often struggling to deal with problems of their own making. They miss deadlines and then have to deal with the stresses and problems that arise as a result. They often find themselves rushing from one thing to the next, unable to focus on what they are doing now. They fail to save money and therefore often run short. They get into fights with their loved ones, and these conflicts take a heavy toll. They report poorer quality sleep. High self-control does not entirely prevent all these problems—but it reduces them significantly.

In general, I see the world in terms of tradeoffs. Often one advantage is offset by some disadvantage. (The various small differences between men and women typically work like this, such that each advantage for one gender is offset by a disadvantage.) But self-control, like intelligence, does not appear to have a downside. The smarter you are, the better off you are—and the same goes for self-control and self-discipline.

For all of these reasons and more, I encourage you to read and enjoy this book. Improving your self-discipline will make life better in many ways—both for you and for the people around you.

THE MANIFESTO

Mindful Self-Discipline is much more than just routine, building habits, managing your time, and keeping on track with your goals. It's about living a fully engaged life, expressing your potential, finding fulfillment, and dying without regrets. It's about self-actualization and wellbeing. It's about being a **purposeful human**.

Purposeful Humans have clear and powerful aspirations.

Purposeful Humans take full responsibility and believe in themselves.

Purposeful Humans think long-term and prioritize fulfillment over comfort.

Purposeful Humans practice meditation, self-reflection, and conscious living.

Purposeful Humans cultivate pausing, awareness, and willpower in their life.

Purposeful Humans persevere on the path until they achieve their goal.

Purposeful Humans are kind to their present self and their future self.

Purposeful Humans have consistent habits and a powerful morning routine.

Purposeful Humans have a plan, work for success, and get up when they fail.

Purposeful Humans have an uncompromising commitment they go Never Zero on.

Purposeful Humans know how to deal with procrastination, distractions, excuses, and doubts.

Purposeful Humans live in alignment with their highest goals and values, day after day.

If you found yourself saying yes to some of the above, then welcome. Mindful Self-Discipline is for you! Turn the page and let's begin this exciting journey.

PREFACE

"Of a thousand principles for success developed over the ages, this one quality or practice will do more to assure that you accomplish wonderful things with your life than anything else. This quality is so important that, if you don't develop it to a high degree, it is impossible for you to ever achieve what you are truly capable of achieving."

Brian Tracy

Take from me everything that I have, everything that I know, all my connections and personal qualities, but leave me with one thing, and I'll get everything back.

That thing is self-discipline.

No amount of talent, money, knowledge, or self-help hacks can compensate for its lack. And in this world of distractions and instant gratification, even a little bit of it goes a long way. Everything around you is designed to break your self-discipline. And now you have a choice: to continue letting that happen, or to take control of your life so you can live more on purpose and achieve your goals.

Self-discipline is the most essential skill for you to achieve your goals in any area of life. It is the king of all virtues, the engine of all growth, and the compass you need to live in accordance with your highest goals and values, day after day.

This is not a genetic lottery, nor a gift from the heavens—it is a learnable skill. The time you spend mastering it will pay you rich dividends. Because self-discipline makes everything else easier in your life.

Do you want to be healthier? Lose weight? Meditate every day? Save more money? Grow your business? Take your career to the next level? Become a better partner or parent? Master a skill? Make a difference in the world?

Are you at a point in life where you need to start again, reset, and reinvent yourself? Or do you simply want to go to sleep every night satisfied with yourself and with the way you've spent your time?

Self-discipline—*mindful* self-discipline—enables you to do all of that. It allows you to live without excuses and die without regrets.

And this book is the ultimate step-by-step guide. If you want to learn this skill, then I believe you will find no other book better than the one you have in your hands right now.

INTRODUCTION

Discipline is choosing between what you want now and what you want most.

Abraham Lincoln

I count him braver who overcomes his desires than him who conquers his enemies; for the hardest victory is over oneself.

Aristotle

SELF-DISCIPLINE: THE KEY TO ALL GOALS

Take a moment to think about the areas of your life that are truly important for you. Think about the changes you want to make—in yourself and in your life—and what they would mean to you.

Think about how you'd feel if, ten years from now, you still have not made those changes.

Now let me ask you a few questions:

- Do you feel that you are making the desired progress in these areas?
- Do you consistently achieve your goals in your career, health, finances, relationships, business or spirituality?
- Are you living the life you had planned?
- Do you always keep the promises you make to yourself?
- Are you fully satisfied with the way you're spending your time, energy, and life?

If you answered *no* to one or more of these, then I'm here to tell you that self-discipline is the missing piece.

Knowing what you want, but not being able to make it happen, is painful. You might be feeling that time is slipping through your fingers, and, while some other people seem to achieve everything they set their minds to, you struggle to move forward. Or you take far more time and effort than is necessary to do tasks and get burned out along the way.

Why haven't you achieved some of your goals yet? Why is it difficult to break certain bad habits, stick to good ones, and have an empowering routine every day?

It's not knowledge that is lacking. Whatever you want to change about yourself or your life, I'd bet that you know what you need to do. It is also not lack of money, support, or time. It's not even lack of motivation. What is lacking is a **deep commitment**, and the **self-discipline** to turn that commitment into effective action day after day, *no matter what.*

When you have that commitment and discipline, then New Year's resolutions don't flop, dreams are not forgotten in a ten-page "bucket list", projects and goals don't get abandoned mid-way, and bad habits don't take over your life. "I decide, therefore I do" becomes your new mantra.

For some people, though, self-discipline has a bad reputation: it's something that is hard and boring; something that hurts, that you are forced to do. However, when seen under the right light, you realize that self-discipline is not self-denial; it is self-affirmation. It is a tool that serves your best interests.

Self-discipline is self-respect.

As long as you wish to grow, there will be the need for self-discipline. Why? Because there will be a gap between the person you are now and the person you want to be. Self-discipline helps you to bridge that gap.

Of course, there are also other elements—such as luck and genetics—but these are things you can't do anything about. Your actions, thoughts, and daily routine are what you can have full control over. The more you take control of these, the more you'll be able to conquer the chaos of life and consistently live on your own terms.

It doesn't matter your age, gender, sexuality, walk of life, political inclination, or belief system. If you have a goal, you need self-discipline. It's as simple as that.

The result of a life lived with self-discipline is fulfillment.

The result of one lived without it is regret.

THE POWER OF MINDFUL SELF-DISCIPLINE

Self-discipline is not just about building habits. Developing habits is one of the main *expressions* of self-discipline, but not the only one. It's also more than time management, having a good mindset, setting effective goals, and taking action—these are just some of its *practices*.

Self-discipline is not just one of the several topics of personal development—it's the *heart* of it. It is the thread that ties together all the numerous self-development topics, such as:

- growth mindset
- habit building
- meditation
- goal setting
- self-control
- productivity
- developing virtues
- positive thinking
- willpower
- finding your purpose
- visualizations
- affirmations
- focus and perseverance

That is why each of the chapters of this book could be a book on its own. In fact, several books have been written about each of the key concepts covered in any of the chapters. My purpose, here, is to bring it all together; to present it in a highly practical and cohesive way, without the typical filler content of academic analysis and endless case studies.

You can talk about goal setting, productivity hacks and brains hacks all day long. Still, all of these require one thing in common: compliance. In other words, you need to *do* it. You need to follow the tools and apply them, even when you don't feel like it. They are, therefore, *disciplines*. So self-discipline is required for all of them.

Okay, but why *mindful* self-discipline?

Because my approach is based on meditation and awareness rather than forcefulness. It invites you to harmonize all parts of yourself in pursuit of a meaningful goal, rather than beat yourself up to stay on track. It evokes the inner power of the *monk* in you—not the soldier.

The mindful approach of self-discipline is more practical and achievable than relying on forcefulness. And it has the added bonus of also giving you many of the proven benefits of meditation practice. If you have tried to be disciplined before but failed, Mindful Self-Discipline may just be the fresh approach that you were looking for.

HOW TO MAKE THE MOST OUT OF THIS BOOK

This book is focused on helping you achieve your goals, live your dreams and values, and make the changes you want to make. It will work for you whether you have one all-consuming purpose, or whether you just need help succeeding at simpler tasks, such as saving money, waking up early and eating better.

Here is how this book is structured.

In the first part of the book, you'll learn what self-discipline is, how it works in your brain, and the benefits of developing this skill. You will see the need to be balanced with your disciplines, so that you live well and don't burn out. We will then discuss the essential role of willpower and how to develop it.

Parts two to four cover each of the three pillars of self-discipline: Aspiration, Awareness, Action.

In the Aspiration Pillar section, you will learn how to find your deepest aspirations in life, magnify them, create specific goals for them, and prioritize them in your daily life. You will see how to deal with self-sabotage, and also how to adopt three powerful virtues that allow you to live your Aspiration more fully: ownership, self-belief, and sacrifice.

In the Awareness Pillar section, we get to the heart of *Mindful Self-Discipline*. Awareness is a quality developed through daily meditation and self-reflection and applied in your daily life with the help of the PAW Method. You will learn three different ways to use your willpower to shift your mental and emotional state, so that you are able to make decisions that advance your goals rather than move you away from them. You will learn how to persevere, no matter what happens. You will also learn techniques to help you overcome distractions and excuses along the way.

In the third pillar section, Action, you will design your action plan by creating milestones for your goals and going through the nitty-gritty of setting up effective habits that will move you forward. Then we will discuss specific methods for overcoming the obstacles of forgetfulness, procrastination and doubt. You will also learn how to plan for failure, so you can graciously bounce back from it. We close with a "golden key" by talking about the Never Zero commitment—which is something you will never forget.

In the final parts of the book, we cover topics that enhance the three pillars. You will learn principles of mindful time management and specific guidelines for building effective morning routines and night routines. We talk about virtues, why they matter, and how to develop them. We also discuss the other lifestyle elements that can make self-discipline easier or harder for you—such as sleep and the company you keep. We then cover the topic of spirituality as an optional layer that can add greater strength and meaning to your self-discipline, as well as grow with it.

I suggest you read this book sequentially, from cover to cover. That, in itself, is an exercise of self-discipline. However, if you are time poor and want to go first to the "quick wins", then read Chapters 17-24 and then 31, 34, and 40. Still, you may ask, "Giovanni, if I *really* only had time to read and implement three chapters, what would they be?" If that is you, I'd recommend you focus on Chapter 17 (The PAW Method), Chapter 31 (Never Zero), and one of the "obstacle chapters" (12, 21, 22, 23, 28, 29, 30) that speaks to your needs.

Most chapters of this book contain several practical exercises. In some cases, you will find links with implementation resources at the end of the chapter (such as for the companion Workbook, meditation instructions, and the Mindful Self-Discipline mobile app). The book is complete in itself; yet these additional resources do make the process of implementing the concepts of *Mindful Self-Discipline* much easier. You can access them all at **MindfulSelfDiscipline.com.** (I chose to keep the Workbook separate to prevent this book from getting too long, to make the reading more fluid, and also not to give it too much of a textbook feeling.)

As you go through this book, please **don't overwhelm yourself**. You don't need to follow every single exercise and try all the techniques. If you learn and truly implement even *one* of the methods, your self-discipline will already have improved. If you implement three to five of them, it will be transformed. As you read, mark the topics that will move the needle the most for you, and focus on integrating those exercises until they are second nature. Then you can come back and try other ones. Refer also to the Implementation Checklist section at the end of the book for a practical guide on how to practice these concepts in your daily life.

This book has some repetition built in. This is deliberate. I will revisit some of the concepts multiple times, from different angles, to really help you absorb these ideas.

The writing style in this book, unlike my first book (*Practical Meditation*), is more direct and "piercing". You might feel at times that my words are putting you under the spotlight, dissecting things deeply, and leaving you with no room to escape. Please understand that this is done in the spirit of service and compassion, not judgment.

As you read these words, allow them to *set you on fire*. But don't go on a guilt trip. Shame and guilt are negative emotions that often keep you chained to bad habits; this is *not* the way of Mindful Self-Discipline, and it's not expected. Nobody is perfect at self-discipline; we are all just learning what we need to learn to take our next step.

SELF-DISCIPLINE AND ME

People say that self-discipline is one of my superpowers. In fact, if you ask any of my close friends or family members what is my top personal strength, most would say "discipline" or one of its variants (perseverance, resilience, willpower).

My wife playfully says that I should change my name to Giovanni *Disciplined* Dienstmann.

Well, it has definitely served me in all areas of life. It is something that I have cultivated over the years—and not a genetic gift (I'm the only one in my family who is disciplined like this).

It is self-discipline that allowed me to thrive in my work in law at a young age, then IT, then blogging. It is self-discipline that allows me to wake up at 2:30am every morning, take a cold shower, do two hours of meditation, and eat only once a day—seven days a week. It is due to this skill that I've practiced over ten thousand hours of meditation, and written a popular book on the topic.

It is self-discipline that enables me to feel calm, centered, and content day after day, no matter what's happening. My moods and emotional states are constant and stable.

It is self-discipline that allows me to say no to addictions to entertainment, information, and other forms of instant gratification. In fact, I have no social media apps on my phone. I check email twice per day. Notifications are mostly all turned off. I watch less than three hours of TV per *week*, and don't waste time aimlessly surfing the web.

And I love my life. I live with the satisfaction of knowing that every moment is dedicated to one of the three main pillars of my life:

- Personal growth (meditation and spirituality)
- Family (my wife and daughter)
- Legacy (my work)

Yet this book is about you—and your pillars may be completely different. The way you want to live your life may be completely different, but the need for self-discipline is the same. It is universal.

Your self-discipline needs may be much smaller than mine, but it's helpful to know what is possible once you follow this system. The level of discipline that is possible for me is most definitely possible for you—if you are open to learn and put in some effort. Self-discipline is not something you either have or you don't. It's a skill that can be learned, a quality that can be developed.

This book is the answer to the question I've been asked countless times: "How can you be so disciplined? How do you do this?" It is my effort of bringing together all the self-development concepts I've studied, practiced, and taught for the past twenty years. Some people have focused on accumulating wealth, building businesses, perfecting their craft, or gaining gold medals. For me, it was all about accumulating wisdom and self-mastery—so this is what I have to share.

Self-discipline is what it all comes down to for me. And in this book, I share with you the pearls I've collected along the way, and the unique way I've strung them together.

WHAT TO EXPECT FROM THIS BOOK

This book is not a compilation of scientific studies, nor an academic research project. Yes, I've consumed those, but I'm not writing a thesis here. I focus on the "how" to do it, rather than "why it's proven to work". (If you want to learn more about those studies and the academic discussions around it, please refer to the notes and references at the end of the book.)

This book doesn't teach a magic formula, nor do I pretend to have discovered something new. This skill is incredibly old. It has been practiced and praised by top performers and wise men and women in all cultures and eras. And *that is why* it is worth paying attention to. It has stood the test of time. It is not a fad.

This book is not—like many other works in the personal development genre—thin with concepts and filled with stories and examples. No. I have a lot to say, and not many words to spare. Every sentence of this book is designed to deliver power and inspiration, without mincing words. This is designed to be your *self-transformation guide*, and not a light and fun read for a Sunday afternoon.

The premise of this book is very simple: if you want to achieve any type of goal, or if you want to change anything in yourself or in your life, you will need to *do* something. In that process, you will meet obstacles—both internal and external—and you will often be your worst enemy. Self-discipline is how you navigate this mess, from where you are now to where you want to be.

This book will likely make you feel uncomfortable at times. If that happens, feel happy—the message is sinking in, and positive change is ahead.

This book will strip you of your excuses. For every challenge in fulfilling your dream, I will give you one (or more) actionable strategies. You won't be able to hide anymore.

It will make self-sabotage become extremely painful—and it is so by design, so you can completely move past it. This approach works and it might be exactly what you need, but perhaps not what you were looking for.

I know, being this straightforward might not win me a place in a coveted bestsellers' list… but this is how I can be at your greatest service. This book will replace the comfort of excuses with the satisfaction of having the power to live the life you want to live.

If you have no goals in life, this book is useless for you. Return it and get a refund if you can.

But if you have goals in life, then I think you will love this—so welcome to the tribe!

Let us now begin.

THE FUNDAMENTALS

CHAPTER 1

WHAT IS SELF-DISCIPLINE?

Everyone must choose one of two pains:
the pain of discipline, or the pain of regret.

Jim Rohn

The ability to subordinate an impulse to a value
is the essence of the proactive person.

Stephen Covey

A disciplined mind leads to happiness. An
undisciplined mind leads to suffering.

Dalai Lama

We begin our journey by clarifying what self-discipline is, and what it is not. This first part of the book, then, is about the *what*. The rest of the book is about the *how*.

Self-discipline is as old as mankind. The Stoics were big on not getting carried away by thoughts and feelings, and often called it the "discipline of assent". The Buddhist monks treated it as the holy grail. The Bible tells us that the whole fall of humanity is due to a failure of self-control: someone traded eternity in the Garden of Eden for an apple… talk about instant gratification!

Let's now have a look at what this thing is that can save us from falling from our ideals.

ONE WORD, MANY VIRTUES

In a nutshell, here is how I define this essential skill: self-discipline is the art of living in harmony with your goals and values.

Here is the longer definition:

> Self-discipline is your ability to live in accordance with your higher goals and values moment after moment. It is your power to overcome internal and external obstacles, commit to what is meaningful to you, and let that guide the way you think, the choices you make, and the actions you take—until you bring your goal to fruition.

The definition above may look simple, but there is a lot in there. Let's now unpack its many layers.

"**Live in accordance**" means your capacity to choose what is in your best interest. It is choosing your higher self and respecting that choice. It's acting in harmony with your goals, not your moods; your decisions, not your emotions; your aspirations, not your desires. It is to have the courage to sacrifice a lower joy for a higher joy.

Goals and values are the things you want to achieve. Examples: living more healthily, writing a book, quitting alcohol, meditating every morning, becoming a great guitar player, being the best mom you can be, building wealth, improving your skills, etc. It is playing the long game, letting go of the illusion of quick gains and overnight success.

Internal obstacles are things like procrastination, excuses, lack of motivation, limiting beliefs, self-doubt, laziness, bad habits, etc. **External obstacles** are things like distractions, social pressure, unhelpful environments, failures, and challenges in your way.

"Let that guide" means that self-discipline brings clarity to your life. It functions as a compass for every decision—a compass with the north of your choice.

"Until fruition", and not "for as long as you feel like it". Self-discipline doesn't ask how you are feeling today. It asks, "How will you live your aspirations today?" and "What choice is true to who you want to become?"

There are many aspects to the skill of self-discipline. On the surface they may look like separate virtues, yet they are all connected. If we look at self-discipline through the lens of what it does for you, we can see that it allows you to:

- Focus on what is most meaningful, despite distractions and shiny objects. Spend your time and energy on the things that really add value to your life. (**Focus**)
- Do what you need to do, regardless of how you feel in the moment and regardless of obstacles on your way. (**Willpower**)
- Stop yourself from doing what you know is not good for you, and coach yourself to do what *is* good for you. (**Self-control**)
- Bypass excuses, procrastination, fears and doubts. Stay on track with your goals and dreams, even when motivation is not there. (**Determination**)
- Keep your promises to yourself (resolutions) and to others (commitments). (**Integrity, Reliability**)
- Live up to your own values, standards, and rules. Match your thoughts, actions, and behaviors to the person you aspire to be. (**Authenticity**)
- Show up as your best self in your life, relationships, and work. (**Generosity**)
- Do what you know you need to do to get the results you want in the different areas of life. Focus on what you can control and accept what you can't. (**Responsibility, Ownership**)
- Live more purposefully, and less impulsively, by considering the long-term consequences of each choice you make. Say *no* to the temptations of instant gratification when they are not in harmony with your long-term goals. (**Vision**)
- Get back up each time you fall, knowing that you are in it for the long-term and will eventually make it. (**Perseverance, Resilience**)
- Stick to your plan even when things don't seem to be working out, and finish what you start. (**Grit**)
- Organize your life—your thoughts, emotions, actions, and habits—in the pursuit of meaningful goals. That makes you unified

and whole. When that happens, all the forces in your personality are pointed in the same direction, and there are fewer internal contradictions. (**Integration, Wholeness**)

- Truly *learn*. The word discipline and the word *disciple* have the same root. (**Growth**)
- Don't be controlled by emotions and impulses in the moment. (**Centeredness**)
- Take your skills and knowledge to the next level and grow as a person. (**Excellence**)
- Make decisions that your future self will thank you for. (**Self-love**)
- Take actions according to the person you aspire to become (future), not the person you were conditioned to be (past). (**Alignment**)

As may be clear by now, self-discipline has an external aspect and an internal aspect. The external aspect is your ability to build and keep good habits, drop bad habits, and act in accordance with your goals.

The internal aspect is self-mastery. This is what makes the external aspect possible. It's our ability to harmonize and coordinate the different elements of our internal world—our thoughts, emotions, impulses, and goals. It means that you have the power to choose which of the conflicting voices inside of you gets to run the show at any given moment. Without this we have no control over ourselves and, thus, over our lives.

Share this concept:
MindfulSelfDiscipline.com/what-is-self-discipline

SELF-DISCIPLINE AS PERSONAL POWER

David Eagleman, author of *Incognito: The Secret Lives of the Brain*, argues that our behavior is simply the result of the many battles between short-term and long-term desires in our brain. If that is the case, then self-discipline is your ability to choose the part of you that should win the battles that matter.

The Greek word for discipline, *enkrateia*, comes from the root *krat*, which denotes control or power. Self-discipline is your core personal power. It is self-mastery. It's the source of all other powers.

Every time you exercise this power, you strengthen it. And you have the satisfaction of knowing that you are doing your best. Do this day after day, expressing the best there is in you, and you can live with the peace of mind of having no regrets—no "what ifs" or "should haves" roaming around your brain.

On the other hand, every time you say *no* to your goals, you *leak* part of your power. This happens whenever you lose sight of what is important for you and get carried away by the distractions and temptations of instant gratification.

It happens whenever you say, "I don't feel like it" or "I'll start next week" or "let me make an exception just this time" or "today doesn't really count."

You are fooling yourself. And every time you do that, you're giving away part of your soul, and becoming powerless. The day soon comes when you begin to feel that your decisions and words don't matter anymore—since they are not respected even by you. This can easily lead to feelings of victimization, depression, and regret.

Instead, honor your personal power. Cultivate it. Exercise it wisely.

Self-discipline is a form of self-regulation, self-control, or self-mastery—it is the benevolent exercise of power within yourself. Like a good king/queen leading a country to a happier, desired future.

This exercise of personal power (self-discipline) is good for you. It leads to happiness, not repression. Indeed, research shows that people with better self-control eat more healthily, do more exercise, sleep better, drink less alcohol, smoke fewer cigarettes, achieve higher grades at university, have more peaceful relationships, are more financially secure, and enjoy stronger physical and mental health. They have higher self-esteem, better interpersonal skills, and more optimal emotional responses.

Honoring and cultivating your personal power also results in you being more satisfied with yourself, more confident in your capacity, and more influential in society. A person with strong self-discipline exudes a natural sense of authority, respect, and trust.

If we don't have that, then we cannot stand out; we must fit in. Or, in the words of the thinker who is known to *deliver his philosophy with a hammer*: "He who cannot command himself must obey." (Friedrich Nietzsche)

Consider the different aspects of your personality as citizens living inside your kingdom, each with different desires, fears, and agendas. There are conflicting interests for sure. Then ask yourself: What does my kingdom look like? Are most citizens harmoniously working toward a mutual goal, or are they fighting themselves? Is there a wise and benevolent ruler sitting on the throne, or a clueless buffoon?

Share this concept:
MindfulSelfDiscipline.com/self-discipline-is-personal-power

SELF-DISCIPLINE AS PERSONAL HARMONY

A gentler way to look at self-discipline is to see it as a way of harmonizing yourself and creating positive rhythm in your life. Rhythm is a form of discipline and order: it is things happening in a reliable way.

Rhythm is all around us.

Our body has its own rhythms, such as the circadian rhythm. We can think of it as the routine of the body, its natural self-discipline. When the body's rhythms are respected and maintained—through healthy meals, regular sleep schedule, etc.—we experience physical health, vitality, and wellbeing. Break them, and we start facing all sorts of problems.

Music is rhythm. Every note, every pause needs to be *exactly* in the correct place—not one second before, not one second later. Otherwise there is no harmony. It's a very strict discipline. Follow it, and you have music; break it, and all you get is noise.

Beauty is also rhythm—a form of visual discipline that values harmony, symmetry, and balanced movement. There is even discipline and form shaping the creative flow of ideas in a story; without that discipline, the story's expressiveness and power are diminished.

Discipline is the foundation for rhythm, balance, and thus harmony. Lack of discipline leads to disharmony, wasted energy, and chaos.

As you can see, discipline already exists in many things around us. In driving, it ensures safety. In medicine, it ensures health and saves lives. In programming, it ensures an app or website that works and doesn't make you pull your hair out when using it.

Consider for a moment the different aspects of your personality—with its different desires, fears, and agendas—as instruments in an orchestra. Then ask yourself: What does my music sound like? Are all instruments harmoniously coordinated to create a masterpiece, or is my life out of tune?

Self-discipline is the maestro. Make sure she/he is the one conducting the show.

Share this concept:
MindfulSelfDiscipline.com/self-discipline-is-personal-harmony

SELF-DISCIPLINE IN YOUR BRAIN

(Note: skip this part if you don't have the need to know how stuff works.)

One useful model to understand how we operate in the world is the *triune brain* model, developed by the neuroscientist Paul D. MacLean. He proposes that there are three layers in our brain.

The oldest part of the brain is the Reptilian System, also known as the *primal brain* or *lizard brain*. It's mostly concerned with threats and survival, and it responds to the environment based on fear and aggression. Most of the times when we respond impulsively in our modern life, and later regret the consequences, we are operating from this primitive brain.

When someone panics when they need to speak in public, or when they get irritated by a rude comment from a family member and lash out, it is the primal brain that is running the show. Unless you really need to tap into this brain for your physical survival, living from the *reptilian consciousness* usually leads to regret.

The second layer is the Limbic System, also known as *mammalian brain* or *emotional brain*. It is responsible for our emotions, coordination of movement, likes and dislikes, pleasure, and pain. When we forget about our resolutions and instead go for the instant gratification of eating that cookie, this is the part of the brain that is speaking the loudest.

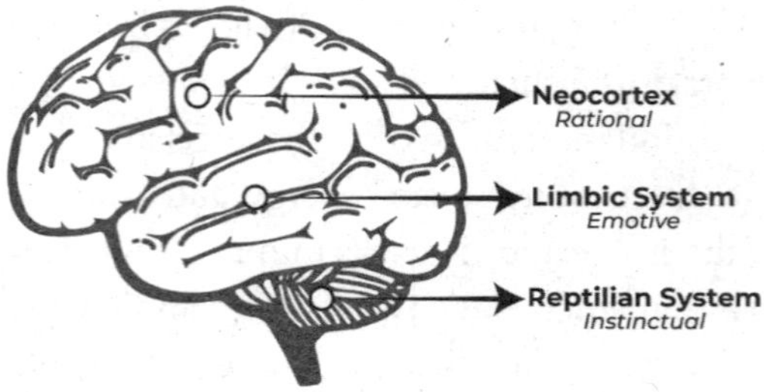

When you find it hard to say *no* to drinking soda, or can't stop aimlessly browsing the internet or social media, it is this layer of the brain that is running the show. The same is true if you want to start running outdoors three times a week but are held back by shame because you worry that people will negatively judge you for being somewhat overweight.

The third layer is the Neocortex, or *rational brain*. It is responsible for language, planning, self-regulation, awareness, rational thinking, and decision-making, among other things. This is the newest and most evolved part of the brain—it's often what we consider to be the noblest part of us.

Self-discipline, willpower, and self-awareness are all functions of the rational brain, the *prefrontal cortex* (part of the neocortex). It is this part of your brain that can differentiate between conflicting thoughts, determine good and bad, consider future consequences of current decisions, work toward a chosen goal, and control your emotions and impulses. In our orchestra metaphor, the prefrontal cortex can be said to be the maestro.

The practice of self-discipline, therefore, is an exercise in human evolution. It is consciously developing our rational brain so that it is no longer overpowered by the reptilian brain or the emotional brain. It is really about outgrowing our "inner reptile", our animal nature, and functioning more as a fully mature human being. Or at least having the option to do so, for the things that truly matter to us.

All the practices recommended in this book, especially meditation, help you strengthen your prefrontal cortex and keep it *online* more often. It's not about killing the inner reptile or the mammal; they are valuable parts of ourselves. It's only about taming their wild nature—making sure that they know their place, and are following the maestro.

KEY POINTS

- Self-discipline is your ability to live in accordance with your higher goals and values moment after moment, overcoming internal and external obstacles. It is your power to commit to what is meaningful to you, and let that guide the way you think, the choices you make, and the actions you take—until you bring your goal to fruition.
- Self-discipline contains, in itself, many virtues—things like focus, willpower, determination, integrity, vision, resilience, alignment, optimism, and excellence.
- It has an external aspect (habits and routines), and an internal aspect (self-mastery).
- It can be seen as your core *personal power* (the king/queen), that needs to be cultivated and exercised. And it can also be seen as *personal harmony* (the maestro), the art of coordinating all the elements in your life to create a masterpiece.
- Self-discipline is a function of the most evolved part of our brain, the *prefrontal cortex*. The practice of this skill, then, is an exercise in outgrowing the more impulsive parts of our nature, so that we have real freedom and agency in our lives.

The rewards of self-discipline are endless. And it's something you can **develop**—you don't need to be born with it. Once you do, it's all about exercising it wisely.

Wisely because, just like any form of power, self-discipline is value neutral. It can be used for "good" or for "bad". Just like language can be used to express deep ideas, declare love, or start a war, self-discipline is simply the power to make things happen. Choosing the right goals to pursue is not in the domain of discipline, but in that of *wisdom* (a topic for another book).

CHAPTER 2

THE BENEFITS OF SELF-DISCIPLINE

The one quality which sets one man apart from another—the key which lifts one to every aspiration while others are caught up in the mire of mediocrity—is not talent, formal education, nor intellectual brightness—it is self-discipline.

THEODORE ROOSEVELT

No stream or gas drives anything until it is confined.
No Niagara is ever turned into light and power until it is tunneled.
No life ever grows great until it is focused, dedicated, self-disciplined.

HARRY EMERSON FOSDICK

For every disciplined effort there is a multiple return.

JIM ROHN

Becoming a self-disciplined person may be one of the hardest things you do, but it will also become one of the most rewarding. Because it's the foundation for growth, wellbeing and achievement in all areas of life.

Here are some examples of what this virtue allows you to do:

- Stay focused on your goals and dreams, day after day
- Get things done, and finish what you start
- Make better use of your time
- Resist temptation and avoid acting on impulses
- Fulfill promises you make to yourself and to others

- Overcome laziness and procrastination
- Continue working on a project even after motivation has faded away
- Exercise every day, even if your mind tells you to skip and watch TV instead
- Continue following your diet, and say *no* to unhealthy food items
- Wake up early every morning
- Overcome bad habits
- Read books from cover to cover
- Meditate regularly
- Avoid wasting time in non-essential activities

The more deeply you understand the benefits of self-discipline, the easier it will be for you to actually practice it. This is the purpose of this chapter—to fire you up, so you have the fuel needed for the journey.

Let's now zoom into some of the key benefits of this practice.

MAKES YOU CONFIDENT AND EMPOWERED

When you blame others and see yourself as a victim, you let go of your personal responsibility—and, thus, of your personal power. You feel disempowered, controlled by external forces. You believe that your thoughts and choices don't matter.

Self-discipline is being self-reliant, and so is the opposite of feeling like a victim. It is for those who are ready to take full responsibility for their lives. It is saying that your will shall shape your future (more of that in Chapter 12).

Let's say your goals are about improving your health and growing in your career. You may choose to begin your day by waking up an hour earlier. With that extra hour, you can then dedicate thirty minutes to work on your professional skills, and in the other thirty minutes you can go for a run. This new routine makes you feel more in control of your life, and more confident that you can make things happen—like losing weight and getting a desired promotion. With this, every day you are growing in things that matter for you. You feel more in charge of your destiny.

Self-discipline is empowering because it leads to self-mastery. And, in the words of Plato, *"The first and best victory is to conquer oneself."*

Practicing Mindful Self-Discipline will put you in touch with an inner strength, an inner power that you didn't dream you had. It will allow you to get out of the waiting room of your life; to stop waiting for the perfect moment, when all the stars align. You can then start taking steps toward your dream life *right now*.

Every time you feel like "just checking YouTube a little bit", playing your favorite game for "just ten minutes", or "Googling some interesting stuff", somewhere inside of yourself you know that you are wasting time and going nowhere. By practicing self-discipline, you gain the ability to say *no*. And every time you do that, your self-esteem goes up. You feel more in control.

What is the result of not having self-discipline? The surface result is not achieving your goals; the deeper result is a sense of low self-worth, low self-confidence, and low self-esteem. You can change that by starting to take control of how you spend your time and energy.

With improved self-esteem also comes better self-talk. Your relationship with yourself changes, and new possibilities open up for you. You start doing things that, before, you felt you couldn't. People around you will notice it, and that will motivate you further. It's a self-reinforcing loop.

Through self-discipline, you don't drift from your goals. You stay focused and start getting results sooner in life. You feel in command of your destiny. You feel like you're in the driver's seat of your life and not merely a victim of your circumstances. Your sense of personal power increases and, with that, the belief that you can achieve anything you set your mind to.

ENABLES YOU TO ACHIEVE YOUR GOALS

It doesn't matter whether you are pursuing success in business, sports, the arts, or life in general: the bridge between wishing and accomplishing is discipline.

HARVEY MACKAY

Self-discipline is the most essential ingredient for achieving any long-term goal. It's what makes people stick to diet plans, exercise regularly, meditate every day, improve the way they show up in relationships, develop professional skills, save money, grow their business, and live a life aligned with their purpose.

A disciplined life is an organized life—a calm, centered and focused life. It's like a boat advancing fearlessly toward its destination, rather than a boat at the mercy of the wind. It doesn't ask, "What's the weather today?" but "Am I on course?"

If you were to ask top performers in any field what are the most important traits that got them there, I'd bet with you that self-discipline would make it to the list for of all of them. Either as "discipline" pure and simple, or disguised as one of its variants: determination, perseverance, "showing up", "not giving up", resilience, grit, dedication, commitment, willpower.

The main reason why most people want to develop self-discipline is to achieve a particular goal. That makes a lot of sense, because in most cases what stands in the way between you and your goals is not lack of knowledge, but lack of commitment and action. You often know what to do, but you can't get yourself to do it.

Do you want to save more, invest better, and build wealth? Do you want to develop your knowledge and skills to be at the top of your game at work? What about growing your business?

For these and many other goals, discipline is the key factor, not motivation. If you wait until you feel like doing things (motivation), you won't stay with them for long. Feelings are fleeting, motivation is temporary—only self-discipline is reliable.

Self-discipline is even more important than intelligence. An American study by Angela Duckworth and Martin Seligman found that a school pupil's self-discipline is a stronger predictor of their future academic success than their IQ,

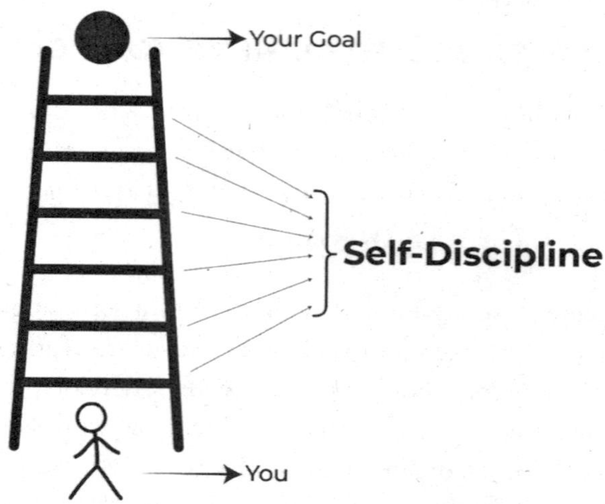

leading researchers to conclude that self-discipline may be the "royal road" to building academic achievement.

The process of achieving any goal always involves a type of transformation, or journey. You are going from point A (where you are now) to point B (where you want to be). And transformation requires consistent action across a span of time, which is only possible with self-discipline. When we put it like that, all this may sound like common sense—but it's far from being common practice.

That is why, without self-discipline, the loftiest goal is just wishful thinking. With self-discipline, even a mediocre goal will take you somewhere.

Discipline allows you to concentrate single-mindedly on your key goals, eliminate distractions, and stick to your chosen path despite obstacles and setbacks. It's a much-valued virtue for top athletes, entrepreneurs, artists, meditation masters, and those in the military. (Yes, that's perhaps one of the only things all these people have in common.)

A disciplined person moves toward his goal like an arrow toward its target, shooting through whatever obstacles come in its way, and not stopping until the goal is reached. Do you want some of that?

When you focus your self-discipline on a single purpose, like sunlight focused through a magnifying glass on a single object, look out! Everybody will get out of your way, open doors for you, and salute as you walk by.

Self-discipline turns you into a force of nature. You become unstoppable.

Let's now pause for a moment and get really specific about how all of this applies to your life. Make a list of all the main areas of your life, and think of up to five ways how self-discipline can help you in each. This will help you be more motivated to learn and apply the skill of self-discipline.

Share this concept:

MindfulSelfDiscipline.com/benefit-achieve-your-goals

GIVES YOU AN UNFAIR ADVANTAGE

We live in a world of distractions. They are all around you, and always with you in your pocket. The opportunities for instant gratification abound, and there is always a new shiny object to go after. Why then, would you trouble to go after hard-to-get goals?

The internet is full of black holes sucking your attention, and many companies are investing millions in making their products more addictive. Everyone is fighting hard to distract you: they all want your attention, even if only for a few seconds. Make no mistake: there is undeniable economical interest in doing so. These people are motivated, brilliant, and extremely well-funded.

And you know what? This is only going to get worse in the next years and decades. Which means that everybody will be more distracted, with shorter attention spans, and lower resilience for pursuing long-term goals.

In the twenty-first century, survival of the fittest means survival of the focused.

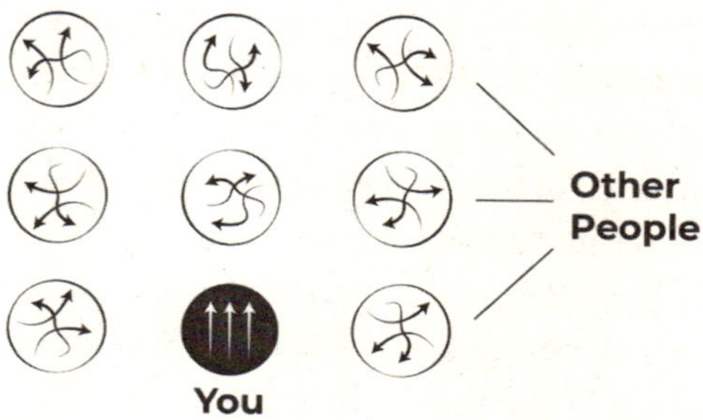

Self-discipline will continue to become more difficult and rare. Having even a little of it will give you a big advantage and take you a long way. You won't need to be more talented than your competitors; you'll just need to be more focused.

We don't have to be smarter than the rest.
We have to be more disciplined than the rest.

WARREN BUFFETT

That is why I say that the disciplined shall inherit the earth.

Share this concept:
MindfulSelfDiscipline.com/unfair-advantage

KEEPS YOU HEALTHY IN BODY AND MIND

Can you say *no* to your favorite unhealthy food items and keep your resolutions? Can you stick to doing your exercises day in and day out, even when tired and demotivated? Do you practice sleep hygiene? Can you coach yourself to stop feeding your negative self-talk, and take positive action even when you feel down?

These are some of the ways in which self-discipline helps you stay healthy in your body and mind. There are so many systems and formulas out there that promise to help you lose weight, gain muscle, eat better, and enhance your wellbeing. There are hundreds of different diets and wellness programs. And yet, every health and wellbeing coach has one thing in common: they give you something to *do*. They give you a practice, a method, a protocol. Unless you are able to do the things they tell you to do and stop the bad habits they tell you to stop, you won't get the results. Here is where Mindful Self-Discipline comes in.

In the 2011 *Stress in America* survey, 27% of respondents said the lack of willpower was the biggest barrier to making healthy lifestyle changes. Chances are that the number is actually much higher than that, and people are just unaware of the causes of their relapses.

With the power of Mindful Self-Discipline, you can stick to your meal plans, exercise regimes, and healthy routines. Without it, the most amazing system in the world can do little for you.

The same is true for mental health. There are studies showing that having healthy routines and improving self-control are essential elements in relieving anxiety and having more stable moods. Good habits and a daily routine also make you more resilient to the ups and downs of life. This is something most people can greatly benefit from.

Whether we are living through times of abundance (which bring with them their own challenges) or through another pandemic, self-discipline keeps you focused on the only thing you can control: yourself. This gives you a firm ground for navigating life, whatever the weather.

IMPROVES YOUR RELATIONSHIPS

Can you remain calm and centered in the middle of a fight? Can you take a deep breath before reacting, and notice that you are angry? Are you able to keep your commitments to your partner? Is it easy for you to remember to practice gratitude, appreciation, and empathy in your relationships?

Welcome to the club. That is why we need to cultivate self-awareness and self-discipline.

Many of the challenges we face in relationships with our family and with our significant other are related to our impulsivity and reactivity. In other words, we sometimes lose control of ourselves and get carried away by our emotions in the moment. Things like anger, defensiveness, fear, and jealousy.

As a result, we say and do things that we later regret. Self-discipline—together with meditation and the awareness practices that come with it—allows us to pause and cool down in the heat of the moment, and resist the temptation to say something we know we shouldn't say.

My Kung Fu master once told me that speaking a word is like releasing an arrow: once it's out, there is no way back. Sometimes words can hurt more than an arrow, and also take longer to heal. Hence, anything that helps you ~~keep your mouth shut~~ speak more mindfully will benefit your relationships. (You see what I did there?)

When you're able to keep yourself calm and collected in the middle of a tsunami of emotions, you've proved your greatness. People respect that, admire that, and feel that you are more reliable. They feel safer when close to you, and thus can trust you more.

Another way that self-discipline improves relationships, especially with your partner, is by facilitating behavior change. Any long-term relationship requires us to make changes and compromises, which often go against old habits and stretch our ways of being. And, of course, you will need self-discipline to make these changes, as they won't happen overnight.

Many perks come with this virtue.

GIVES YOU PURPOSE, POWER, PEACE

The self-disciplined life is a life of purpose, power, and peace. *Purpose* in your actions, and the values you choose to pursue. *Power* to align your life and your goals and bring them to fruition. *Peace* in living without regrets, mastering yourself, and purifying your mind of useless noise.

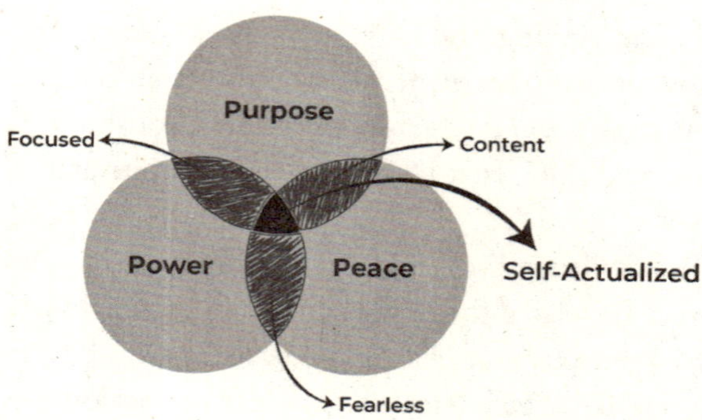

A disciplined life is a life without regrets. It's a life where you can look back and say, "Yes I've made mistakes, had many failures, and sacrificed a lot of things. But I lived life on my terms, and achieved many of the things I really wanted. I was true to myself."

The opposite is a life without discipline. Instead of purpose there is *chaos*: you are a puppet of the strongest forces at play in the moment. Instead of power there is *frustration*, as you can't make things happen, and your important goals are not fulfilled. Instead of peace there is *disturbance*, as unhelpful thoughts, limiting beliefs and negative emotions get the best of you.

A life without discipline may still be full of pleasure—but it won't be *pleasant*. Time is filled with many activities that bring instant gratification but are devoid of meaning and take you nowhere. You may be busy, well-fed and comfortable—but not fulfilled. You are living on the surface, coasting, and you haven't touched your true potential.

Something deep inside your soul knows it. Ignore that voice at your own peril.

CHAPTER 3

MISCONCEPTIONS ABOUT SELF-DISCIPLINE

Discipline without freedom is tyranny.
Freedom without discipline is chaos.

CULLEN HIGHTOWER

Discipline is the ability to control our conduct by principle rather than by social pressure.

GLENN C. STEWART

Self-discipline is a form of freedom. Freedom from laziness and lethargy, freedom from the expectations and demands of others, freedom from weakness and fear—and doubt. Self-discipline allows a person to feel his individuality, his inner strength, his talent. He is master of, rather than a slave to, his thoughts and emotions.

HARVEY DORFMAN

Self-discipline, despite being an essential skill, is not really a popular topic. Many people have misconceptions about it and resist the idea. As a self-discipline coach, part of my work is to help my clients overcome limiting beliefs and negative self-talk; in this chapter we will do this around the concept of self-discipline itself.

WHAT MINDFUL SELF-DISCIPLINE IS NOT

Mindful Self-Discipline is FOCUS, Not Restriction

The first negative belief is thinking that to be disciplined is to live a *restrictive* lifestyle, full of rigid rules, dos and don'ts, like a robot. People imagine that they will have no freedom, no spontaneity, and that all the fun of life is gone.

That is not the case. Self-discipline doesn't ask you to do anything that you don't want to do. In fact, it only asks you to do things that you **do** want to do. It allows you focus on what matters most. And yes, that comes with the understanding that every choice in life is a tradeoff—whenever you say *yes* to one thing, you say *no* to a thousand other things. It can't be otherwise.

Self-discipline is there to help you focus on your goals; to empower your best self to come forward, and your best life to materialize. It is something you do *by yourself, for yourself.* It is choosing your values, choosing yourself, and having the maturity to accept that there is a price to pay for them, in the form of temporary physical or emotional discomfort.

Self-discipline is often viewed as limiting, but when practicing it you quickly realize how limiting it is to *not* have discipline. It limits what you can achieve in life. It limits your ability to actualize yourself, to make your dreams come true. It places a low ceiling above your head.

Without discipline, you live a reactive life. You live how you were *conditioned* to be. Your bad habits and addictions reign freely, and you don't get to say *no* to them. Your energies are scattered, and your future is a repetition of your past.

With discipline you live a creative life. You live how you *design* your life to be. Your aspirations and values run the show. Your energy is focused, and your future is molded by your goals.

Mindful Self-Discipline is

Not		But
Restriction	→	Focus
Repression	→	Awareness
Inflexibility	→	Power

This is confirmed by studies that show that higher levels of self-control are linked to higher levels of satisfaction in life. When you practice self-discipline, you feel more confident about who you are, and get more of what you *really* want. So self-discipline doesn't kill the joy in your life—it gives you more meaningful joy, and in a more reliable way.

Mindful Self-Discipline is AWARENESS, Not Repression

Another misconception is thinking that self-discipline involves beating yourself up, suppressing your desires, and shaming yourself whenever you give in. Or thinking that it is forcing yourself to do stuff you don't want, with the whip of willpower.

Perhaps self-discipline has a bit of that taste to it, for some people—but not the type of self-discipline we are talking about in this book. Mindful Self-Discipline is not an act of self-violence. It is not about self-denial, suppression, or punishment. It is about self-love and choosing yourself. It's letting go of a smaller pleasure now for a greater gain later.

It is not about suppressing the desire for the donuts, but about *remembering* who you are, who you want to be, and what is really at stake when you say yes to this short-lived pleasure. When that is super clear, no force is required. The attractiveness of the temptation diminishes by itself.

You also cultivate self-acceptance, knowing that sometimes you will choose the donuts, despite knowing that it's not the best for you. When that happens, you just notice it, and gently bring yourself back to your goal—no shame, guilt or self-blame required. In fact, these negative emotions only harm your self-discipline. (More on this in Chapter 16.)

Self-discipline is basically the art of bypassing self-control conflicts (by using the tools that we will discuss later in this book); and, when that is not possible, resolving them in favor of your highest goals and values.

Mindful Self-Discipline is *not* based on shame, self-denial, and morality; and it's not suffocating. Rather, it is based on healthy goals and living in accordance with your own values. It is there to serve your true needs.

In fact, we all already have some self-discipline in our lives. We brush our teeth after meals, whether we feel like it or not; most of us also go to work every weekday, whether we feel like it or not; a good mother is there nourishing her baby multiple times a day, even when she is overwhelmed and sleep deprived.

We may take these for granted, but they are essential—without them, we would end up toothless, jobless, and childless.

The purpose of this book is not to give you impossible-to-meet standards or make you a superhuman that never fails, but to expand your self-awareness and self-discipline so that you can live a life more in accordance with your goals and values. In the journey to that ideal, you will fail many times. That is not only okay, it's *expected*. When that happens, you will use the skills you learn in this book to bounce back, without ever resorting to shame or guilt.

Mindful Self-Discipline is POWER, Not Inflexibility

It is not about being a slave to yourself, to time, to rules. Quite the opposite—it is freedom and power. Slavery is when you cannot do what you want to do; discipline is precisely the opposite. It allows you to do what you *really* want to do.

Self-discipline is freedom from the grip of your temptations, from the reptilian brain, from the lower self. It is the power to be led by your higher goals and ideals. It is you being the boss of yourself, the **author of your own life**. It is you deciding what you will do and what you will not do.

When you press the power button on your remote control, the TV turns on. It is always so. It's *inflexibly* so. And if it weren't, we would consider the remote to be faulty, or to need new batteries. Whether you decide to turn it on or not, it's your choice; but if you do press that button, it must turn on.

Likewise, when you make a resolution to yourself, self-discipline allows you to follow it *always*. It makes no sense to say that this is inflexible, because you are the one in control here. Being able to do what you want to do is not inflexibility; it is power.

When designing your ideal routine, you get to choose every element of it—and it is wise to keep a balance between effort and relaxation, work and fun, chasing goals and cultivating relationships. If you decide that you want to meditate every morning at 7am for twenty minutes, you do so because you *want* to, because you *choose* to. You do so because it is an important part of the person you aspire to be. Self-discipline gives you the power to keep that commitment to yourself.

Share this concept:

MindfulSelfDiscipline.com/what-self-discipline-is-not

HOW TO BALANCE SELF-DISCIPLINE

Self-discipline is a virtue, and every virtue casts a shadow—unless it's balanced by its opposite virtues. You may want to read that sentence again, as this is a rare insight. It took me years to realize the depth of this truth, and, unfortunately, I don't hear many people talking about it.

Too much humility makes you self-deprecating. Too much vitality makes you hyperactive. Too much kindness makes you a doormat. Too much patience makes you lenient. Too much perseverance makes you obsessive. Too much focus makes you narrow.

Your greatest strengths can be the source of your greatest weaknesses. The way to avoid that is not to diminish your strengths, but to develop wisdom about how to use them, and to balance them with opposing strengths.

In the case of self-discipline, some of the opposing strengths are flexibility and playfulness. Without these, you can go to the extreme of being rigid, stubborn, and obsessive.

Cultivate Discipline for The Right Reasons

The first thing to watch out for is that you are practicing this virtue for the right reasons. Ideally, you want it to be based on a dream, a vision, or a goal that you have for yourself—not based on the feeling that you have to do more to be "good enough". In other words, Mindful Self-Discipline is based on self-love, not shame; on self-respect, not self-punishment.

Balance Your Self-Discipline

The flame that burns twice as bright burns half as long.

LAO TZU

If being disciplined for you means burning the midnight oil for weeks or months on end, obsessively pursuing a goal or activity at the expense of all other things—such as your relationships or physical wellbeing—then you are in for trouble. This is not sustainable. It leads to willpower fatigue and, eventually, to burnout.

Having very strong willpower and self-discipline is definitely a good thing. If, on top of that, you can incorporate some healthy indulgences in your life without a sense of guilt, then you are safe. But if you end up living a workaholic life devoid of pleasure, then that's what is called *hyperopia* in scientific literature. Hyperopia is when, due to an excessive productive orientation, or excessive "indulgence guilt", you always avoid pleasure, feeling that it's immoral or shameful to indulge. This is not what Mindful Self-Discipline is about.

Balancing self-discipline is especially important for people who are type-A overachievers by nature. Studies show that hyperopic people experience more and more regret over time, for being too inflexible and not enjoying life. This, in turn, can lead you to being overly puritanical and judgmental about other people's choices.

The point for most of us is not to become an ascetic, nor to live one-sided lives. Therefore, part of your self-discipline must include taking care of yourself. This involves:

- Getting enough sleep, and proper meals
- Scheduling breaks, time off, and fun activities
- Having cheat days
- Keeping some areas of your life undisciplined and spontaneous
- Balancing work, relationships, and health
- Indulging, with moderation, in your favorite "guilty pleasures" (without the guilt)

Having some wiggle room for failure is not only healthy but can also help you maintain self-discipline in the long run. Otherwise, if you are too strict with yourself, it becomes very easy for you to fail, feel disappointed, and then give up. Your standards are too high, and your expectations, unreasonable.

If you have a tendency toward hyperopia, then you need to be disciplined about indulgences and rewards as well. Plan for them. Put them on your calendar. Make sure it happens—and when it does, enjoy it without inhibition. Remind yourself that if you don't do it, you may regret it. And please, celebrate your small wins along the way!

Fire and Water

To take this concept of balance one step further, I'll have to be a bit metaphorical and philosophical in my language. Bear with me for a minute, if that is not your cup of tea.

We can say that there are two forces in our personality.

One of them is like fire. It's the dynamic energy of desire, ambition, focus, and productivity. It makes you dissatisfied with the present moment, and gives you the fuel to move forward, make a change, and achieve things. The more dissatisfied you are—in other words, the bigger the gap between your current state and your desired state—the stronger will be your drive.

The other force is like water. It's the cooling energy of satisfaction, relaxation, gratitude and connection. It makes you happy in the present moment. It accepts things as they are, and accepts you as you are, having no urge to go anywhere. The stronger this energy is in you, the more you will feel peaceful and content, here and now; and, conversely, the weaker will be your fuel for change.

For increasing the water aspect, cultivate the feeling that your reality exceeds your expectations, rather than expectations exceeding your reality. For increasing the fire aspect, focus on the gap between expectations and reality; when that is eventually bridged, then create new and higher expectations.

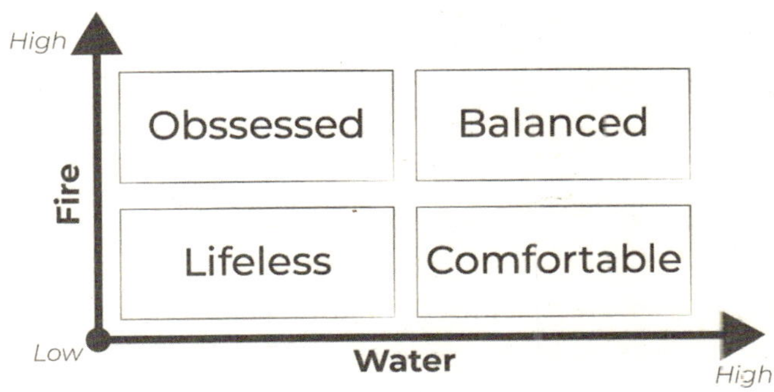

Self-discipline gives shape and reality to your inner fires. But please don't forget to also use it to protect your inner waters.

Living a life that is healthy, happy, and fulfilling involves striking the right balance between the fire and the water in you. How to actually do that? Well, that is one of the questions that I myself live with.

I don't think there is one true answer for it. It's different things for different people. Perhaps in one area of your life you want to be predominantly like fire, while in another you want to be like water. Or maybe these two elements need to be present in every area of your life, but in different proportions.

Let's leave it at that. Perhaps, like me, you just need to live with this question—and make adjustments as you go. Just don't forget that balance is key.

Share this concept:
MindfulSelfDiscipline.com/balanced-self-discipline

KEY POINTS

- Mindful Self-Discipline is *focus*, not restriction. It is something you do by yourself, for yourself. It enables you to become who you want to be.
- Mindful Self-Discipline is *awareness*, not repression. It is not about beating yourself up, but about healthy goals and self-acceptance.
- Mindful Self-Discipline is *power*, not inflexibility. It allows you to keep your promises to yourself, and be the author of your own life. It is self-respect.
- Cultivate self-discipline for the right reasons (going after a vision rather than running away from something).
- Balance self-discipline by getting enough sleep, taking breaks, time off, and keeping a balanced lifestyle.
- Have a balanced mix of the energies of fire (goals and productivity) and water (relaxation and gratitude).

Implementation resources: see the companion Workbook for exercises to help you achieve the right balance of self-discipline in your life. You can download it for free at **MindfulSelfDiscipline.com/workbook.**

CHAPTER 4

WILLPOWER, HABITS, AND ENVIRONMENT

Willpower is the key to success. Successful people strive no matter what they feel by applying their will to overcome apathy, doubt or fear.

DAN MILLMAN

There are no shortcuts to any place worth going.

BEVERLY SILLS

I think of self-discipline as something like a muscle. The more you exercise it, the stronger it gets.

DANIEL GOLDSTEIN

What is the difference between self-discipline, self-control, willpower, and habits? Do we still need self-discipline if we are able to build habits more effortlessly by "hacking" our environment? Some authors say that self-discipline and willpower are not dependable, because they are finite resources—is that true?

The purpose of this chapter is to clarify these points.

KEY DEFINITIONS

Let's bring some clarity to this conceptual maze of self-discipline.

Self-regulation is a broad term that encompasses many internal skills, including willpower, self-discipline, self-awareness, and motivation. It is the conscious, effortful regulation of the self, by the self.

Willpower is your ability to control your attention, emotions, and actions, despite the presence of competing stimuli, and resolve conflicts between your short-term desires and your long-term goals. It includes your capacity to delay gratification, override unwanted thoughts and feelings, and shift your internal state. For example: staying focused on the task at hand despite distractions, or saying no to soda despite the tempting can sitting in front of you.

Self-control is often cited as being synonymous with willpower. The authors who differentiate the two argue that self-control is more limited to impulse control, being your power to prevent yourself from doing things (the "I won't" power), while willpower includes also your ability to make yourself do things (the "I will" power).

Self-discipline is the continuous application of self-awareness and willpower over time, for the purpose of living in accordance with your higher values and choosing behaviors that are in harmony with your long-term goals.

Habit is when the exercise of self-discipline has crystallized over time, and now has become mostly automated and effortless. But habits can also be formed unconsciously in our lives.

Motivation is an emotional state of being energized to do something. It is the desire to engage in a certain activity.

A short example will help illustrate the differences.

> *Sarah goes for a coffee with an old friend she hasn't seen since college. When they meet, Sarah is impressed seeing how her friend is in perfect shape and beaming with energy. Her friend then talks about her healthy eating and exercise routine. This sparks Sarah's* ***motivation*** *to take healthy eating and physical exercise more seriously. She makes a decision there and then to stop eating ice cream (one of her top junk food items), and to run every weekday after work.*
>
> *Monday comes, the workday is over, and Sarah doesn't really feel like running. She is tired after a particularly stressful day at work. She just wants to lie on her couch and relax. There is zero motivation to*

*run. Then she remembers her commitment to run every Monday (**self-awareness**) and pushes herself to do it (**willpower**).*

*After the run, she opens her freezer and sees her favorite pot of ice cream—the one she and her partner always eat together while watching TV at night. There is a strong impulse to go for it, but she decides to instead close her eyes, shut the freezer door, and grab an apple for a healthy snack (**self-control**). After some time, the urge passes, and she feels pretty happy with herself.*

*This process repeats itself, in one way or another, every week. Every time she practices the skills of willpower and self-control to keep herself on track with her commitment, for the achievement of her goals, she is practicing **self-discipline**.*

*After a couple of months, all of this becomes automatic. Running every weekday is non-negotiable for her. There is no question about it anymore, no internal conflict to be fought—she just does it, regardless of how she feels. The pot of ice cream looks less tempting because she knows she won't go for it. At this point, Sarah has formed a **habit**.*

Willpower is basically the power of your decisions—it's how much what you say to yourself counts. Each time an obstacle or temptation comes your way, and you say NO to it and re-affirm your initial decision, this strengthens your willpower. So, in a way, willpower overlaps with determination, resilience, and mental toughness. Much of what is said in this book about self-discipline is also true about willpower, and vice-versa.

If we see willpower/self-control as the thread, then self-discipline is the process of weaving it all together to make a piece of clothing. Motivation is what got you started knitting in the first place.

It's important to note that habit-building is one of the main functions of self-discipline, but not the whole of it. Self-discipline is the guiding force that allows you to take action in accordance with your goals; some of these actions can be turned into habits, but not all of them.

For example, let's say that one of your goals is to fix your broken relationship with your son. To do that, you will need to behave in certain ways with him, to build rapport and connection. It is not about building a *habit* of doing something—such as journaling every night—but about responding to the needs of the moment in a way that advances your cause. The dynamic and unpredictable nature of human relationships is such that building habits cannot be the (only) solution; you need the self-discipline to act in accordance with certain principles.

Self-discipline includes building habits, but it is more than that. For building habits, setting up triggers and modifying your environment are good hacks (see Chapter 26); for other manifestations of self-discipline, there are no shortcuts. You need to be aware and exercise willpower as per the needs of the moment.

The rest of this chapter is focused on willpower, which is one of the two core elements of self-discipline. (The other one, as we'll see, is awareness.)

Share this concept:
MindfulSelfDiscipline.com/willpower-definition

IS WILLPOWER A LIMITED RESOURCE?

Is self-discipline/willpower a finite resource? One that we only have a limited amount of, and should avoid using too much, so that we have enough of it in the tank for when we need it?

Looking at the research on the surface, it seems that willpower is a limited resource—one that we should save up. This is known as the Ego Depletion model, which compares willpower with a battery that depletes over time, or a muscle that is fatigued with overuse. Once you dig deeper, however, you see that although this theory sheds important light on the topic, it's only half of the story. The other half is the psychological aspect of willpower: your beliefs and mindset.

Before we dive into theory, let's have a look at a well-known phenomenon called *decision fatigue*.

Decision Fatigue is Real

While we can debate whether willpower is finite or not, there's one thing we cannot deny: that decision fatigue is real.

What is it, actually? Every decision we make takes effort and is thus a form of stress. Making decisions takes some mental energy, and it is proven that after a long period of decision-making, the quality of our decisions deteriorates. We become tired of thinking things through properly, exercising self-control, and being thorough in our thinking. This leads people to:

- Make impulsive decisions
- Over-rely on cognitive biases, assumptions, and other mental shortcuts
- Have less energy for exercising self-control

A famous study found that the decisions judges make are strongly influenced by how long it has been since their last break. The percentage of favorable rulings dropped gradually from about 65% to nearly zero the more time had passed since their last break, and returned abruptly to 65% after a break.

Speaking to the concept of decision fatigue, Barack Obama once said in an interview:

> "You'll see I wear only gray or blue suits. I'm trying to pare down decisions. I don't want to make decisions about what I'm eating or wearing. Because I have too many other decisions to make."

Self-control is a big energy consumer in the brain, and that is a problem because the brain's primary purpose is survival (*not* self-actualization). For survival, saving energy is important. That means that the brain has a natural resistance against exercising self-control or willpower; it prefers to take the easier path (often the one of instant gratification) and save energy.

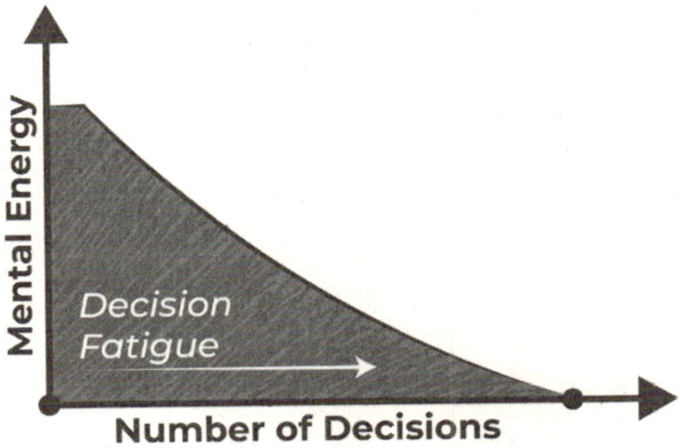

Understanding the phenomenon of decision fatigue teaches us one essential lesson: the value of simplicity and energy management. Do you want to experience less decision fatigue? Reduce the number of trivial decisions in your day-to-day life. Here are some ideas:

- Have a routine whereby you sleep, wake up, and eat at the same times every day.
- Predetermine the clothes you will wear. Donate half of the clothing items in your wardrobe so you have fewer options to choose from.
- Don't spend time on choices that don't matter much—such as "should I eat in the Mexican restaurant or the Thai place today?" Choose randomly if needed, or toss a coin, or make the decision once and then don't think about it anymore.
- Practice simplicity and minimalism in different areas of your life. Go on fewer social events, cultivate fewer (but deeper) friendships, process less information, subscribe to fewer newsletters, watch less news, etc.
- If possible, leave important decisions and self-control challenges for after a replenishing activity such as meditation, napping, or listening to music. Or make them earlier in the morning, after a full night of sleep.
- The more you can keep stress at bay, the more willpower you will have at your disposal. This one of the reasons why meditation, as a powerful stress release exercise, is important for Mindful Self-Discipline.

Decision fatigue is real, and it gives important lessons for us to better manage our energy. But does it prove that willpower is limited?

Nobel Prize winner and physiologist Archibald Hill argues that exercise fatigue may not be caused by muscle failure, but by an overprotective monitor in the brain that wants us to avoid exhaustion. He concluded that fatigue should no longer be considered a physical event, but rather a sensation or emotion. If that is the case, then what you believe about your capacity and about willpower is as important as how many decisions you've made today. At the very least, it means that our willpower is not as limited as we may feel.

The true limit for your willpower is much beyond the first signals of low glucose that your brain sends. The Navy SEALs have what is called the "40% rule", which states that once you get your first feeling of fatigue or tiredness, you have only used 40% of your actual power. This is as true about mental tiredness and willpower as it is about physical tiredness and muscle use.

We will get back to this topic in a moment. But before that, let's talk about the theory that, in explaining the mechanism of decision fatigue, concludes that willpower is limited. Many authors have used this theory to argue that you should not rely on willpower nor attempt to train it.

The Ego Depletion Model

Glucose is the fuel for the brain, and it's used in all mental operations, including exercising willpower. So it's possible (although unproven) that the reason why people fail to exercise willpower in certain challenging situations is due to lack of glucose in the blood. This idea can explain the phenomenon of decision fatigue. Indeed, for many years, the academic discussions on self-control and willpower were dominated by the Ego Depletion model proposed by Roy Baumeister, which is based on this observation.

The Ego Depletion model proposes that willpower is like a battery with a limited capacity: the more you make use of it, the more you deplete it, until it gets to a point where you can no longer use it unless you recharge it. The willpower battery is recharged by restful activities—like proper sleep, meditation, taking a break—and by replenishing your blood sugar through healthy meals.

This theory has been challenged by new studies that demonstrate that the amount of willpower you have is affected by the amount of willpower you *believe* you have.

Yes, you read that right. Your beliefs about your willpower capacity influence how much of it is at your disposal. People who believe in the limitations of willpower experience more self-control failures than those who don't believe that their willpower is limited. Other things that influence your willpower are your level of motivation, how you frame the self-control challenge ahead of you, and how you believe willpower works. Therefore, the Ego Depletion model doesn't fully explain what is going on here. And it has also fallen prey to the "replication crisis" in psychology.

You cannot believe that your smartphone is at 100% charge and with that make it last forever. Your thoughts about its battery level don't influence it; but your thoughts about willpower do. So, willpower is not like a depleting battery. The bottleneck for your willpower—and thus your self-discipline—is more likely in your mind than in your glucose levels.

A more accurate belief about willpower is that it works like a muscle. That means that:

- You strengthen it by exercising it; you weaken it by not using it (use it or lose it)
- It becomes temporarily weaker immediately after intense exercise
- After recovery, it becomes stronger than its prior capacity (this is known as *supercompensation*)

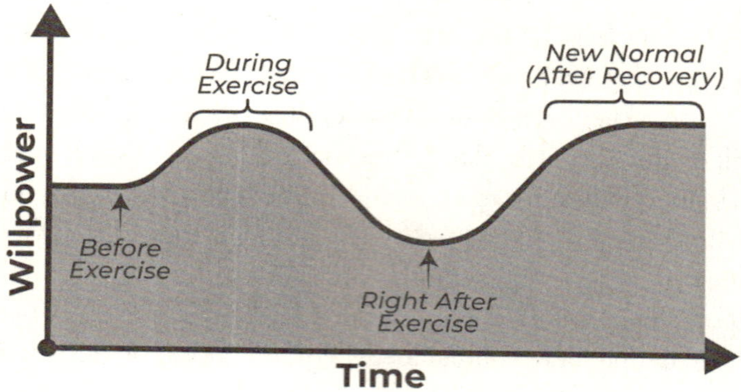

Hence, willpower is not like a hopelessly depleting battery. Willpower is a muscle that needs to be exercised—and the more you do, the stronger it becomes. And while there is arguably a correlation between willpower and the glucose levels in your blood, there is still a lot you can do to enhance your willpower or at least tap into deeper reserves.

Share this concept:

MindfulSelfDiscipline.com/willpower-is-like-a-muscle

AS YOU THINK, SO IT BECOMES

It's important to contextualize the findings of the Ego Depletion model research by noting that a lot of that research is testing the *average* individual, not the *self-disciplined* individual. This is like wanting to understand the nature and limits of a muscle by doing research on people who don't lift weights. What you get from such research is only half of the picture.

This distinction is well made by Stanford University Professor of Psychology Carol Dweck, author of the bestseller *Mindset: The New Psychology of Success*. Dweck observes that:

> While decision fatigue does occur, it primarily affects those who believe that willpower runs out quickly. (...) People get fatigued or depleted after a taxing task only when they believe that willpower is a limited resource, but not when they believe it's not so limited. (...) In some cases, the people who believe that willpower is not so limited actually perform *better* after a taxing task.

Since the majority of people believe that their willpower is scarce, the phenomenon of decision fatigue *seems* to be a universal truth about human experience simply because most studies don't distinguish between people holding various beliefs. These studies, attempting to draw conclusions about human nature, ignore the outliers and focus on the average. But the average just demonstrates the status quo; it shows what is common. The outliers show what is *possible*.

Okay, but what about the actual levels of glucose in the blood? Surely that functions as a general ceiling to the amount of willpower we can exercise, doesn't it? Dweck's insights again differ from the conclusion of previous studies, and confirm the experience of those who have systematically trained their willpower:

> We find that sugar improves self-control *only* for the people who believe in limited willpower. (...) We think that people who believe in limited willpower are always checking to see how fatigued they are. If they feel fatigued, they show a deficit. If you give them sugar and they get a surge of energy, they don't show a deficit.

If willpower is like a muscle that can be trained, which is an idea that Roy Baumeister eventually proposed, then that means that glucose is not the whole story. Regularly going through activities that strengthen your willpower—such as cold showers, fasting, meditation, behavior change and habit building—does *not* increase the level of glucose in your blood, of course, but it does indeed increase your willpower. Prof. Baumeister told me in an interview that he was able to replicate these findings in his lab, and explained them by saying that what's actually happening is that we are training ourselves to tap into deeper glucose reserves. But it's entirely possible that something else is happening because, as Dweck proposed, our mindset and beliefs have a lot to do with it.

It seems, then, that both the Ego Depletion theory and the mindset theory are right; each of them tells half of the story. That is, willpower is a *psychological force* with a biological basis (glucose levels). You can enhance it by increasing the level of glucose in your bloodstream, or by developing more positive beliefs about your capacity. So it is smart to observe both of these facts. In practical terms, this means that you need to both **manage** your willpower reserves *and* **strengthen** your willpower by exercising it daily and cultivating an empowering mindset.

Having said all of that, if you really want to *grow* your willpower, then I recommend that you emphasize the mindset aspect. Why? Because otherwise you tend to focus on your limitations. What you believe about your capacity becomes a self-fulfilling prophecy. Believing that you have limited willpower limits the amount of willpower that you can tap into. It closes your access to your deeper willpower reserves, making you accept defeat too soon under the pretext of "Sorry, I'm out of glucose". As the author Richard Bach once wrote, "Argue for your limitations, and sure enough they are yours."

So we can say that there are two types of people.

The first type focuses on the idea that willpower is limited and hopelessly depleting throughout the day like a dying battery. Therefore, they depend solely on habits and environment to make sure that they are in the best possible shape to make good decisions—and if not, they have a great biological excuse to justify their limitations. They emphasize the biological limits of self-control, don't attempt to exercise their willpower, and believe that "willpower doesn't work".

The second type of people believe that willpower is mostly limited by their minds. They see it as a muscle to be strengthened. They seek conducive environments and create habits to save time and prevent decision fatigue, but they don't shy away from exercising this core skill whenever they can. They feel tired after exercising self-control multiple times (just like the "limited theory" believers do), but they don't take those feelings as a sign that they have depleted a limited resource and that they cannot continue further. They feed on challenges, eat stress for breakfast, and feel energized when they meet resistance. They take full responsibility for their decisions and believe in the greatness of their potential.

Who will you choose to be?

Yes, it's a choice. You can choose to focus on the biological limits of willpower—or you can choose to focus on its psychological plasticity. This has profound implications about how you feel, and about your relationship with your willpower. Which person is strongest: the one who avoids using their muscles as much as possible because they believe they are doomed to eventually fail, or those who *believe themselves strong* and systematically exercise their muscles?

Hence, it is wiser to believe that you can train your self-control, tap into deeper sources of willpower within yourself, and thus experience more energy and willpower in your daily life. That does not mean that you will instantly have a limitless amount of willpower just by believing that you do. But you will have *much more* than the next-door neighbor who believes that his willpower is scarce and that there is nothing he can do about it.

Practical Conclusions

Do you want more self-discipline in your life? Then believe that you can exercise it, and train yourself to tap into an endless source of willpower within you. And, of course, be pragmatic and also make the changes in your life that you need to make to help this process.

First and foremost, **exercise your will** (just like you exercise your muscles). Take it seriously. Rely on it as if your life depended on it—because in some aspects it does. Believe in your power. Exercise it daily. Grow it daily.

Second, **manage your energy**. It makes sense to be aware of decision fatigue and to organize your routine around it. This means, among other things: starting the day with the most willpower-consuming tasks; diminishing the amount of trivial decisions you need to make on a daily basis; and learning to manage stress.

Third, optimize your **lifestyle**. Just like your physical muscles, your willpower muscle can be overloaded if you don't take breaks and build strength over time. Commit to exercising your willpower regularly, yes, but also develop a supporting lifestyle that includes good fuel and good rest. Things like eating healthily, having regular physical exercise, sleeping enough, and practicing meditation daily will go a long way.

Finally, cultivate **patience and perseverance**. Muscles don't go from flabby to toned overnight. You have to put in a considerable amount of effort before that happens, and if you expect too much too soon, you will feel disappointed and give up. The same happens with your willpower muscle. If you think that you can psych yourself up to have superhuman willpower by the time you're done with this chapter…you're in for disappointment.

So believe in your capacity, but be patient about the process of actualizing it. Aim for having small willpower wins consistently, day after day. This will help you further believe in yourself, and thus expand your capacity. (I'll cover this concept in depth in Chapters 21, 28, and 31.)

In summary, here are the four aspects of cultivating willpower:

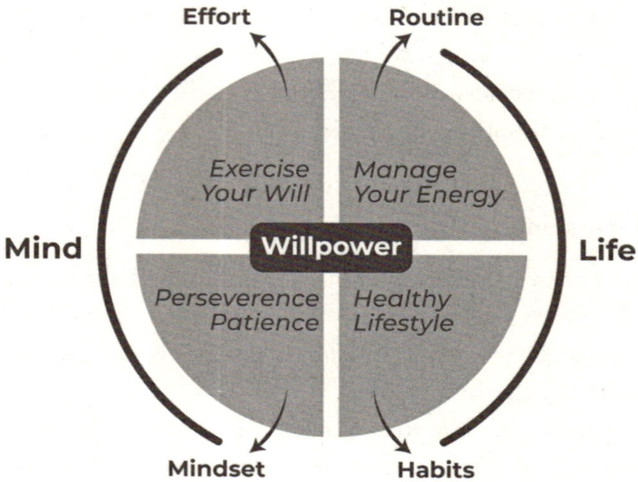

Share this concept:
MindfulSelfDiscipline.com/train-your-willpower

HABITS ARE ESSENTIAL, BUT NOT ENOUGH

It is trendy these days to write articles titled "willpower is dead" and "the self-discipline myth". You can see many bloggers embracing this trend. These ideas, although well-meaning, are misleading and can be harmful.

Yes, it's true that willpower takes effort, and self-discipline is hard work. And it's true that habits, once established, are automatic and almost effortless. But that doesn't mean that you can replace the need for willpower in every area of life just by building habits.

First, because developing good habits does require some willpower in the beginning. You can make it as easy as possible for yourself to build that habit, and start really small, but you still need some willpower. The example of Sarah wanting to run and stop eating ice cream illustrated this point.

When building good habits, you can, and should, tweak the environment and use reminders to make it easier. These things are good and helpful, and we cover this topic in Chapter 26. Yet they are the training wheels of willpower; if you can only ride with them on, then you've limited yourself.

Habit will take you to the gym; willpower will pull the weights and make you do another rep even when you are tired. Habit will keep you in a relationship; willpower will enable you to change deep patterns in yourself, so you can *thrive* in your relationship. Habit stops you from buying chocolate cake when you go to the grocery store; willpower allows you to say no when a delicious dessert is available under your nose. Habit takes me to my cold shower every morning; willpower turns on the tap.

The second reason why habits don't fully replace willpower and self-discipline is because life is dynamic and unpredictable. You can't make sure that you will always act in harmony with your values and goals by trying to make a habit out of everything. Life will throw curveballs at you. It will catch you unprepared. It will require you to control your impulses and make difficult decisions when you least expect.

When you need to go to work but don't feel like it; when you wish to respond aggressively but shouldn't; when you desperately need to sleep but your baby won't stop crying; it is willpower that comes to the rescue—not habit.

We all have moments like these. Sometimes on a daily basis. In these challenging situations, self-discipline—which is the ability to act in accordance with your highest goals and values—comes to the rescue. If you have developed it, it will be there for you. If you haven't, then you'll be carried away by the strongest impulse in the moment.

Habits are essential, but not enough. They are the result of practicing self-discipline and willpower, not a replacement for it. *Mindful Self-Discipline* is both about building habits and about growing willpower.

If all you need to do is to move a heavy box from A to B, then please use wheels, not your muscles. But if your purpose is to become strong, then let go of those wheels and push that box—or go to the gym and pull heavy weights for that purpose. Likewise with your willpower: if you want to strengthen it, you'll need to make use of it. Just as with any other muscle, the only way you'll develop willpower is through friction and resistance.

If you are struggling to change your diet, or to get yourself to work on a side business, or to go to sleep early, then probably just getting the habit established, at whatever cost, is the priority. But eventually you will need to do things to strengthen your willpower. You will need it in life—especially if you are pursuing difficult goals. For these things there are no shortcuts.

Do you want to grow beyond your current limits in your career and personal life? Then you will need willpower every single day. Just having habits won't be enough. Habits make you show up; willpower makes you excel.

In a nutshell: please make use of the habit-building principles in this book to create habits in the easiest possible way, but don't shy away from exercising your willpower. Scientific research shows that willpower is the greatest single factor for success in life. You will always need it.

Share this concept:
MindfulSelfDiscipline.com/habits-are-not-enough

ENVIRONMENT IS ESSENTIAL, BUT NOT ENOUGH

The "willpower doesn't work" believers argue that willpower will always eventually fail, and the environment will always eventually win. They argue, then, that we should rely on improving our environment rather than training our willpower.

This idea attempts to average us down to the lowest human denominator—and that is incredibly limiting and uninspiring. Besides, you cannot always avoid exercising willpower in your life by seeking to build the perfect supportive environments around you all the time. Sometimes it's not possible, or not desirable. What if you want to stop eating ice cream everyday but removing it from your freezer is not an option because your partner is an ice cream aficionado?

Those authors speak from the point of view of "what usually happens"—of your conditioning. I am speaking from the point of view of "what's possible for you"—your potential. Mindful Self-Discipline is not about who we are conditioned to be. It's about who you can become. It's about your *potential*, not your current limitations.

People say that "willpower doesn't work" because they haven't fully developed it; so it's not dependable *for them*. By the same token, with the way digital distractions are increasing in our modern life, soon enough future generations will be saying that "focus doesn't work", because nobody can concentrate anymore!

If you never rely on your willpower, you will never be *able* to rely on your willpower. That's not a good place to be, because willpower is essential for both success and happiness. Environment is important, but it's only half of the story—and often the half we have less control over.

You Will Always Need Willpower

Unless we are perfect people (with no internal conflicts) living in a perfect environment (with everything around us fully supporting our goals), we will *always* meet some form of resistance or obstacle. That is the case especially if we are trying to develop ourselves, stretch beyond our current limits, or achieve anything difficult.

We can't escape that fact. And when we do meet obstacles, we will need willpower to overcome them. We will need to have the discipline to make choices that are difficult, choices that are against what our external environment is triggering us to do, or against what our internal environment (impulses) is pushing us to do.

It is a great idea to also focus on resolving internal conflicts, of course. When all the aspects of our personality want the same thing, and there is no self-sabotage or internal contradictions, it is much easier to move forward. There are many tools to help us get to that state, such as meditation, self-reflection, therapy, coaching. It is also a great idea to seek the most suitable environment for our goals, or attempt to shape our existing environment to be as helpful as possible. There is no need to swim upstream when there is an easier path available.

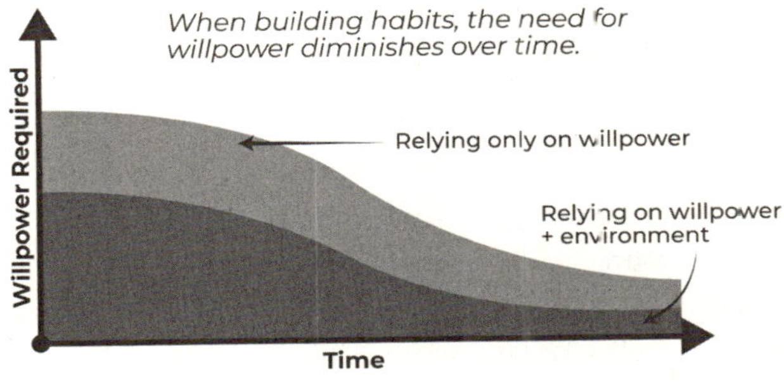

Still, we will *always* meet resistance on the way to our goals. When that happens, we will need willpower. It is futile to try to design a life where we won't need it, just so we can avoid the pain of exercising it. Such life would be stale—devoid of growth.

Exercise your willpower so you strengthen it. Make use of your environment, if possible, to make things easier; but don't depend on it.

Willpower Can Fail—So What?

Emphasizing that willpower is an exhaustible resource and saying that in the end the environment always wins, is just like saying that our muscles are an exhaustible resource, and that at the end gravity (the weights) always win. Even if that is true, it doesn't mean that exercise is futile. The whole point is that we transform ourselves in the process.

Perhaps it's true that the natural tendency of willpower in the human mind is to eventually exhaust itself. So what?

It's also the natural tendency of the body to get dirty and sick. Does that mean we shouldn't clean it and attempt to keep it healthy? Does that mean that healthcare doesn't work?

It's the natural tendency of love to fade away after years of marriage—does that mean we shouldn't attempt to keep it alive? Does that mean love doesn't work?

It's the natural tendency of our mind to get distracted—does that mean we shouldn't exercise our power of focus? Does that mean focus doesn't work?

Many of the most valuable things in life require effort to be achieved and then maintained; and our effort may not always succeed. But it is worth it. The price of giving up exercising our willpower, self-care, love, and focus, is much, much higher.

Self-Reliance is Evolution

It's a sign of evolution to be able to choose your environment, or improve it. But it's also a sign of evolution to be able to *thrive* despite your environment—because we will always meet unhelpful environments.

Let's look at nature and the evolution of species. The less evolved the animal is, the more it lives and dies by its environment. Humans are the animals with the greatest ability to survive despite the environment, because we are resourceful. We can create tools and methods to master our environment, and we refuse to be controlled by it.

Being able to thrive despite the environment is a great strength—and a much needed one. It invites you to focus on what you can *control* (your choices), and not on what you can at best only *influence* (the environment). The exercise of self-discipline allows us to continuously master our *inner* environment; to act according to our goals and aspirations, despite environmental triggers; and to succeed even when the odds are against us.

The well-known Stanford marshmallow experiment illustrates this point perfectly. In this study, published in 1972, a child was left alone in a room with a marshmallow, and she had two choices: to eat that yummy marshmallow straight away, or to wait until the researcher returned and get two marshmallows instead. The choice was between an immediate reward, or a bigger reward for those who had used willpower to delay gratification.

In follow-up studies, the researchers found that children who were able to delay gratification ended up having better life outcomes. They got higher SAT scores, had better social skills, earned more money, engaged less in substance abuse, had lower likelihood of obesity, could cope better with stress, and had overall better physical and mental health.

Today, willpower and self-discipline are essential for you to survive and be happy. We live in times where the survival of the fittest means survival of the *focused*.

Use Your Environment, But Don't Be Dependent on It

Using your environment to your favor—e.g., removing temptation or placing reminders all around you—is a great hack for building habits. This is something we will explore later (Chapter 26). It's a shortcut, and we love that. We live in a shortcut-obsessed society.

The problem is when we overuse the shortcut, we become dependent on it. We get to a point where we can't do the work without it anymore. Or we may try the available shortcuts to achieve our new goal and give up when they fail—because we've lost the ability to rely on ourselves and exercise our willpower.

If you focus on environmental triggers, you will be able to build some good habits. But if you focus on your environment *and* your willpower, you will have both good habits and strong willpower. It's funny how that works!

That is why, unlike some self-help gurus out there, I don't put too much emphasis on environment. It's good to use it as an aid, and it is a useful shortcut.

But, at the same time, you need to be prepared for *life*, and in life many times we have no control over our environment. So we need to be able to stick to our goals and values regardless of the environment. That is only developed by exercising our willpower in adverse conditions.

Yes, I do make use of environment to achieve my goals, but I also exercise my willpower daily. It is the environment that makes my alarm clock ring at 2:30am every morning. It is willpower that makes me immediately get up. It is habit that takes me to the cold shower every day; it is willpower that turns on the tap.

Willpower doesn't work if you haven't trained it. It works if you have.

Like love, focus, and good health, willpower takes constant effort.

Even if you could design your life so that every environment is perfectly supportive of your goals, please don't. It's like designing a life where you never need to lift anything heavier than five pounds—it's comfortable, but it won't make you strong. And sooner or later you'll need those muscles!

Conclusion: make use of your environment to help you stick to good habits, but don't depend on it fully. Continuously seek to stretch yourself, meet resistance, and exercise your willpower. This is how true greatness and inner strength are born.

Share this concept:
MindfulSelfDiscipline.com/environment-is-not-enough

EXERCISE: STRENGTHEN YOUR WILL

To build a muscle, you must apply resistance to that muscle, embrace the pain, and push through. Likewise, with willpower and self-discipline—they grow through friction. Embrace that pain, and don't shy away!

Remember the talk of *Fire vs. Water* in Chapter 3? Well, exercising your willpower in the direction of your goals will increase your inner fire because friction creates heat. When exercising your muscles, it's physical heat. When exercising willpower, it's psychological heat. In the spiritual traditions of India, this psychological heat is called *tapas* (not to be confused with Spanish snacks). *Tapas* is considered the main element of self-transformation. Unimaginable things are possible through willpower and *tapas*.

You can mold a piece of iron to your desired shape only if you strike it while it's hot. Likewise, exercising your willpower daily generates the needed inner heat that allows you to mold your life—and yourself—as per your design.

Don't shy away from this inner heat. Invite it. Rejoice in it. Seek to exercise your willpower, in one form or another, every day of your life.

How do you do that? Practicing self-discipline with your goals and aspirations is a natural way of exercising your willpower. This is what the rest of this book is all about.

Another way is to focus on exercising the willpower muscle by itself, by choosing to do something difficult every day, on purpose. It doesn't matter how small it is. If it generates psychological heat, if it stretches you, it is a form of *tapas.*

The idea is to choose a small commitment every morning—something that is meaningful and challenging for you—and keep to it throughout your day, *no matter what.* Here are some examples of challenging daily commitments:

Today I will	**Today I will not**
Take a cold shower for five minutes	Complain about anything
Practice intermittent fasting for eighteen hours	Use any swear words
Feel grateful whenever I say "thank you"	Slouch
Cultivate contentment and optimism	Drink coffee
Speak out when I see injustice	Eat sugar
Breathe deeply before unlocking my phone	Argue meaninglessly
Be in bed at 10pm sharp	Use any social media app/site
Have one difficult conversation	Interrupt anyone who is speaking
Do something I've been postponing	Watch TV or play games
Exercise thirty minutes more than usual	Snooze my alarm
Hold eye contact with people	Have any junk food
Say "no" when I need to say "no"	Bite my fingernails/lips/cheeks
Be friendly toward everyone I meet	Check email outside working hours
Think before I talk	Check or send any text message
Do something I was avoiding	Gossip
Be on time for everything	Indulge in negative feelings
Speak kindly and truthfully at all times	Say any harsh words

These are just some ideas, to get your juices flowing. Some of them may not be an issue for you at all, so they are not good candidates for this exercise. Choose whatever is challenging and yet meaningful for you. Focus on a different challenge from the list (or make one up) every day, for twenty-one days. This simple practice exercises not only your willpower, but also your self-awareness skills.

In following this exercise, you may notice a tendency to want to avoid that particular temptation you've decided not to indulge in, so that it's easier for you to complete your daily commitment. That is cheating and defeats the purpose of this exercise. Instead, live your life as normal, and meet the challenges as they come. Or, if you are feeling ambitious, turn the heat up by purposefully exposing yourself to more temptation.

What happens at the end of twenty-one days? Your willpower will be more reliable. You can then use it to change any particular behavior you want; or you can go through the list again, narrow down to five main challenges, and this time stay twenty-one days on each one.

Finally, don't worry if these challenges feel unachievable at this point. The point is not doing it perfectly, but just to get you to exercise your willpower muscle and to show you what is possible. The rest of this book will teach you many practical tools to make this process easier.

Share this concept:

MindfulSelfDiscipline.com/willpower-challenge

KEY POINTS

Definitions

- Willpower is your ability to control your attention, emotions, and actions, despite the presence of competing stimuli, and resolve conflicts between your short-term desires and your long-term goals. It includes your capacity to delay gratification, override unwanted thoughts and feelings, and shift your internal state. Self-control is often used as synonymous with willpower.
- Self-discipline is the continuous application of self-awareness and willpower over time. Much of what is said in this book about self-discipline is also true about willpower, and vice-versa.
- Habit-building is one of the main functions of self-discipline, but not the whole of it. Not all of your goal-promoting actions can be turned into a habit.

The Nature of Willpower

- Knowing that decision fatigue is real, simplify your daily life so that you need to make fewer decisions, keep stress at bay, and follow a regular routine.
- People who focus on the limited theories of self-control experience more self-control failures than those who don't believe that their willpower is limited. What you believe about your capacity becomes a self-fulfilling prophecy. Believing that you have limited willpower limits the amount of willpower that you can tap into.
- Willpower works like a muscle. That means that you strengthen it by exercising it and you weaken it by not using it (use it or lose it). Just like a muscle, it will be temporarily weaker immediately after intense exercise, but after recovery it will be stronger than its prior capacity (*supercompensation*).
- Willpower is a *psychological force* with a biological basis (glucose levels). You can enhance it by increasing the level of glucose in your bloodstream or by developing more positive beliefs about your capacity.

- To increase your willpower, exercise it regularly (as with any other muscle), with patience and perseverance (muscles don't grow overnight). Also, cultivate high levels of energy by eating well, doing physical exercise, and sleeping well.
- Believe in your power. Exercise it daily. Grow it daily.

Habits Are Essential, But Not Enough

- You cannot replace the need for willpower in every area of life by just building habits. Not everything that requires discipline can be turned into a habit. Besides, building habits still requires some willpower in the beginning, even if you tweak your environment.
- Habits make you show up; willpower makes you excel.

Environment Is Essential, But Not Enough

- You cannot always avoid exercising willpower in your life by seeking to build the perfect supportive environments. Environment is important, but it's only half of the story—and often the half we have little control over.
- We will always need to have the discipline to make choices that are difficult—choices that are against what our external environment is triggering us to do, or against what our internal environment (impulses) is pushing us to do.
- Willpower doesn't work if you haven't trained it. It works if you have.
- Make use of your environment to help you stick to good habits, but don't depend on it fully. Continuously seek to stretch yourself, meet resistance, and exercise your willpower. This is how true greatness and inner strength are born.

Exercise: Strengthen Your Will

- To build a muscle, you must apply resistance to that muscle, embrace the pain, and push through. Likewise, with willpower—it grows through friction.

- That friction generates an inner heat known as *tapas* which allows you to mold yourself and your life as per your design.
- Seek to exercise your willpower, in one form or another, every day of your life. Do that by developing self-discipline in relation to your goals, and also by choosing to do something difficult every day, on purpose. (See examples for a twenty-one-day willpower challenge.)

CHAPTER 5

THE THREE PILLARS OF MINDFUL SELF-DISCIPLINE

The Three Pillars are the heart of Mindful Self-Discipline. They contain everything you need to know and do to become self-disciplined in all areas of your life. They are: Aspiration, Awareness and Action.

You need all three pillars. If even one of them is missing, your self-discipline will not be reliable. I recommend that you learn these pillars in order but focus first on the ones you are weakest in.

The opposite of the three As of *self-discipline* are the three Fs of *chaos*: **F**ragmentation, **F**orgetfulness, **F**utility.

Self-discipline is a skill that you can learn. The first time you go through this whole process for a habit you want to build, it may feel cumbersome, hard, artificial. But, after that, it becomes easier with each habit added. Eventually, this becomes second nature.

The next several chapters deal with each of the three pillars in depth. You will learn all the concepts you need, and a variety of exercises. Please don't feel overwhelmed. You don't need to understand everything or practice everything. Explore which pillar(s) you are weakest in and start with the one or two exercises that feel most promising.

PILLAR 1

ASPIRATION

CHAPTER 6

THE WHAT AND THE WHY

Inspiration follows aspiration.

RABINDRANATH TAGORE

The greater danger for most of us lies not in setting our aim too high and falling short; but in setting our aim too low, and achieving our mark.

MICHELANGELO BUONARROTI

A person without a purpose is like a ship without a rudder.

THOMAS CARLYLE

Your aspiration is your purpose, your dream, your *why*. It is the goal, desire, or ambition that moves you to action. It's what you want to achieve, experience, or become. (Throughout the rest of this chapter, I use the terms aspiration and purpose interchangeably.)

Desire motivates action. Desire creates a void in you, by conceiving a reward that will fill it perfectly. The bigger the void—in other words, the aspiration—the greater the fuel that's available for you.

That fuel is essential for you to overcome the challenges that will eventually come your way. Challenges such as things not working out as expected, self-doubt, procrastination, confusion, criticism, and rejection. As the philosopher Friedrich Nietzsche said, "He who has a *why* can bear almost any how."

START WITH PURPOSE

Your aspiration is the reason you are starting the journey in the first place. Without it, self-discipline becomes difficult at best—if not outright meaningless. You're unlikely to go through pain, discomfort, and sacrifice without a good reason for it. Your aspiration is that good reason.

Let me give you a simple example from my personal life. My wife ~~insists~~ encourages me to use a face cream every night before going to bed, to prevent wrinkles. She reminds me that I am constantly appearing on videos, seeing clients, and giving interviews, and argues that appearance matters a lot. She points out that other men in my family got face wrinkles early, so there might be a genetic predisposition for it. Besides, "it only takes two minutes", she says.

Yet none of that seems to make any impression on my mind. I don't seem to care that much. As a result, I never end up using the cream for more than a few days in a row, even when the environment is conducive (that is, the cream is clearly visible on my bedside table). Because it's not connected to any deeper aspiration for me.

If the habit you are trying to build or the change you are trying to make are not connected to a deeper why, then self-discipline will feel forced—a chore. But if they are connected to a heart-felt purpose, then self-discipline can feel exciting, meaningful, and promising.

Let's say we want to encourage Mark, an executive in our company, to meditate. If Mark is simply told to "sit quietly every day for ten minutes and watch your breath", because "it's good for you", he is unlikely to follow it. Or, even if he does, his meditation practice will lack depth and vitality—it will not be transformational.

Compare that to Mark having clarity that the most important thing for him is to master his mind so he can live without anxiety, sleep without using pills, and begin to explore his deeper potential as a leader and as a man. Then have him magnify that feeling by evoking the understanding that he can never be a true leader in his company if he is not a leader of himself, and that lasting legacy and influence can only be had if he is more *calm, centered, and focused* in his daily life. Show him the difference between living and leading from the monkey-mind versus the monk-mind. Explain that meditation is a powerful tool that supports this transformation—and *then* encourage him to meditate.

Can you see the difference?

Every activity that you can connect to a deeper purpose will be energized with meaning and vitality. This changes everything.

Indeed, studies show that people with a stronger sense of purpose:

- live longer
- experience less depression
- have better immune systems
- are more engaged at work
- are less likely to experience cardiovascular diseases and Alzheimer's
- feel more love and connection in intimate relationships
- experience a greater sense of abundance in their lives

We all need to aspire to something and feel that we are going somewhere. Otherwise, there is a sense of boredom in life. Our daily routine feels stale and unengaging. As a result, we seek relief through bad habits, and seek engagement through mindless entertainment, news, social media, games, etc.

When you have a purpose, you are not waiting for things to happen—you are making them happen. You are not waiting to *feel like* doing the work; you do so regardless of how you feel. Because it's key to who you are.

Your aspiration is the source of your motivation and commitment. It's the spark, the fuel for the journey. If you don't have it, it will be easy for you to get distracted, give in to temptation, forget what's important, and run after the next shiny object.

Despite being extremely important for living and thriving, most people don't have a deep aspiration. The current climate of busyness, materialism, and cynicism doesn't help either. As a society, we are living in a *crisis of meaning*. Dr. Viktor Frankl, PhD, calls it the "existential vacuum", which he deems responsible for the three major societal ills: aggression, addiction, and depression. His book, *Man's Search for Meaning*, is a masterpiece on the topic of purpose.

> *The mass of men lead lives of quiet desperation,*
> *and go to the grave with the song still in them.*
>
> HENRY DAVID THOREAU

Having no sense of purpose kills us from the inside, little by little, without us even noticing. If we feel that we are not needed, that we cannot contribute and make a difference, that we have no mission… then our life will feel empty. We may attempt to fill it with pleasure, money and fun, but we will never be *fulfilled*. Not until we touch that deeper pain or deeper desire that exists within.

You need a noble aspiration. Something that stretches you, that keeps you engaged, and that is deeply meaningful for you. And if you can connect this aspiration to an ideal greater than yourself, that's even better. With that, you will also have access to strength that is also greater than yourself.

Aspiration Pillar Steps

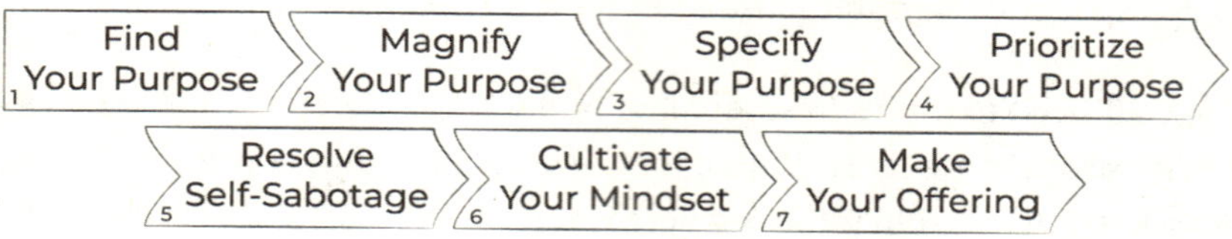

At this point, you may be thinking: "Giovanni, I got this book just because I need to start exercising, save some money, and stop eating donuts. I'm not into all this soul-searching stuff." If that is you, then you may want to skip Steps 1 and 2 of this Pillar for now and start from Step 3 (Chapter 9).

Share this concept:
MindfulSelfDiscipline.com/start-with-purpose

GOALS VS ASPIRATIONS

Let's take a moment to clarify the differences between a goal and an aspiration. In the table below, we start with the goal, which is more specific, because that is usually what people are aware of. Then we cover an example aspiration that could be sitting behind that goal, and some of the strategies (tactics) that can be used to accomplish it.

Goal	Aspiration	Possible Strategy
Lose forty pounds	To feel young, healthy, full of life; to have plenty of energy for the activities I care about	Daily treadmill for thirty minutes and intermittent fasting on a low-carb diet
Double my business	To feel that I have made it as an entrepreneur, and experience financial abundance	Hire a marketing consultant, improve my systems, and launch a new product
Master cooking	To better express my feelings of love and nurture for those I cook for, so they feel how much I care	Find a good cookbook, buy the ingredients and utensils, try a new recipe every day
Meditate daily	To be less impulsive, and more centered; to explore the spiritual side of life; to master my mind	Practice three minutes a day, and gradually increase; join a good program or community
Be more productive	To feel that I am making good use of my skills; to keep challenging myself and show up as my best	Use better tools; implement the GTD system; schedule time for distraction-free work

The goal is the vehicle for your aspiration; the strategy is the vehicle for your goal. Two people with the same goal may have completely different aspirations; or they may have the same goal and aspiration but completely different strategies to achieve that goal.

The aspiration is the *deeper why behind your why*. Discovering what that is will unleash tremendous energy for your journey, and lead to greater fulfillment. This important step is usually skipped in many other books in this genre, which focus more on the technicalities.

If you think of your life as a boat journey, your strategy is the map, the destination is the end goal, and your aspiration is why you want to get there. If the destination is not clear, you will be continuously tempted to choose another destination midway, when the journey gets rough, and settle for the distractions on the way (islands).

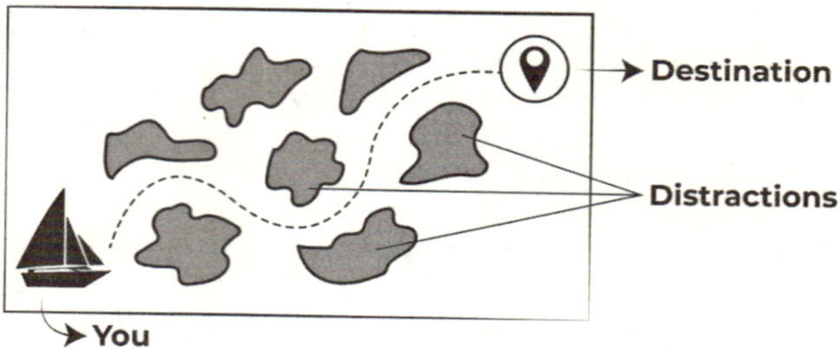

Indeed, in this book, I could have simply given you a proven framework for self-discipline—with all the tools, tips, and exercises—so you can reach whatever goal you are pursuing. But that wouldn't necessarily serve you, because your goal is only half the story. You need to touch the *aspiration* behind it.

Your goal needs to be a proper *vehicle* for your aspiration. Yet for most people there is a disconnect between the two. It could be because:

- Your goal was borrowed from someone else. Perhaps you were told that this is what you *have to* pursue. Or perhaps this goal embodies the values silently imposed by your parents, society, or the media.
- You are unaware of your aspiration, and so you cannot choose a goal that is well aligned with it. This, again, will make you gravitate toward other people's goals and worldviews.
- You are aware of your aspiration but lack the courage or support to fully *embrace* it. Perhaps you believe that it is not right for you to pursue it, or that it's "not practical", or that you are not good enough for it.

Whatever the cause, when your goals don't match your deeper aspiration, achieving your goals will leave you unfulfilled. You will have successfully climbed to the top of a ladder you actually didn't need to climb. No amount of money, ovation, or perks can compensate for the emptiness you'll feel.

Self-discipline empowers you to achieve your goals. *Mindful* self-discipline empowers you to fulfill your *aspiration* by achieving the right type of goals.

Share this concept:
MindfulSelfDiscipline.com/goals-vs-aspirations

WANT-TO VS. HAVE-TO GOALS

Is your goal a "have-to" goal or a "want-to" goal?

Do you want that new BMW because all your friends have it, and you believe that you are lagging behind? Or do you want it because ever since you were a kid you saw your dad enjoying his, and you dreamed of the sense of freedom and independence that you believe you'll experience once you drive your own?

In the first case, it's a *have-to* goal; it only makes sense if you can show it off, and it loses meaning if nobody knows you own one. In the second case, the drive is a bit more intrinsic, and regardless of whether people know about it or not, you'll enjoy having it; it's a *want-to* goal.

Do you take a shower every day because you're *supposed to*, or because you enjoy feeling clean? Do you want to get a PhD because of status, or because you want to take your research skills and career to the next level? Do you want to eat healthy because you have no other option, or is it because you know and *feel* that it's good for you?

Self-control studies show that students with have-to motivations experience more obstacles and temptations than those with want-to motivations. As a result, they had to make more effort, and wear out their willpower more easily. (To read about the details of this and all other studies mentioned, check out the references section at the end of the book.)

A goal, habit, or activity that is a vehicle for your true aspiration will feel like something you *want* to do, not something you *have* to do. The need will come from within you, not from other people or from society. It will fit what you deeply want for yourself, and not something you do just because you're supposed to, because people expect you to, or because of status benefits.

All right, but what to do if your current goal feels like a *have-to* goal? You have three options:

1. Change your attitude toward this goal, so you can want it for its own sake.
2. Find a different strategy for achieving the same goal, so you can enjoy the process.
3. Choose a new goal.

Option number one is about telling yourself a different story about your goal. For example, if you need to start eating more salads and you hate it, try to condition your mind to enjoy it. Or tell yourself that eating salads is not just about enjoying tasty food, but about having the health and energy levels you want. (We will explore these two strategies in Chapter 19.)

Sometimes rewording your self-talk from "I have to" to "I get to" can do the trick. "I get to spend time with my kids every night" feels very different from "I have to spend time with my kids every night", doesn't it?

Option number two is about finding a different way of achieving the same goal. For example, if you need to exercise but hate going to the gym or running, try tennis or another sport you may enjoy more. If you want to grow your business but hate using social media, try ads or partnerships. When the goal-promoting activity is enjoyable, it's easier to want it for its own sake.

If options one and two don't work, then you will need to resort to option number three and change your goal. Otherwise, self-discipline will feel like a battle, take a lot of effort, and involve constant fights with yourself. And, at the end, achieving your goal would be less fulfilling than you imagine.

Share this concept:
MindfulSelfDiscipline.com/want-to-and-have-to-goals

KEY POINTS

- Your aspiration is the fuel for your self-discipline, the source of your motivation and commitment. The stronger your purpose, the easier it will be for you to be disciplined. So spend some time clarifying and magnifying your purpose.
- Goals and aspirations are different things. Your aspiration is the deeper why behind your why. Your goal is a vehicle for your aspiration, and thus needs to be in sync with it. When your goals don't match your deeper aspiration, achieving your goals will likely leave you unfulfilled.
- Make sure your goals are "want-to" goals and not "have-to" goals. If they are not, you'll have to change your attitude toward your goal, find a different strategy for achieving it, or choose a new goal.

CHAPTER 7

ASPIRATION STEP 1: FIND YOUR PURPOSE

Aspiration Pillar Steps

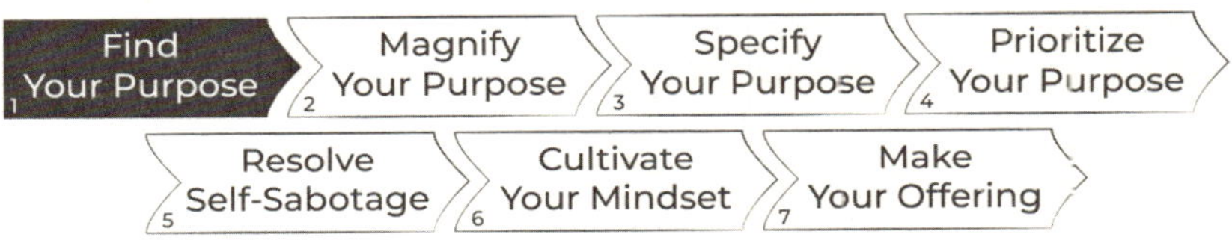

Perhaps you have a good idea of what you wish to achieve. It could be losing forty pounds, doubling your business, breaking a bad habit, meditating daily, controlling your anger, reinventing yourself, writing a book, improving your relationship, or mastering a new skill. However, these things are actually the goals, not the *aspiration*.

We all have a deep aspiration inside of us, waiting to be discovered, owned, and realized.

There is big pain in not living our life in accordance with that higher purpose—but most of us are out of touch with that. We are distracted from that pain (and, thus, from that fuel) by the busyness of our daily lives and the instant gratification of food, the internet, games, sex, money, and other things. As a result, we are living life on the surface.

That more existential aspiration is usually:

- related to some deeper pain we carry (often from early life experiences)
- an expression of our core values and drives in life
- the result of years of accumulated life experiences and insights
- inspired by someone we admire, or an ideal that moves us

Some people say it's hard to figure out what this deeper aspiration is. But from my years of self-development and coaching, I can tell you this: we often already know what that is. Perhaps we are just not paying attention, or we are avoiding looking because we are afraid that what we'll find will require too much change, or that we won't like it.

The exercises in this chapter are a starting point for you to begin your search. As you go through them, don't think of the consequences of recognizing something as your aspiration. That will only bring in fear, attachment, and the chains of your social identity—all of which will interfere with your process. Just be committed to look within, be honest with yourself, and see what you find. Don't edit your findings; just let them come up.

At times, saying *yes* to your aspiration can feel risky. Something inside of you knows that, once you see it, you can't un-see it. You may feel that it's better to live a "normal life" and pursue the approved goals of society—you know, the stuff that everyone else thinks they should be doing because it's what everyone else thinks they should be doing.

I call that the *lukewarm life*. It's safe, maybe even pleasant—but not exciting, not deep, not purposeful. As a wise man once said, "Since you are like lukewarm water, neither hot nor cold, I will spit you out of my mouth" (Revelation 3:16).

It is much better to be aware of what deeply moves you than to pretend you don't know and live your life on the surface. You can't find fulfillment like that—only lukewarm water.

Let's now review the four brainstorming exercises to clarify your aspiration. Each of these can take from thirty minutes to two hours to complete, so if you are pressed for time you may want to just read about them now, and go through them carefully at a later time.

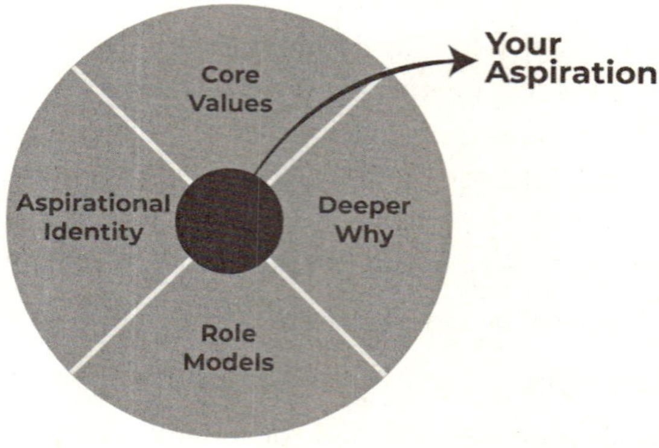

EXERCISE #1 — FIND YOUR CORE VALUES

Mark Twain once said: "The two most important days in your life are the day you are born and the day you find out why." Discovering your core values is a good starting point for finding your *why*.

Your core values are the feelings, experiences, and activities that you care about the most in your life. They are what you want to experience more of, and grow into. They are the stuff that your aspiration is made of. Here are some examples of values (the list is endless):

Ambition	Assertiveness	Beauty	Enjoyment	Exploration
Family	Loyalty	Freedom	Friendship	Productivity
Prosperity	Purpose	Respect	Security	Fun
Communication	Compassion	Confidence	Awareness	Control
Creativity	Curiosity	Growth	Happiness	Health
Strength	Honor	Humor	Individuality	Innovation
Wisdom	Intuition	Joy	Leadership	Logic
Love	Mastery	Service	Skill	Spirituality
Empowerment	Energy	Excellence	Meaning	Order
Originality	Passion	Peace	Playfulness	Truth
Recognition	Art	Knowledge	Home	Legacy

Go through the list above—or through your own list—and highlight your top five values. Then go through these powerful questions below and see what other values your answers reflect.

1. How do you spend most of your **time** (apart from work)?
2. Where do you spend most of your **money** (apart from life essentials)?
3. In what area of your life are you naturally most **focused**, reliable, or disciplined?
4. What do you most **think** about, desire, and dream about?
5. What do you love to **learn**, read about, and explore?
6. What **inspires** you the most?
7. What types of **injustices** really piss you off?

8. What **virtue(s)** do you admire the most?
9. What do people who know you well say that you were **born** to do?
10. Fast forward your life ten years and look back. You are **proud** of achieving one thing. What is that?
11. Think of three **peak experiences** in your life, when you were at your best. What was going on at that time? What values were you living?
12. What **relationships** or people have most influenced your sense of purpose? How have they inspired you?
13. If you had unlimited **resources** (time and money), what would you set out to do?
14. If your efforts **could not fail**, what would you choose to do, be, have, or achieve?
15. If you had only two years to live, what would be the **most important** things you would do in that time?
16. Suppose every experience of your life, including all your failures and successes, was planned to train you for your **destiny**. What has your whole life prepared you to do?

When you are done with these questions, look for patterns in your answers. What are the handful of values they are all pointing to? Group together similar values in themes, and rank your themes from most important to least important.

This exercise requires some time and attention. If you plan to finish it in ten minutes, the value you'll get from it will be limited. Give yourself time and space to explore these questions. If you are struggling to find clarity, then get the support of someone who knows you really well, or of a coach.

The result of this exercise is that you will understand the things that you really care about. Collectively, they are your North Star. Your aspiration(s) in life will always be an expression of one or more of these values.

Clarifying your core values, and formulating aspirations and then goals out of them, is a top-down approach. Let's now explore a bottom-up approach: starting with your current goals and finding the *why* behind them.

Share this concept:

MindfulSelfDiscipline.com/find-your-core-values

EXERCISE #2 — THE DEEPER WHY

If you want to develop self-discipline, you probably already know the behavior that you want to perform, the task/skill you want to master, or the person you want to become. But why do you want that?

Sometimes it's hard to get clarity on your values and aspirations, but you have clarity on your goals. In that case, you start with one of your current goals and try to find the underlying value or aspiration. To do that, ask yourself why that goal is important for you, and then follow up the answer with as many "why" questions as you need. This exercise has been inspired by the Fivefold Why exercise from Josh Kaufman.

For example, if your goal is to "lose twenty pounds", this inner questioning could unfold like this:

1. *Why do I want to lose twenty pounds?* Because I want to be fit.
2. *Why do I want to be fit?* So that I feel good about my body.
3. *Why do I want to feel good about my body?* So I feel more confident.
4. *Why do I want to feel more confident?* Because I want to feel more confident.

In this case, feeling confident and empowered is the core value or aspiration behind the fitness goal. Knowing this is helpful because it makes the goal more meaningful. And it also makes us think of other ways to fulfill that core need or desire.

Take the habit that you want self-discipline to help you create, or the goal you want to achieve. Keep asking yourself "why?" for every answer until you get to the bottom of it; you may need to ask it several times. Once you get to a point where it's impossible to go any further, you have come to an intrinsic value. This is what the aspiration behind your goal is truly about.

The Deeper Why process is especially important if your current goals are focused on what is called *extrinsic values* in positive psychology. Extrinsic values are things like money, fame, beauty, and power. This process allows you to see the *intrinsic values* that might be sitting underneath those surface goals.

Your strategy is the *why* for your actions. Your goal is the *why* for your strategies. And your aspiration is the *why* for your goals. So "*why*?" is a powerful way to find what lies beneath your choices and desires.

Share this concept: **MindfulSelfDiscipline.com/the-deeper-why**

EXERCISE #3 — YOUR ROLE MODELS

Set your life on fire.
Seek those who fan your flames.

RUMI

Would you love to be driven, more "on fire" with your goals? Then spend time with people who are on fire with theirs—until you find something that resonates with you. *Inspiration* begets *aspiration*.

Seek role models in the area you are pursuing. Listen to them. Read their biographies. Learn about their daily grind. Understand what fired *them* up and see if that moves you too. If it doesn't, then learn about somebody else. This is a very simple exercise, and Rumi summarizes it beautifully.

When looking for role models, dream big. Don't compare their results (where they are now) with your process (where *you* are now) and think that you can never achieve that. The purpose is not to become like them, but to get inspired. You may end up doing something very different, and yet be inspired by the same drive. Knowing what that drive is helps you figure out your aspirations.

Knowing who your role models are, in different areas of your life, will also be important for exercises in other chapters of this book, so it would be a good idea to spend some minutes thinking about it now.

Share this concept:
MindfulSelfDiscipline.com/role-models

EXERCISE #4 — DESIGN YOUR ASPIRATIONAL IDENTITY

Every aspiration is, at the end of the day, about self-transformation: becoming a new person and living a new life. We need self-discipline because we want to achieve a goal, get somewhere, stop a bad habit, transform ourselves, live better. In other words, we want a new identity; we want to be a better version of ourselves.

We can call this "your best self", "your ideal self", or "your aspirational identity". It is the person you want to become; the *why* behind your goals. It is where you will arrive at once you fulfill your aspirations to a certain degree—your designed life. In a way, then, your aspirational identity is both the result of your aspirations, as well as their driving force.

This concept of aspirational identity is key to Mindful Self-Discipline. In this chapter, we will use this to help you clarify who you want to become, and then find the true aspirations that are a natural expression of that end state. The concept is simple: you **decide** who you want to be, and then see the **gaps** that need to be covered to get there. The drive to fill these gaps is your aspiration(s).

1. Review the insights gained from the three exercises in this chapter.
2. See what patterns emerge. Ask yourself, "What are all these things really about? If I actualize these values, fulfill the deepest *why* behind my goals, and come close to that which inspires me in my role models, who will I become?"
3. Describe your aspirational identity to yourself:
   a. What do you feel?
   b. What does a typical day of your life look like?
   c. What will people admire in you and know you for?
4. Now look at your current identity. Identify three areas where there is a big gap between who you are now and who you want to become. For example: "In my aspirational identity I have mastered singing, I'm well known for my work, and I make a living from it."
5. In each of those gaps is a potential aspiration. In this case, "to master singing" might be the main aspiration.

Share this concept:

MindfulSelfDiscipline.com/aspirational-identity-design

EXERCISE #5 — DEEP-LONGING MEDITATION (BONUS)

The four exercises covered thus far are very analytical and will help you to get clarity about your aspirations using reason and self-reflection.

There is also another way to acknowledge your aspirations: through intuition. Something inside of you already knows exactly who you are, and who you want to become. It knows what is important, and what is a waste of energy. It doesn't need to go through B and C to arrive at D. It's direct knowledge.

Analysis: A → B → C → D
Intuition: A → D

The reason why we can't often tap into this mode of knowing is because we so rarely listen. Our minds are super busy processing thoughts and inputs. We over-rely on analytical thought, so we get disconnected from our intuition and our gut feeling.

You can also use meditation to help you to temporarily turn off your analytical mind and then explore this question of "what are my true aspirations?" through your intuition. You do that by posing that question to yourself, rejecting every answer from your analytical mind, and staying quiet and receptive.

DON'T GET STUCK

If you have completed the exercises above but feel you still can't find a powerful *why*, please don't panic. This is a process and can take some time.

Our understanding about what is truly important for us will evolve with time. Self-reflection is very important and a good start, but sometimes clarity only comes by taking action, trying things out, and seeing how we feel. There is no need, then, to obsess about the perfect goal or "one true aspiration" before moving forward. It's better to have an okay goal to start with, and have the perfect capacity to execute it (self-discipline), than a lofty end goal but no ability to make progress in it.

If your more existential aspirations are not yet clear, then start where you are. Identify one or more key areas in your life where you wish to become more self-disciplined. Think about why they really matter to you, and what will be possible once you achieve those goals. Use this sense of purpose to go through the other steps discussed in the following chapters.

It doesn't matter how small you start. Any goal is a good training ground for self-discipline. As you grow in awareness and willpower, and as you start ticking off some of your existing goals, your deeper aspirations will begin to emerge.

Conclusion: please do the work in these exercises sincerely. Give it some time and thought. Get the help of a coach if you need it. But don't stay stuck in analysis paralysis. Start developing self-discipline towards whatever goal feels meaningful in your life right now; that will give you momentum, and in time your deeper aspirations will become clearer.

KEY POINTS

- You learned about the following exercises:
  - Your core values
  - The Deeper Why
  - Inspiring role models
  - Designing your aspirational identity
  - Deep-Longing meditation
- You don't need to follow all of them. Exercises 1 and 4 are the most important ones—the others are optional.
- Don't get stuck in analysis paralysis. Don't obsess about the perfect goal or "one true aspiration". If your more existential aspirations are not yet clear, then start where you are. Identify one or more key areas in your life where you wish to become more self-disciplined, and use that as your purpose.

Implementation resources: download the step-by-step instructions for the deep-longing meditation at **MindfulSelfDiscipline.com/meditations** (no email required for access).

CHAPTER 8

ASPIRATION STEP 2: MAGNIFY YOUR PURPOSE

Aspiration Pillar Steps

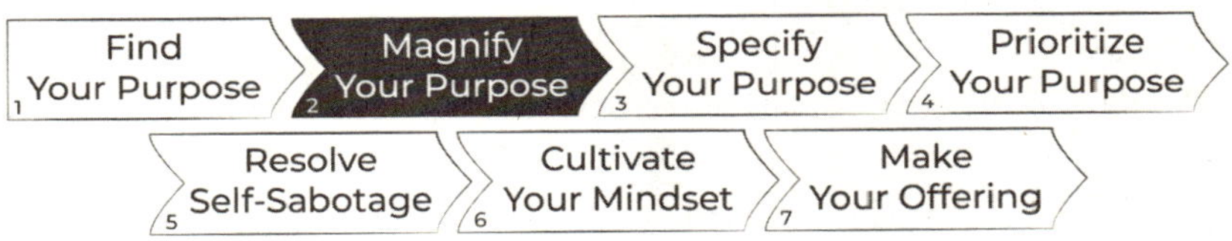

Now that you know your aspiration, the next step is to magnify it. Because *big purpose* equals *big motivation.*

How do you magnify your purpose? By enhancing your awareness of the **pain** of not actualizing your aspiration, and of the **rewards** of actualizing it, in all the different areas of your life. The more benefits you can connect to actualizing your aspiration, the better. Likewise, the more pain-points you can connect to not actualizing it, the more driven you will be.

Deep inside our brain, our core drives are all about escaping pain and experiencing pleasure. When you expand your perception of pain and pleasure associated with this aspiration, it takes deeper roots in you.

Now let's get to the practical exercise. We will take as an example the aspiration to be always calm and centered, and the goal of *meditation*. This is how you might strengthen your purpose and thus generate more motivation and energy for it, by linking it to pain and pleasure in the eight different areas of your life.

"To be always in control of my emotions, calm and centered" (Meditation)	**Impact of fulfilling my aspiration (*pleasure*)**	**Impact of neglecting my aspiration (*pain*)**
Health	I have better immunity, mental health, and increased longevity	Having harmful stress hormones in my body; poorer health
Career	I am seen as a natural leader, more reliable and professional	Making decisions I later regret, due to my impulses
Finances	I'm able to save more	Emotional spending
Love Life	My partner feels safer with me	Lack of trust and connection
Fun	n/a	n/a
Family and Friends	I create more positive experiences for those I love	Reacting out of fear and anger, and thus create negativity
Social Contribution	I have headspace and energy to serve at my best	Working on my mission wears me out and feels like a chore
Growth and Spirituality	I'm able to develop myself spiritually, be at peace, and really apply what I learn	I keep making the same mistakes; it seems I'm not practicing what I believe in

Now it's time for you to go through a similar exercise:

1. Draw a table with three columns and nine rows. You can use a piece of paper or your favorite digital tool.
2. Write your aspiration on top. (Do this exercise once for each aspiration.)
3. Write the eight areas of life in the first column. If you like, you can give them a multiplier, from one to five, to represent how important each area is for you.
4. For the second column, ask yourself how actualizing your aspiration may help you better fulfill or enjoy that area of life.

Think of the things you will gain from achieving your goal. Feel the joy, excitement, and satisfaction—make it real.

5. For the third column, think about how, by not actualizing that aspiration, your goals in that area of life will be harder to achieve. Think of the regrets, missed opportunities, and challenges that may come up. Feel the pain.
6. For steps four and five, list as many items as you can, aiming for at least three to five.
7. To enhance this exercise, you can add an image that represents your current self (your conditioned life) on the left, and an image for your aspirational identity (designed life) on the right.
8. Once done, take a moment to step back and appreciate how important your aspiration is for you. If you did this exercise well, at this point you feel more motivated to work toward your aspiration.

Now that you have a clear aspiration behind your goals, and you have magnified it by enhancing your awareness of the consequences of fulfilling that aspiration or not, you are much better off than you were at the beginning of this book.

Eventually, you will begin to experience the *pull effect*: something inside of you will be strongly attracted to pursuing that aspiration. This will naturally make you more disciplined in it. It will be more top of mind for you, which will make it easier for you to make decisions in your daily life that help you take a step toward your aspiration rather than away from it. Your aspiration gives you something worth fighting for—something that enlivens you and motivates you.

With this, self-discipline becomes easier, commitment comes naturally, and staying focused "just happens." This method can even turn have-to goals into want-to goals.

Internalize Your Aspiration Deeply

There is a special method of meditation, from the wisdom tradition of Yoga, that is useful for imprinting your aspiration deep in your subconscious mind, in the form of a resolution (*sankalpa*). This will enhance the power of your purpose and give you the confidence that you *will* actualize it.

This technique is called Yoga Nidra, and it has many different variations—some of them focus more on relaxation and sleep, while others focus on self-actualization. Look for a guided meditation on Yoga Nidra that emphasizes the *resolution* aspect of the practice, and then follow it daily for a few weeks until your intention is fully internalized.

Share this concept:
MindfulSelfDiscipline.com/magnify-your-aspiration

KEY POINTS

- Enhance your awareness of the pain of not actualizing your aspiration and the rewards of actualizing it, in all the different areas of your life.
- Consider practicing the Yoga Nidra meditation using your aspiration as a resolution, for strengthening your purpose and imprinting it in your subconscious mind.

Implementation resources: see the step-by-step instructions for my *Yoga Nidra for Aspirations* meditation at **MindfulSelfDiscipline.com/meditations**, or join the app to access the guided audios. Check also the *Black and White* exercise in the workbook (**MindfulSelfDiscipline.com/workbook**).

CHAPTER 9

ASPIRATION STEP 3: SPECIFY YOUR PURPOSE

Aspiration Pillar Steps

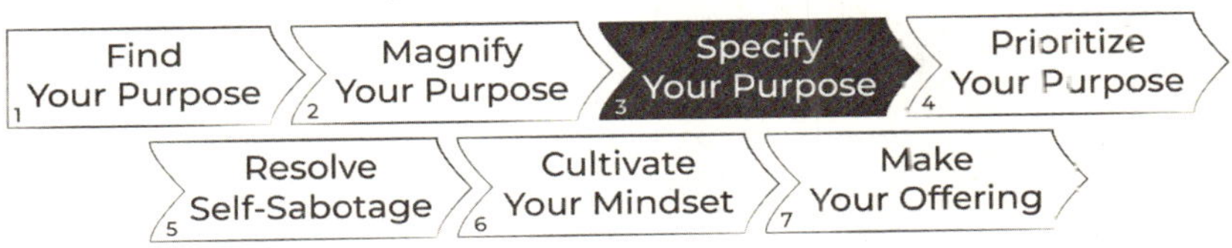

At this point in the journey, you know your aspirations, and you have magnified them. You feel that they are something worth fighting for. The next step is to set effective goals based on them. One of the best frameworks for this is SMART goals.

A SMART goal is a goal that is *specific*, *measurable*, *achievable*, *relevant*, and *time bound*.

Specific means that the goal is concrete and detailed enough that you know what success looks like. "I want to be healthy and full of energy" is an aspiration, and it's not specific—you can't know when you have achieved it, or what the logical next steps are. Translating this to a specific goal might look like, "To lose thirty pounds and sleep seven to eight hours every night." (This goal will later be translated into habits, as we'll see in Chapter 25.)

Measurable means that the success item is quantifiable, so that you are able to track your progress and stay focused. Ask yourself: "How can I know that I'm getting close to my goal?" There may be a single variable that you are measuring (e.g., money saved, pounds lost, hours practiced, people contacted); or, for more complex goals, you'll need to break it down into milestones.

Achievable means that your aspiration needs to be expressed as a goal that is realistic and attainable for you. You need to feel that you can do it, otherwise you will soon lose motivation. Ask yourself: "What steps am I able to take to achieve this goal?" Think of the attitudes, skills, and resources you need to make it a reality. If the goal is not achievable, either get the resources you need to make it achievable or set a different goal.

Relevant, in the context of Mindful Self-Discipline, is whether or not the goal is aligned with your values and aspirations. Goals are *relevant* if they move you toward your aspirations, and irrelevant if they don't. The goal also needs to be a bit challenging and stretch you, otherwise it will feel too easy and thus lose importance.

Time bound is a goal that has a (realistic) deadline attached to it. If you don't have this, you may just end up procrastinating forever.

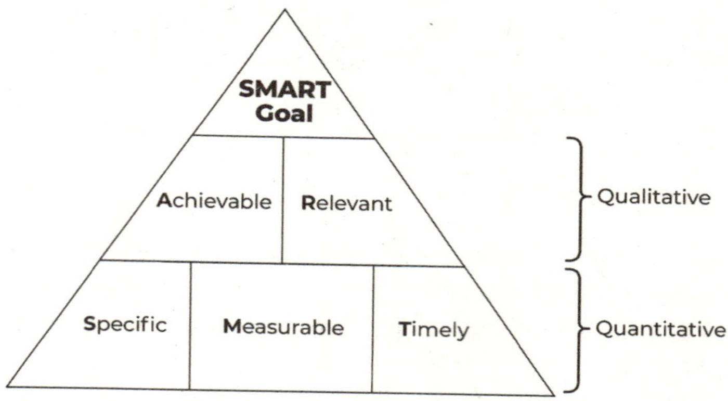

SMART goals are clear goals—and with clarity comes strength, conviction, and the motivation to be disciplined in your chosen journey. If your goals are not SMART, it's less likely that you will achieve them.

Aspirations regarding personal growth, relationships, and spirituality might be more difficult to translate into SMART goals. Don't let that stop you. It's also possible to create specific and measurable goals connected to these more intangible aspirations—and it's equally necessary and beneficial. For example, if you have a personal growth goal to be more positive and optimistic, you could keep a diary of how many times per day you complain or worry needlessly; then your goal would be to diminish that to a specific number.

It is easy to hide ourselves behind a lofty aspiration—and the higher the aspiration is, the easier it is for us to hide. This is a form of self-sabotage few people are aware of. To prevent it, translate that lofty aspiration into a couple of

SMART goals that will hold you accountable, so that you can't hide anymore. You will then know exactly what you are supposed to do and whether you are on track or not.

WRITE DOWN YOUR SMART GOALS

Consider what are your top aspirations—ideally no more than three, so you remain focused. Create one SMART goal for each of your aspirations.

ASPIRATION #1: ______________________________

SMART GOAL: ______________________________

ASPIRATION #2: ______________________________

SMART GOAL: ______________________________

ASPIRATION #3: ______________________________

SMART GOAL: ______________________________

Please don't just think them through and move on. It's very important to actually **write down** your goals. This makes them more "official," and it becomes more real for your brain.

Dr. Gail Matthews, a psychology professor at the Dominican University in California, ran a study on goal setting and found that people who write down their goals are 42% more likely to achieve them. Your goals become more top of mind, more real and motivating.

If you want to get the most benefit out of this principle, then don't just write it down on a piece of paper somewhere. Make it visible. Put it in a place where you will see it often. Frame it on your bedroom wall if needed, or make it your phone's wallpaper.

You can also have a symbol, object, or image that helps you keep the goal top of mind.

Conclusions:

- An aspiration without a goal is just a wish
- A goal that is not SMART is not a goal
- A goal that is not written down is not a goal

Share this concept:
MindfulSelfDiscipline.com/smart-goals

BE GOAL-ORIENTED *AND* PROCESS-ORIENTED

Should you be focused on what you want to achieve (the end goal), or on the process to get there? You need a healthy balance of both.

As we've seen, being focused on the end goal is important. Yet, if you are focused too narrowly on your end goal and keep measuring to see if you are making progress or not with every step you take, then you may end up getting impatient and discouraged.

This nervous attitude of constantly monitoring the process can easily burn you out, or make you doubt yourself or your chosen path—and that can make you want to give up. It's like removing a plant from the soil every day, to check in and see if it's taking root or not. Or opening the oven every minute to see if it's warm enough—every time you do that, some of the heat dissipates.

On the other side of the scale, we have focusing on the process rather than the end goal. Focusing on the process is especially important when your goal is far-fetched. In that case, it is better to make the routine itself be the goal. So "writing a book" becomes "write 500 words every morning" and "losing fifty pounds" becomes "follow this diet six days a week and exercise for twenty minutes every day". You still have a goal, but are not constantly obsessed about it; you are not worried about how far you still need to travel and how long it will take. You just take a step in the right direction every day. This helps you stay on track and not give up.

Just as a narrow focus on the end goal alone is not healthy, a narrow focus on process alone is also not healthy. If you are too focused on the process, you can get to a state where you are just lifelessly going through the motions. You don't stop and analyze what is working or not anymore. You've built the habit, but perhaps lost the emotional connection to your aspiration; as a result, you may feel unmotivated and lack energy in your efforts.

The metaphor of a boat traveling to a destination makes this point clearer.

The end goal is the destination; the process is the work you do to get you there. Without regularly checking if your boat is sailing in the right direction (goal), you may end up not getting where you wanted to go. On the other hand, if you are too busy checking the direction all the time and just looking at the map, instead of actually sailing your boat, you won't get to your destination either.

You need a healthy mix of both. You need to pay attention to the end goal *and* to focus on the process.

Share this concept:

MindfulSelfDiscipline.com/process-oriented-and-goal-oriented

KEY POINTS

- Translate your Aspiration into SMART goals: *specific*, *measurable*, *achievable*, *relevant*, and *time bound.*
- If your goals are not SMART, it's less likely that you will achieve them. It's easy to hide behind goals that are not specific, measurable and time-bound.
- Write down your goals. Put them in a place where you can see them often. Keep them top of mind.
- Have a balance between being goal-oriented and process-oriented. Focus on the process, enjoy the process, but still be connected to the end goal.

CHAPTER 10

ASPIRATION STEP 4: PRIORITIZE YOUR PURPOSE

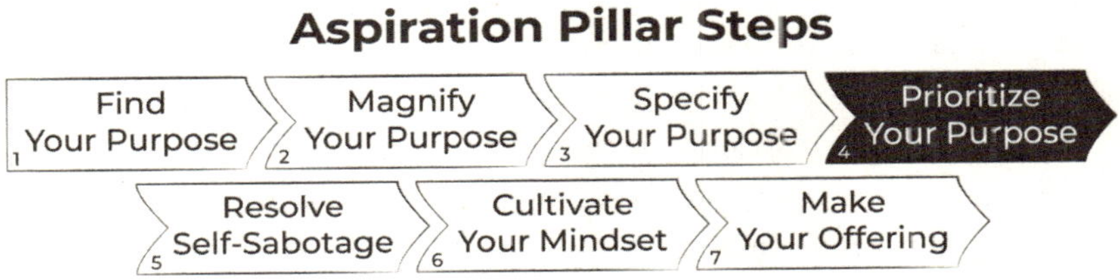

Now that you have a clear SMART goal to express your aspiration, it is time to prioritize it with your time, energy, and resources.

You need to create space in your life—and on your calendar—for your aspiration. This is how you test the strength of your aspiration: **Are you ready to *commit*, or are you merely "interested"?**

Simply being interested is not enough. It doesn't tap into the deep resources that you have inside yourself. Nobody has ever achieved anything great just by being interested.

If you are not spending some of your time, money, and energy on it, it's not real. That shows it's not really important to you.

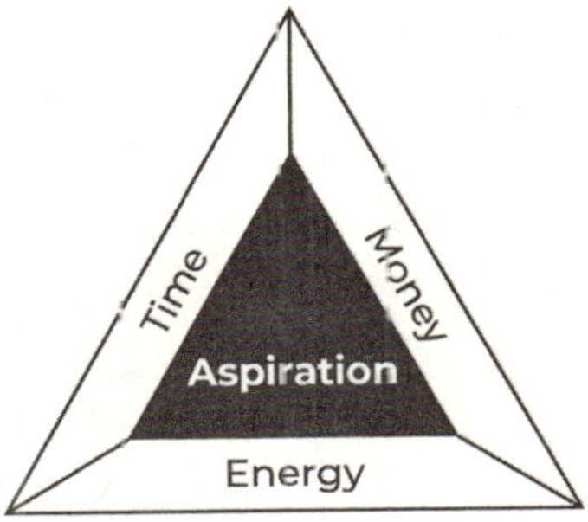

So how do you make your aspiration real?

Prioritize with your **time** by making the goal-related activities part of your daily routine. That means adding it to your calendar, so nothing else is booked in its place. Or it could mean adding an alarm on your phone to remind you to do that activity. At least in a certain segment of your day, following through with your goal should be your number one priority, and you should protect this time slot with all your might.

Prioritize with your **money** by investing on whatever tools, classes, and mentors you need to help you stay focused in that area of your life. With the right tools and guidance, you can grow more quickly, and save yourself a lot of frustration. Is there any better use for your resources than to empower your dreams?

Prioritize with your **energy** by giving it *attention*. This means that it's something you often think about, plan, and remember. It also means that you create a distraction-free environment where you can really focus on that goal. For example, if sharing your life wisdom through writing a book is an aspect of your aspiration, that could mean leaving your phone in airplane mode for two hours a day while you just focus on writing.

Now, let's get pragmatic. Most of us live complex lives nowadays, with other obligations and goals competing for these three scarce resources. So there is no need to go overboard with this, at least not in the beginning. Just make sure that you are dedicating some of your time, money, and energy for your aspiration—according to your capacity in this phase of your life. The amount of resources you invest depends on the type of aspiration it is, and the place it has in your life.

If you are unwilling to invest any of these three, at least to some degree, then it's time to ask yourself: "Do I really want this? Is this aspiration important for me?"

THE TRIPLE COMMITMENT

1. *How will you spend your time for your goals?* Decide right now, and create a recurring calendar event or an alarm on your phone. Don't postpone this simple step.
2. *How will you spend your money for your goals?* Consider if there are any products, courses, mentors, or services that could accelerate your progress in this area.
3. *How will you spend your energy on your goals?* Create a distraction-free environment for this activity, and also some sort of reminder to help you keep your aspiration top of mind.

For establishing the reminder mentioned in the last item above, there are many options. Some people have a meaningful image that reminds them of their end goal, or a relevant quote as their desktop background image, or an object that's always with them. Select whatever works for you, and associate that in your brain with your aspiration.

Share this concept:
MindfulSelfDiscipline.com/triple-commitment

KEY POINTS

- Simply being "interested" is not enough. You need to be committed.
- Prioritize your aspiration(s) by dedicating your time (add it to your calendar), money (get the tools and mentors you need), and energy (create a distraction-free environment to focus on it).

CHAPTER 11

ASPIRATION STEP 5: RESOLVE SELF-SABOTAGE

Aspiration Pillar Steps

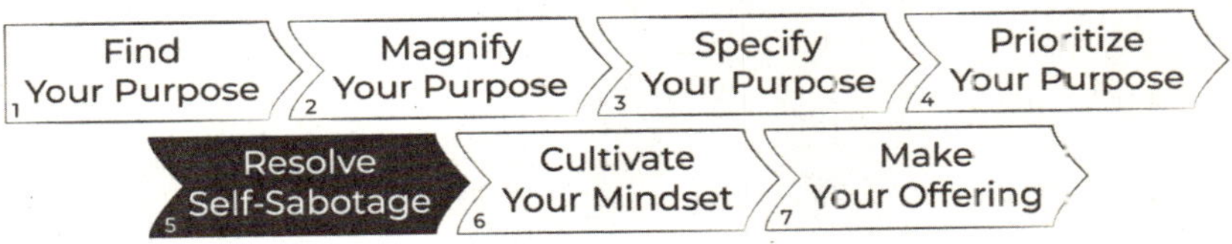

At this point in the Aspiration Pillar, if you have followed the exercises, you have identified and magnified one or more aspirations, translated them into SMART goals, and prioritized them by allocating resources to make them happen. Now it's time to face the one big obstacle that can prevent you from moving forward; the one big challenge that is so powerful that it can render all your efforts futile.

You.

There are different parts or "voices" inside of us. We can actually call them different aspects of our personality. This is a brilliant insight developed by Richard Schwartz, creator of the Internal Family Systems; and also Dr. Hal Stone and Dr. Sidra Stone, creators of Voice Dialog Therapy.

Each part inside of us has its own function and agenda, and it varies from person to person. There is the resentful-self, the "I know it all" self, the dreamer, the hurt child, the "control freak", the needy-self, the optimist, the protector-self, the anxious-self, the conqueror, the workaholic, the inner bully, etc.

Here is the challenge that you may face: part of you really wants to achieve your goal and actualize your aspiration, and part of you doesn't. There may be aspects of yourself that don't want what you say you want. This is known as self-sabotage, or internal conflict. Your heart is divided; your mind hesitates; your energy is not focused.

Some examples:

- You say you want to procrastinate less and work on that dream project, but part of you loves to hide behind procrastination so you don't experience disappointment or failure.
- You say you want to get fit, but part of you is afraid of what will happen if you become more attractive, or you are unwilling to do the work required.
- You say you want to double your business, but part of you is afraid that success will bring shame, make you lose your friends, make you greedy, or lead you astray.
- You say you want to speak out more, but part of you is afraid of being heard and judged.
- You say you want to stop using social media, but part of you is afraid you will lose connections, be seen as the "weird one", and end up alone.
- You say you want to be kinder and control your anger in your relationships, but part of you feels that this would make you weak and a pushover.

In coaching, we call these things "secondary gains". It's when there is a benefit for you in not changing your behavior, and not achieving your goal. The examples are endless, and most people engage in self-sabotage in at least one area of their lives.

Are you self-sabotaging your aspiration? If you were paid to hold yourself back, would you be rich or poor?

Share this concept:
MindfulSelfDiscipline.com/resolve-self-sabotage

THE RED-PILL TEST

There is a simple test I use with my coaching clients to figure out if there is self-sabotage in them or not. I call it the Red-Pill Test. For example, if I am working with somebody that wants to overcome anxiety, I'll ask: "*Suppose I have a red pill here in my hand. Once you swallow it, you will never experience anxiety again. Will you take it?*"

Some clients will say, "YES, just gimme that #@&*% pill!" Their answer is truthful, wholehearted, and immediate. But other clients hesitate. Or they will say a "yes" with their mouth, while their body is telling a different story. Something in them doesn't want to overcome anxiety, and it's usually because they believe anxiety somehow protects them or pushes them forward in life.

Take a moment now to ask yourself: "If there is a red pill that will give me right now what I want, will I take it?" Be very aware of what happens next.

- Does the answer come immediately or is it delayed?
- Is it a "Hell yes" or an "I guess so"?
- Is there any part of your body that slightly contracts or pulls back?
- Are you present and energized when you answer this question?

If there is any part of you that doesn't want the transformation you are after, then you need to address that. Otherwise you won't be able to move forward wholeheartedly, and your path will be longer and harder than it needs to be.

If two different aspects of your being are in conflict and want different things, then we can say that there is self-sabotage in you. In this case, here are the two things you need to do.

First, become *aware* of it. Take a moment to really see that part that resists your goal. Spend some time clarifying what your secondary gain is. In other words: What are the benefits of remaining as you are, and not having the transformation you say you want? What are the bad things that may happen if you actually achieve your goal? What does that other part of you want? Why is it afraid?

Awareness is key to Mindful Self-Discipline, and it plays an important role here too. You can develop awareness through a daily meditation practice, through journaling, or with the help of a trusted coach or a therapist in the aforementioned modalities. Sometimes you may need a combination of these.

Second, *resolve* the inner conflict. This is not always straightforward, and it's a big topic, beyond the scope of this book. The way for this inner resolution will be unique for each person, depending on their personality and life history. It often will require some external support, because we all have blind spots. In fact, this is one of the main reasons why people come to me for self-discipline coaching—to integrate all aspects of their being so that they can move forward wholeheartedly.

Still, I don't want to leave you hanging, so let me at least outline that there are two main methods to work out inner resistance or self-sabotage. Through a lot of self-reflection, awareness, and inner work, you need to either: (a) come to a point where you no longer need that secondary gain; or (b) fulfill the secondary gain in a way that doesn't conflict with your aspiration.

Becoming aware of the different aspects of yourself is self-knowledge. Bringing together these different aspects, so that you are more unified and whole, is self-mastery. This is the journey of a lifetime.

As a side note, it might be that you love the journey more than the destination itself, and that is why you can't pass the Red-Pill Test. In this case, I wouldn't consider that self-sabotage, provided that you are actually taking action toward your aspiration, and are not procrastinating. It simply means that you are not in a hurry; you are taking your time and enjoying the scenery.

Share this concept:

MindfulSelfDiscipline.com/red-pill-test

KEY POINTS

- There are different voices inside of us; different "selves", each with its own agenda.
- If one of your inner voices or selves doesn't want what you want, then there is self-sabotage. Your heart is divided; your mind hesitates; your energy is not focused.
- "Secondary gain" is the hidden benefit you get if you don't achieve your goal. It's the unconscious incentive for remaining as you are and not changing.
- The Red-Pill Test will show you if you have self-sabotage. If you do, you need to become acutely aware of it, and find a way to resolve that inner conflict.

CHAPTER 12

ASPIRATION STEP 6: CULTIVATE YOUR MINDSET

Aspiration Pillar Steps

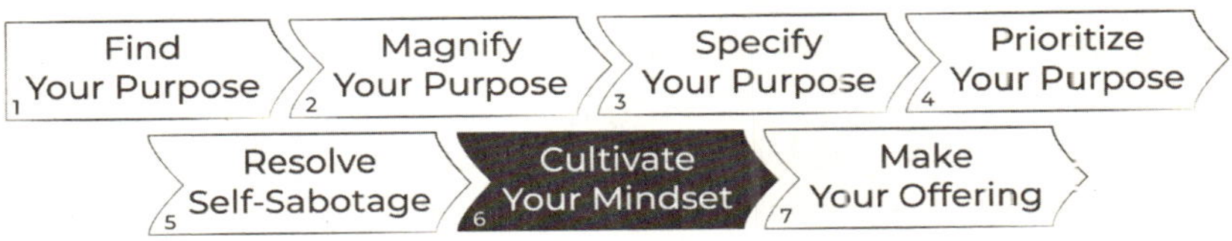

At this point, if you have already gone through the exercises in the previous steps, your aspirations are now clear, strong, specific, and prioritized. You are also aware that there might be self-sabotaging tendencies inside of you, and what to do about them.

Now we need to talk about three core virtues/mindsets that are necessary for you to live a purpose-driven life. They are ownership, self-belief, and sacrifice. If you have an aspiration but you don't believe that you are responsible for your life (ownership), or if you don't believe that you are capable of fulfilling that aspiration (self-belief), or if you are not ready to pay the price for it (sacrifice)—then it's not an aspiration, but just a wish.

So let us see what these empowering mindsets are about. Step 6 is about the first two mindsets, and Step 7 is about the third one.

THE VIRTUE OF OWNERSHIP

Taking complete ownership of your outcomes
by holding no one but yourself responsible for them
is the most powerful thing you can do to drive your success.

Gary W. Keller

Ownership is the attitude that, "I am responsible for my life, my wellbeing, and my goals." Ownership is power, because you can never change anything that you don't take responsibility for.

The opposite of ownership is victimization. Feeling yourself to be a victim keeps you stuck, because when you are a victim there is nothing you can do to change things. You then feel that you have no control, no power. You can only blame, be miserable, and play "poor me" so others will come and help you.

Ownership is not "victim blaming". Whatever other people did that was wrong is their responsibility, and they need to pay for it. Yet your wellbeing is ultimately your own responsibility. In this scenario, ownership is about taking responsibility for *your* life, your emotions, and your healing process. It means that you are not waiting for an apology before you can move on. You are not waiting for anything outside of you—you are taking charge and moving forward by yourself.

Self-discipline starts with taking responsibility for your life, and that is not possible in a state of victimization. The fruits of self-discipline are achievement, wellbeing, and happiness. The fruits of victimization are self-pity, resentment, and a limited life.

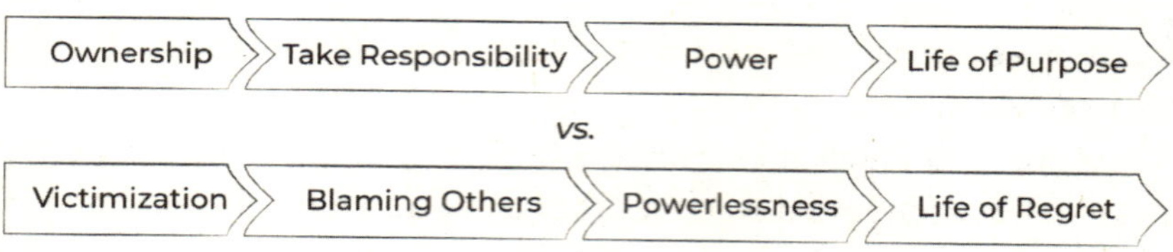

If you were fully stuck in a victim mentality, you'd have never picked up this book. The words "self-discipline" would have repelled you. Yet there might still be some traces of victim mentality somewhere in your life. Here are a few questions to help you dig deeper:

- How am I excusing myself for my lack of progress or change?
- How is the situation I am in "not my fault"?
- Who do I blame for the bad things that happened in my life?
- On a scale from one to ten, how much of a complainer am I?
- Do I often dwell on thoughts of having suffered injustice?

These questions will point out potential victimization patterns in you, and the excuses you have been making. Lack of ownership is one of the reasons why we make excuses about breaking our resolutions. (For more on excuses, see Chapter 25.)

It is easy to get into a victim mentality, especially if you have had experiences of trauma, betrayal, or being manipulated. For some people more than others, it is a default way to seek emotional relief, or to explain why things went wrong. Be that as it may, it is never a good place to remain in. As long as you remain a victim, your life and your wellbeing will keep spiraling down.

There are many things in life we cannot control—the thoughts and reactions of other people, the weather, politics, external events, etc. These things are just happening; they are not happening *to you.* It is better to simply acknowledge these things, and then focus on the things you can control: the stories you tell yourself, the decisions you make, the actions you take. This is your only business.

You do not need to go on a guilt trip or shame trip in order to take responsibility. That is not what it's about. To have ownership, it is enough that you see how you have contributed to the current state of things, and how you are able to change it. Then you take action, self-disciplined action, in that direction.

Own your life by taking full responsibility for your decisions and actions. Focus on what you can control and accept the rest. Just don't get caught up in complaining, blaming, and a victim mentality. Don't cause needless suffering for yourself.

Without ownership, your aspiration is just wishful thinking, your awareness is incomplete, and your action is half-hearted.

Share this concept:
MindfulSelfDiscipline.com/ownership

THE VIRTUE OF SELF-BELIEF

The greatest sin is to think yourself weak.

Swami Vivekananda

As we saw in Chapter 4, the amount of willpower you have available depends on your beliefs. Your beliefs about yourself are the limits of your willpower and the ceiling of your achievements. Self-belief may not guarantee success, but self-doubt very often guarantees failure.

Self-belief is one of the greatest gifts you can give yourself. With it, self-discipline is possible; without it, it is not, for you will sabotage yourself.

Self-Belief vs. Self-Doubt

The opposite of self-belief is self-doubt. It is thinking that you can't do something, that you are not good enough, that "it will never happen". Self-doubt prevents you from jumping in wholeheartedly, by saying that you don't have the needed skills, intelligence, time, resources, or experience. You defeat yourself before you even try.

When you believe in yourself, you have more motivation, more resources, more energy to overcome obstacles on your way. When you don't believe in yourself, every setback you encounter is interpreted as a confirmation of your suspicions—that "I'm not gonna make it", that "this is not going to work".

Self-belief doesn't mean believing that you are perfectly ready for every challenge or that you already have all that you need to succeed. Rather, it means having complete trust in your ability to learn and grow. It is knowing that you can develop whatever you may lack in order to fulfill your aspiration.

True self-belief doesn't mean arrogance. You still reflect on your shortcomings and prepare for what can go wrong, but you rely on your strengths. Self-reflection is a virtue; self-doubt is a poison. Wisdom tells the difference.

Growth Mindset vs. Fixed Mindset

Your beliefs about yourself are not truths, but opinions. Yes, you can always look back at your life and find many reasons to reinforce those beliefs; but you could probably do the same for the opposite belief, if you were to dig deep enough. Your beliefs are simply a model for you to navigate the world.

If that is the case, then why should you, in the words of Vivekananda, "think yourself weak"? Rather, think of yourself strong. Develop the self-talk that your willpower is unlimited, and that you are gradually unlocking it. Tell yourself, constantly, that **you can achieve anything you set your mind to, and that anything that is difficult today will be easier tomorrow**.

This is one aspect of what psychologist Carol Dweck called the *growth mindset*. It is the opposite of the *fixed mindset*. In her own words (Dweck, 2015):

> In a fixed mindset, people believe their basic qualities, like their intelligence or talent, are simply fixed traits. They spend their time

> documenting their intelligence or talent instead of developing them. They also believe that talent alone creates success—without effort.
>
> In a growth mindset, people believe that their most basic abilities can be developed through dedication and hard work—brains and talent are just the starting point. This view creates a love of learning and a resilience that is essential for great accomplishment.

When you meet an obstacle in your way that you can't figure out how to overcome, one of two things can happen. If you have a fixed mindset, you will look at it as a proof that you can't make it (confirmation bias). If you have a growth mindset, you will see it simply as a sign that you need to develop certain skills to be able to move forward. You can then make use of self-discipline to push past that obstacle.

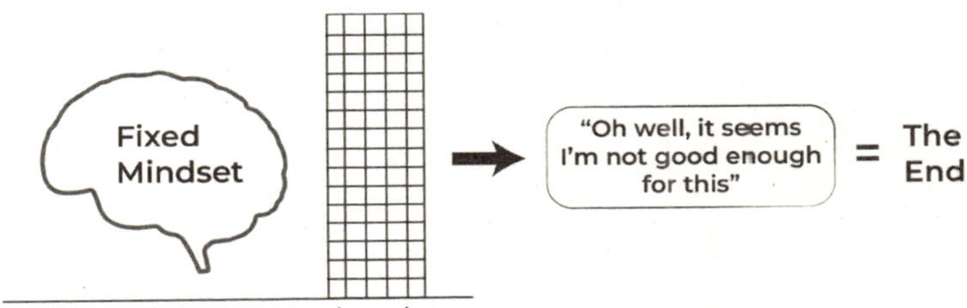

Fixed Mindset meets obstacle

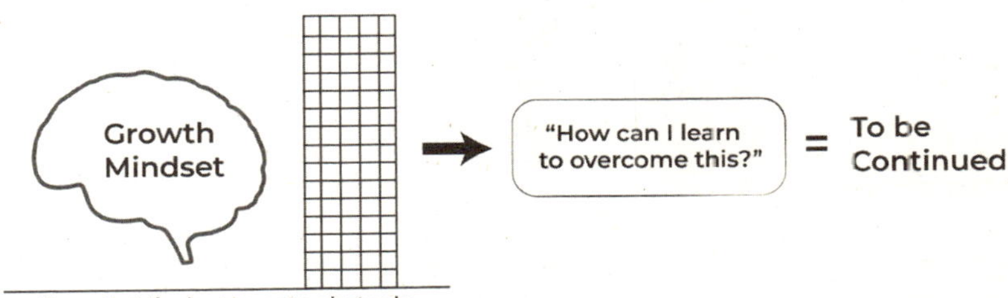

Growth Mindset meets obstacle

With self-discipline and a growth mindset, you will experience more energy, hope, and optimism in your life. You will be confident in your ability to learn and grow. Every obstacle will be like a comma, not a full stop.

Achieving your goals or changing yourself requires consistent effort over a period of time. But you won't make that effort if you believe that you can't change (fixed mindset). And if you keep doubting yourself, your effort will be weak and inconsistent. Therefore, developing self-belief is an important ingredient for self-discipline.

Think of the aspiration you are pursuing, or the specific goals you want to achieve. On a scale from one to ten, how would you rate your self-belief in that area? The more challenging is your goal, the higher you need the rating to be in order to succeed.

Share this concept:
MindfulSelfDiscipline.com/self-belief

HOW TO DEVELOP SELF-BELIEF

We will cover five methods to develop self-belief and self-confidence. Focus on the two that you feel will be most impactful.

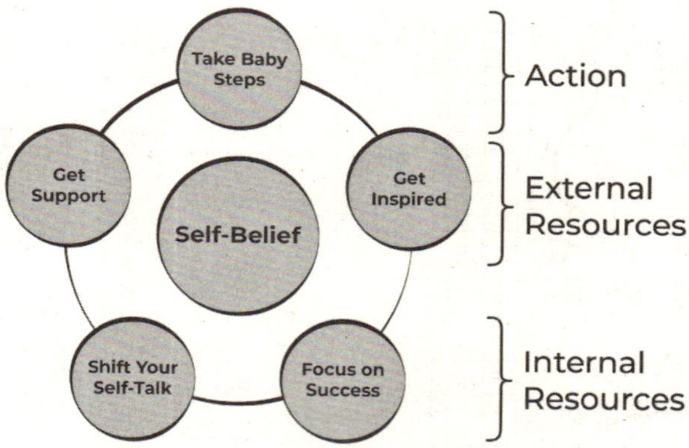

Focus on Success

The first method is to teach your brain how capable you are by highlighting your past successes. This means looking back on your life and seeing all the times that you accomplished something difficult. Perhaps you look at times when you were facing big obstacles, unforeseen challenges, or an unexpected loss—and nevertheless you persevered, survived, and found resources to move forward.

Spend some time remembering those moments and reinforcing the feeling of "I can do it" and "eventually I figure things out" that comes from reflecting on those experiences. It doesn't matter in which area of life your difficult wins happened, or how big or small they were. Anything that you can find as evidence that "I can make it" is good enough.

While you could do this exercise in two minutes in your head, you will gain much more from it if you actually write it down. You could keep a journal or a file of your accomplishments, so you can review it whenever your self-confidence is low.

Self-doubt looks at your past mistakes and projects them onto the future, thinking, "I'll probably fail there too". Self-belief looks at your past successes and thinks, "I have accomplished difficult things in the past, learned new skills, and surpassed my limits when facing big challenges—so there is no reason for me to believe that I won't be able to do that again."

What if, after thinking about it, you still feel that you haven't accomplished anything difficult in life? Well, then begin now! Choose something that makes you uncomfortable, and then go do it. It could be to start learning a new language, skill, or sport; focus on the small wins you'll experience in the process (they are there from the beginning, if you know where to look). Tidy up your house. Make that difficult phone call. Stretch yourself in some way.

Whenever you overcome difficulty, you naturally build confidence and self-belief. Prove to yourself through small experiments that you can go much further than you thought your limits were, and remember all the times that you have already overcome challenges in your past.

Take Baby Steps

A simple way to build confidence is to break down a big task into smaller tasks, also known as Baby Steps. If your action/project feels overwhelming, scary, or confusing, you may doubt your ability to move forward. But once you break that action into small easy steps, you will be able to move forward. Baby Steps give you the taste of success early and often—and this builds confidence in your abilities. With more confidence, you achieve more success.

We will cover the Baby Steps method in greater detail when discussing how to use it to overcome procrastination (Chapter 28).

Shift Your Self-Talk

Your self-talk is the way you talk to yourself and think about yourself. These thoughts you have about yourself—including those of self-doubt—are only habits, not truths. In fact, many of them are *lies repeated a thousand times*, and thus they feel like truths.

One of the key insights gained through meditation is that *you are not your thoughts*. The deeper you go in the practice, the more clearly you see this. And this is really great news, because it means that you then have the power to shift the way you think. You can choose what you want to believe in—and, through that, shape your character and your destiny.

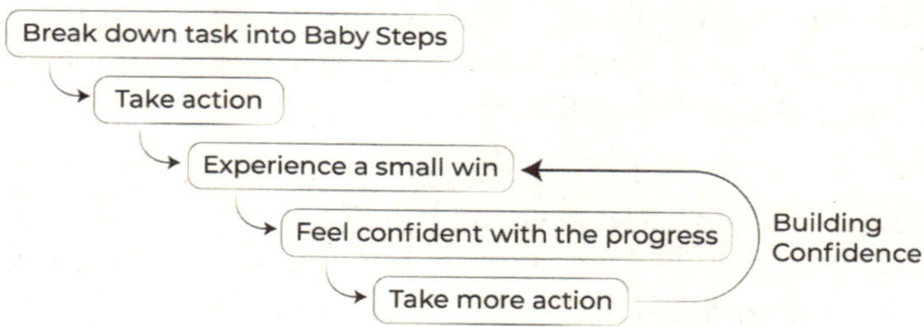

Shifting the way you think sometimes means correcting what in cognitive-behavior therapy is called cognitive distortion, or "thinking error". At other times it means telling yourself a ~~better lie~~ better story. Self-doubt tells you a story that your past wins were due to luck, or weren't that hard, and that to believe that you "can achieve anything" is a lie. Well, that story itself is a lie, and a dis-empowering one! Why not change it?

Argue for your limitations, and sure enough they're yours.

Richard Bach

At the root, it's as simple as this: **You can believe in your limiting thoughts, or you can believe in your limitless potential. Your choice.**

Self-doubt is a voice inside of you. Self-belief is also a voice inside of you. You are not these voices, but you can choose which one gets the mic. Here lies your power.

Once you have made your decision about which version of yourself you want to feed, then it's all about reinforcing it repeatedly through your self-talk, affirmations, and visualizations.

Suppose you are about to attempt running your first marathon. There is naturally some level of self-doubt in you. You don't know if you'll be able to finish it or not. You are afraid of failing or having health complications during the run. You catch your mind telling you,

"*Who am I to think I can do this…? I'm not an athlete. I'm not even sure I'll be able to finish, and it will be embarrassing. Six months ago I couldn't even run a mile, and now I'm attempting twenty-six! I'm not ready… What am I thinking?! I've failed many times in the past on tasks much simpler than this one… Maybe I should cancel this one and prepare more for next year.*"

Again, this self-talk is not the reality of things. It's simply the habitual way that you talk to yourself. Here is how you can use the different personal growth tools to overcome this limiting self-talk:

- **Visualization.** For three months before the marathon, visualize yourself going through the race, feeling tired at times, but persevering and succeeding at the end. Practice it for five minutes every morning, and right before the marathon.

- **Affirmation.** Create a short sentence that encapsulates your commitment to this goal, and your self-belief about your capacity. It could be, "I can do this—I will finish this no matter what!" Repeat it to yourself ten times every morning and evening.

- **Reflection.** Question the assumptions behind this self-talk. Poke holes in your limiting beliefs—look for reasons to "doubt the doubter" and reasons to believe in your capacity.

- **Shifting.** Whenever self-doubt creeps in during the day, replace the negative narrative with a positive one. Use the skills you developed through meditation to redirect your attention away from the old narrative, to let go of the negative thoughts, and to focus on the present moment.

Shifting Your Self-Talk

- Visualization
- Affirmation
- Reflection
- Shifting

Once you have shifted your mindset using any of the methods above, then take action. Act as if your new narrative, your more empowering beliefs, were already a reality. Action is the ultimate confirmation of belief. It consolidates the whole process.

Act as who you want to be, not who you were conditioned to be. Act as a person of great self-confidence, and you will feel great self-confidence.

Get Inspired

In Chapter 7, you went through the exercise of choosing your role models. These are people who have achieved some of what you wish to achieve in life. They represent what is possible for you; they inspire you to take action.

Now you can use your role models as a means of developing self-belief. There are two ways to do this: *learn from their experience* and *absorb their virtues*.

To learn from their experience, get to know about their lives as much as possible. Read their biographies, watch their interviews, and talk to them (if at all possible). Get to know about the times where they too experienced self-doubt, fear, and failures; and learn how they overcame those difficult moments. What made them keep going? What was their self-talk? What were their decisions and their commitment? See how you can tap into similar resources in your own life.

To absorb their virtues, there is a special type of meditation that allows you to absorb the qualities of that person into your own personality. Since this can be used to develop any quality or skill, not only self-confidence, it is covered at the end of the book (Chapter 38).

Get Support

The final method to overcome limiting narratives and develop self-belief is to get the support of a skilled mentor, a coach, or a therapist. Someone who can hold space for you, help you see through your biases, and question your assumptions. Sometimes a wise and patient partner will also do!

It is often very difficult to see how we are sabotaging ourselves. It's as though something inside of us doesn't want to be seen. That part will try to sabotage *even this process* of seeing it. It becomes a blind spot; and whenever there is a blind spot, we need something or someone outside of us to help us see. We need a mirror.

Share this concept:

MindfulSelfDiscipline.com/develop-self-belief

KEY POINTS

Ownership

- Ownership is taking full responsibility for your life. You can't change what you don't take responsibility for, so ownership is power.
- The opposite of ownership is blaming, victimization, and making excuses. These things keep you stuck and miserable. You can't practice self-discipline from this place.
- You do not need to go on a guilt trip or shame trip in order to take responsibility. It is enough that you see how you have contributed to the current state of things and how you are able to change it.

Self-Belief

- Self-belief is having complete trust in your ability to learn, grow, and overcome challenges along the way. The opposite is self-doubt—thinking that you can't do it, that you are not good enough, that "it will never happen".
- Self-belief may not guarantee success, but self-doubt very often guarantees failure.
- Develop a growth mindset, as opposed to a fixed mindset.
- You can develop self-belief by contemplating on your past successes, taking Baby Steps, shifting your self-talk, getting inspired, or getting support.

CHAPTER 13

ASPIRATION STEP 7: MAKE YOUR OFFERING

When I let go of what I am, I become what I might be.

LAO TZU

The most important decision about your goals is not what you're willing to do to achieve them, but what you are willing to give up.

DAVE RAMSEY

Nothing is impossible to a willing heart.

JOHN HEYWOOD

Aspiration Pillar Steps

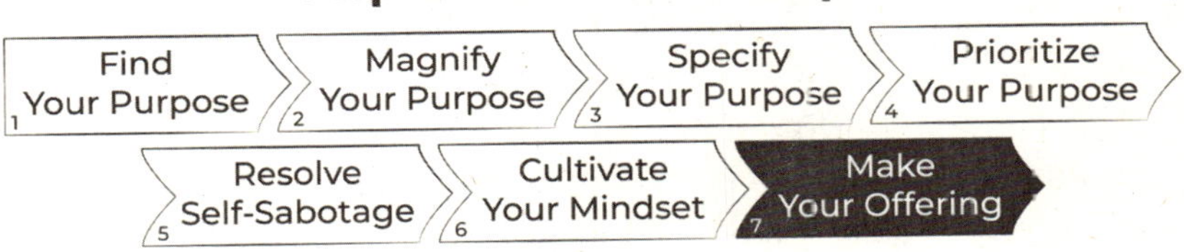

To make space for the new, you need to let go of the old; to transform yourself, you need to sacrifice yourself. You do that by letting go of everything that is not aligned with your goals and values, thus creating space in your life for what matters most.

Self-discipline can be hard because it requires some sacrifice. The sacrifice of, at times, not doing what would feel pleasant in the moment, or the sacrifice of doing something that feels unpleasant. That is not really appealing for our lizard brain, because it just cares about the pleasure or pain that is in front of us right now.

Mindful Self-Discipline is about outgrowing that primitive view of the world. It involves our capacity to sacrifice, our willingness to let go of a small short-term gain (instant gratification) for a greater long-term gain (delayed gratification). It is trading a small value (comfort) for a larger value (fulfillment). It is following your bliss, yes—the *higher* bliss.

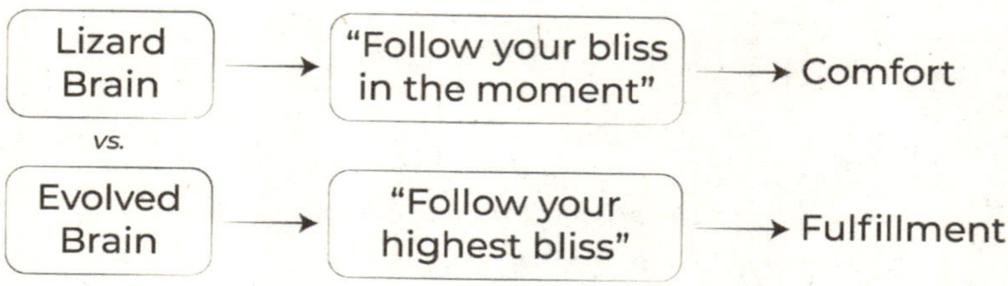

The concept of sacrifice is as old as humankind, and is found in the lore of all ancient philosophical and spiritual traditions. You give up something of value now to get something of greater value later. This requires faith, because there are no guarantees. The only guarantee you have is that if you don't make your sacrifice, you will never get the end goal.

The word "sacrifice" comes from two Latin roots: *sacra* (sacred things) and *facere* (to do or perform). To make a sacrifice is to do something sacred—and make something sacred. From the point of view of self-discipline, to be willing to make a sacrifice means that you are getting attuned to what is most sacred inside of you—your highest values and aspiration.

It is almost like life wants you to prove how much you want something. And if you thus prove yourself, then you can get whatever you desire.

Share this concept:
MindfulSelfDiscipline.com/sacrifice

MAKE YOUR OFFERING

In order to achieve your goals and fulfill your aspirations, you need to make an offering. Your offering is the price you are willing to pay for what you want—it's your commitment, your skin in the game. The bigger the offering you make, the bigger the reward you can reap. The more you are willing to give, the more you are ready to receive.

Often what we need to sacrifice are the usual suspects: part of our time, money, and energy. But it could also be other things. It could be sacrificing relationships that are no longer serving you, habits that are holding you back, or many opportunities for instant gratification (when they distract you from your goals).

Sometimes, the only thing we need to sacrifice is our old self. It is letting go of our limiting beliefs, excuses, and the old stories we have been telling ourselves for years. At other times, we need to sacrifice holding on to two opposing desires at the same time—such as the desire to snooze the alarm vs. the desire to have a productive morning, or the desire to eat chocolate every day vs. the desire to be fit and healthy.

How much time, money, energy, and pleasure are you willing to offer in return for success in your goal? How much of *yourself* are you willing to offer? The more you are willing to offer, the more energy you generate toward your aspiration.

The more you give, the more you get. Empty yourself fully, and there is nothing you cannot receive.

You cannot cheat this system. People keep trying to avoid paying the price by using hacks, magic pills, and empty promises of overnight success from greedy internet marketers. It rarely works—and if it does, it is neither sustainable nor fulfilling.

If you don't get what you want, it's a sign either that you did not seriously want it, or that you tried to bargain over the price.

Rudyard Kipling

The Buddha said that life is suffering—and that is so, unless you become a Buddha yourself! Whether you believe in the Buddha or not, it is axiomatic that a life without any pain or discomfort is not possible. You cannot choose to never experience pain. But you can choose your pain. You can choose the pain of self-discipline, or the pain of regret and wasted potential.

The bad news, then, is that sacrifice is inevitable. With any choice we make in life, we are sacrificing something—we are saying *yes* to one thing and *no* to a thousand other things. The question is not *if* you will sacrifice, but *what are you already sacrificing?*

The good news is this: you can choose your sacrifice—and, with that, your future.

You can choose the life you want to live, and the person you want to be—but it won't come for free. You can choose your goals and aspiration, but not their price.

- What are you willing to let go of in the pursuit of your aspiration?
- What is your offering? What will you sacrifice?

Take a few minutes to reflect on these questions. It will be time well spent.

You won't make a sacrifice if you have no faith in yourself. If there is doubt about the importance of the goal, or about your capacity to achieve it, sacrificing your present-moment comfort will not make much sense. If you have a solid aspiration and self-belief, then you will be willing to commit yourself to your goal.

Own your aspiration. Have faith in your capacity to actualize it. And then take a step forward every day, accepting discomfort and boredom as a small fee to pay for the transformation you desire. You will not regret it.

Share this concept:
MindfulSelfDiscipline.com/make-your-offering

REFRAMING SACRIFICE

Do not consider painful what is good for you.

Euripides

The fact that you need to make an offering doesn't mean that you need to suffer. You can actually make the sacrifice easier by changing your perception about it. It does not need to feel like passive resignation or self-denial.

When you see things under the right light, the potential pain of self-discipline is not really a sacrifice, but an investment. And like any other investment, there is the potential of a big reward at the end—but also a risk of no reward at all. Sacrifice simply increases the probability of a better future for you by creating a psychological state where change and progress can happen more easily.

Those who make the offering may or may not get the end reward—but those who do not definitely won't get it. So how can you make this offering feel less of a sacrifice? By changing the way you look at it. There are a few different ways to do that.

First, you can see sacrifice as something that you are doing *for* yourself, not against yourself. Your offering is you saying *yes* to yourself, to your aspiration. It is you deciding to live a life in harmony with your higher self. It is you investing in self-mastery and personal growth—and there is a sense of satisfaction that naturally comes with that.

A disciplined life is a good life. In a way, self-discipline is its own reward—because it brings inner strength, equanimity, wellbeing, and several other virtues. And if, at the end of your effortful journey, you also achieve your goal, that is a lovely bonus. The cherry on top.

It may take some time to adopt this new way of thinking. Give yourself that time, because it's worth it. Once you do, there will be less friction in your path. Self-discipline becomes *mindful* self-discipline.

If you see the offering like paying taxes, then you'll likely want to escape it. But if you look at it as an expression of your deepest goals and values, you will welcome it with an open heart.

Making an offering makes things real. It shows that your aspiration is true. It is the ultimate proof that you have found something to live for—a true sense of purpose and meaning. And that brings more happiness than the small pleasures given up on the way.

Working hard toward your goal is also an investment in your future happiness—it guarantees that you will be more satisfied with the result. We don't value things that come effortlessly into our lives; we value things that we have to pay a big price to get, be it in the form of effort, money, time, or sacrifice. Therefore, making an offering also means that you are able to enjoy the end reward more. It builds up contentment.

Finally, making an offering, even if you don't have 100% faith in yourself, creates buy-in. It forces your brain to generate that self-belief, because you don't want to lose on both fronts. In case you were not committed, it makes you commit.

Share this concept:
MindfulSelfDiscipline.com/reframing-sacrifice

A BALANCED OFFERING

If you are truly ready to do *whatever it takes*, then you will achieve your goal. There is no doubt about it. It's just a matter of time.

But that is not always practical. You might have a determination like that regarding your deepest aspiration. But that feeling likely won't be there in relation to your smaller goals (for which you also want to be more disciplined in). And that's okay.

It's not about investing all you've got into every single goal you have. That might be too high a price to pay, depending on the goal. That could potentially require you to sacrifice your health, or your career progression, or your life's savings, or important relationships. For most goals and aspirations, that is *not* a good idea. It would lead you to have a life of pure fire and no water, thus losing the balance (see Chapter 3). This is not what Mindful Self-Discipline is about.

If you are a 21-year-old with no dependents, no responsibilities, and nothing to lose, then you can do whatever you want, and risk everything at every step of the way. For the rest of us, we live complex lives, and want to grow in more than one area of life. Therefore, we need to look at our lives holistically and pursue our goals responsibly, according to the phase of life we're in.

That doesn't change the fact that each goal has a price. You need to be fully aware of that, be fully honest with yourself, and then pick goals and paths that are realistic for you, given your other roles in life.

EXERCISE: PRACTICE CHOOSING DISCOMFORT

Mindful Self-Discipline is about doing what is good for you. The challenge is, what is good does not always *feel* good; and what *feels* good is not always good. Therefore, make decisions based on how things are, regardless of how they feel. For that, you need to separate the search for what is good from the search for what is comfortable.

A recurring theme of self-discipline is the willingness to go through discomfort—be it physical, mental, or emotional. It's the ability to experience uncomfortable emotions, without that stopping you from doing what you need to do. This is key. In the words of a friend and podcast guest, Dr. Rick Hanson (PhD), "the limits of our life are the limits of the emotions we are unwilling to feel".

If you are willing to feel everything, without resistance and without running away, self-discipline becomes easy because you then have the superpower of "acting regardless". You can choose to act regardless of fear, boredom, laziness, tiredness, doubt, etc. You just keep on moving forward, no matter what.

You can train yourself to be like that. One of the ways to do that is to practice what the Stoic philosopher Epictetus calls *voluntary discomfort.* It is deliberately putting yourself through uncomfortable situations so that discomfort no longer holds you back. You basically schedule a form of sacrifice into your daily routine, until it ceases to feel like a sacrifice. This builds great willpower and emotional resilience. Another Stoic philosopher, Marcus Aurelius, called it *voluntary hardship.*

If the fitness adage of *pain is weakness leaving your body* is true, then we can also say that *discomfort is weakness leaving your mind.* Move toward meaningful pain, not away from it. This will make you stronger.

(Note: please don't go overboard with this, and don't do anything silly. It's about developing strong willpower, and not becoming a masochist or hurting yourself. Be mindful.)

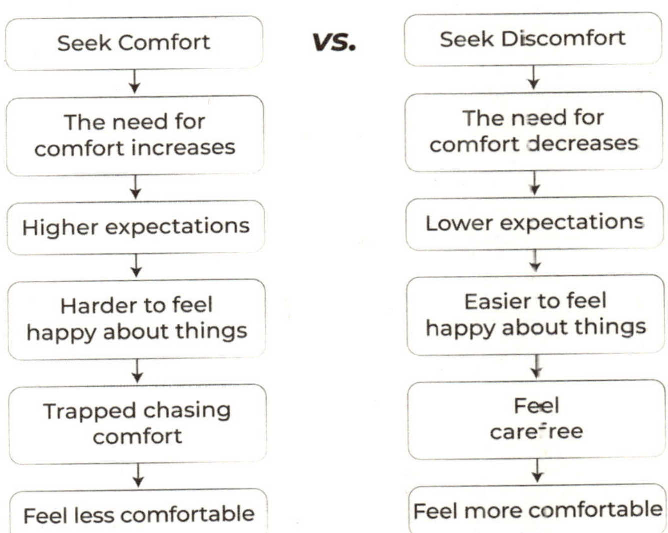

Choose one difficult thing to do every day. Once that becomes easy, then choose something else. Always exercise your willpower muscle, and never fall into inertia. Use the examples at the end of Chapter 4 for ideas about how to put this into practice, but always remember to keep things balanced so you don't burn out (Chapter 3).

Once you overcome attachment to comfort, your life becomes much easier. Whether you feel comfortable or not doesn't matter that much anymore. As a result, you need less stuff. You complain less. You fear less. You are more content with everything. And you are naturally more disciplined.

Paradoxically, **choosing discomfort makes your life *more* comfortable**. You become more care-free, and your threshold for discomfort becomes much higher. What used to be uncomfortable in the past will now feel like nothing.

Many people seek to become *financially independent*—and that's great. Even better, though, is to become *comfort independent*. For true wealth is not endless money in the bank, but endless contentment in your heart.

Share this concept:

MindfulSelfDiscipline.com/choose-discomfort

KEY POINTS

- In order to achieve your goals, you need to be able to let go of short-term gains (instant gratification) for a greater long-term gain (delayed gratification); trading a small value (comfort) for a larger value (fulfillment). This requires strong aspiration and self-belief.
- Your offering is the price you are willing pay for what you want—it's your commitment, your skin in the game. The bigger the offering you make, the bigger the reward you can reap. Your offering could be time, money, energy, bad habits, limiting beliefs, or contradictory desires.
- You cannot cheat this system. Your goals won't come for free. You can choose your goals and aspiration, but not their price.
- Sacrifice is inevitable. Life without pain is not possible; but you can at least choose your pain.
- Make sacrifice easier by reframing it as something positive. To sacrifice is to make an investment in your future and to say *yes* to yourself. It is you investing in self-mastery and personal growth—and there is a sense of satisfaction that comes with that. A disciplined life is a good life; it is its own reward.
- Your offering needs to be balanced, so that it won't hurt other areas of your life that are also priorities for you. So we need to look at our lives holistically and pursue our goals responsibly.
- What is good for you does not always *feel* good; and what *feels* good is not always good for you. Therefore, make decisions based on how things are, regardless of how they feel.
- To make this possible, separate the search for what is good from the search for what is comfortable by practicing Voluntary Discomfort.
- Choosing discomfort actually makes your life *more* comfortable. You become more care-free, and your threshold for discomfort becomes much higher. Obsessing after comfort makes you less comfortable.

Implementation resources: go through the Make Your Offering exercise in the Workbook (**MindfulSelfDiscipline.com/workbook**).

CHAPTER 14

BE TRUE TO WHO YOU ARE

Robert Cialdini, PhD, in his excellent book *Influence*, speaks of the principle of Consistency. According to this psychological principle, human beings are moved to do things that makes them feel consistent with their previous choices, desires, and identity—even if they are painful.

Having a clear aspiration—and committing to it by creating specific goals and writing them down (Step 3)—taps into the psychological drive of Consistency. When we then prioritize those goals by dedicating our time, energy, and resources to them (Step 4), we make this drive even stronger. Every time you remember your Aspiration (Pillar 2) and then take action on it (Pillar 3), you reinforce the need you have to live in consistency with it.

Self-discipline is the art of living in harmony with your highest goals and values. In other words, it is the art of integrity or consistency—it is being true to who you are. It uses this natural programming of your brain in your favor.

Being clear about your goals (e.g., being a successful writer) or values (e.g., taking care of your health) makes it painful for you to act in ways that are not in harmony with who you are. You write every morning because you are a writer, and that is what writers do. You don't drink soda because you are health-conscious; that's just not something that you do. Breaking those rules would contradict your self-image, and that would be painful.

In a way, then, the whole process of Mindful Self-Discipline can be summarized thus: know who you want to be (aspiration), and live accordingly (awareness and action). Affirm your aspiration, and let the consistency bias kick in. Believe the "ideal you" to be who you are already, and prove that to yourself with your actions. Bring your future into the present; let your ideal identity become your current identity—and transformation will follow naturally.

If you want to be healthy and full of energy (your ideal self), then affirm that that is who you are right now, and act accordingly. Make choices that a healthy and energetic person makes. Never mind that, for a while, you will *not yet feel* healthy and energetic. Affirm your aspiration repeatedly, and the reality will catch up with it very soon. Focus on what you are creating ("I am healthy") and not on the feedback of the present moment ("I don't feel healthy yet"). **Let your aspiration bend reality.**

If you want to be wealthy, think like a wealthy person. If you want to be confident, act confident. If you want to be a writer, write. If you want your life to make a difference in the world, then make a difference in the world. If you want to run a marathon, then do what marathon runners do (run every day). And, in the words of Jocko Willink, "If you want to be tougher, *be* tougher."

You will become who you believe yourself to be—because that is how you will act. That is how you will choose. That will be the lens through which you see the world—and through which the world will see you. Therefore, changing your beliefs about yourself, by affirming your Aspiration, is one of the most powerful methods of Mindful Self-Discipline.

Decide who you want to be. Affirm it. Be ready for it. This is the Aspiration Pillar.

Then be true to who you are. Remember it. Act on it. This is the purpose of the Awareness and Action Pillars.

Share this concept:

MindfulSelfDiscipline.com/be-true-to-who-you-are

CHAPTER 15

THE BIG PICTURE OF ASPIRATION

People often say that motivation doesn't last.
Well, neither does bathing—that's why we recommend it daily.

ZIG ZIGLAR

Your aspiration is the source of all your motivation and drive. It's what gets you started on the journey of self-discipline, and gives it meaning. These seven steps of the Aspiration Pillar will give you an aspiration that is *clear* (Step 1), *strong* (Steps 2, 3, and 4) and *wholehearted* (Steps 5, 6, and 7).

Now you have a clear aspiration, magnified and translated into SMART goals. You have prioritized it by committing part of your time, money, and energy. You have become aware of any self-sabotage tendencies you need to deal with on the path. You have developed the mindsets of ownership, self-belief, and sacrifice needed to actualize your aspiration.

The framework of self-discipline taught in this book works for whatever aspiration or goal you may have—from the most trivial to the most existential. Having said that, the deeper goals will, of course, bring with them more motivation. When your aspiration is deep, you will be powerfully driven. You will become like a force of nature, and nothing will be able to stop you.

Once your goals are clear, the next step is finding a good strategy for making progress with them, and then keeping yourself on track with it regardless of obstacles. The strategy is domain-specific—for example, the right exercise regime or the right business plan—but *keeping yourself on track* is all about self-discipline. And self-discipline is aspiration's best friend.

The next two pillars will teach you how to keep yourself on track and how to live a life true to your aspirations.

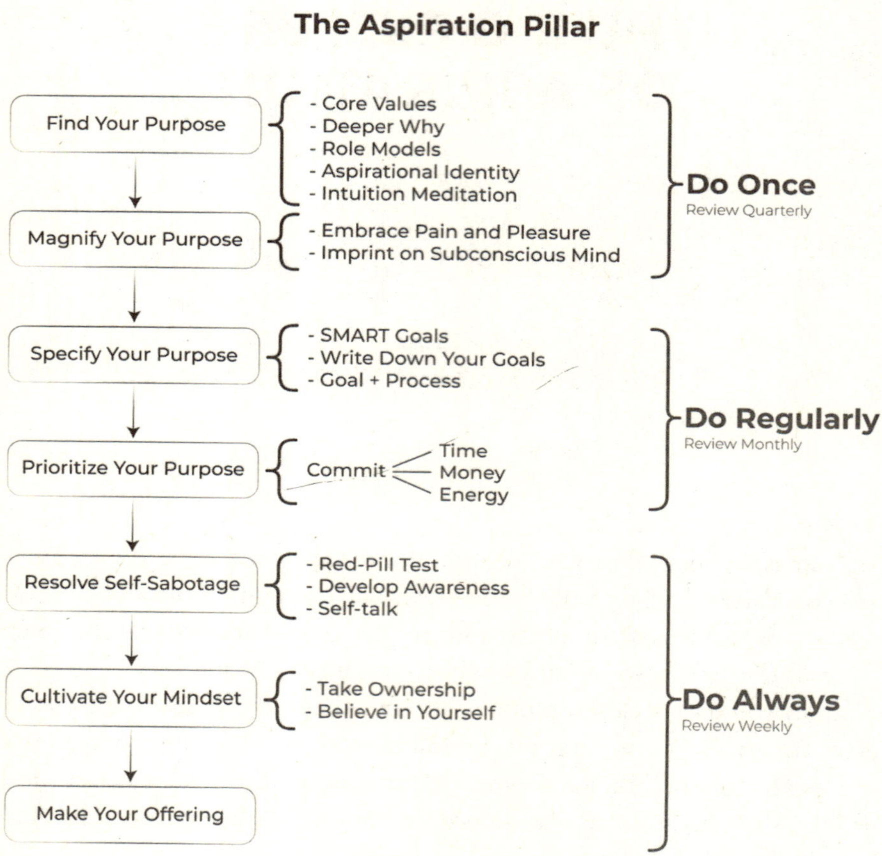

PILLAR 2

AWARENESS

CHAPTER 16

THE WHY AND HOW OF AWARENESS

Awareness is like the sun: when it shines on things, they are transformed.

THICH NHAT HANH

What is necessary to change a person is to change his awareness of himself.

ABRAHAM MASLOW

Awareness, awareness, awareness—that's the name of the game in Mindful Self-Discipline. If self-discipline is the father of all virtues, self-awareness is the mother.

By *awareness* we mean that quality of noticing what's happening inside of you. It's the ability to look inside, reflect, and contemplate. It is seeing things as they are, with presence of mind and radical self-honesty. In other words: mindfulness. Being awake to your inner world.

Self-discipline is a combination of two things: **remembrance** and **action**, or attention and intention. To practice self-discipline, day after day you need to remember your aspiration (attention), and then decide to act on it (intention).

THE POWER OF SELF-AWARENESS

Self-awareness brings with it many benefits to your inner life and outer life.

First, self-awareness is the foundation for conscious living. Whenever you are not self-aware you are living by default, not by design; you are being reactive, not creative. In other words, without self-awareness, you are just playing out your conditioning. Your future becomes a repetition of your past—sadly predictable.

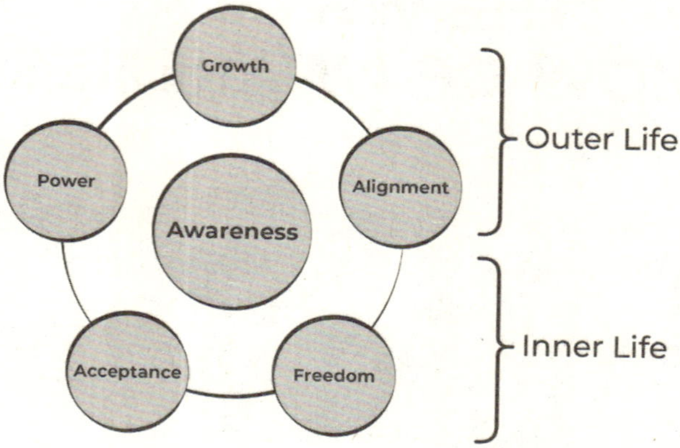

When you are self-aware, you have a choice. There is a pause—a space between the inputs from your environment and how you choose to respond. The wider that space, the more freedom you have. Your future becomes the result of your choices in the present moment.

You can't choose the thoughts, emotions, and impulses that spontaneously arise. But you can be aware of them, and this gives you the space to choose your response, instead of just being pushed by the loudest voice inside of you.

More awareness brings more **freedom**.

Your thoughts, emotions, and actions are the master sculptor of your character and of the reality you experience. They determine the life you live. Hence, it's essential that you pay attention to them. Without this type of awareness, you are just not in control of your life. Self-discipline is the art of transforming yourself. But you cannot change what you are not aware of.

More awareness brings more **power**.

Mindful Self-Discipline is about awareness, and not about beating yourself up. With self-awareness comes self-compassion: you see your flaws and limitations without any sense of shame or disgust, because you understand your human nature and your past conditioning. You don't hold on to unrealistic expectations.

This means that you may have a clear goal about eating healthily, and yet sometimes you become aware that there is a strong desire for the junk food that is in front of you. You may even become aware that the desire is overpowering you—despite your knowledge about what is best for you—and that you are deciding to do something that goes against your aspiration. Then you become aware that you did it, and how that felt in your body and mind.

All of this is good self-awareness, because it's clear and honest. Even when you choose something that is not in your best interest, be aware of that. "*I know that I'm choosing to take a step away from my aspiration right now. I don't know how to stop it, but I'm aware of what's happening.*" Self-awareness needs to be radically self-honest.

Self-awareness also brings the understanding that shame and guilt are negative emotions that produce only suffering, and not growth; with that realization, you are able to let them go, and replace them with compassion and understanding. Self-transformation is a process that needs to be cultivated, not a result you can whip yourself into.

More awareness brings more **self-acceptance**.

It is awareness that allows you to keep your goal in mind, to track your progress, and to keep coming back to the habits you are trying to create. Awareness reminds you of the new identity you are cultivating. It also makes you more aware of what triggers you; with this knowledge, you can then choose better environments and be ready to exercise your willpower when the situation calls for it.

The more you have self-awareness, the easier it becomes to exercise willpower and self-control. First, because you remember to do it before it's too late! And second, practicing awareness brings a natural pause to your automatic reactions, gives you options, and allows your aspiration to come alive again.

More awareness brings more **alignment**.

If you become acutely aware of what is happening in your body and mind the moment you drink a can of soda, or smoke a cigarette, or spend five minutes mindlessly scrolling social media, you will naturally develop a distaste for it. It won't happen all at once, but every time you *meditate on your temptations* like this you will get closer to seeing them for what they are.

As you can see, self-awareness has the potential to help you outgrow your addictions. And it does so *organically*, without you needing to force anything. Just as we organically outgrow our fascination for children's toys as we become aware of greater things in life.

Self-awareness is, thus, the catalyst of **growth**.

All the methods in this chapter are here to help you cultivate your awareness, remember your aspiration, and translate it into action. Awareness is the bridge that connects who you want to be (Aspiration), and how you decide to show up (Action). It empowers you to live a more authentic life.

Share this concept:
MindfulSelfDiscipline.com/the-power-of-self-awareness

THE QUALITIES OF SELF-AWARENESS

There are many ways to define awareness. The way a neuroscientist would define it is different from the way a philosopher or a spiritual master would define it. For the purposes of Mindful Self-Discipline, awareness has three main qualities: clarity, neutrality, and acceptance.

Clarity means that you see things for what they are, without fooling yourself. I like to call this *radical self-honesty*. You don't avoid or color the truth, however painful. Even when you are breaking your own rules and would otherwise like to "turn a blind eye", you instead see it clearly, and articulate to yourself what is going on.

> *"I know that I made a commitment to not eat any sweets for thirty days—because this is an expression of my aspirations. And I can see that I'm telling myself a story that today doesn't count, because it's my brother's birthday and his wife brought my favorite ice cream to the party. I can see that I'm trying to rationalize why today is an exception. I feel the urge to eat the ice cream, and a pull to give in."*

That is radical self-honesty. It will make you more likely say *no* to the excuse and thus keep yourself on track. But even if you still go forward and break your rule, at least you are not lying to yourself. You are not fooled by your rationalization—you know and see what is going on.

Radical self-honesty means catching yourself procrastinating, making excuses, self-sabotaging, or giving up on your goals. It means realizing that part of yourself doesn't want your goal, at least not right now. However painful that realization is, awareness doesn't shy away from it. It sees it, accepts it, and works from there.

Quick Exercise: take a moment right now to think of three times this week/month when you fooled yourself with your self-talk, rationalizing something that deep down you knew wasn't right for you. Make a commitment to be aware of it next time it happens.

Neutrality is the second element of awareness. This means observing your experience with a sense of curiosity, without getting attached to it nor developing aversion toward it. Attachment and aversion make you partial; they blind you. Awareness is neutral, because that's the only way it can truly see.

In very practical terms, for the purpose of Mindful Self-Discipline, neutral awareness means noticing what's happening without adding stories of shame, guilt, or self-criticism. All of these forms of deprecating self-talk only make it harder for you to achieve your goal. They create emotional stress—which is a form of pain—and then the lizard brain kicks in wanting a dopamine shot to relieve that pain through instant gratification. The researchers Polivy and Herman aptly called this vicious cycle the *what-the-hell* effect.

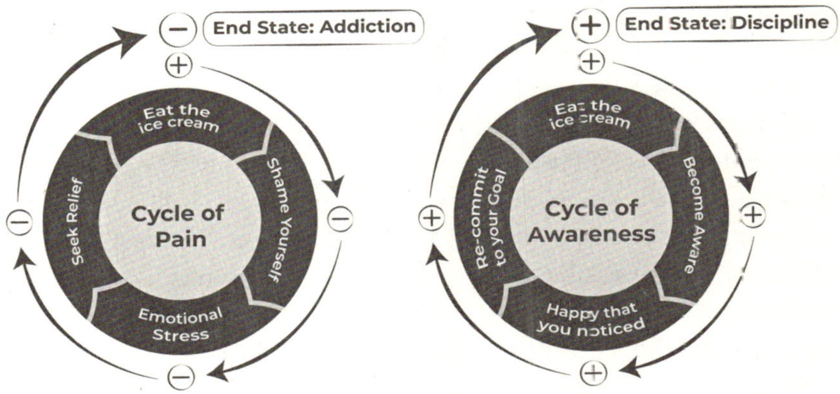

Instead of shaming yourself, just practice neutral awareness: notice what happened, and then feel glad that you noticed it! That moment of awareness is a big step forward. And then realize that you now have a moment of choice again: do you want to give up your goal, thinking that you are not good enough for it, or do you want to re-affirm it?

Many people resist this idea. They are afraid that if they let go of self-criticism they will become lenient, lazy, and not try hard enough. But that is not the case. If your aspiration is strong and clear, you will have all the needed fuel to put in your best effort. You won't need to add shame and guilt to the mix in order to keep yourself motivated. Shame, anger, and other negative emotions can also work as powerful fuels, but they are not used in *mindful* self-discipline, because they are an engine of suffering. We use our values and aspirations instead.

Awareness has an element of self-compassion in it, of *allowing* things to be as they are, without fighting. It is not even about self-forgiveness, but more fundamental than that. You only need to forgive yourself if you have first bashed yourself. Neutrality is about not adding that negative spin in the first place. Then there is no need to even talk about self-forgiveness.

This all leads to the third element of awareness: **Acceptance**.

Mindful Self-Discipline is about self-awareness, not self-punishment. Whatever negative emotions or harmful urges show up for you, you see them and accept them for what they are. This means no repression and no suppression—no self-violence.

There are several scientific studies showing that repressing thoughts and urges doesn't work very well. One of the reasons for this is that your mind keeps itself busy with the very thought it wants to get rid of. "Don't drink anymore", "Stop doing that", "Forget about your anger"—these thoughts affirm the very thing they want you to forget or overcome.

D. M. Wegner ran an experiment where he asked the participants to ring a bell whenever they thought of a white bear. There was a control group who were told to actively think about a white bear. The result? The group that was told *not* to think of the white bear ended up ringing the bell more often than those who were actually encouraged to think about it. This happens because asking us to suppress a thought sets up a mental process that is constantly comparing each thought with the unwanted thought; and when we stop doing that, the suppressed thought returns with renewed strength. Forcefully suppressing a thought is like pressing down a spring: the moment you release the control, it comes back up even stronger.

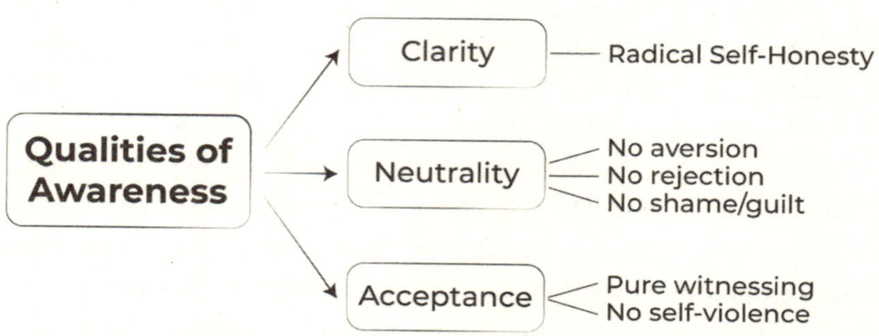

Another study showed that smokers who were told to suppress all thoughts about smoking ended up smoking more, in the long run, than the other group who were encouraged to think about smoking *as much as they could.*

The message is clear: **whatever you resist, persists**. Suppressing thoughts and emotions like that doesn't work. They will stay there somewhere inside of you, silently influencing your life without you noticing it.

The alternative to suppression is **awareness**—which is neutral and accepting. To be the witness of your thoughts, emotions, and urges without repressing them.

"All right, Giovanni, I got it! Self-awareness is one of the seven wonders of the world—but how do I practice it?" There are three core practices of awareness: meditation, reflection, and integration. If you practice them daily, you are practicing the Awareness Pillar in your daily life.

Share this concept:
MindfulSelfDiscipline.com/the-qualities-of-self-awareness

PRACTICE #1: MEDITATION

Meditation gives you space and clarity.

Meditation is the first of the core trainings for awareness. It strengthens your prefrontal cortex—which is the part of your brain where self-awareness and willpower reside—reduces stress, improves your moods, and gives you the ability to pause rather than act impulsively. All of these are essential elements for self-discipline.

With meditation you develop the power to pause, slow things down, and zoom out. It disentangles you from the thoughts and impulses in the moment, and by doing that it gives you the clarity to see what's really happening and what needs to be done.

Meditation is something you practice at the beginning of your day (ideally), to kindle your awareness. You can start by practicing five minutes per day, and then increase one minute per week until you get to at least ten minutes. Ideally you will grow your practice to twenty minutes per session, but with ten minutes you will already experience some benefits.

As you will see in Chapter 37, there are many different styles of meditation. Here is a simple method for you to start with:

1. Sit with your back straight and unsupported. You could sit on the edge of your bed, or on a chair, or cross-legged on a cushion on the floor. The position of your hands and legs is irrelevant.

2. Close your eyes. Take a few deep breaths—in through your nose, and out through your mouth, releasing all tension.
3. Close your mouth and breathe normally through your nose. Allow yourself to fully arrive in the present moment. Feel grateful that you are taking the time to cultivate awareness and ground yourself.
4. Bring all your attention to your breathing. Notice if it is shallow or deep. Notice if it is fast or slow. Notice if it is jerky or smooth. If by being aware of your breathing it changes its rhythm, that is okay. Simply allow it to be as it is.
5. Begin to count your breaths backward, from ten to one, both when breathing in and when breathing out. Breathing in, "ten"; breathing out, "ten". Breathing in, "nine"; breathing out, "nine". All the way to "one—one".
6. When you get to one, start again from ten. If you get lost and forget what you were doing, become aware of that fact. This is self-awareness. Now bring your attention back to the breath, and start again from ten, with the resolve of staying with the breath moment after moment. This is willpower.
7. As an initial goal, see if you can count from ten to one three times in a row without getting distracted.

If you already have a meditation technique that you enjoy, you can do that one instead.

Right after meditation, when your mind is clear and focused, **review** your aspiration and **recommit** to your goals. Then make a **resolution** to live your aspiration during the day. Affirm the intention to be aware of it, and then allow it to be the driving force behind your decisions during the day.

Action step: start a daily meditation practice. If you already meditate every day, and know the best style of meditation for you, then see how you can take it to the next level by better integrating it into your daily life.

Share this concept:
MindfulSelfDiscipline.com/awareness-practice-meditation

PRACTICE #2: REFLECTION

Reflection develops perspective and accountability. It is studying yourself. It is learning deeply about your motivations, emotional triggers, thought patterns, and biases.

There are three main ways to do this:

- Journaling
- Tracking
- Deep conversations

One of the best ways to practice reflection is through **journaling**, at the end of your day. There are many different methods of journaling, but all of them essentially have the same effect: they prompt you to reflect on your day, on your behaviors and on your choices, thus making you more self-aware and more accountable. You are teaching your brain to be more aware during the day, since it will have to answer your journaling questions every night.

For the purposes of Mindful Self-Discipline, your journaling practice is simply taking a couple of minutes to answer these three questions every night:

1. How have I taken a step toward my aspiration today? (Gratitude)
2. How have I taken a step away from my aspiration today? (Awareness)
3. What can I do better tomorrow? (Intention)

The second method of reflection is **tracking**. Tracking involves regularly taking note of your habits, routines, and goal-promoting activities, using a habit tracker, wall calendar, spreadsheet, or habits journal. It can also involve rating yourself, from one to ten, in particular qualities or behaviors you are trying to develop. For example, if you want to develop more confidence, you could rate yourself every day from one to ten on how much you have practiced confidence that day. Finally, it includes the practice of attributing either a +1 or a -1 to your decisions during the day—a concept that we will explore in the next chapter.

However you implement it, tracking gives you black-and-white clarity about your patterns, and it will enhance your commitment and self-awareness. Consider it an essential piece of Mindful Self-Discipline.

The third method of reflection is harder to implement, because unlike the first two, it doesn't depend only on you. It involves having **deep conversations** with a wise friend, a coach, or a therapist. Someone who knows how to "hold space", ask the right questions, and be a mirror for you. This often goes to much deeper places than journaling and tracking, because it is very hard, if not impossible, to see through all our biases on our own. We often need some support.

> **Action step:** start a daily journal for self-reflection, and also some form of tracking of your habits and the steps you are taking toward your goals. If you are able to, find a way to also have deep psychological conversations with someone who can help you become aware of your biases and thereby gain perspective.

Share this concept:
MindfulSelfDiscipline.com/awareness-practice-reflection

PRACTICE #3: INTEGRATION (PAW)

Integration is applying awareness in your daily life. While meditation and reflection are practices you do in a specific time and place, *integration* is something you do all the time, throughout your day. It's about being consciously present to yourself and your life as it happens, moment after moment, in real time. In a way, it is taking meditation beyond the cushion.

The key element of integration is **observe thyself**. It means to be constantly watching what's going on in your mind and body. It is to be aware of your "inner weather", including:

- the thoughts and feelings that you are having
- the triggers that were fired
- the impulses that are pushing you
- the effect of the environment on you
- the mood fluctuations you're experiencing
- the desires, fears, and biases that are coloring your perception

For instance, if you are having a difficult conversation, or experiencing a moment of temptation, and you are aware of your inner weather, then you are *integrating* awareness into daily life. If not, then awareness practice is still limited to certain moments of your day (meditating in the morning, journaling at night). Without being constantly aware of your inner weather, it's very difficult to navigate life effectively or be disciplined in relation to your aspirations.

This practice will be explored further in the next chapter.

Action step: make a decision to constantly *observe yourself* throughout your day. Set up reminders for it (perhaps post-it notes or notifications on your phone/computer), to check in with yourself several times a day.

KEY POINTS

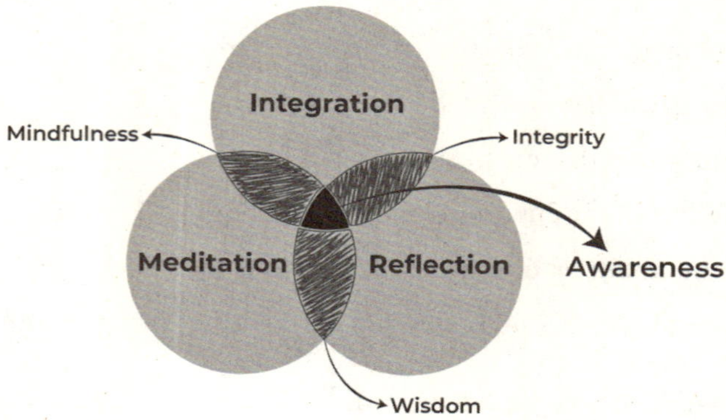

- Self-discipline is a combination of two things: attention and intention. To practice self-discipline, day after day you remember your aspiration (attention) and then decide to act on it (intention).
- Awareness gives you acceptance of who you are, freedom from your thoughts and impulses, power to choose your actions, alignment with your higher values, and organic growth.
- Self-awareness is developed through three core practices: meditation (in the morning), integration (throughout the day), reflection (at night).
- Reflection happens through journaling, tracking, and optionally through deep conversations.
- Awareness, for the purposes of self-discipline, has three core qualities:
  - Clarity: seeing what is happening with radical self-honesty
  - Neutrality: observing your experience without adding shame or guilt
  - Acceptance: embracing what is here without repression or suppression

Implementation resources: For an up-to-date list of my recommended tools for *meditation*, *journaling*, and *tracking*, visit **MindfulSelfDiscipline.com/tools**.

CHAPTER 17

THE PAW METHOD

Mindful Self-Discipline is the art of living in harmony with your goals and values. To make that happen, you need to apply your willpower to shift your mental and emotional states, so that you can make decisions that help you advance toward your aspiration, rather than move away from it. But you cannot use your willpower unless first you are aware, and you cannot be aware if you are living on autopilot.

Therefore, you need to pause, then be aware, then apply your willpower. This is the natural order of things, and this is what the PAW Method is all about. PAW stands for *pause, awareness, willpower*. It is the *integration* practice of awareness, and the master thread for all of the exercises in the Awareness Pillar. If you remember just one thing from this pillar, let this be it.

You will notice that, even though we are talking about the Awareness Pillar, the word *awareness* is just in the middle of the PAW Method. That is so for a couple of reasons. First, because you can only practice full awareness if first you are able to *pause* (P); and practicing awareness often reveals the need to shift your state of mind by using your *willpower* (W)—so these are all part of a single process. Second, both the *pause* and *willpower* elements are, in themselves, practices of awareness.

The practices of meditation and reflection train you to practice PAW more effectively; without them, practicing PAW becomes harder.

PAW STEP 1: PAUSE

The ability to pause is one of the main superpowers of meditation practice; it gives you space, clarity, and presence. When you pause, you experience more peace of mind, groundedness and wellbeing. You can slow things down to make more sense of the chaos of daily life. You feel more in control.

On the other hand, if there is not enough pausing in your daily life you can't practice awareness. When everything is happening too fast and you have no breaks, you likely won't even notice the self-control conflicts that are right in front of you! You won't notice that you forgot your aspiration and are taking steps away from it. Your mind is too busy juggling ten different things—there is no space left in your working memory to deal with a temptation.

You can't exercise your willpower in a state like this. You are living on autopilot—reacting to life instead of responding. And you're also enjoying your life less. Since you are not present, even your indulgences feel less satisfying.

Research shows that when you are eating or smoking in a distracted state, you tend to eat more junk food and smoke more cigarettes. The participants in a study actually ate 20% more food when distracted, and also felt less full. As a result, they ended up eating more food later on too, since they were not satisfied.

Pausing and being more consciously present in your daily life means that you will be less distracted, more aware of your goals, and thus more likely to follow through with them. As you can see, pausing is both a prerequisite for awareness, as well as a practice of awareness in itself.

Practicing Pause

How do you become good at pausing and slowing things down?

Through meditation and mindfulness. Pausing in your daily life is a natural effect of keeping a daily meditation practice. In a way, it's a skill that builds up effortlessly over time. However, you can accelerate this process and enhance it by deliberately practicing pausing during your day.

The simplest way to bring more pause into your daily life is through conscious breathing. When you breathe consciously, deep and slow, you calm down your nervous system, down-regulate your impulses, and awaken the most evolved part of your brain (the prefrontal cortex). Your emotions are then more manageable, and you suddenly feel more aware and in control.

The Stanford scientist behind the marshmallow study (discussed in Chapter 4), Walter Mischel, attributed the willpower success or failure of participants to the brain's "hot and cool" system. He explained that the cool system of our brain is our cognitive portion (i.e., it is the thinking system, with our rational decisions). The hot system reacts immediately based on emotions and impulses. This distinction is helpful for practicing self-discipline, because it illustrates the shift we need to make in order to stay on track with our long-term goals: from the hot system to the cool system, from impulsive to rational, from lizard brain to evolved brain, from unconscious to conscious.

Pausing helps you make that shift, and it does that through breathing.

There are multiple breathing techniques that have been developed by meditation masters throughout the centuries; some of them are quite elaborate and intense. But for the purpose of getting started with the PAW Method, the easiest way is simply to take three deep abdominal breaths. I call this the 3-Breath Rule:

- Place your hands on your belly
- Imagine your belly being a balloon
- As you breathe in, expand your belly
- As you breathe out, relax your belly
- Let your breaths be *slow*, *deep*, and *even*
- Take three breaths like that

To breathe *slowly* is to be unhurried, to take in air little by little, in a long breath. To breathe *deeply* is to take in plenty of air, using your full lung capacity. To breathe *evenly* is to keep a constant rhythm, without spikes or jerks in the breath. These three principles apply equally to the inhalation and exhalation.

For meditation, we breathe in and out through the nose. For this particular breathing practice, however, if you are very tense you may choose to breathe in through the nose, and out through the mouth three times, having a long sigh each time. After that, you breathe in and out only through the nose.

When you breathe slowly, deeply and evenly three times, you bring calming moments into your day. It's like taking a short break from the never-ending flow of thoughts and emotions. This pause is essential for awareness—**there is no awareness without pause.**

Step 1 of PAW

A more elaborate method of breathing that you can also practice any time is Box Breathing. In this technique you set a particular rhythm to your breath:

breathing in for four seconds, holding your breath for four seconds, breathing out for four seconds, and holding empty for four seconds. If four seconds is difficult, you can do it with three seconds; if it is easy, you can do five or six. Other than that, the same guidelines apply: breathe abdominally and keep a rhythm that is slow, deep, and even.

Mini-Meditations

If you can't pause, you have no choice. There is no space between you and your impulses.

When you pause and breathe consciously, you shift your state of mind. You shift your nervous system. In this new state, you are then able to see your habitual patterns of behavior—mindlessly going for your phone, getting irritated for nothing, drinking an extra can of soda—and change them.

The trickiest part of practicing PAW is remembering to pause. In our fast-paced life, this can be challenging; we are always busy, and so we forget. The first step, then, is getting into the habit of pausing. For that, I recommend that you create three short moments in your day for cultivating pauses. I call these "mini-meditations".

A mini-meditation is a one-minute informal meditation that you practice anywhere, anytime. It could be while you are commuting, eating, walking, waiting for something, or preparing for a difficult conversation. You could even do it with your eyes open—nobody needs to know what you are doing.

For the mini-meditations, keep your body still (if possible), and practice your favorite style of meditation for a minute or two. That could be just doing some deep conscious breaths, repeating a mantra in your mind, doing a quick body scan, or any other calming technique. The most challenging part is not the mini-meditation itself, but remembering to do it. For that, you can use alarms on your phone, or use the resources at the end of this chapter.

Cooling Down

Pausing is important for self-discipline, regardless of your goals. Having said that, if your goal is to overcome certain impulses or drop bad habits, pausing becomes even more important. It allows the hot system of the brain to cool down.

If your urges are very strong, you might need to get away from the temptation, until they cool down. In these cases, it could be helpful to take a break from your impulses by getting busy with something else, or find a way to not have the temptation under your nose anymore. You can leave the store, hang up the call, take a break, close your eyes, count from fifty to one, shut down your computer. Do whatever you need to do to walk away from the temptation, until things cool down.

Summary: Whenever you find yourself in a willpower conflict—between short-term desires and long-term goals—take a moment to pause and breathe deeply three times. To make it more likely that you'll remember, create the habit of pausing multiple times a day through mini-meditations. Finally, if you are facing an overpowering urge and can't just pause and watch it, then get busy with a positive activity.

Share this concept:
MindfulSelfDiscipline.com/paw-step-one

PAW STEP 2: AWARENESS

Once you have paused and slowed things down, you are now in a position to practice self-awareness and see things more clearly. For the purposes of the PAW Method, this means having awareness of your options and awareness of your drives.

Awareness of Your Options

Every decision we make matters. Every decision we make is either a step toward to our goals, or a step away from them. The problem is that we are usually not aware of this. Without this awareness, self-discipline is not possible.

The simplest way to enhance this awareness is to create the habit of labelling every option you have as either +1 (if it takes you closer to your goal) or -1 (if it takes you away from it). You can do that in your mind, but in the beginning I highly recommend that you actually keep this balance in writing. You can use a small notebook that you have always with you, a spreadsheet, a notetaking app—whatever you are comfortable with. You can also try the mobile app I created for this purpose: **MindfulSelfDiscipline.com/app**.

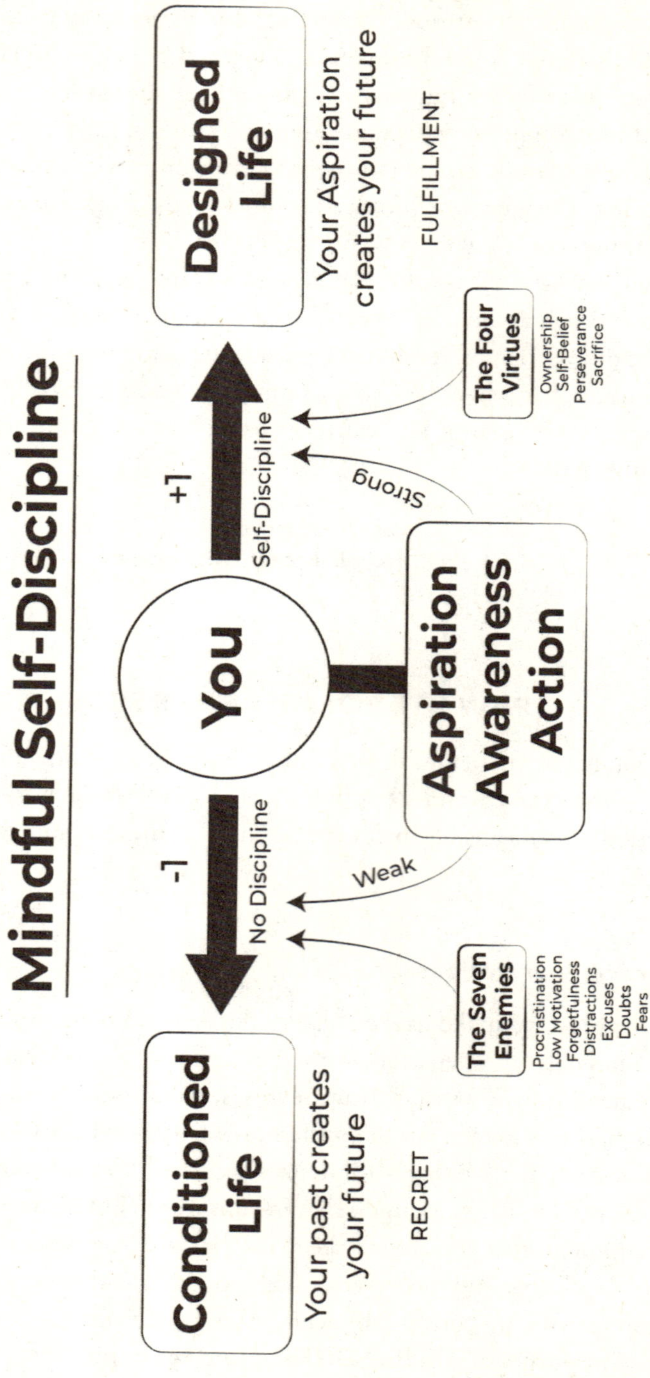
Mindful Self-Discipline
Conditioned Life
Your past creates your future
REGRET
-1
No Discipline
Weak
The Seven Enemies
Procrastination
Low Motivation
Forgetfulness
Distractions
Excuses
Doubts
Fears
You
Aspiration
Awareness
Action
+1
Self-Discipline
Strong
The Four Virtues
Ownership
Self-Belief
Perseverance
Sacrifice
Designed Life
Your Aspiration creates your future
FULFILLMENT

Here are some examples, using the aspiration "to be perfectly healthy and full of energy":

- I hit the snooze button when the alarm rang this morning (-1)
- After I woke up, I took a cold shower (+1)
- I skipped breakfast, as I'm practicing intermittent fasting (+1)
- On my way to work, I felt a strong urge for sweets. I stopped at the donut shop and got some for dessert after lunch (-1)
- I felt sleepy this morning, so I drank two extra cups of coffee (-1)
- I choose to eat salad instead of fast food for lunch today (+1)
- On my way home, I stopped by the gym and did half an hour of cardio (+1)
- I had a smoothie for dinner (+1)
- Daily score: +2

If you want to take this to a whole new level and become a *Willpower Jedi*, then do that with your thoughts as well: +1 when they are positive/empowering, -1 when negative/limiting.

This process forces you to develop clarity about where you are putting your energy, and what kind of life you are creating for yourself. It is a practice of radical self-honesty. The fact that you need to be very black-and-white with this (it's either +1 or -1) means that you cannot hide in the middle—because there is nothing in the middle.

Following this process helps you understand the real costs and benefits of each decision. You begin to see that that every time you say *no* to your self-discipline, you are moving away from your designed life (your aspiration), and back into your conditioned life (the *status quo*). This is a choice you make in every moment of your life.

Of course, not all plus-ones are equals, and likewise with the minus-ones. So if you like, after you have built the habit of labelling like this, you can then add nuance to this by choosing different weights depending on how helpful or unhelpful the behavior was. This is not really necessary, and can add complexity to the system, thereby slowing down the process—but some people prefer this more nuanced approach.

The way of Mindful Self-Discipline is simple: make sure that your points balance at the end of each day is always positive. When it is, you go to bed satisfied with your day, and feeling proud of yourself. When it is not, you look for the lesson (without shame or guilt) and commit to do better tomorrow. That is all. Over time, the compound effect of this small practice will be huge.

It is unrealistic to expect that you'll be able to follow this process with every decision. We make thousands of decisions every day, and there is not enough time to pause for each one. You just need to follow this process regarding a dozen or so of your key decisions every day. The more you practice the P of PAW (*pausing*), the more you'll be able to apply this technique throughout your days and accumulate the points you need to propel you toward your goal.

At the end of your day, add up your points, and review. See what you can learn. This nightly review is part of the third practice of awareness, *reflection* (Chapter 16). It will make you acutely aware of every time that you are taking a step toward your goal, and every time you are taking a step away from it. I know of no better means to achieve this self-awareness.

Awareness of your Drives

Awareness of your options helps you identify the best decision you can make. Yet *knowing* the best choice is very different from actually *making* the best choice—hence the need for self-discipline. Once you are aware of your options, it's then time to look inside yourself and examine the psychological forces at play.

To help you make the best choice, you need to develop awareness of what is happening inside of you in that moment. You need to be aware of when you are feeling demotivated, or when you feel like quitting, or when you begin to rationalize and make excuses. You do that by honoring the three qualities of awareness: with radical self-honesty (clarity), without shaming yourself (neutrality), and without repressing yourself (acceptance).

Here are the four core questions that help you develop clarity about what's going on inside of you in the moment:

1. What *stories* am I telling myself?
2. What *emotions* are here?
3. What *urges* am I feeling?
4. What are my secondary *gains* from this? (See Chapter 11)

What's Next?

Sometimes the simple act of pausing and becoming aware of your urges is enough to down-regulate them. This works because it creates a sense of distance between you and your emotions, and helps you move away from the *hot system* (lizard brain) and toward the *cool system* (the prefrontal cortex). Making a decision that promotes your aspiration becomes much easier.

Many times, though, practicing pause and awareness is not enough. You realize that your internal state is such that it will push you to take a step away from your goal. In order to prevent that from happening, you need to shift your internal state—and that inevitably involves an exercise of your intention, your willpower. That is what the third step of the PAW Method is all about.

Share this concept:
MindfulSelfDiscipline.com/paw-step-two

PAW STEP 3: WILLPOWER

You've paused. You've seen clearly what's going on inside you—your options and your drives. And now you may need to do something about it. You may need to use your willpower to shift your state. In Chapter 4, we defined willpower as "your ability to control your attention, emotions and actions, despite the presence of competing stimuli" and "your capacity to delay gratification, override unwanted thoughts and feelings, and shift your internal state".

Awareness is Seeing. Willpower is Doing.

If we compare the PAW Method to crossing a busy intersection on the road, then:

- *Pause* is stopping your car at the intersection
- *Awareness* is looking around and seeing if it's safe to proceed
- *Willpower* is about deciding what to do next, and doing it

The last step of PAW is to shift your state by using one of the three techniques explained in the following chapters. It's good to learn them all, but you don't necessarily need to practice them all. You may find that one of the techniques works better for you every time, or that you need to use different techniques for different self-discipline challenges.

In other chapters of the book you will learn variations of the PAW Method specifically focused on overcoming excuses, distractions, procrastinations, and doubts. The approach is always the same: we start with *pause* and *awareness*. It is only the third step, *willpower*, that varies according to the challenges you are facing. PAW is an extremely versatile technique, and any approach that you use to shift your state remains true to the *willpower* step.

Share this concept:
MindfulSelfDiscipline.com/paw-step-three

KEY POINTS

- The PAW Method is the master thread for all of the exercises in the Awareness Pillar. It is how you integrate awareness into your daily life, improve your self-control and willpower, and remain true to your aspiration. It is at the heart of Mindful Self-Discipline.
- **Pause** is slowing things down so you can make better choices and live more mindfully; practice the 3-Breath Rule and mini-meditations.
- **Awareness** is becoming aware that every decision matters, and it's either a +1 or a -1 in relation to your goals. Become aware of your drives—which are the stories, emotions, and urges playing out in the present moment—by using the questions in this chapter.
- **Willpower** is intentionally shifting your state so that you can choose what is in line with your aspiration. In the next chapters, I'll discuss three techniques for applying your willpower.

Implementation resources: see my list of recommended tools for *pausing* and for *tracking* here: **MindfulSelfDiscipline.com/tools**. For the interactive version of the PAW Method, together with the +1/-1 tracker, check out our custom app at **MindfulSelfDiscipline.com/app**.

CHAPTER 18

TECHNIQUE #1: SHIFT YOUR FOCUS

Imagine it's time for you to go for your run, and instead you feel a strong temptation to skip, grab a pot of ice cream, and watch your favorite Netflix show. Then something inside of you remembers, "No! I should use the PAW Method for this…" Here is how it might look:

- **P**: You pause and take a few deep breaths. The urge to sit down with Netflix and ice cream cools down a little but is still there.
- **A**: You become aware of your options: ice cream and Netflix are clearly a -1, while going out for a run is clearly a +1. Then you become aware of the stories, emotions, and urges that are playing out in the moment. You see exactly what the problem is, yet the temptation continues.
- **W:** You now need to shift your state in order to make the right decision and stay on track with your aspiration. You do that by "zooming out" and refocusing on your aspiration and your future self. This way you remove yourself from your immediate cravings and see the bigger picture.

The more you develop the right perspective on what is really going on, the less forceful your approach needs to be to get yourself back on track. By refocusing on your values and long-term goals, exercising willpower to win the self-control conflict that you're facing becomes easier. The temptation becomes weaker, and your aspirations can then drive your decision. This is what this first willpower technique is all about.

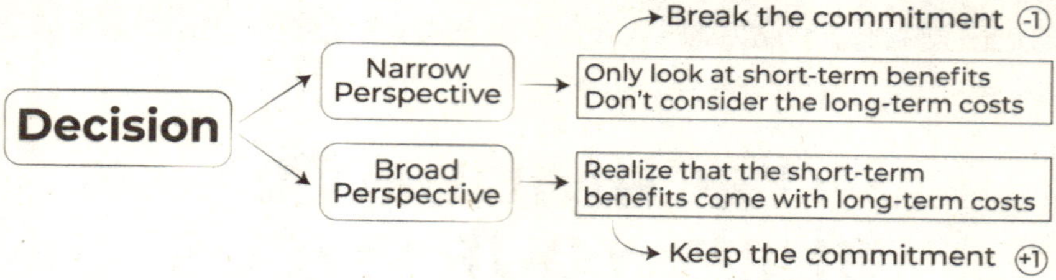

Shift Your Focus involves three core steps: *zoom out* so you get perspective, *remember your aspiration* so you realign yourself with your values, and *be kind to your future self* so that the benefits of remaining on track with your goals become more real to you. Let's dive into each of these now, starting with the first one.

STEP 1: ZOOM OUT

Skipping the run and going for the Netflix/ice cream combo may feel so tempting because you are not seeing the long-term consequences of this decision. You are just considering it in a vacuum: the effort of running *versus* the pleasure of ice cream and watching TV. To shift that, remember the score of the decision you're tempted to make (+1 or -1), and ask yourself: *What are the costs of making this decision a habit?*

Become aware that every time you choose to procrastinate, you are training your brain to be a good procrastinator. Every time you choose to make an exception to your rule, you are making it easier for you to make that exception again. Every time you say yes to a temptation, you are making it more addictive. By skipping your goals today, you are training yourself to skip them tomorrow.

On the flipside, every time you say *yes* to your aspiration, you are strengthening it. Every time you go for the run, you are making it easier for you to run again. Every time you choose to stick to your commitments, you are making it less likely that you'll break them in the future. Every time you take a step forward, you increase your momentum; every time you skip, you slow it down. Small decisions compound over time, and will either propel you forward (+1), or hold you back (-1).

The problem is that we often don't see this clearly in the moment it's happening. We live under the impression that our small daily choices have no long-term consequences, because we see them in isolation. Sure, eating ice cream *once* and skipping your run *once* has basically zero health consequences in the long term—yet this is *not* what's going on here. What is really at stake is this: are you training yourself to stay on track, or are you training yourself to make exceptions and go astray from your goal? Which habit are you reinforcing right now?

This technique of zooming out and thus shifting your perspective is an expression of what academics call *broad bracketing*. When making decisions, if we zoom into that choice in isolation and just consider its consequences, this is known as *narrow bracketing*. If we instead zoom out, see that decision as an instance of many identical decisions over time, and consider the costs and benefits of that series of decisions as a whole, this is known as *broad bracketing*. Assuming that you care about your future, broad bracketing is a wise strategy.

You've got to remember: it's not about the ice cream. It's not about skipping "just today".

It's about choosing which version of your future you are voting for. It's about your life, your aspirations, the person you want to be. Will you sacrifice those ideals for a short-lived pleasure?

The right way of seeing that decision is not, "Do I want the pain of running, or the pleasure of watching TV?" It is, "Do I want the pain of poor health and carrying all of this extra weight, or the pleasure of feeling fit and light, and having high energy levels? Is it worth sacrificing that for a few minutes of mindless entertainment?"

As long as the bad decision made does not bear fruit, the fool thinks it is like honey; but when it ripens, then the fool suffers grief.

BUDDHA (DHAMMAPADA, V.69)

That which is good for you in the beginning and bad for you at the end, is bad for you. That which is bad for you in the beginning and good for you at the end, is good for you. Remember this, and you'll be proud of your decisions, rather than regret them.

When we are not aware of what is really going on—the values that are at stake with every decision—we often don't even notice that we are facing a self-control conflict. As a result, we just mindlessly indulge. To avoid this problem, we need to zoom out and gain some perspective. We need to see the long-term effects of the decision we are facing, and ask ourselves: "Am I happy to make this a habit?"

When gaining perspective like this is difficult, you can also imagine that you're observing a friend going through this situation and facing the same self-control conflict. Can you describe what she's doing, the challenges she's facing, and the real values at stake? Can you help her make a decision she won't regret? This helps you temporarily suspend your own biases, and think outside the box. Then you can re-apply the same thinking back to yourself more impartially.

In summary: zoom out of the temptations in the present moment, so you can think long-term. It will then be much easier to use your willpower to take a step in the right direction.

STEP 2: REMEMBER YOUR ASPIRATION

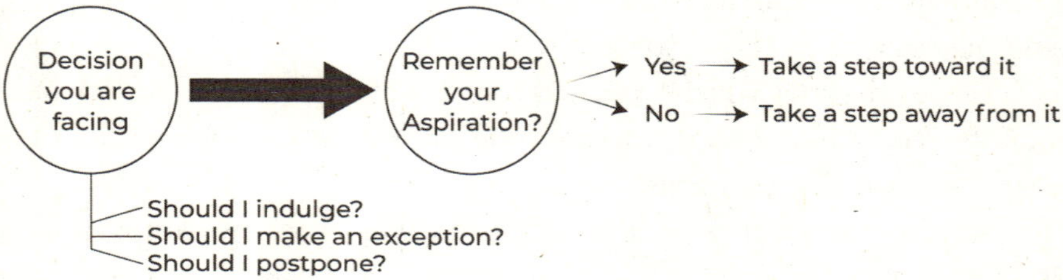

The first step of this Shift Your Focus technique, *zooming out*, makes you more aware of the values at stake. The second step is to enhance the values that you want to come out on top in the self-control conflict. You do that by reconnecting emotionally to your aspiration and strengthening it.

Bring to mind your goals and aspiration, then ask yourself:

- *Why are my goals important for me?* Review the exercise in Chapter 8.
- *How will I feel once I actualize my aspiration?* Take a minute to connect yourself emotionally with the benefits of achieving your goals; get excited about your vision once again.
- *How will I feel if I delay my goal—or perhaps even give it up—for the sake of the temporary pleasure that is in front of me?* Feel the pain that would cause, and how you'd rather not go there.

You can even exaggerate your perception of pain and benefits, if needed, so that the decision becomes a no-brainer for you. That will help you feel more strongly about the values in conflict. For example, if the habit you want to build is making time to work on a side project, you can tell yourself that if you don't do that, you will eventually experience a lot of regret in life and feel miserable; and that if you make it happen you will feel on top of the world, proud, and fulfilled. The more black-and-white the distinction is in your mind, when making any choice, the less willpower and self-control you will need to exert. Having clarity about your values and the tradeoffs of every choice makes it easier to choose your aspirations over instant gratification.

The more you keep your goals and aspirations in mind, the easier it will be for you to consider the impact of small daily life decisions on them. In practical terms, whenever deciding whether you should say "yes" to an impulse, first check in with your aspiration to see if it's okay. If you want every decision to move you toward your aspiration, use your aspiration as the compass for every decision. This leads to a life lived in harmony with your goals. This is Mindful Self-Discipline.

This only works, of course, if you actually remember your aspiration in times of "temptation". Hence the importance of pausing and awareness—the P and A of the PAW Method. If you have strong and clear goals, and are training your awareness regularly, then you'll be able to keep your aspiration top of mind, and use it as the compass for every decision.

At the end of this second step, you might have already resolved the self-control conflict in front of you in favor of your higher goals. If not, it is likely because you don't care enough about the long-term consequences of your actions—there is a sense of apathy or indifference toward your future self. If that is the case, then proceed to Step 3 of this technique.

STEP 3: BE KIND TO YOUR FUTURE SELF

Ask yourself: "What will this decision do to my future self? Who will I become if I say yes to this temptation?"

The main challenge with the Shift Your Focus technique is that our present self feels much more real than our future self. Brain scans show that, for most people, thinking of their future self is almost like thinking of another person. It doesn't feel like "me". When you imagine a future experience, the brain areas associated with thinking about "self" are not activated.

There are several studies indicating the effects of this curious dissociation, and the resulting tendency we have to burden our future self.

- Researchers at Yale demonstrated that when people had the choice between a healthy food item and a large cookie, 57% chose the cookie; unless they are told that they will have the same options the following week, then 83% chose the cookie—most of them rationalizing that they would choose the healthier option "next time".
- Researchers at the University of Wisconsin and at Duke University, in a study about exercise equipment, noticed that people tend to overestimate how much exercise they would do in a month. When participants were then specifically asked to "be realistic" in their estimates, they overestimated even more.
- In another study, the participants were asked how much time they would like to volunteer for a given good cause. On average, students were willing to sign up their future selves for 85 minutes, but their present selves for only 27 minutes.

If your future self feels like a stranger to you, of course you will opt for procrastination and instant gratification—you won't even register that there is a self-control conflict at play. Why would you give up comfort right now and undertake a long and effortful journey to benefit a stranger sometime in the future?

You wouldn't do it. Rather, you'd decide based on what is comfortable right now, even if that might hurt you in the future. This is called the *personal discount rate*, which is how much you are willing to trade your future wellbeing for your present wellbeing—the higher it is, the more you are bent toward instant gratification.

With a high personal discount rate, you fool yourself often, and make decisions that are short-sighted. It is one of the main reasons why self-discipline can feel so difficult; and regret, so commonplace.

- You give in to a temptation today because you believe that tomorrow you'll control yourself.
- You overspend today because you believe that in the future you will save more and spend less.

- You get distracted today, thinking that in the future the distractions will be less distracting.
- You postpone important work today because you believe that your future self will be better equipped to do it and have more willpower to follow through.
- You don't act on your aspiration today because you think that in the future you will have more time, more money, more determination, and more focus to follow through.
- You think that tomorrow will be different and believe that somehow you will change and start making better decisions.

With each decision like this, you burden your future self. You make life more difficult for yourself, and the effect of these small decisions compound over time. I call this *self-discipline debt*. Either you'll pay this debt with interest (change will be harder in the future), or you'll go bankrupt (live with feelings of regret and lack of fulfillment).

If you keep making decisions that will put your future self in trouble, how do you think he/she will feel about you? Disappointment. Shame. Resentment. Self-hatred.

The way to reverse this, and prevent future self-discipline debt, is to create a strong connection with your future self, so that it feels like "me". There are a few different ways to accomplish this shift.

Self-Reflection: The first way is to reflect repeatedly on the fact that your future self is *you*, and that today you are the future self of yesterday. Contemplate that your core identity, preferences, and tastes are likely to stay the same. See that the joys and sorrows of tomorrow will be as real for you as are the ones you experience today. Reflect on the fact that making a decision that brings you comfort now, but challenges later, is like spitting against the wind—you'll suffer it eventually.

Letter Writing: A second way is to communicate with your future self. Kelly McGonigal, PhD and author of *The Willpower Instinct*, suggests that you can write an email to your future self, telling him/her what you are doing today to meet your long-term goals. You can use a service such as **FutureMe.org** for that.

Visualization: You can also visualize your future experience in great detail. Go into a relaxed and calm meditative state, then imagine two versions of your future life: having achieved your goal (designed life) and not having achieved it (conditioned life). Experience each of these two futures in great detail, and in first-person. Feel the pains of the conditioned life, and the joys of the designed life; see how your life looks on the outside, and how you feel on the inside. Make it as real as possible.

Aging Software: Finally, you can look at a likely version of your future self. Researchers have proved that using age-progression software can also help you envision your future self and create a stronger sense of continuity. So you might want to use certain third-party apps to visualize your aged self. You then look at your future self and ask yourself, "Which decision will make my older self happier? What advice would he/she give me right now?"

If you still struggle connecting to your future self, then you can teach your brain about the benefits of the action you want to take by attaching an external reward to your desired behavior. (This is covered in greater detail in Chapter 27.)

How would you live if you knew that all your actions were being constantly observed by your future self? It's good to spend some time answering that question—because they are.

Nowhere can you hide from your conscience. It will haunt you.

Neither in the sky nor in the middle of the ocean nor in the depths of the mountains—nowhere in the world is there a place where one may escape from the results of one's bad decisions.

BUDDHA (THE DHAMMAPADA, V. 127)

If your future self doesn't feel real for you, it will be almost impossible to make this technique, Shift Your Focus, work. If that is you, you will need to establish a stronger connection with your future self by using whichever of the four methods above work best for you.

If you struggle connecting with your future self, it would be a great idea to do these exercises daily for some time—perhaps right after your morning meditation practice, or after journaling at night. Then, when a self-control conflict shows up in your life, you will be able to think of the future self *first*, and prioritize his/her happiness over the temptation that's in front of you.

Live with the awareness that every decision matters; that every decision is building up your future self and future life. Link your present with your future, and you will have a present you can be proud of, and a future you can truly enjoy.

THE RESULT: NO MORE CONFLICT

The Shift Your Focus technique gives you three different ways to shift your perception about the values at stake. As we saw, the real value conflict in our example is not "running" vs. "Netflix?" It is "being healthy and energetic, looking great, achieving my goals, and being the person I want to be" vs. "delay all of that good stuff for a fleeting pleasure that will soon be forgotten and does not really build toward anything".

Do you feel the difference?

In the first case, there is an internal conflict and you need to make a difficult decision: running vs Netflix. In the second case, the values are so wide apart that the decision becomes nearly automatic. There is simply no comparison, so it's a no-brainer: you'll choose the goal-promoting option.

With every step in this technique, your aspiration becomes stronger for you, and your temptations, weaker. Your focus is shifted from the short term to the long term.

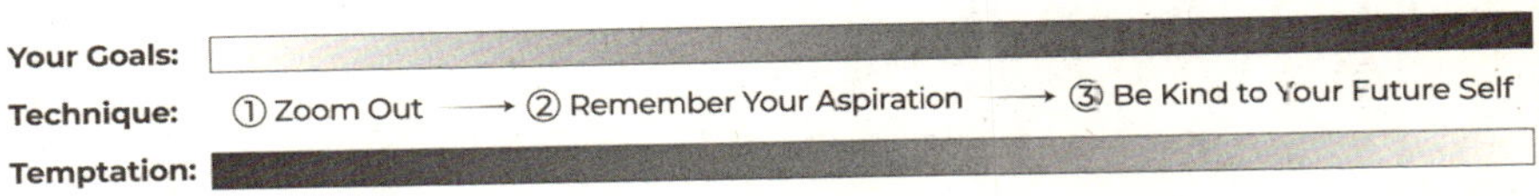

The end result of following through with this technique is that you have increased the delta between the two values and bypassed the self-control conflict. In this new state, it is much easier to apply your willpower to do what you need to do—you are now no longer fighting an uphill battle. That is why it's essential to be clear on your values and aspirations by going through the exercises in the Aspiration Pillar.

> **Exercise:** Think of the last three times you broke one of your resolutions or good habits for each of the goals you want to be more disciplined in. How could you have *shifted your focus* at that time? Write the exact words you would use in your self-talk to make that shift. Commit to trying that the next time it happens.

Mindful Self-Discipline is not really about punishing yourself when you go off track and rewarding yourself when you remain on track. It's about *enhancing awareness* of the natural consequences of going off track, and the benefits of staying on track. The more you are aware of these, the less you will need to be forceful with yourself.

Every decision matters much more than it may seem in the moment. Become aware of the real costs and benefits of each decision by zooming out, remembering your aspiration, and connecting to your future self. With that habit in place, every day in your life will be a step toward your goals; without it, every day might be a step toward regret.

Share this concept:
MindfulSelfDiscipline.com/shift-your-focus

KEY POINTS

- The more you develop the right perspective on the real value conflict at play, the less forceful your approach needs to be to get yourself back on track. By re-focusing on your values and long-term goals, exercising willpower to "win" the self-control conflict that you're facing becomes easier.
- **Step 1:** Zoom out by seeing the consequences of making your decision a habit.
- **Step 2:** Remember your aspiration and re-connect emotionally to it, to strengthen its weight in the decision making.
- **Step 3:** Connect to your future self so that you care more about your long-term goals, by using either visualization, letter writing, self-reflection, or aging software.

Implementation resources: for a list of third-party tools that you can use to enhance the connection with your future self, visit **MindfulSelfDiscipline.com/tools**. For instructions for the meditation version of the Shift Your Focus exercise, go to **MindfulSelfDiscipline.com/meditations**.

CHAPTER 19

TECHNIQUE #2: SHIFT YOUR PERCEPTION

Self-discipline begins with the mastery of thought.
If you do not control your thoughts, you cannot control your needs.
Self-discipline calls for a balancing of the emotions of your heart
with the reasoning faculty of your head.

NAPOLEON HILL

Self-control is strength.
Right thought is mastery.
Calmness is power.

JAMES ALLEN

If technique #1 is shifting what you focus on and how you think about temptation, technique #2 is shifting how you feel about it. It makes use of a principle that has been employed by stoics and monks for centuries, and is known as *cognitive reappraisal* in modern psychology. Cognitive reappraisal is most often used to reduce stress and anxiety, but it can also be used for helping you be more disciplined with your goals. In simple terms, it is your ability to change how you feel about a certain thing or activity by deliberately choosing to see it differently and assign it a different meaning.

The reasoning behind this technique is very simple: when you consider something attractive, you'll desire it; when you consider it repulsive, you'll want nothing to do with it. What makes things attractive or repulsive is subjective—it depends on how you look at them, what you pay attention to, and the stories you tell yourself.

From meditation we learn that our thoughts are not reality, but they create our reality—or *color* it, at the very least. That means that we have the capacity to shift the way we feel about things by shifting the way we perceive them. We can turn pleasure into pain, or pain into pleasure, by choosing where we put our attention.

Where you focus your thoughts and attention determines how you feel about a given temptation, experience, or task. The cognitive reappraisal techniques are as effective as your ability to visualize, and your ability to turn thoughts into reality by focusing on them. With the daily practice of meditation, these mental faculties are sharpened, and applying these methods becomes easier.

NEGATIVE REAPPRAISAL

Suppose you have made a resolution to stop drinking soda. You have done well for a week, but now you are out with friends and everybody is having one. The urges have suddenly come back, and you start thinking, "Surely, drinking just one can will do no harm". Memory of the pleasurable sensations of drinking soda floats around in your brain, your mouth starts salivating, and you feel that this time you'll make an exception so that you can feel "more connected with the group".

Time to apply the PAW Method!

You pause and take a couple of deep breaths (P). You notice the urges, stories, and feelings related to drinking soda, and become aware that giving in means getting a -1 in relation to your goals (A). You then decide to shift your state by changing how you feel about the temptation in front of you, using cognitive reappraisal (W).

(Warning: skip the next paragraph if you are having a meal right now.)

To do that, you start developing a sense of disgust toward the soda. You think of how bad that is for your body. You remember the bloated feeling of gas in your stomach. You look at that black liquid and associate it with dirty water or sewage. You imagine that it will taste extremely bitter and make you want to puke. You say to yourself that drinking it is like drinking poison.

Now, are you ready to go forward and grab yourself a can? Not so appealing anymore, is it?

The stronger your imagination is, the more effective this method will be. You are telling yourself a different story about the tempting object, and believing it to the point where it feels real. That reverses the urge: you will now want to move away from that object rather than toward it.

(Just make sure that you keep this whole process to yourself. Let other people enjoy their soda if they want to!)

You can enhance the perception of negative consequences associated with the soda by linking it to your aspiration and ideal life. For example, you can ask yourself: "Do I want to be the type of person who is overweight, doesn't prioritize health, and can't say *no* to junk food?" Reframing the self-control conflict in this way can help you turn your self-talk from "I can't drink soda" to "I don't drink soda"—it's just not who you are anymore. The former ("I can't") feels like a restriction; a rule you wish you could break. The latter ("I don't") is a choice made consciously, based on your ideal self and aspiration; you are being authentic, and true to who you are (see Chapter 14).

So contemplating the defects of the object of desire and focusing on the negative consequences of indulging in it are two powerful ways to practice negative reappraisal.

A **third way** to practice negative reappraisal is taking your mind to the state of being saturated with that pleasure. When we are saturated with a particular pleasure—be it food, sex, TV, or whatever—we are done with it. In that moment, that activity has no more pull for us, and we don't perceive it as desirable. The spell has been broken.

Desire makes an atom look as big as a mountain before it is fulfilled and a mountain look as small as an atom after it is fulfilled.

RAMANA MAHARSHI

So the next time you feel a strong urge, try this: imagine that that urge has already been fulfilled. Take your mind to the state you experience once you are done with that activity, or have been saturated with it. Try to re-create the feelings in your body associated with being saturated with that activity.

If this is difficult for you, then go through that indulgence as mindfully as possible, paying attention to how it feels in your body and mind afterward. Then take a "mental snapshot" of that post-indulgence experience, so that you can remember it the next time the urge comes up, and use it to re-create the state of saturation.

Finally, the **fourth method** of negative reappraisal is to physically associate painful sensations to that urge. Some people use a rubber band on their wrist and snap it whenever they are about to do the undesirable behavior; others use a device such as the Pavlok wristband to achieve the same end. This is known as aversion therapy, and it does work; but this book is about *mindful* self-discipline, so we won't emphasize this method.

"Negative reappraisal" can be used to break habits and prevent you from acting on your impulses. In some wisdom traditions—such as Buddhism and Yoga—this is described as "contemplating the defects of the objects of the senses". It is known to be one of the most effective ways to overcome strong desires.

Science backs it up. Studies show a 50% decrease in cravings for unhealthy food items after the negative reappraisal. Another study showed a 37% decrease in cravings for smoking when the participants did a mindfulness exercise while smoking—in this case, it seems that simply paying attention to the natural "defects" of the experience of inhaling smoke was enough.

Keep in mind that this method can be used with anything (not only food). No thing, person, or event can lure us away from our chosen goal unless we allow it. Nothing has the power to shake our resolutions unless we allow it. As Epictetus put it, "Men are disturbed not by things, but by the view which they take of them."

Negative Reappraisal
- Contemplate the defects
- Focus on the negative consequences
- Create a state of saturation
- Associate painful sensations

Share this concept:
MindfulSelfDiscipline.com/negative-reappraisal

POSITIVE REAPPRAISAL

Negative reappraisal is used to stop us from a behavior we don't want to do. Positive reappraisal is used to encourage us to do a behavior we want to do but don't feel like doing. Here are some examples:

- eating a healthy food item that we just don't enjoy
- doing effortful physical exercise
- having a difficult conversation with our partner
- doing boring work that we have been procrastinating about
- waking up early when we feel like snoozing
- drinking water instead of sugary drinks

This method is summarized perfectly in the quote of Euripedes, a stoic philosopher: "*Do not consider painful what is good for you.*" And it works. Studies show that individuals who were asked to focus on the vitamins and minerals in healthy food items, and how that will make them strong, ended up eating more healthy food and less junk food.

So how do we program our mind to find a particular effort or experience attractive and delightful? This is very simple: we do the polar opposite of the negative reappraisal methods. In other words, we can:

Positive Reappraisal

- Contemplate the qualities
- Focus on the positive consequences
- Create a state of desire
- Associate pleasant sensations

Are you feeling too lazy to go for a run? Think about how you will feel energized, light, and alive in your body after a few minutes of running; and how good you will feel later on in the day as a result of it. (Method A)

Are you procrastinating doing some boring tasks at work? Focus on the positive consequences of getting that work done; feel the sense of accomplishment and relief of ticking off those tasks; think about how it will increase the likelihood of you being promoted. (Method B)

Do you find yourself resisting drinking water because it's tasteless, and instead going for soda? Imagine that you are feeling very thirsty, and that only water can quench your thirst. Think about how cool and fresh a cup of water will taste, and imagine it being a refreshing experience. (Method C)

Do you find it hard to stop snoozing and wake up on time? Associate waking up on time with a comforting cup of great coffee. Create a rule for yourself that you can only have that coffee if you wake up on time, without snoozing. (Method D)

When you have the option to use both negative and positive reappraisal, which should you go for? While there is research indicating that positive appraisals may be more effective, at the end of the day you have to use what works for you. You are the judge.

Share this concept:

MindfulSelfDiscipline.com/positive-reappraisal

REDUCING FRICTION

On the path to fulfilling your goals, you will likely have to do a lot of things that you don't naturally enjoy. You may desire the end result of looking fit, or having a brilliant book published—but dislike the experience of daily exercise, or the pain of writing.

Sure, you can use willpower to *get it done* regardless. You can boost the Aspiration Pillar so much that it crushes your dislike to pieces, or implement the Action Pillar so well that you do what you need to do regardless of how you feel. You can keep yourself accountable to people, associate external negative consequences with not keeping your good habits, and external rewards with keeping it. You then become really good at doing something that you hate.

All of this works, but if the process is not awareness-driven, there is still a lot of friction—it's like you become so strong that you can run while still attached to an iron ball and chain. This is not the way of Mindful Self-Discipline. Get rid of the chain first, remove friction first, and then you'll achieve the same results with less willpower expenditure. How to do that? By using the tools of the Awareness Pillar.

Awareness reduces friction by helping you transform the behavior you hate to do (but have to do) into something that, at the very least, you can accept. It does that by making the activity you resist more desirable by aligning it with your highest values (Shift Your Focus) or by allowing you to change how you feel about that activity (Shift Your Perception). Awareness also teaches you how to let go of aversion and resistance toward certain activities, so you suffer them less—a concept we will explore in the next chapter.

When pursuing your goals, it is very likely that the path will be long and the results, short-lived. The results are just the carrots that lure you forward in life—the real goal is the path itself. The real goal is the growth that happens on the journey: you become a more virtuous, conscious, and empowered individual. If that is the case, why not learn how to enjoy the path itself? If you can do that, keeping your discipline will depend less on forcefulness, and more on mental mastery. This is one of the ways in which Mindful Self-Discipline is different.

Enjoying the path comes naturally if you use positive reappraisal (Shift Your Perception), and also if keep yourself aligned with your values and aspiration at all times (Shift Your Focus). This is the ideal way to move forward. This is how to get the most bang for your willpower buck.

When that is not possible, making the right choice can feel like a sacrifice. In order to stomach that experience, you'll need to learn how to *embrace the pain*. That is the topic of the next chapter.

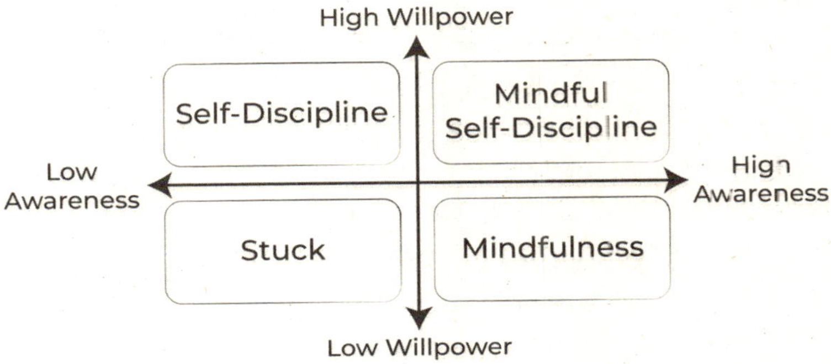

Mindfulness	Pure non-judgemental observation. See clearly. Let things come and go.
Self-Discipline	Make yourself do the things you need to do. Suffer 99 days; enjoy the result on the 100th.
Mindful Self-Discipline	Aspiration. Awareness. Action. Learn to enjoy the 99 days of effort; the end result is just a bonus.

KEY POINTS

- Change the way you feel about things through your self-talk and through how you focus your attention. This is a technique used by monks and Stoics and called *cognitive reappraisal* in psychology.
- Negative Reappraisal: Develop feelings of disgust toward the object of temptation by contemplating its defects, focusing on the negative consequences of indulgence, creating a state of saturation, or associating painful physical sensations with it.
- Positive Reappraisal: Create feelings of attraction toward the activity that you need to do by contemplating its qualities, focusing on the positive consequences, creating a state of desire, or associating pleasant physical sensations with it.
- The better your ability to visualize, imagine, and believe your thoughts into reality, the more effective this technique will be. These abilities can be developed through meditation.
- Learn how to enjoy the path and the efforts required to achieve your goals, so you can move forward with less friction. This is the approach of Mindful Self-Discipline.

CHAPTER 20

TECHNIQUE #3: EMBRACE YOUR PAIN

At times, self-discipline can feel like hard emotional labor. In the pursuit of a higher ideal, you are asked to let go of certain things that you like, and accept some form of physical or emotional discomfort. Be prepared for that. Some sacrifice will always be required; and, as we've seen in Chapter 13, it paradoxically leads to a *more* comfortable life.

The problem is that we have a deeply-ingrained desire for comfort. We like to avoid discomfort whenever possible, because discomfort is a form of pain—and our lizard brain is programmed to avoid pain at all costs. By doing that, however, we shelter ourselves not only from pain, but from life too. We stop growing. **There is no growth without discomfort.**

- If you hate discomfort, you hate growth. Your potential will remain untapped.
- If you want growth, suspend your desire for comfort (or at least limit it).

You only develop muscles by going through effort, sweat, and pain. You only write a great book by squeezing your mind and bleeding your soul through every sentence. You only develop inner strength by going through suffering with an open heart.

Charles Duhigg, author of classic *The Power of Habit*, explains how habitual behaviors are not linked to the conscious decision-making part of the brain, but to other areas. This means that when something becomes a habit, you are not making conscious decisions about it anymore; it just becomes second nature, part of who you are. Thus, expect that changing your habits will feel difficult—perhaps even wrong. It will feel like you are going against your nature. Your brain wants to save energy, and it does that by relying on your existing patterns of behavior. Changing your behavior, on the other hand, takes effort, and can feel like swimming upstream.

That is the nature of the human mind, and the challenge of self-discipline. So what are your options? You can either give it all up and remain as you are, or you can accept the discomfort and make a change. After some time, the new behavior will become the new normal, and inertia will then work in its favor; until then, however, you'll need to face some form of discomfort. That is not optional.

Expect Discomfort

Once you have committed yourself to your goal, it is better not to assume that you will *feel like* doing the activity. It is better to assume that your goal-promoting activities will often include some level of discomfort or pain. Even though that might not always be the case, it sets your expectations right, so you are ready to act despite your feelings, when the moment comes.

Let me share a quick example. In the first months of my daughter's life, the shift from 4am to 7am was mine. Before starting that schedule, I knew that waking up at 4am would be difficult. I knew that I would face an irresistible temptation to snooze, and to go back to bed "just for ten more minutes…" (yeah, right!). I had tried in the past and I knew that waking up at 4am would involve fighting with myself for three to four minutes just to get my eyes to stay open, then dragging myself to the bathroom. A pain!

What I did was the following. Every night right before sleep I would tell myself, "Tomorrow, the first ten minutes of my day will feel like hell". As counterintuitive and exaggerated as this may sound, it worked perfectly. It made me ready for the challenge and boosted my willpower. (The first ten minutes never really felt like hell, which was a relief.) By exaggerating the pain and being ready for it, I was allocating more willpower to the task than it actually demanded; as a result, it felt easier than expected.

So adjust your expectations. Expect that you will need to act despite not feeling like it. Expect that it will be painful, and be ready to face that without fear, without hesitation, without shying away.

Some days you will not be feeling at your best, and there will be a temptation to skip the things you have committed yourself to do. Still, it is better to stick to your plan and at least go through the motions, rather than skipping altogether. It is better to have a "below average" meditation session than to not meditate at all; it is better to do ten sloppy pushups than zero pushups; it is better to write 300 bad words than to write zero words.

Mindful Self-Discipline is about taking consistent action in the direction of your goals. Self-discipline doesn't ask, "How are you feeling about this?" It asks, "What will you do about your goal?" The emphasis is on action, not mood; on commitment, not motivation. You do what you need to do to live in integrity with your aspiration, with your ideal self.

Whatever your aspiration may be, some level of discomfort will likely always be part of your path. If you can learn to love it, as we learned in Shift Your Perception, then great. If not, let's see how you can go through the experience without running away. This is especially helpful when you need to do something that you don't feel like doing. The trick is learning how to be inside that pain without letting it control what you should do or should not do. It is about releasing resistance. Doing this will expand your limits, little by little.

Share this concept:

MindfulSelfDiscipline.com/embrace-discomfort

HOW TO EMBRACE DISCOMFORT

When you find yourself facing a self-control conflict where you know you need to do something, but part of you doesn't want to do it because it might bring some emotional or physical discomfort, then you will need to take a deep breath, and—in the words of Mark Twain—*eat a live frog*.

That frog could be the experience of fear. Maybe fear of failure, and the shame and loss you project you would experience. Maybe fear of being judged, disappointing others, and being rejected. Maybe fear of the unknown; or even fear of success.

That frog could be the boredom of the task ahead of you, when compared to all the more pleasant ways you can spend your time. Or your self-doubt and feelings of inadequacy.

That frog could be the experience of unpleasant sensations in your body—in the form of physical effort (exercise), sleepiness (waking up early), pain (cold showers), or unfulfilled urges (temptations).

Whatever the frog is for you, whatever the physical or emotional discomfort that you fear, embrace the pain. Whatever you resist, persists. Don't resist it—move *toward* it. Take a step toward the discomfort with a fearless heart, saying "yes" to the pain, then you will be free even in the midst of it.

Learn to embrace boredom, discomfort, and pain, and there is nothing you cannot achieve. Get into the habit of "eating a frog" every morning. This is the price for your aspiration—and if your aspiration is true, it will be worth it. There will be no frog too hard to swallow.

There are two ways of eating the frog.

One way is forceful and bellicose—you just force yourself to do it, regardless of how you feel. Become so strong that you can fight that uphill battle, and still win. We could call this the *David Goggins method*. Goggins is an ultra-endurance athlete and retired U.S Navy Seal who hates to run, yet runs several hours every week, because he is committed.

The other way is the *mindful* way—you open your heart to the experience of discomfort, focus on it as simply unpleasant sensations in your body, and breathe through them.

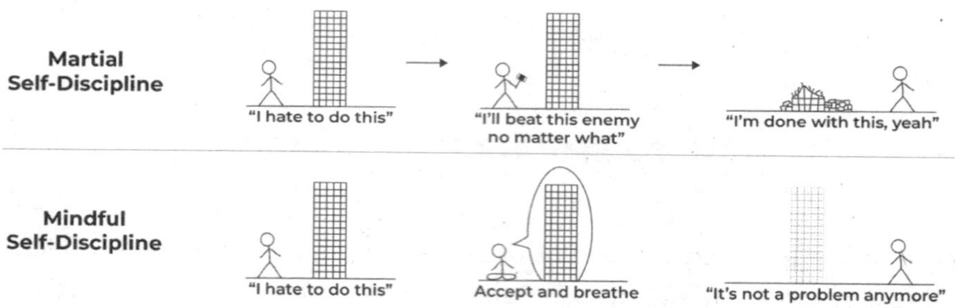

THE ROAR METHOD

All discomfort, be it physical or emotional, is just sensations in your body. The emotions that you are afraid of feeling—such as anxiety, shame, fear, grief—are only unpleasant sensations in your body. You don't need to run away from them. You don't need to let them tell you what you should or shouldn't do. They are just warning signals.

It's the same thing with the cravings that push you to do things you don't want to do. They are just sensations in your body. You don't need to chase them. You don't need to obey them. You can just be aware.

The technique itself is very simple. I call it the ROAR Method:

- **R**ecognize the emotion or urge that is here. Label it to yourself, "Anxiety is here" or, "Boredom is here".
- **O**bserve it in your body as pure sensations. See where they are, and what they are like. Stay for some moments in the place where they are the strongest.
- **A**ccept the sensations as they are, without rejecting them, without aversion, without contracting. Just stay with them. Create room for them. Let them be there, as if it makes no difference for you.
- **R**elease the sensations with every out-breath. Imagine that you are breathing in and out through those sensations in your body, and that with every exhalation they are dissolving.

Do this for a couple of minutes, and it will shift your state. In most cases you will be ready to move forward. This is how you *mindfully* embrace your pain. The ROAR Method is so important that I often recommend my clients to have a screenshot with the word ROAR as their phone wallpaper, for a constant reminder.

Share this concept:
MindfulSelfDiscipline.com/roar-method

KEY POINTS

- We have a deeply-ingrained desire for comfort, but growth requires accepting physical and/or emotional discomfort. This can be done forcefully or mindfully.
- The mindful way is to open your heart to the experience of discomfort, by using the ROAR Method. You recognize it, observe it as simply unpleasant sensations in your body, accept it fully, and release it through conscious breathing.
- The emotions that you are afraid of feeling—such as anxiety, shame, fear, grief—are only unpleasant sensations in your body. If you are willing to feel them without running away, then you can be free.

Implementation resources: to learn more about the ROAR Method, and get the wallpaper images and the step-by-step guided meditation for it, consider getting the Mindful Self-Discipline app (**MindfulSelfDiscipline.com/app**).

CHAPTER 21

AWARENESS BRINGS PERSEVERANCE

Never give up on something that you can't go a day without thinking about.

WINSTON CHURCHILL

We are what we repeatedly do. Excellence, then, is not an act but a habit.

ARISTOTLE

Perseverance is the ability to continue on the journey regardless of the challenges and obstacles on the way. It is to get up every time we fail, with renewed commitment and enthusiasm. It is to pursue our goals for long enough until they get fulfilled.

Perseverance is an umbrella virtue that contains in itself many other virtues—such as patience, determination, grit, willpower, diligence, and resilience. It relies on the foundation of the Aspiration Pillar, and it's a test of how true your purpose is.

Perseverance is self-discipline applied over time. Difficult goals take time. Real self-transformation takes time. The path to it is never a straight line. You need effort and dedication for a long time before you reap the end result.

Why is the virtue of perseverance within the Awareness Pillar? Because it is awareness and the PAW Method that allow you to process the negative emotions that would otherwise push you to give up or give in. It is awareness that allows you to accept failure without shaming yourself and without overreacting. Finally, it is awareness that helps you to let go of limiting beliefs that make it hard for you to continue on track.

TRAP #1: PAINFUL EMOTIONS

If you can master your emotions, you can persevere at anything, for as long as you wish.

The opposite of perseverance is giving up, or giving in. It is when you break your commitment, abandon the project midway, and forget about your aspiration. This decision is almost always preceded by an experience of emotional distress when facing an obstacle, or by boredom and apathy as your motivation toward reaching your goals wanes. In any case, there is an unpleasant emotional state that pushes us to make that decision.

How, then, are we to deal with these negative emotional states? As covered in the previous chapter, there is the forceful approach and the mindful approach. The forceful approach is to ignore pain and power through by the force of your will. The mindful approach is to accept the pain and release all resistance. Both ways work, and they both build the emotional resilience you need to persevere in your path.

In order to persevere, you sometimes need to close your eyes and just stubbornly charge forward. Just like concentration is blind to distractions, and faith is blind to doubt, perseverance is blind to adversity. You need to keep your eyes on your goal and your attention on your action steps, ignoring all the pain until the storms clear up. This is the forceful approach.

The mindful approach is to learn how to sit with the difficult emotions, the pain and the discomfort inside yourself. It is allowing those emotions to be there, but not making any decision based on them. Refer to the ROAR Method explained in the previous chapter for details on how to do this.

Our greatest glory is not in never falling,
but in rising up every time we fall.

OLIVER GOLDSMITH

Knowing how to resolve painful emotions is key to perseverance. Still, it always helps to learn how to not create negative emotions inside ourselves in the first place. In Chapter 16, we talked about not engaging in shame, self-blame, and emotional suppression. Let's now address another way we create negative emotional states for ourselves: unrealistic expectations.

Share this concept:
MindfulSelfDiscipline.com/perseverance

TRAP #2: FALSE HOPE SYNDROME

Holding on to unrealistic expectations guarantees emotional friction and disappointment. These things make you feel like giving up, which makes perseverance difficult.

One common type of unrealistic expectation is the false hope syndrome. It is expecting that the path to your goal will be easy, that your aspiration will be fulfilled quickly, and obstacles overcome painlessly. You are either impatient about the process or deluded about it. In any case, there is a false hope about the process, which then leads to frustration and loss of motivation.

Our society is addicted to the myth of overnight success. The media promotes it, because people love the rush of dopamine they get when they believe they can quickly achieve their dreams. Many companies promote it too, because promising instant results is great marketing. Think of the many "get rich quick" programs and "lose fat while you sleep" ads.

What about "get rich slow" or "lose fat by working out hard"? That doesn't sell as well—it requires perseverance, and most people don't have it. Instead of developing this essential skill, they want to spend money to compensate for its lack. And, sure enough, somebody is willing to monetize on that.

As the Dalai Lama once joked, "In the West, people would like enlightenment to be fast, easy, and, if possible, cheap." (From *Why Meditate*, by Matthieu Ricard.)

As a remedy to the false hope syndrome, accept that the path will probably be harder than you think, and take longer than you expect. Therefore, focus on the process, expect it to take time and be challenging, and stick to your commitment no matter what (See Never Zero, Chapter 31). On your chosen path you will fail many times, doubt yourself, and get disheartened. Know that that is the case and be ready to patiently get up as many times as you fall.

To better adjust your expectations to reality, consider going through a "challenges audit" exercise, where you take note of all the likely obstacles you will meet on the way. This will help you avoid underestimating the journey ahead of you, be ready for what life brings, and persevere through the ups and downs.

Changing yourself, and your life, is very hard. Changing reality around you is even harder. Without perseverance and self-discipline, it is impossible.

Share this concept:

MindfulSelfDiscipline.com/false-hope-syndrome

TRAP #3: PERFECTIONISM

The second common type of unrealistic expectation is perfectionism. It is expecting that you will be perfect at every step of the way, that you will perform flawlessly, that you will never skip a day or make mistakes. When you think like that, you will treat many of your results as failure, engage in "not good enough" thinking, and fall into the pit of self-criticism and shame.

Being excessively hard on yourself is not conducive to Mindful Self-Discipline. And it's not healthy either. As a remedy, accept that you will mess up from time to time. Accept that perfection may be a noble thing to aim at, but it will never be something that you actually achieve. Remember, Mindful Self-Discipline is built on the foundation of awareness, and it is the nature of awareness to see and accept things *as they are*.

If you are the type of person who beats yourself up whenever you fail, then naturally you will fear failure—which leads to procrastination and perfectionism. On the other hand, if you habitually practice self-compassion, then you know that if you fail you will still be okay; this leads to taking more steps in your life. It leads to courage.

You can always edit a bad page. You can't edit a blank page.

JODI PICOULT

Know that you are not alone. Know that other people have gone through similar challenges and felt the same way. Be kind to yourself. This is a process, and you will never be perfect. That is okay.

Share this concept:
MindfulSelfDiscipline.com/perfectionism

KEY POINTS

- Perseverance is our ability to continue on the journey regardless of the challenges and obstacles on the way. It is to get up every time we fail, with renewed commitment and enthusiasm.
- In order to persevere, you need to master your emotions. You can do that through the forceful approach (just be blind to the adversity and push forward) or the mindful approach (accept and release the negative emotions with the ROAR Method).
- Holding on to unrealistic expectations about the path ahead (false hope syndrome) or about yourself (perfectionism) will make it harder for you to persevere.
- False hope syndrome is expecting that the path to your goal will be easy, quick, and painless. To overcome it, accept that the path will probably be harder than you think, and take longer than you expect. Focus on the process, and commit to getting up as many times as you fall.
- Perfectionism is expecting that you will be perfect at every step of the way, that you will perform flawlessly, that you will never skip a day or make mistakes. To overcome it, accept that you will mess up from time to time, and be kind to yourself.

Implementation resources: If you want to go deeper in the topic of *self-compassion*, or get a template for the *challenges audit* exercise, download the free Workbook at **MindfulSelfDiscipline.com/workbook**.

CHAPTER 22

AWARENESS OVERCOMES DISTRACTIONS

When a person can't find a deep sense of meaning, they distract themselves with pleasure.

VIKTOR FRANKL

Conquer your bad habits or they will conquer you.

ROB GILBERT

When you are habitually distracted with instant gratification and trivial things, you eventually become indifferent toward your goals. You are satisfying the human need for fulfillment and purpose through small pleasures that promise you both, deliver neither, yet keep you addicted for more.

Mindful Self-Discipline aims to break this vicious cycle and deliver you happiness on your own terms.

Socrates taught us that every person always seeks their own good, in every situation, as perceived in the moment. When you drink alcohol or spend hours on social media, you do so seeking what feels good; and so too when you work on an important project, engage in altruistic action, or choose to work out every morning. When you yell at your partner, you also do that because it feels good. The criminal who pulls the trigger also does so because it feels good—or because he thinks it will help him get things that will feel good.

The concept of good varies from person to person, but not the basic fact that we all seek what *feels good*. To know what our higher good is, and the right way to seek it, is the pursuit of wisdom, philosophy, and spirituality (see Chapter 39).

Your brain is wired to want to *feel good*. It spends part of its energy wanting to survive, and the rest of it seeking what feels good in your body, mind, and emotions. Once the brain is feeling good, for that moment this *seeking energy* (motivation) subsides, as you feel satisfied and there is no point in making any further effort. When the experience then wears off, the cycle begins again.

You cannot change how the brain works, but you can decide how you spend your "seeking energy"—the type of *good* you pursue. If you spend it pursuing quick bouts of pleasure, there will be no energy left to pursue your deeper good—your aspiration.

Pleasures are the *fast food* of happiness. You can get them quickly and inexpensively, but they won't fulfill you. They don't have the nutrients you really need. In the long term, they will only make you sick.

Pleasures are a depreciating asset. The more you have them, the less happiness they deliver. Self-discipline is a much better investment.

There is an emptiness in your soul that needs to be filled by actualizing your aspiration, living your values, and achieving your goals. That process takes time and often involves much effort. Meanwhile, you are tantalized by instant gratification. Every time you engage in it, though, you make a poor investment of your precious motivation energy.

It's okay to have pleasure and comfort too, in a balanced way. Self-discipline needs to be balanced, otherwise you may burn out (see Chapter 3). But if that is how you quench most of your brain's thirst for happiness, then you are settling for very little. You are living on the surface.

THE CHALLENGE

Between long-term goals (purpose) and short-term pleasures (instant gratification), what option will your brain often choose? Instant gratification. Unless you have developed a deep aspiration and effective awareness tools (the first two pillars of Mindful Self-Discipline).

Distractions and temptations make you look away and forget about your goal; as a result, you lose part of your mojo. Your purpose loses power. You become a bit indifferent to it. So it is extremely important, in the path of Mindful Self-Discipline, that you learn how to manage distractions and temptations by developing greater self-awareness and self-control.

These skills will only become more essential, as in our modern world the distractions and instant gratification opportunities are becoming more abundant, easier to access, more engaging and addictive. Self-discipline will become rarer. This means that those who have discipline will easily stand apart and reap greater fruits. They will lead, and they will push the world forward. Even a little self-discipline will go a long way.

This is the purpose of this chapter: to learn how to deal with distractions and temptations, so we don't become indifferent to our long-term goals. Let us start by looking at how dopamine—the brain chemical for motivation and wanting—works. If you have any addictions or bad habits you wish to drop (who doesn't?), this section will probably be one of the most important ones for you in this book.

Share this concept:
MindfulSelfDiscipline.com/the-challenge-of-distraction

DOPAMINE AND YOUR BRAIN

Do not bite at the bait of pleasure till you know there is no hook beneath it.

THOMAS JEFFERSON

Contrary to popular belief, dopamine is not the "pleasure" chemical; it is the *arousal* chemical. Dopamine is the neurochemical your brain releases whenever it recognizes an opportunity for a reward, either real or imagined. This chemical creates feelings of alertness, craving, and arousal. We become motivated to take action in order to get that reward—and until we do, we are in a state of anxiety and restlessness. When we do achieve the reward, dopamine quiets down, and *that* relief is perceived as a state of pleasure or satisfaction.

In her best-seller, *The Willpower Instinct*, Kelly McGonigal, PhD, makes the point that dopamine itself is not a feeling of happiness or pleasure. Rather, it is a state of restlessness, stress, and discontentment—often accompanied by a burning sensation or feeling of life-and-death emergency. Even if you know from past experience that the reward doesn't live up to the expectation, dopamine will still show up and tempt you.

Once you do achieve the object of desire, however, you get more pleasure from the ending of the restless state of mind created by craving, than by the enjoyment of the object of desire itself. In a way, you are just back to the status quo. McGonigal concludes along the same lines as the Buddha and other spiritual masters, saying that we confuse desire with happiness. We are all addicted to dopamine, and we are exposed to thousands of marketing messages every day that are skillfully designed to exploit that human weakness.

Cycle of Dopamine

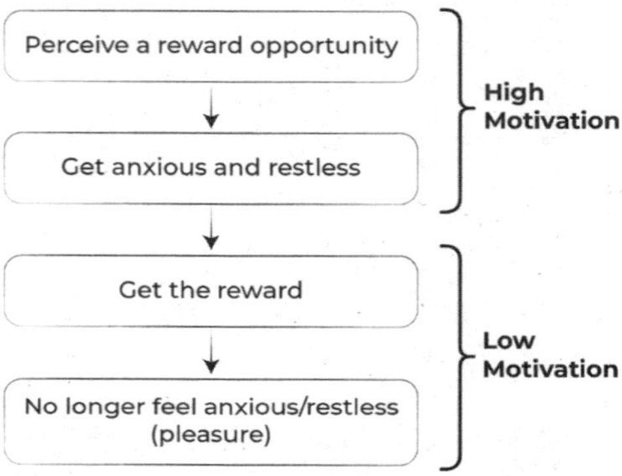

Yet dopamine is not bad. It is not a defect of the brain. It has many positive functions in our life, such as promoting healthy motivation, focus, working memory, and a bunch of other things. If we are low in dopamine we will experience low vitality, poor concentration, low sex drive, fatigue, apathy, and difficulty sleeping. In fact, mental health challenges such as depression, ADHD, and addiction are characterized by a dopamine deficiency. So we need adequate dopamine levels to be a functional human being.

Dopamine is not the problem; the way you seek to experience it is. When you can delay the experience of the reward, dopamine motivates you to stay on track; it keeps you focused and resourceful. However, when you seek to experience high but brief bursts of dopamine repeatedly (instant gratification), that wears out your motivation. It can also lead to addiction.

Right after experiencing the reward we were so anxiously seeking, dopamine levels often drop considerably—and, with it, our ability to motivate ourselves and keep focused on long-term goals. Not only that, but constant over-exposure to dopamine causes the dopamine receptors to leave the membrane, making the membrane less sensitive to stimulation. Your body does that to protect itself from overstimulation. That is why the tenth scoop of ice cream doesn't feel as pleasurable as the first. This is known as *pleasure downregulation*—the more pleasure you have, the less joy you get from it.

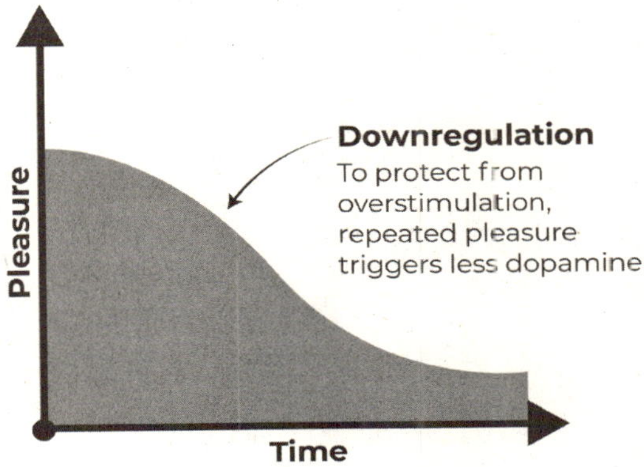

Psychologist Douglas Lisle, in his TEDx talk on *The Pleasure Trap*, describes a curious bird experiment. When a bird in a cage had the ability to hit a button that would flood its brain with cocaine, it did that all the time. It skipped eating and mating, and just kept pushing that button until it died, fourteen days later.

Dr. Lisle explains that the bird's brain was acting on the primal instinct of doing what feels good and, at the same time, saving energy; yet it was actually leading to self-destruction, because of a wrong cue from the environment. He concludes that whenever you use a supernormal stimulus, you get addicted and run a risk of making huge mistakes and harming yourself. (The term *supernormal stimulus* was coined by the Nobel Prize-winning biologist Nikolaas Tinbergen, and refers to a stimulus that is not part of our natural environment, and thus our brain is not prepared to handle.)

Our modern life is not too different from that bird in the cage. While we (thankfully) don't have a button that floods cocaine into our bloodstream, we do have many other buttons that give us an instant rush of dopamine. We have multiple sources of high stimulus, equally as accessible and seemingly inconsequential.

In fact, everything around us is designed to distract us, and to lure us in with the power of dopamine. It's all around us in shopping centers, social media, and in almost every app on our phones. We are being trained to be addicted to easy dopamine, because that is very profitable for most companies. Indeed, promises of quick dopamine are the engine of marketing. This is a big problem, because repeated short bursts of dopamine lowers our baseline dopamine levels and, by doing that, it reduces our motivation, willpower, and ability to focus. A lower dopamine baseline has also been linked to depression and suicide.

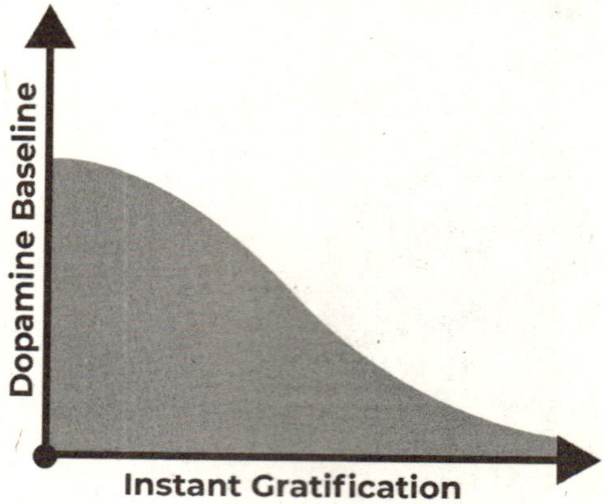

Dopamine is what generates energy that drives us to pursue our goals. If you keep bringing that energy back to zero every day by indulging in instant gratification, is it at all surprising that you don't feel so driven to seek your long-term goals?

The Trap of Easy Dopamine

Our appetite for easy dopamine is what makes self-discipline difficult. Every time you get a like on your Instagram picture, watch another funny video, play an addictive game, get sexually aroused, drink alcohol, or go for that chocolate cake, your brain produces a strong hit of dopamine. And it doesn't take much effort!

Once you fall into the habit of seeking easy dopamine, it becomes increasingly harder to motivate yourself to go after your higher goals and values. With every indulgence, your self-discipline and willpower weaken, and your important goals become more distant. Endless access to quick dopamine leads to a meaningless life.

The worst part is that, after a while, your habit is completely automatic. You hurt yourself little by little, without even noticing it. Just like that unfortunate bird in the cage.

The way to reverse this vicious cycle is to first develop the ability to see what you are doing (awareness), and then to refrain from activities that give you a quick shot of dopamine (willpower). Instead of seeking instant gratification, you then do activities that increase your *dopamine baseline*—such as physical exercise, learning, working on long-term goals, and meditation. This will make you more motivated, more focused, and less dependent on constant stimulation.

Dopamine: Anticipation & Motivation

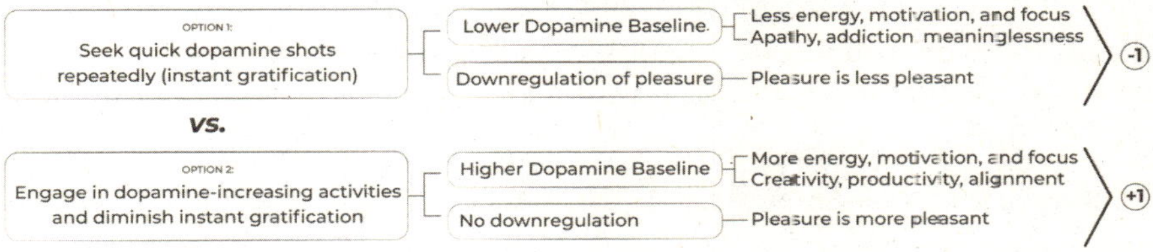

By developing self-discipline and learning how to manage your dopamine, you experience not only more long-term fulfillment but more pleasure too. Because you are no longer desensitizing yourself. Such is the paradox of pleasure: seek it, and you will lose it; forsake it, and it will follow you like a shadow.

Coming back to our opening point: your brain is hard-wired to seek what feels good. It will always push you toward the highest perceived reward in the moment. The problem is that the highest reward is often not the highest *perceived* reward. The way around this is to increase the perceived reward for your long-term goals, in relation to short-term pleasures (Aspiration Pillar), and to keep this insight top of mind day after day, especially when you find yourself facing self-control challenges (Awareness Pillar).

Remember, the brain's first priority is to survive and avoid pain; the second is to seek pleasure. For survival, saving energy is important. That is why instant gratification is so appealing to your brain: it promises what it wants (pleasure) with minimum expenditure of energy. This ancient mechanism of the brain worked well when the only goal was survival; but it is self-defeating, in our modern life, when the goal is self-actualization, growth, and fulfillment.

Quick dopamine makes you indifferent to your aspiration and higher values, because you satisfy part of that thirst for achievement and satisfaction a hundred times each day, through small pleasures that distract you from your goal and disperse your energy. Naturally, when you are able to do that so easily and (apparently) without consequences, you will begin to feel less strongly about the most important goals in your life—which are uncertain and require a lot of effort to achieve.

Constantly seeking quick bursts of dopamine also hurts your long-term goals in another way: by keeping your working memory busy. It is like part of your awareness is always unavailable, because it is trapped in pleasure-seeking thoughts in the background. The temptations then more easily enter your mind and capture your attention, because they are there right in front of you. They feel more concrete and tangible than your long-term goals. That is why it is essential to cultivate awareness so you can redirect your attention back to your goals; otherwise, you will just indulge without even noticing.

Finally, habitual overindulgence in instant gratification can actually hurt your brain. This has been seen when studying brain scans of addicts. The prefrontal cortex area—responsible for awareness, conscious thinking, and willpower—gets weakened and less active. That is the hidden sacrifice you are making through overindulgence in your addictive activity of choice.

It Won't Suck

At this point, you may have clearly seen the costs of junk dopamine and be intellectually convinced of its harm. Yet there may still be resistance in you. Part of you may feel that giving up pleasures means giving up the joys of life. You may fear that your life will become dull, boring, and dry.

This is not what happens. You might experience that for a few days or weeks in the transition phase, but soon it becomes clear that your quality of life has actually increased. Researcher Wilhelm Hofmann and his colleagues did some studies on this topic, with the purpose of understanding how practicing self-control affects life satisfaction. They found that even though people experienced pleasure when indulging in a temptation, that spike of happiness was short-lived and soon received a "correction". People felt less happy after indulging.

There are several possible reasons for this. First is that experiencing pleasures, even repeatedly, does not increase your baseline happiness. They may offer temporary relief from feelings of boredom or emotional distress, but they do nothing to change how you feel in the long-run.

Second is that there is also pleasure and a sense of satisfaction in pursuing long-term goals—you feel good about yourself, and this feeling often lasts much longer than indulging in short-term pleasures. We need to enhance our awareness of this fact by remembering it often.

Third, many of the pleasurable activities we seek come with considerable side effects to our physical or mental health. Think of obesity, alcoholism, social media addiction, and short attention spans.

Finally, as already covered, there is a natural downregulation of pleasure in our nervous system; the more we have it, the less we appreciate it. Do you want to live a more meaningful and also more pleasant life? Sacrifice thy pleasures at the altar of thy aspiration!

Having more self-control is not only good for your long-term goals and aspirations, but it actually makes you live a better life. Research shows that people with strong self-control are happier with themselves, experience fewer negative emotions, and actually appreciate pleasure even more.

A self-disciplined life is a good life. Wise sacrifice leads to fulfillment, not self-denial.

More Self-Control

- More self-esteem
- Stronger willpower
- Greater life satisfaction
- Better health

What Sacrifice Are You Making?

In Chapter 13, we saw that sacrifice is inevitable; that whenever you choose one thing you are saying *no* to a thousand other things. Well, when you say *yes* to instant gratification in an unconscious or unbalanced way, you are saying *no* to your goals, and weakening your willpower. You are saying *no* to your aspiration. You are delaying the actualization of your highest values and hurting your future self.

Success, growth, and fulfillment require some sacrifice. Otherwise, everybody would be healthy, wealthy, wise, in shape, accomplished, and enlightened. Yet look around you.

What about you? What are your sources of quick dopamine? How are you leaking your own energy of will, focus, and motivation? Spend some time reflecting on that, so you can become more aware and make changes.

Once you are fully aware of the problem, how it plays out in your life, and its consequences, let's talk about what you should aim for instead.

Share this concept:
MindfulSelfDiscipline.com/dopamine

THE SHIFT: FIRST PURPOSE, THEN PLEASURE

The secret to success is learning how to use pain and pleasure, instead of having pain and pleasure use you.

ANTHONY ROBBINS

A good life has space both for your aspirations and your pleasures—and this is what Mindful Self-Discipline is about. It is balanced. (See Chapter 3.)

This balance is achieved by prioritizing your long-term goals, but leaving space for short-term joys too. Otherwise, if your self-discipline gets unbalanced, you are more likely to experience willpower fatigue; and, with that, indulging in easy dopamine hits becomes much easier.

So it's not that you should remove all sources of pleasure or instant gratification from your life. It is, rather, about prioritizing the most important things in your life, and allowing the pursuit of pleasure to be secondary. **It's about having islands of pleasure in a sea of meaning, and not islands of meaning in a sea of pleasure.**

The most important thing is to keep the most important thing the most important thing.

DONALD P. CODUTO

For most of us, the pursuit of pleasure is taking far too much of our time, attention, and energy. We have allowed junk dopamine to become ubiquitous in our society, and in our lives, unaware of the consequences. We are enjoying fun, comfort, and distractions compulsively, and at the expense of our more important goals. If we want to radically change for the better, reclaim our power, and fulfill our goals, we urgently need to review the role of pleasure in our life.

Instant gratification should be a treat or reward—not our default. It should be something that we indulge in *consciously*, not compulsively. It should be something that lightens up our life, and not something that attempts to cover up an underlying emptiness.

There is an analogy that illustrates this point. It's an old story popularized by Steven Covey, author of *The 7 Habits of Highly Effective People*. Imagine your life is like a jar, and next to it you have rocks, pebbles, and sand.

- The **rocks** are your meaningful goals and your higher values, and all the steps that help you achieve them. They are the things that truly give you a sense of lasting satisfaction and fulfillment; without them, there is a sense of emptiness in life, and you experience regret.

- The **pebbles** are things that are important, but not critical; they are the minor goals, activities that are urgent but not essential, and external values such as money, status, recognition, and pleasing others.
- The **sand** is pleasure, comfort, pastimes, busyness, and everything else.

If you fill your jar first with sand or pebbles, there will be no place left for the rocks. But if you first put in all the rocks, then the pebbles, and then the sand, there is space for everything.

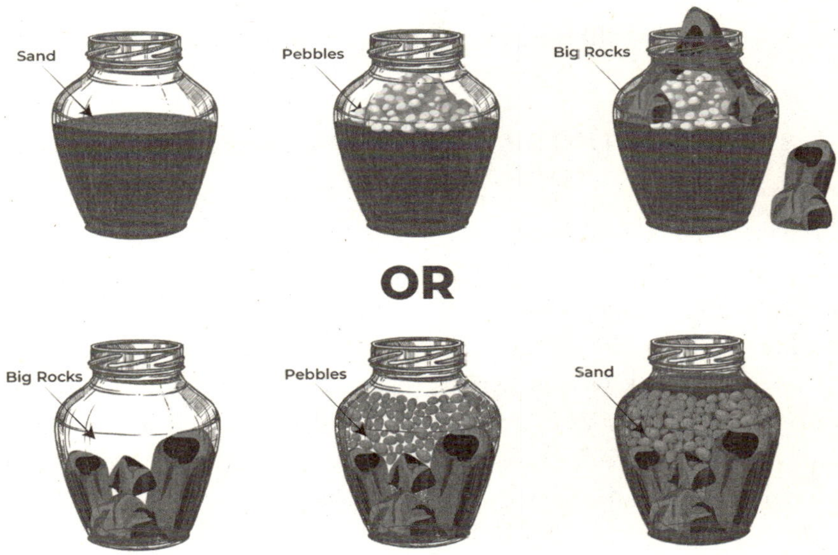

How is the jar of your life?

Mindful Self-Discipline is about prioritizing your highest values, your aspiration and long-term goals. Start with that, and then pleasure can fill in whatever gaps are left. This will allow you to replace the "junk dopamine" hits by longer-term and healthier dopamine. It will also allow you to enjoy the small pleasures of life guilt-free, and appreciate them much more.

This is the only way I know how to have the cake (aspiration) and eat it too (pleasures). You can then enjoy life's pleasures freely, as long as you keep your balance.

If you need a more practical guideline, think of applying the Pareto principle:

dedicate 80% of your available time, money, and energy to things that advance your highest values and goals; and 20% in pleasures and distractions. Or, if you are really ambitious, you can make it 90/10.

How do you make this shift from seeking pleasure to seeking fulfillment, from favoring short-term goals to favoring long-term goals, from junk dopamine to healthy dopamine? You can use the Shift Your Focus method (Chapter 18) to zoom out from the temptation in front of you and re-focus on your long-term goals, or the Shift Your Perception method (Chapter 19) to make the distraction feel less appealing. Or you can use one of the three methods explained in the rest of this chapter, which are specific to dealing with distractions.

Share this concept:
MindfulSelfDiscipline.com/first-purpose-then-pleasure

METHOD #1: THE MONK WEEK (DOPAMINE DETOX)

The first method is to go on a dopamine detox: a period in your life where you avoid all junk dopamine and cultivate presence, contentment, and focused work. You basically go into *monk mode* on all distractions and temptations. It's a true life reset! Consider this your initiation ritual into Mindful Self-Discipline.

During the Monk Week, you completely cut out all your sources of distractions and junk dopamine, or at least you keep them to the bare minimum if related to real family needs or work needs. Here are some examples of things to cut out during this experiment:

- Comfort food (sugar, snacks, coffee, alcohol, fast food)
- Email and messaging apps
- Gaming
- Social media
- News
- Pornography
- Aimless browsing
- Time-wasting websites
- Daydreaming

- Downloading new apps
- Entertainment
- Emotional addictions (arguing, gossiping, complaining, shaming, etc.)

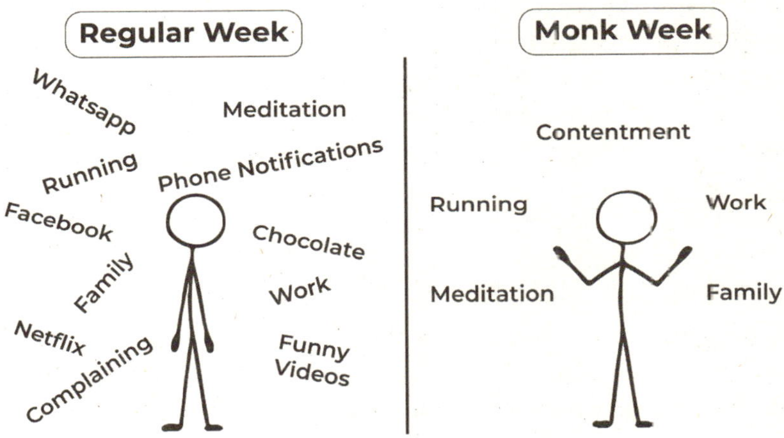

You may not be able, right now, to completely let go of any of these things—and that's okay. But you are certainly able to take a one-week break from them. Even if that becomes the hardest week of your life (unlikely), you *are able* to do it. (The harder it feels, the more it shows how addicted you had become.)

Where should you do it? You can do it in your own home, or you could change your environment for this dopamine detox—such as going on a retreat. The latter does make things easier; having said that, you need to be very mindful about how you transition back to your daily environment. Otherwise, your brain could associate that change with the new environment, rather than see it as your new way of being overall.

How long should it be? I suggest you try it for a week, and so I call this the Monk Week.

What happens at the end? After the week is finished, review which forms of instant gratification are really worth it, and which ones you can do without. You can then add them back as needed, but this time in a more intentional and controlled manner, with awareness and temperance. Be conservative, and ruthlessly eliminate the ones that you haven't really missed.

For example, let's say that you have the habit of jumping into your email or social media multiple times a day—as soon as a notification dings on your phone or computer, or whenever you have fifteen seconds of downtime. It keeps you addicted to junk dopamine, keeps your mind scattered, makes you less present, and breaks the flow of your work. It also makes you more tired and restless, as your attention is fragmented.

During the Monk Week you would limit checking your email to once or twice a day, for work purposes, and take a complete break from social media (among other things). After the Monk Week is over you may realize that you don't need to check email more than twice a day anyway, and you might also decide to only check social media twice a day, ten minutes each time, and limited to a single platform.

What's the effect of all of this on your motivation? During the Monk Week, you cultivate your hunger for meaning and enjoyment, but you don't satisfy it through trivial activities. You have removed those options for the time being. With every source of junk dopamine that you sacrifice, your energy and motivation rise. Remove one distraction and your focus on your goals will increase. Remove ten distractions and your focus will be ten times better.

Stay Hungry.

STEVE JOBS

What happens when you cut all the sources of instant gratification from your life for a short period of time? Your brain will rebel, and you will need to find another way to experience dopamine. You then make use of that opportunity to train your brain to seek satisfaction through long-term goals. This happens by focusing all the freed-up time and energy on your aspiration—review it daily, and act on it daily. Let that be your only source of dopamine.

Seek boredom, and then working on your goals will feel like a welcomed distraction—a joy! For this to work optimally, though, you need to cut **all** sources of distraction during this experiment. If you leave a single other source of quick dopamine available, there is a good chance that your brain will channel all its hunger for pleasure there.

One of the concepts behind the Monk Week is that it's easier to experiment with these (somewhat radical) changes all at once, for a short period of time, than one at a time. This allows you to focus your energy better and see the impact that all of these small dopamine addictions have on your life as a whole.

It is often easier to completely abstain than to try to gradually diminish your consumption over a long period of time. The former has very clear, black-and-white rules; the latter involves playing with fire, making many decisions, and being involved in a protracted self-control battle. Echoing this idea, physician Dr. Dean Ornish, in his research on intensive lifestyle change, found that it was easier for people to ditch lots of bad habits all at once rather than little by little.

The biggest challenge, for most of us, is digital media (apps, websites, social media, news, YouTube, etc.). Unlike other sources of quick dopamine, in modern life this is not something that we can completely go without. Yet these big, shiny dopamine buttons are hijacking your brain with chronic overstimulation—they are destroying your motivation and fragmenting your attention. It's the polar opposite of what meditation and self-discipline are all about.

Therefore, it's essential to improve our relationship with digital media. The radical reset of the Monk Week can be a great beginning for that.

During the Monk Week, make sure to eat enough, sleep well, meditate daily, exercise, and stay connected to your loved ones—or to whatever keeps your heart warm. These things help replenish your willpower, and they also balance the emotional hardships that you might face during the week.

After you finish your Monk Week, and if you are feeling ambitious, you can try your first Monk Month. Or you can include a Monk Day once a week. You can even choose to go into *monk mode* in relation to one addictive activity, completely abstaining from it for good. At the very least, you can practice a Monk Hour at the beginning of your day, every day, as a morning routine (Chapter 34).

Your next step is very simple: book a time on your calendar for your first Monk Week.

Share this concept:

MindfulSelfDiscipline.com/monk-week

METHOD #2: PROCRASTINATE DISTRACTION

A difficult lesson to learn:
Your most persistent distractions will seem justified to you.

JAMES CLEAR

The Monk Week (and other *monk mode* variants) is a great reset. Yet, it is something that you schedule for a particular time of the year, or a particular day of the week. But how do you deal with distractions at other times? Here is where methods #2 and #3 come in.

We all know how to procrastinate, but we are all procrastinating the wrong things. We procrastinate doing things that are meaningful but uncomfortable; rather, we should procrastinate things that are trivial yet comforting. I call this Procrastinating Distraction. The method is simple: when there is a strong urge to indulge in a distraction, procrastinate it. Keep focused on the work you are doing and leave the distraction *for later*. Postpone it, so that the instant gratification is no longer so *instant*.

When does "later" become "now"? That is up to you. For the distractions that you want to completely let go of, due to their harmful effects or time-wasting nature, the answer is *never*. For other types of distractions, you can allow yourself to engage in them as a reward for having made progress in your important goals; in any case, wait at least half an hour before indulging.

Again, doing this doesn't lead to a boring life devoid of pleasure. Rather, it makes you cherish the pleasures even more. You first deprive yourself, and then you enjoy it as a treat. The happiness you extract from the experience will be much greater.

The one requirement for this method to work—actually, for all methods to work—is pausing and awareness. You cannot apply it if you are just indulging automatically, without even noticing. If that is the case for you, review the three core awareness practices of meditation, reflection, and integration (Chapter 16). The more you can slow down and live more mindfully, the easier it will be to become aware of your compulsions and make a different choice about them.

Procrastinate Distraction is, thus, a variant of the PAW Method (Chapter 17)—the only difference is that the third step, *willpower*, is about postponing the distraction and re-focusing on your goal.

- Start by using the 3-Breath Rule for pausing (P): whenever you are being tempted by distraction or any type of urge, pause and take three deep breaths.
- Then become aware of the distraction and notice how tempting it feels (A).
- Finally, make a conscious decision to leave the distraction/pleasure for later, and re-focus on your goal-promoting activity (W).

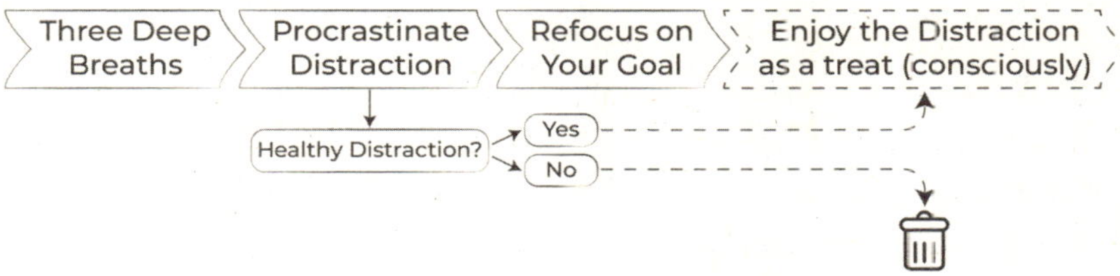

Do the above process as many times as needed, until you complete the work you had set yourself to do. And you don't need to make this hard for yourself; help your focus by removing the distraction from your line of sight in the meantime. This could mean closing a browser tab, putting your phone in airplane mode or face down and in silent mode, or putting the chocolate bar back in the pantry. (Learn more about using the environment to improve your focus in Chapters 26 and 33.)

Slowing down your impulses allows you to see things more clearly and make better choices.

At this point, you may wonder why we simply don't resist the temptation altogether with a definite *no*. It's because in most cases that doesn't work so well. It feels like it's forever a "no", and so your mind will rebel and reject that instruction. The renowned psychologist Roy F. Baumeister, co-author of *Willpower: Rediscovering the Greatest Human Strength*, relates an experiment that explains why this works:

> (...) people who had told themselves *Not now, but later* were less troubled with visions of chocolate cake than the other two groups... Those in the postponement condition actually ate significantly less than those in the self-denial condition...The result suggests that telling yourself I can have this later operates in the mind a bit like having it now. It satisfies the craving to some degree—and can be even more effective at suppressing the appetite than actually eating the treat.

They conclude that, "It takes willpower to turn down dessert, but apparently it's less stressful on the mind to say *Later* rather than *Never*. In the long run, you end up wanting less and also consuming less."

Alcoholics Anonymous also use a version of this principle. The commitment they make to follow their program is: "I will not drink *today*". This is much more doable than "I will never drink again". You trick your brain by postponing the temptation every single day, indefinitely.

Unlike the Monk Week, this method is simple and easy to implement. Take a moment right now to choose one distraction that you will procrastinate on. Make a firm commitment to remember to practice *procrastinating distraction* in relation to that temptation; or have some form of external reminder to bring you back to this exercise. Journal about it every night for extra accountability and self-awareness.

Share this concept:
MindfulSelfDiscipline.com/procrastinate-distraction

METHOD #3: COMMITMENT DEVICES

A commitment device is a deliberate choice that you make today to restrict your options of tomorrow, with the intention of helping your future self to practice self-control and stay on track with your goals. It is designed to create a buffer against your future urges and environmental pressures.

The classic example of commitment device is the story of the Sirens in Greek mythology. The Sirens were dangerous creatures who lured nearby sailors with their enchanting music, causing them to crash their ships into the rocks. In the ancient tale, Ulysses (Odysseus) wanted to hear the Sirens' song without jumping overboard or crashing his ship, so he ordered his men to lash his body to the mast of the ship. That choice was a *commitment device* which restricted his future choices, preventing him from acting on impulse.

What are your Sirens? How will you tie yourself to the mast?

In our modern life, a commitment device could be choosing to delete social media apps from your phone, or block time-wasting websites on your browser so you can't use them when you feel bored or want to procrastinate. It could be buying a long-term gym membership or online subscription, so that breaking your commitment has financial consequences. Another example is not keeping chocolate or chips in the house, so that unhealthy snacks are just not an option when you wake up at 2am looking for something to munch. There are also several browser plugins that you can use to limit your time on certain websites, wipe out your Facebook or Twitter feeds, and hide the black hole known as "Related Videos" on YouTube.

Some people like to formally create a contract with a friend or family member, where they commit to achieve a goal within a certain time frame, and place a deposit. You only get your deposit back if you achieve your goal; if not, you lose it in favor of an anti-charity (an organization that you'd hate to give your money to). Or, instead of a financial consequence, it could also be a social one—for example, in case of failure your friend has to release embarrassing photos of you on social media.

There are many ways to create a commitment device, and you can get creative. The whole purpose is making your self-control failure impossible, or at least adding a consequence bad enough to stop you in your tracks and prevent you from indulging.

Share this concept:

MindfulSelfDiscipline.com/commitment-devices

KEY POINTS

In this chapter you learned about dopamine, the trap of instant gratification, and the need for prioritizing your aspiration on top of pleasures. You learned three powerful methods for dealing with distractions, in addition to the previous methods of the Awareness Pillar. In case you feel unsure which one to focus on, here is a quick map of how they all fit together.

Distraction Solutions	Monk Week	Do once, for a big reset
	Procrastinate Distraction	Practice whenever distractions show up
	Shift Your Focus	
	Shift Your Perception	
	Commitment Devices	Optional extra help

- Indifference happens when you don't care enough about your goal or aspiration anymore because you got distracted with something else. You are satisfying the human need for fulfillment and purpose through small pleasures that promise you both, deliver none, yet keep you addicted for more.
- Pleasures are the fast food of happiness. You can get them quickly and inexpensively, but they won't fulfill you. They don't have the nutrients you really need.
- You cannot change how the brain works, but you can decide how you spend your "seeking energy"—the type of *good* you pursue. If you spend it pursuing quick bouts of pleasure, there will be no energy left to pursue your deeper good—your aspiration. This is a poor investment.
- You need healthy levels of dopamine to function well in life, so the problem is not dopamine, but the way we seek to experience it. When you can delay the experience of a reward, dopamine motivates you to stay on track; it keeps you focused and resourceful. However, when we seek to experience high but brief bursts of dopamine repeatedly (instant gratification), that wears out our motivation and can lead to addiction.

- Our brain doesn't know how to deal with the many sources of supernormal stimuli in our modern environment, so it becomes addicted to easy dopamine. You need to end this vicious cycle by developing awareness, limiting activities that give you a quick shot of dopamine, and instead focusing on activities that increase your baseline dopamine—such as physical exercise, learning, and meditation.
- Prioritizing long-term goals over instant gratification will not make your life boring or dry. On the contrary, research shows that with greater self-control your happiness and life satisfaction actually increase. Short-lived pleasures, on the other hand, soon get a "correction" and don't change how you feel in the long-term.
- A good life has both aspirations and pleasures. This balance is achieved by prioritizing your long-term goals, but leaving space for short-term joys too (rocks, pebbles, and sand analogy). This will allow you to replace the "junk dopamine" hits by longer-term and healthier dopamine hits. It will also allow you to enjoy the small pleasures of life guilt-free, and appreciate them much more.
- Instant gratification should be a treat or reward—not our default. It should be something that we indulge in *consciously*, not compulsively. It should be something that enhances our wellbeing, and not something that attempts to cover up an underlying emptiness.
- Pareto principle: dedicate 80% of your available time, money, and energy on things that advance your highest values and goals; and 20% in pleasures and distractions. Or, if you are really ambitious, you can make it 90/10.
- Method 1 — *The Monk Week*: Go on a dopamine detox for one week, where you avoid all distractions and temptations, and instead cultivate presence, contentment, and focused work. Satisfy your hunger for meaning and enjoyment through long-term goals, rather than instant gratification.
- Method 2 — *Procrastinate Distraction*: When there is a strong urge to indulge in a distraction, procrastinate it. Keep focused on the work you are doing, and leave the distraction *for later*, so that the instant gratification is no longer so *instant*. This is a variant of the PAW Method.

- Method 3 — *Commitment Devices*: Make a deliberate choice today to restrict your options of tomorrow, with the intention of helping your future self to practice self-control and stay on track with your goals.

Implementation resources: review the *Mindful Technology Use* checklist and go through the *Dopamine Audit* exercise in the Workbook (**MindfulSelfDiscipline.com/workbook**). For an up-to-date list of recommended commitment devices and *digital detox* tools, go to **MindfulSelfDiscipline.com/tools**.

CHAPTER 23

AWARENESS OVERCOMES EXCUSES

Argue for your limitations and they're yours.

RICHARD BACH

It's one thing to lie to ourselves. It's another thing to believe it.

STEVEN PRESSFIELD

A person either buys his dream by surrendering his excuses or he buys his excuses by surrendering his dream.

ORRIN WOODWARD

An excuse is something you tell yourself to justify making an exception to your commitment, skipping your habit, or doing something you know will be a -1 in your life. It is rationalizing your emotional impulses so that you don't feel bad about acting on them.

Find a procrastinator, and you'll find someone who is an expert in excuses. Find an addict, and you'll find a gold medalist in this sport. We are great at rationalizing; we can justify breaking any rules.

As with many of the challenges with self-discipline, there is a neurological basis for our habit of excusing ourselves. We have seen that the top priorities of our primitive brain are first to save energy and survive, then avoid pain, and then experience pleasure. The rational brain (neocortex) and all its goals are relatively new to the game. So, when engaging in excuses we attempt to get the rational brain out of the way in order to justify following our impulses, by talking to it using its own language: reason.

Creating bad habits is easy: simply take the path of least resistance. Follow what *feels good* in the moment, regardless of long-term consequences. Creating good habits is difficult: it takes effort and perseverance. You need to follow what you *know is good*, regardless of how it *feels* right now.

Excuses are a way to avoid making that effort, while at the same time avoiding feeling bad about it (emotional distress). "Prevent pain plus save energy at the same time? Oh YES!" —that's your primitive brain's reaction to excuses, and why it loves them.

This genetic predisposition works great if our goal is only survival. But for the modern human who seeks fulfillment, achievement, and meaningful contribution, it is self-defeating. It is you rationalizing why it's okay for you to be less than you can be, and not express your full potential.

> *If you deliberately plan on being less than you are capable of being, then I warn you that you'll be unhappy for the rest of your life.*
>
> ABRAHAM MASLOW

Some excuses prevent you from starting, or even dreaming about it. Others come later on, preventing you from being consistent, or preventing you from giving your all.

Examples of excuses for not trying (or not trying wholeheartedly):

- It will probably never work for me anyhow, because _____
- Maybe I'm too old for this
- I don't have the time/money/support to accomplish this

- I'll go for it after ______ (something in the future)
- I'm not talented enough/connected enough/smart enough/experienced enough
- I'm not like ________ (role model), because I had a difficult childhood
- I've missed my chance. Now it's too late
- There is no guarantee that I'll succeed
- I can't do it. I've never followed through with anything...

Examples of excuses for skipping the habit, procrastinating, or breaking a resolution:

- Now is not the right time. I'll start it when ______
- I'll make an exception just this time, because ______
- I'm now too tired/busy/demotivated to do ______
- I don't feel like it right now
- I'm not getting anywhere with this anyway
- Let me think about it for a while
- One bite/cup/round never killed anyone
- This will help me feel good and relax
- Skipping this time does no harm
- This week is not a good week. I'll start again on Monday
- Everybody is doing this
- Tomorrow

Which ones are your go-to excuses?
What sacrifices are you making by believing these excuses?

Share this concept:
MindfulSelfDiscipline.com/excuses

ALL-OR-NOTHING THINKING

One of the most common excuses I hear from people who come for coaching is what is known as *all-or-nothing thinking*. So let's spend some time unpacking this one.

All-or-nothing thinking is when you break your rule once, and then you justify to yourself breaking your rule even further by thinking that your case is already lost. You then burden your future self with the task of starting over again. This is a very common, and very limiting, thought pattern.

It kind of goes like this… You commit to running twenty minutes on the treadmill every day. You do twenty minutes on Monday and twenty minutes on Tuesday. You skip Wednesday because you were busy. Thursday you feel tired, and tell yourself, "Oh well, I've already skipped yesterday, so I'll consider this week as wasted, and I'll start afresh next week."

Or you made a commitment to go for thirty days with no junk food and no sugar. On the fifth day you go to a birthday party and everyone is drinking soda, so you join in. You then think, "Oh well, I've already drunk soda today so I might as well eat some hot dogs and the cheesecake too." Or, "Tonight I have a party and will probably eat badly, so I might as well consider this as a wasted day and eat junk for lunch too!" Or, "I've already cheated on my partner by kissing this person, so I might as well go forward with the whole thing…"

All-or-nothing thinking is like slashing three good tires because one of them is flat, and you can't drive anyway.

The way to reverse this tendency is first to consider every choice *individually*. Don't bundle them all together as part of one day/week/month, and then consider the whole as a +1 or a -1. Every choice by itself is either a +1 or a -1. Doing your treadmill on Monday and Tuesday, then Friday and Saturday, is much better than not doing it at all—at least you got four +1 points that week. Likewise, with the junk food: just having some soda is -1, but adding the hot dog and cheesecake on top makes it a -3 for your health goals.

Temptations are often like this: you give them your little finger, and they want to take your whole hand. Please remember that it's much better to lose your little finger than your whole hand!

All-or-nothing: "It's either a +7 or a 0!"
Realistic expectations: "A +4 is much better than a 0!"

The second element here is letting go of unrealistic expectations and perfectionism (see Chapter 21). You believe that one "failure" spoils the whole thing, so you want to re-set and start again. You believe that one failure means that you are not good enough, and won't be able to build this habit, so you might as well indulge right now. This will make this habit a problem to your future self.

To counter this, expect that there will be failures, setbacks, and challenges. As soon as you are aware that you went astray, cut your losses and move on. Make your best effort from that moment onward. That is enough.

This skill is developed in meditation: as soon as you notice that your attention got distracted, you bring it back to the meditation object (breath/mantra). You don't say to yourself, "Oh well, I had a thought, so I guess this meditation is wasted. I may as well stop now and try again tomorrow." Instead, you just become aware and bring your attention back as soon as possible. The same applies to all other habits and goals in life.

Let's now cover the methods that you can use to overcome other types of excuses.

Share this concept:

MindfulSelfDiscipline.com/all-or-nothing-thinking

METHOD #1: CHALLENGE YOUR EXCUSES

Imagine that the resistance you experience is a barbell in your mental gym. Each time it shows up, you can either walk away and get weaker or pick it up and get stronger.

PATRICK EDBLAD

Excuses are thoughts, so they can be tackled by changing the way you think about things. This shift is done through the PAW Method covered in Chapter 17.

Let's say that you have committed to practice meditation every day, and the excuse is that today you are busy, and you also don't feel like doing it. Following the PAW Method, the first step is to **pause**, slow things down, and interrupt the pattern of excusing yourself; meaning that you don't act on your excuse just yet, but instead take a deep breath.

The second step is to become **aware** that you are telling yourself a story; to see clearly the thoughts that came up, and where they will take you (+1 or -1). Labeling your thoughts can help you a lot. This could be as simple as saying in your mind, "Excuses are coming up", or "Rationalizing". Or you can take this to the next level by objectifying the voice of excuse in your mind—give it a name, so you can separate it from yourself. For example: "Mr. I-can't-do-it is here", or "The Complainer is speaking".

The third element, **willpower**, means to intentionally shift your state—in this case by challenging your excuses, and shifting your self-talk. Here are some examples:

Excuse	Challenging	Shifting
I'll do it tomorrow...	Yesterday you said tomorrow!	If I don't do it now, I will never do it. Nothing will be different tomorrow.
Today was a tiring day, and I don't feel like exercising.	Which day isn't? If you only exercise when you are not tired, how far do you hope to go?	It doesn't matter how I feel. I'll just go and do the bare minimum, but I won't skip!
Making an exception and indulging today will help me relax and feel good...	Yes, it will, but at what cost? If you always think like this, who will you become?	What healthier alternatives do I have for relaxing and feeling better right now?
Everybody spends time on social media...	"Everybody" is also more anxious and depressed than ever before... This is just herd mentality!	What will I be able to achieve if I dedicate half of my social media time to my goals?
I don't have the time and money to pursue this dream	There are many examples of people with fewer resources than you who succeeded	Is this really important for me? If so, what can I do now to take a step forward?

The next time you find yourself making excuses, apply the PAW Method. Pause. Become aware of your self-talk. Use your willpower to shift it to something that empowers action. Do this repeatedly, as many times as needed, until the old excuses no longer show up.

Don't wait for it to "feel right". Push through laziness and discomfort and come out the other side with something you can be proud of. Take a step toward your ideal self. Use the Embrace Your Pain technique if necessary (Chapter 20).

Refuse to feel sorry for yourself. Don't make a victim out of yourself—even if, objectively speaking, you actually were a victim of injustice (see Chapter 12). Know that you always have a choice, and simply focus on making the best possible choice you can in every moment. Accumulate as many +1s as you can, until there is a critical mass that pushes you forward toward your goal, or the change you want to make.

Exercise:

1. Think of three goals or areas of your life in which you want to be more disciplined.
2. Think of the last three times you broke a resolution/intention for each of these goals.
3. Identify the excuses you used to rationalize that choice.
4. Below each excuse, write how you can challenge or poke holes in that story.
5. Then write what self-talk you can use to reframe the situation and shift yourself to action.
6. Commit to remembering to make that shift the next time that excuse comes up.
7. Review this list daily for twenty-one days, or until the new ways of thinking become second nature for you.

Share this concept:
MindfulSelfDiscipline.com/challenge-your-excuses

METHOD #2: POWER VISUALIZATION

When people in the personal growth movement talk about visualization, they often mean visualizing that you have effortlessly achieved your goal and are enjoying the end result, as inspired by the "law of attraction" concept. This is not what I mean by visualization.

For the sake of overcoming excuses, resistance, failures, and other challenges on your way, you need to visualize the process of overcoming them—and not only the happy end result. As a matter of fact, researchers Heather Kappes and

Gabriele Oettingen published a study showing that visualizing the end result can actually be harmful, since it drains your motivation. Your brain thinks it is all done, and so there is less energy available to make the needed effort on your path.

Visualization as a tool of Mindful Self-Discipline is about rehearsing perseverance. You imagine yourself doing the action that you need to do, facing obstacles, and then successfully overcoming them. I call this the POWER Visualization. You can use this visualization as a complement to Challenge Your Excuses (method above), or also as a technique on its own.

POWER Visualization

Here is the process:

1. **Preparation.** Sit or lie down comfortably. Close your eyes. Get to a calm state of relaxation by using your favorite meditation technique.
2. **Obstacle.** Visualize yourself working toward your goal or ideal, and then facing obstacles on your path. Visualize them with as much detail as possible. Feel how it feels at that moment—the fear, excuses, or doubts that may come, the irritation or confusion, the distractions, failures, and discouragement.
3. **Willpower.** See yourself pausing (P), becoming aware of the situation (A), and intentionally making an effort to shift your state (W). Visualize yourself remembering the tools that you have learned and using your willpower to apply them.
4. **Energy.** Experience the state of heightened energy that comes as a result of tapping into your inner resources and overcoming the obstacle. Feel how empowering and enlivening this feels.
5. **Result.** Visualize yourself overcoming that obstacle and moving forward. Feel how good it feels.

For example, if success for you means a great relationship with your partner, you visualize the *conflicts*, the misunderstandings, the fights that are likely to happen. You feel the frustration, the confusion. And *then* visualize yourself finding the *tools*, the *clarity*, and the *energy* to successfully work through them, coming out of the storm stronger and more united. This is *very* different from simply visualizing eternal honeymoon moments. This is practical and realistic.

Let the whole visualization be as vivid as you can, as if you were actually there. If you are not good at visualizing, then just imagine it in whatever way works for you. The important thing is to make it feel real and to experience it first-hand, so that you are truly priming your brain to behave in a different way.

Share this concept:
MindfulSelfDiscipline.com/power-visualization

OTHER SOLUTIONS

In Chapter 29, about overcoming doubts, you will learn two techniques that also work well for overcoming excuses: the Not Now Technique and the Remove Your Options Technique. They are great wildcard techniques that remove many internal obstacles all at once. If none of the techniques in this chapter worked for you, you might want to try those.

Finally, you may also want to consider getting some form of accountability (Chapter 35). Most of us are experts at fooling ourselves. We are unable to either see our excuses or consistently act in spite of them. We may need someone to be a mirror to us and help us stay on track. So if you can have an accountability partner who is bold and psychologically savvy (i.e., understands how the mind works), that would be of great help. Or you may also consider hiring a discipline coach.

Excuses are a form of self-sabotage. Overcome them by whatever means necessary, so you can move forward without having the handbrake on.

KEY POINTS

- An excuse is something you tell yourself to justify making an exception to your commitment, skipping your habit, or doing something you know will be a -1 in your life. It is rationalizing your emotional impulses so that you don't feel bad about acting on them.
- All-or-nothing thinking is when you break your rule once, and then justify to yourself breaking your rule even further by thinking that your case is already lost. To reverse it, consider each choice *individually* (not bundling it with others), and let go of the unrealistic expectation that you will be able to follow through perfectly from the beginning.
- Method 1 — *Challenge Your Excuses*: Apply the PAW Method (Chapter 17) to interrupt the thought pattern, notice the story you are telling yourself and its consequences (+1 or -1), and shift the story by challenging your excuses. Create a list of shifts for your most common excuses.
- Method 2 — *Visualization*: Visualize the process of overcoming excuses, resistances, failures, and other challenges on your way, by using the POWER Visualization (Preparation, Obstacle, Willpower, Energy, Result). Don't just visualize the end result, as that can actually de-motivate you.
- Other solutions for overcoming excuses are the Not Now Technique and Remove Your Options technique (Chapter 29), or getting some form of accountability.

Implementation resources: see the step-by-step instructions for the POWER Visualization meditation at **MindfulSelfDiscipline.com/meditations**.

CHAPTER 24

THE BIG PICTURE OF *AWARENESS*

The Awareness Pillar is the foundation of Mindful Self-Discipline. It gives you the freedom to choose how to respond to life as it happens, thus helping you live in alignment with your goals and values. Without it, true self-discipline is not possible because you are living in automatic mode—your future will be a repetition of your past. With awareness, you can design your future according to your aspirations.

Self-awareness has clarity in it; it sees things as they are, with radical self-honesty. It is neutral—it doesn't reject nor shame. And it accepts you as you are, without self-violence.

You cultivate awareness via the three core practices of **meditation** (every morning), **integration** (throughout the day), and **reflection** (journaling in the evening). Integration is practicing the PAW Method—including the three *willpower techniques*—throughout your daily life, so that you can take steps forward toward your aspirations (+1s) and avoid taking steps away from it (-1s). This is the heart of the Awareness Pillar.

The Awareness Pillar

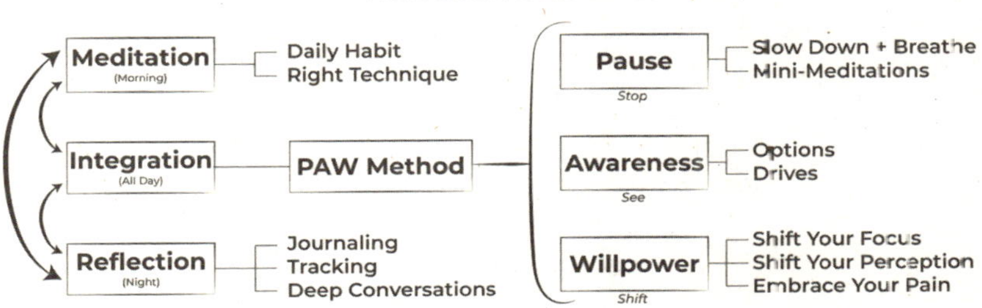

The PAW Method and other awareness practices also help you directly overcome three of the biggest obstacles of self-discipline: lack of perseverance, distractions and excuses.

- To **persevere**, you use awareness to release difficult emotions via the ROAR Method, and also to let go of unrealistic expectations (perfectionism and false hope syndrome).
- To overcome **distractions**, you have a dopamine reset with the Monk Week, use the Procrastinate Distraction method and the willpower techniques from PAW; optionally you use Commitment Devices to turn up the heat.
- To overcome **excuses**, you use a variant of the PAW Method known as Challenge Your Excuses and also the Power Visualization.

Now take a deep breath. You know what you want (your aspirations) and have the awareness tools to stay on track with your goals. It's now time to dive into the third and final pillar of Mindful Self-Discipline.

PILLAR 3

ACTION

CHAPTER 25

ACTION STEP 1: DESIGN YOUR PATH

Your ability to discipline yourself to set clear goals, and then to work toward them every day, will do more to guarantee your success than any other single factor.

Brian Tracy

Do first what you don't want to do most.

Clifford Cohen

Self-discipline is the ability to make yourself do what you should do, when you should do it, whether you feel like it or not.

Elbert Hubbard

Aspiration without action is wishful thinking. Awareness without action is powerless. Your resolutions and intentions, without action, are useless.

This third pillar is all about taking action—the final essential element of Mindful Self-Discipline. It is here that the rubber meets the road. But it's not enough to just take action. Your action needs to be purposeful, consistent, and effective.

In the first step of this pillar, you will learn how to translate your aspiration and goals into milestones and habits, and then overcome the four remaining obstacles to disciplined action: forgetfulness, procrastination, doubts, and rigidity.

Taking action requires effort, and your brain doesn't like effort. Indeed, ten thousand years ago laziness was often a virtue—it meant saving energy and thus increasing the chances of survival. Nowadays laziness means the exact opposite: you will struggle to pay the bills. Besides, if your goal is not only surviving but also thriving, laziness is not an option.

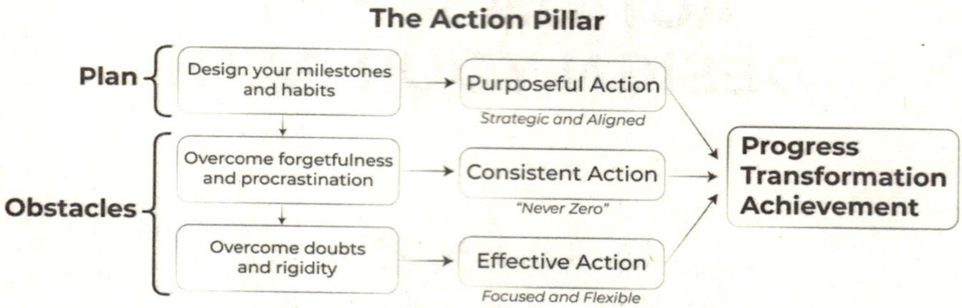

Your Action Plan

To move forward with your aspiration, you need to take *organized* action. For that, you will need an action plan, which is your map of the territory. Otherwise, it's easy to end up putting in a lot of effort without really knowing what you are doing, and then not experiencing the results you are after. That leads to frustration and giving up.

Having an action plan like that can help you avoid two pitfalls on the path:

- Underestimating the journey
- Underestimating yourself

When you underestimate the journey, there is an unconscious tendency to allocate fewer resources than the task really demands. You think that the tasks will take less time, less energy, less patience and willpower than they actually will. As a result, the natural challenges, obstacles, and uncertainties of the journey take you by surprise. When that happens, you may feel disheartened and burn out.

When you underestimate yourself, you look at the path ahead and feel overwhelmed. You think, "There is no way I can accomplish all of this." You don't have a clear path forward, therefore you feel discouraged and start doubting yourself.

Breaking down your journey into milestones and then action steps allows you to avoid these two pitfalls. You will have a better grasp of what is needed in order to achieve your goal, thus developing a healthy dose of respect for the work that lies ahead. And you also won't get overwhelmed, because the next steps are always clear, and small enough that you can tackle.

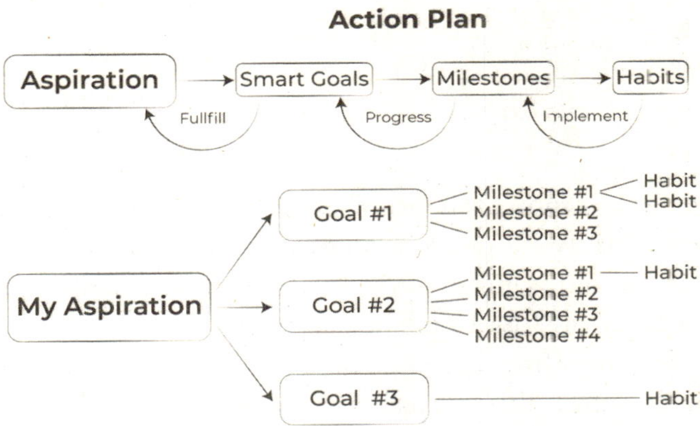

Let's now get started designing your action plan!

Share this concept:
MindfulSelfDiscipline.com/design-your-action-plan

CHOOSE YOUR MILESTONES

Your aspiration is the end benefit. It's your new identity—who you want to become. In Chapter 9, we translated that into SMART goals, which are more specific and time-bound. Now we need to further break down some of your SMART goals into milestones.

An aspiration can have multiple goals under it, covering the different aspects of that dream, value, or project. And each goal often has at least a couple of milestones. Milestones are the key phases that you go through to achieve a goal. Here are some examples of how this might look.

Aspiration	*Happy family life*	*Share my wisdom*	*Health and vitality*
Goal #1	*Marry a smart and loving partner before I turn thirty-five*	*Write an influential book on leadership by end of next year*	*Lose forty pounds by Christmas this year*
Milestone 1	*Work on myself*	*Research and plan*	*Lose the first ten pounds*
Milestone 2	*Find a good partner*	*Write first draft*	*Lose ten more pounds*

Milestone 3	*Build our relationship*	*Get it published*	*Lose ten more pounds*
Milestone 4	*Get married*	*Promote it*	*Lose the last ten pounds*

As you can see, for some goals the milestones will be different types of tasks or sub-projects (first two aspirations above). For other types of goals, more quantifiable in nature, the milestones will be different landmarks of progress in the same type of activity (third aspiration above).

You can also benefit from having a start and end date for each of your milestones. These dates are a plan, not reality. Reality will rarely be like any of your plans; yet planning is still extremely useful. Having clear start dates and deadlines helps you keep your momentum, build a sense of urgency, and channel your resources properly.

So here are your next steps in your journey of Mindful Self-Discipline:

1. Select an aspiration to focus on, and one of its SMART goals
2. Break down that goal into milestones
3. Add a start date and deadline for each milestone
4. Repeat the steps above for every aspiration and goal

Milestones allow you to focus your energy better and to avoid overwhelm. They clarify the steps ahead, help you feel more motivated, and give you a taste of success more quickly. You can dream as big as you like, but you need to break down that dream into SMART goals and those goals into achievable milestones.

If your big aspiration is not yet clear, then simply get started with a SMART goal of improving a specific area of your life and developing the habits that you need for that purpose.

Action step: Break down your goals into specific milestones.

Share this concept:
MindfulSelfDiscipline.com/milestones

CHOOSE YOUR HABITS

Once you have clear milestones, you then break down each of them into habits. Your habits are the specific things you need to do to complete each milestone. They may change as you progress from one milestone to the next.

A habit is a commitment to your goal. It is you allocating time and energy to advance your cause. If your aspiration is not translated into habits, it will never get fulfilled.

There are three types of habits, depending on the nature of your milestone.

- **Action Habit.** What you need to commit to is a single activity, such as, "Meditate for twenty minutes every morning," or "Write in my gratitude journal before going to bed".
- **Replacement Habit.** When your self-discipline is about breaking a bad habit or overcoming a harmful urge, your habit will then be about replacing the action that you take after a given cue, with a healthier one. For example, "Whenever I feel like smoking, I will instead do five minutes of conscious breathing".
- **Project Habit.** When your milestone is a complex sub-project with different types of activities (e.g., launching a blog, or buying your dream house), your habit will be in the form of a time commitment, such as, "To work on my project from 7 to 9pm, five days a week". During that allocated time, you will then go through the tasks needed to advance your milestone, in order, one after another.

There are many different ways to achieve a goal; and, therefore, there are different habits that could be useful for that purpose. Each habit, thus, represents a different strategy. If your goal is to lose weight, your food-related habit could be to follow a low-carb diet or it could be to practice intermittent fasting by eating once a day (OMAD diet)—there are different possible habits for achieving the same result.

List Your Habits

Your next step is to figure out the specific habits you need to create in order to support your goal. Who will you need to become in order to actualize your aspiration? What are the habits and behaviors of the ideal version of yourself—the one who has achieved his/her goal?

Look at your first milestone and make a list of all the important activities you need to perform to fulfill it. These are the daily rituals that help you make progress toward your goal. Here are some questions to help you figure this out:

- What changes do I need to make to achieve my goal?
- What activities help me make progress toward my goal?
- What are the different strategies to achieve that goal, and their steps?
- What new beliefs and ways of thinking will I have to develop?
- What are the habits, routines, and virtues of people who have achieved my goal?

For the last question above, you can use the role models you listed while going through the exercises of the Aspiration Pillar (Step 1). Deconstruct what makes them who they are. This will give you a list of things you need to do, and qualities you need to develop. Alternatively, you can use your ideal future identity as a base for these questions.

Once you have your list of activities ready, review it and try to figure out what are the one or two essential habits you need to create. These are the things without which no real progress is possible.

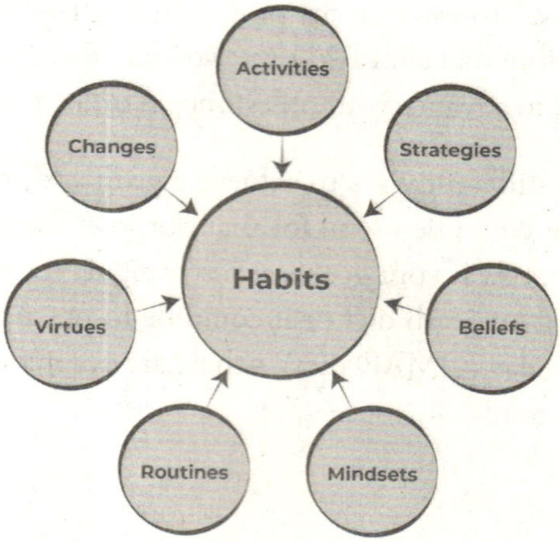

For health, the essential habits might be daily exercise and a regular sleep schedule, or daily exercise and portion control. For wellbeing, it might be meditation and a break from our busy lifestyle. For wealth-related aspirations, it might be saving and reviewing investment opportunities. For career, it might be spending an hour each day learning an important skill. For relationships, it might be becoming more empathetic and practicing daily appreciation. For personal growth, it might be journaling and reading good books.

Find Keystone Habits

There may be many habits that you want to create in your life. Habits for your health, career, personal growth, hobbies, and relationships. However, you don't need to start with all your habits right now. In fact, that would probably be overwhelming, and not a good idea. In my experience as a self-discipline practitioner and coach, this rarely works.

Instead of overwhelming yourself, choose one or two keystone habits, and get started with them. Keystone habits, according to Charles Duhigg (author of the seminal *The Power of Habit*), are "small changes or habits that people introduce into their routines that unintentionally carry over into other aspects of their lives". In other words, it is a single habit that has a positive domino effect, making self-discipline easier with other habits too.

Here are some examples of keystone habits:

- Daily meditation
- Regular physical exercise
- Sleep hygiene
- Morning routine
- Journaling

These are keystone habits that are universal—everyone can benefit from them. There will also be keystone habits unique to your goals and aspiration. If you want to write a book, a relevant habit may be to spend the first hour of your day offline, just writing uninterruptedly. If you want to improve your craft, it may be spending the first hour of your practice sessions focused on mastering the basics. If your goal is creating a happier family life, it may be making the dinner time sacred, technology free, and engaging.

Exercise: Choose your first keystone habit—it could be a universal habit such as meditation, or something specific to your goal. Write down, in simple language, the minimum action and the ideal action for the first habit you want to create.

Share this concept:
MindfulSelfDiscipline.com/choosing-your-habits

FINE-TUNE YOUR HABITS

Now that you know which habits you need to build in order to take steps toward your goals—and thus actualize your aspiration—it's time to fine-tune them so they are more effective. Effective habits need to be specific, time-bound, and ideally enjoyable.

Make Your Habits Specific

Effective habits tell you exactly *what* to do, *when,* and *where.* If your habits are vague, it is very unlikely that you will follow them for any length of time. Here are some examples.

SMART Goal	Ineffective Habit	Effective Habit
Lose thirty pounds in two months	Do some exercise every morning	Do thirty minutes of CrossFit at 7am every morning at the local gym
Write a 200-page book, by March, on the topic of leadership	Write every night before going to bed	Write a thousand words every night right after dinner, at my home office
Improve our marriage satisfaction from 60% to 90% this year	Talk more often about our needs and wants in our relationship, and how we can improve	Have a twenty-minute relationship review every Friday night, using questions XYZ
Never again yell at my kids	Commit to being calmer and remember to breathe when I'm angry	Do a five-minute conscious breathing session before family time, wherever I am
Spend no more than thirty minutes a day on YouTube	Have a sticky note reminding me to limit YouTube time	Turn on a countdown timer on my phone whenever I start watching YouTube

Make Your Habits *Enjoyable*

One of the elements of effective habits is specificity, as we saw above. The other element is removing friction—because it is hard to focus on the process if you hate the process, or don't understand it. To stay on track with your long-term projects and aspirations, you need to focus on the process, and not only the end goal. This is what habits are about: focusing on the process.

We naturally tend to procrastinate or get distracted when doing tasks we dislike, find boring, or find meaningless. On the other hand, if you can derive some sense of satisfaction from the process itself, then being disciplined to achieve your goal will come more naturally. You will be more wholehearted in your process.

For a habit to be effective, see if you can learn how to enjoy the process itself. If you can learn to truly enjoy the activities required to achieve your goal, then it will be much easier for you to stay focused on them and keep those habits for the long-term. For that, love not only the goal, but also the path itself. Let the path itself be the goal. This approach is not only more enjoyable, but also more effective.

The way to do this is simple: when pursuing your aspiration, find a process that you can enjoy, or learn to enjoy the process you've found. The end result of both is the same: you'll be present, dedicated, engaged. Perseverance will come more naturally, failures will matter less, and it will be easier for you to stick to your plan until fruition.

There are many different ways to achieve a goal. If you want to get in shape, for example, there are hundreds of different physical activities. If you hate running or lifting weights, then you can try tennis, martial arts, or any other sport you find interesting. Even if these options have been proven to be objectively less effective for your particular goal, they would still be more effective *for you*, because you'll be able to focus better, put in more effort, and stick to the activity for longer.

This is *finding a process you can enjoy*. When that is not possible or desirable, you then need to learn how to *enjoy the process* of doing something that you naturally dislike. For example, if doing CrossFit every day is the most effective way to achieve your goal, you might as well learn to *enjoy* it.

How do you learn to enjoy an activity you dislike? By adding rewards to that activity, a topic that we will cover in depth in Step 2 (the next chapter). But let us have a brief overview right now, for the purposes of choosing your habit.

You can make an activity intrinsically rewarding by using positive reappraisal

(Chapter 19): contemplate the qualities of that activity, focus on its rewards, change your self-talk about it, etc. If that is not possible, you can attach extrinsic rewards. One way to do that is known as "temptation bundling"—a term coined by Professor Katherine Milkman. This technique involves pairing indulgence with a goal-promoting activity. You can do that, for example, by listening to music while walking on the treadmill.

Despite this concept being highly praised by other experts in the field, I don't see temptation bundling as an ideal solution—definitely not from the meditation point of view. We already live in a distracted world. Temptation bundling splits your attention and makes you less focused on the activity itself, only to make it bearable. It's also not something that you can use effectively for activities that require concentration (such as work or study).

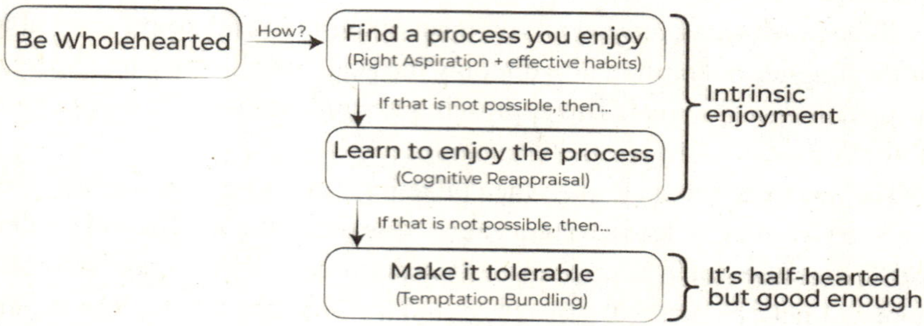

For these reasons, I almost didn't include this technique in this book. However, it is still better than hating what you are doing and counting the minutes to finish it. So keep this method as your last resort, in case you couldn't choose a process you love and couldn't make positive reappraisal work.

One area for which this method can work well is when the temptation comes *after* your goal-promoting activity, rather than together with it. For example, "I will only watch my favorite TV show after cleaning up the kitchen", or "I will have a piece of chocolate only after I write 500 words". However, this is not really temptation bundling, but what I call temptation sequencing.

Conclusion: make sure you pick an enjoyable habit. If that is not possible, take a moment to decide how you will make it enjoyable—or at the very least tolerable.

Share this concept:
MindfulSelfDiscipline.com/make-your-habits-specific-and-enjoyable

Prepare the Ground

Now that you know the *what*—the habits, activities and qualities you need to cultivate—it's time to decide the *how* and to get prepared.

Do you need any special tools, knowledge, or other external circumstances in order to be able to do your habit? If so, your first step is to get these things ready, otherwise you won't be able to start. It might be buying your running shoes, finding the right mentor or online course, downloading the apps you will need to make your work easier, buying a journal, organizing your calendar, making space in your house for that new activity, having a conversation with your family members about your new schedule and what they can expect, finalizing a project that is pending, etc.

Don't let this be an excuse for procrastinating or for feeling that you are not ready yet. To prevent that from happening, take a moment now to decide on a start date for your new habit or activity. Put that on your calendar and get all the preparations you need done before that. Then, when the date comes, get started whether you feel ready or not, whether you have finalized everything or not.

Implementing Your Habits

Here are the action steps for setting up your habit, based on what we've covered so far:

1. Decide on the two most important habits you need to build
2. Make them specific and time-bound
3. Make them enjoyable
4. Get the tools you need and do the preparation beforehand

In *Step 2* of the Action Pillar, you will learn all the nitty-gritty of habit mechanics, including how to choose the ideal cue or trigger for your habits, harness your environment, choose your minimum and ideal action, and make your habits more rewarding. By the end of it you will have everything you need to take purposeful and consistent action toward your goals.

SCHEDULE YOUR REVIEWS

What if you are taking action that is purposeful and consistent, but in the wrong direction? You would be putting in a lot of effort but progressing slowly. And if you are unwilling to learn and course-correct, you fall into the trap of *rigidity*.

It's important to not only persevere, but also *adapt*. Mindful Self-Discipline is not about blindly pushing forward; it's about awareness and thoughtfulness.

Maybe you are religiously following your diet and exercise regimen, but not losing weight as desired. Or you are practicing your meditation every day without fail, but not experiencing any benefits. You could keep on doing what you are doing, but there is no guarantee that you will start having different results. Maybe you need to tweak something.

Don't just push through stubbornly, with a brute force approach, hoping that eventually it will all add up. Don't just "set it and forget it", leaving your habit or process lifeless. Always be caring. Always be curious. Be open and coachable.

Stay foolish.

STEVE JOBS

You need to constantly fine-tune your process. One effective way to do this is to have regular reviews, where you look back and see what is working, what isn't, and what you need right now. You can do this weekly, monthly, or quarterly.

When you go through your reviews, you will need to ask yourself, "Do I need to persevere on this strategy, or is it time to change things up?" There are no rules of thumb here. Sometimes you will need to change because circumstances have changed, or because you discovered that a certain approach doesn't work particularly well for you. At other times you just need to stick with it for longer, as you haven't put in enough time on that line of action to draw any meaningful conclusions yet.

You will need to see it case to case, check in with your gut, educate yourself, and potentially get the help of a mentor in that field. Even if you don't have a clear idea of what to do next, don't skip this review process. Don't stop asking the right questions, even though you may not get any immediate answers.

Have a plan. Have a strategy. Execute it consistently. And never cease to learn and adapt.

Share this concept:
MindfulSelfDiscipline.com/your-reviews

KEY POINTS

Design Your Action Plan

- Break down your aspiration and SMART goals into milestones and habits, then take action that is consistent, focused, and flexible.
- Having an action plan will help you avoid underestimating the journey and underestimating yourself.

Create Your Milestones

- Select an aspiration to focus on and one of its SMART goals.
- Break down that goal into milestones.
- Add a deadline for each milestone.
- Choose when you will start the first milestone.
- Repeat the steps above for every Aspiration and goal.

Create Your Habits

- A habit is a commitment to your goal. It is you allocating time, space, and energy to advance your cause.
- There are three types of habits: action habit, replacement habit, and project habit.
- For choosing your habits, think of the changes, action steps, routines and mindsets that will help you move forward with your goal.
- Instead of trying to build many habits at the same time, choose one or two keystone habits, and get started with them. Keystone habits have a positive domino effect, making having self-discipline for other habits easier.
- For a habit to be effective, it needs to contain exactly *what* to do, *when,* and *where*. And it should be something that you either enjoy or can learn to enjoy.
- Prepare the ground by getting the tools, knowledge, and

circumstances needed so you can perform your activity with less friction; but don't let friction be an excuse to procrastinate.

Review Often

- You need to have regular reviews, to see what is working and not working. Be open and coachable. Never cease to learn.

Implementation resources: if you would like to use an app to better track your goals and milestones, see my list of recommended third-party tools at MindfulSelfDiscipline.com/tools.

CHAPTER 26

ACTION STEP 2: DESIGN YOUR HABITS

Success is nothing more than a few simple disciplines, practiced every day.

JIM ROHN

You'll never change your life until you change something you do daily. The secret of your success is found in your daily routine.

JOHN C. MAXWELL

Bad habits are easy to form, but hard to live with. Good habits are hard to form, but easy to live with. And as Goethe said, 'Everything is hard before it's easy.'

BRIAN TRACY

In the beginning of this book I said that most people think that building habits is all there is to self-discipline. By this point, if you have read all the preceding chapters, you might have already realized that while building habits is an important part of self-discipline, there is much more to it than that. As defined in Chapter 1:

> Self-discipline is your ability to live in accordance with your higher goals and values moment after moment, overcoming internal and external obstacles. It is your power to commit to what is meaningful to you, and let that guide the way you think, the choices you make, and the actions you take—until you bring your goal to fruition.

Everything that we have covered so far empowers you to build good habits and to let go of bad habits. They are the timeless principles of Mindful Self-Discipline. In the previous chapter you translated your aspirations into specific goals, milestones, and effective habits. In this chapter we go into the nitty-gritty of habit building.

HABITS AND SELF-DISCIPLINE

How long does it take to build a habit? There are different studies on this, and the opinions of the experts in this field differ. Some say it takes as little as eighteen or twenty-one days; others say it takes 254 days. In any case, after this relatively short period of setup time, the behavior tends to become automated and require very little self-control or willpower to be maintained. Therefore, habits can be thought of as shortcuts to self-discipline.

For this reason, most people put a lot of attention on building habits, and very little on self-discipline as a whole. Their hope is to "hack their way" into building a habit as quickly as possible, using the latest apps and tricks, and then to hopefully reap the fruits of an automatic good behavior for the rest of their lives, with no more effort required.

This is rarely the case. As we saw in Chapter 4, not all actions that we need to be disciplined in can be automated. Some of them will always take an effort of willpower (such as cold showers in the winter); others are too dynamic to be predictable (such as managing conflicts in a relationship).

Besides, however long it takes to *build* a habit, that is only half of the journey; the other half is *maintaining* it. You may take a month to build a habit, but it will take you a lifetime to maintain it. Even well-established habits can vanish from one month to the next, especially if your environment or schedule changes with a new job, a relationship break up, travel, moving homes, family dramas, etc.

Self-discipline is not the type of thing that you practice once and then forget all about it. It is not a simple "setup cost" for building good habits. You can never truly retire from it; when you do, you start relapsing. For as long as you have goals, for as long as you desire growth in any area of life, you will need self-discipline. That is why I wrote this book—to be a sort of *manual for living*.

If you let go of cleaning your body, it will get dirty by itself. If you let go of taking care of your relationship, it will decay by itself. If you let go of focusing your mind, it will get distracted by itself. It is the nature of the body to get dirty and sick; the nature of the mind to get distracted; the nature of relationships to need maintenance. Likewise, it is the nature of our brain to prefer comfort over effort, instant gratification over long-term goals, junk dopamine over healthy dopamine. If you stop disciplining yourself, your important goals and aspirations will automatically lose momentum, and your energy will dissipate.

The quality of your life is a reflection of the quality of your habitual thoughts and actions. So having the right habits is extremely important for you to live well and achieve your goals. Let's now learn how to build habits by understanding the three core elements of automatic behavior: cue, action, and reward.

(Note: the following pages focus on building good habits. While some of the principles here also apply to breaking bad habits, if that is where you need to focus on the most, have a look at my step-by-step system as outlined in this article: **https://liveanddare.com/how-to-break-bad-habits-with-meditation/**).

Share this concept:

MindfulSelfDiscipline.com/habits-and-self-discipline

CHOOSE YOUR CUES (*WHEN*)

The *cue* is the trigger in your environment. It prompts you to take action, in order to experience an end reward. We all have many versions of the Cue-Action-Reward loop in our lives. They can be what I call "automatic habit loops", if they were formed without you realizing it, or "purposeful habit loops", if they were intentionally created.

Here are some examples of automatic habit loops:

Cue	Automatic Action	Reward
Phone notification dings	Pick up the phone	Excitement, fun, information
Smell of coffee	Have a cup of coffee	Feel more awake and comfy
Wake up feeling tired	Press the snooze button	Rest more
Pile of papers on your desk	Procrastinate	Feel temporary relief
Feel emotionally drained	Watch TV mindlessly	Feel okay
Meet your partner	Start complaining	Avoid responsibility

Here are some examples of purposeful habit loops:

Cue	Purposeful Action	Reward
See your running shoes by the door	Put them on and go for a run	Feel healthy and energetic
Alarm rings, reminding you to meditate	Meditate	Feel calm, centered, clear
Open the pantry looking for snacks and find only fruits	Eat fruits	Feel good for eating healthily
Find your journal on top of your pillow	Do gratitude journaling	Feel more content
Alarm rings at 7am on a weekday	Go to the gym	Feel on track with your health goals
Finish lunch	Write on my food journal	Feel in control of my diet
Notice I'm emotionally triggered	Do a short deep-breathing meditation	Feel well again

In the path of Mindful Self-Discipline, what we want to practice is to be *aware* of our automatic habit loops (so we can change bad habits), and *create* new purposeful habit loops (so we can build good habits).

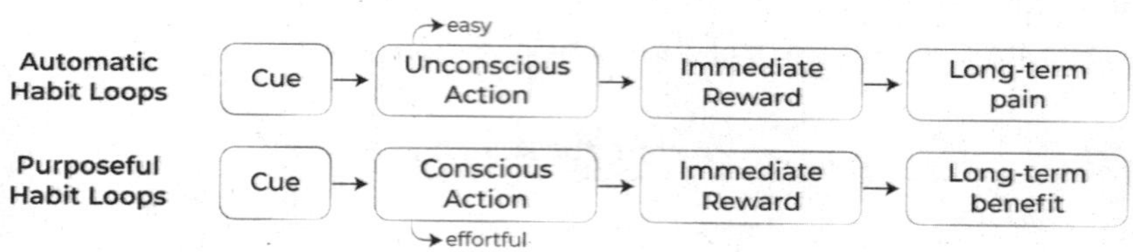

The practice of becoming aware of the *cues* that lead to negative behavior is pretty self-explanatory. You need to start noticing the times of the day, places, people, feelings, interactions, and other inputs that trigger you to do something that you would rather not do. That is the first step of breaking a bad habit.

Let's now discuss how to create cues for your goal-promoting habits.

Choosing Your Cue

In the last chapter you selected the habits that you want to create in order to push your goals forward and actualize your aspirations. To implement these habits, you need to choose a cue/trigger that will remind you to do them.

This is you using your environment as a support for your self-discipline. You make changes to your environment (time, space, people) so that the action you want to perform becomes easier. You create a trigger to remind yourself to take a step toward your ideal self.

Using a cue for habit building is basically telling yourself that "*When X happens, I will do Y*" or "*After X, I will Y*". This formula expresses your intention and your resolution of following through with your new habit (Y) whenever you encounter the chosen cue (X).

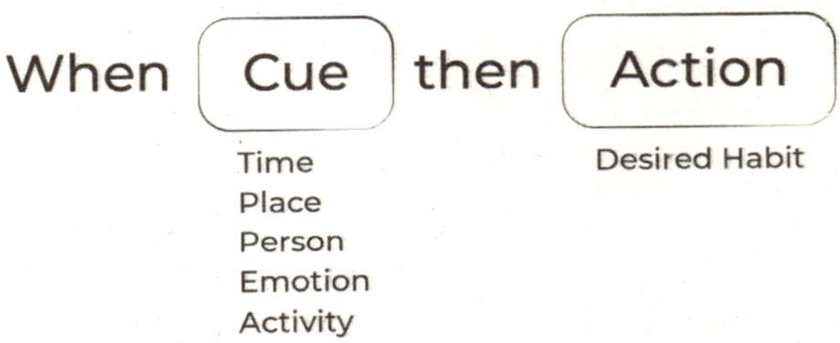

Most people find that setting up alarms on their phone, and events in their calendar, are some of the best cues for new behaviors. These are *time* cues.

Do you want to make sure you spend the first hour of your day working on your priorities? Create a recurring calendar event called "Focused Work". This makes sure nothing else will be booked at that time, and it's also there for you to see it every day. Do you want to make sure you do ten minutes on the treadmill before work? Put an alarm on your phone for 7am saying "Exercise now!" Want to sleep by 11pm? Put an alarm for 10:45pm with the label "Prep for Sleep".

Time cues work great, but you also have other options.

- **When** my alarm rings at 10pm, **I will** begin my night routine.
- **When** I see my kids at the end of the day, **I will** hug them and spend time with them.
- **When** my salary hits my account every month, **I will** plan my monthly budget.

- **When** I'm done brushing my teeth in the morning, **I will** go meditate for ten minutes.
- **When** I feel anxious, **I will** pause and do three minutes of deep breathing.
- **When** I am at the table, **I will** put my phone in airplane mode.

Establishing your habit using the "When X, I will Y" formula helps you avoid decision fatigue. You make this decision only once, and then every time after that it is clear what you need to do. When the cue happens, you do the behavior. Nothing new to think about or decide.

So how to choose the best trigger for your habit? You need a cue that is reliable, and specific to the habit you want to build.

If you want your habit to happen *every day*, you need to attach it to a cue that also happens every day—or create one. If your habit is about the things you need to do when you are in a certain place, then attach it to that place. If it's about actions you want to take when you meet a certain person, then attach it to meeting that person. If it's about how you want to react when you feel a certain way, then attach it to that feeling. This all may sound pretty obvious, but sometimes it's helpful to state the obvious.

The more specific and reliable your cue is, the easier it will be for you to do the desired action. "After brushing my teeth in the morning" is a good cue for a new meditation habit because it is something that (hopefully) happens every morning without fail, even though the exact time for it may vary. If the cue also happens always at the same time ("alarm rings at ten"), that is an added bonus, as it brings greater consistency to your routine. This is desirable, but not essential—so work with what you have.

"When I see my kids at the end of the day" may not happen always at the same time, but it is still a great cue for the behavior "spending quality time with them", because it's directly related to that trigger. However, that would be a bad cue for doing a daily meditation practice, for example—because on the weekends you could be seeing your kids all day long, so your cue would not work then. Or perhaps your kids are on vacation or spending the night at a friend's house, and then your habit probably won't happen that day.

Linking your desired habit to an existing habit is an effective strategy recommended by many experts in this field. B. J. Fogg calls this "using an anchor habit", and James Clear calls it "habit stacking". Whatever you want to call it, the idea is to piggy-back on one of your established habits/routines, using it as the cue for the new behavior.

The order of the habits in your routine can also matter. If your new habit is difficult, unpleasant or boring, consider performing it right after something you enjoy (a), or as a condition for you to enjoy something else (b). As an example for (a), if you need to go through some boring research, do that right after a relaxing shower or good meal, so that your willpower is replenished and more easily accessible. An example for (b) would be to read some pages of your favorite book as soon as you wake up, but only if you get up without snoozing. (We will explore this second approach in greater detail in the next chapter.)

Having a cue doesn't mean that you will *feel like* performing the new behavior. No. The cue is just a trigger, a reminder. You will likely still need to apply some willpower so that you can perform that action even if you don't feel like doing it. (We will cover the concept of commitment versus motivation in Chapter 31).

Before closing this section, let's talk about a couple of problems people sometimes face with establishing cues for their habits.

The first one is: what do you do if your cue stops working?

That is a very common challenge I see with some coaching clients and meditation students. If the cue is no longer working, it's either because it was never properly set up in the first place, or it got worn out before your desired behavior could turn into a habit. If that's happening for you, then consider re-establishing that same cue with a firmer intention, or else change the cue to something new and more effective.

The second challenge is: can we use cues for activities that involve creativity?

As a coach, I've worked with several artists, and one common objection is that, "We can't simply schedule inspiration into our day". No, you can't control inspiration; but you can make yourself *available* for it—and here is where self-discipline and habit building is useful. Many accomplished artists have a routine for creative expression.

The screenwriter Raymond Chandler had this simple rule for writing: "*Either write or nothing. I find it works. Two very simple rules, a. you don't have to write. b. you can't do anything else.*" In the same line of thought, someone once asked Somerset Maugham if he wrote on a schedule or only when struck by inspiration. "I write only when inspiration strikes," he replied. "Fortunately it strikes every morning at nine o'clock sharp."

Exercise: Spend a few minutes choosing the cues for the next three habits you want to create. Take the steps needed to implement those cues right now. Consider the order of the habits if relevant, and be ready to still need to exercise some willpower after the cue.

Share this concept:
MindfulSelfDiscipline.com/habit-cues

IMPROVE YOUR ENVIRONMENT

There is no denying that your environment affects you. It is easier to focus on your work if your desk is clean, your office quiet, and your computer desktop is not littered with fifty different files and leftovers of abandoned tasks. It is easier to get into the mood of doing exercise when you are in the gym, as opposed to working out alone in your garage. You go more easily into a deep meditation session if you have a corner of your room dedicated to this activity, with its own calming vibe, rather than meditating seated on your couch in the living room.

Your environment can make self-discipline harder or easier. While we don't want to be dependent on the environment—because it's not always possible to control it, and it doesn't always work (see Chapter 4)—it is wise to improve your environment to make things easier for you, whenever possible.

The general principle is to harness the *power of default*:

- Make bad habits as hard as possible (default to not doing)
- Make good habits as easy as possible (default to being reminded to do it)

Breaking bad habits, thus, is made easier by changing your environment and removing sources of temptation. Do you want to stop smoking? Don't hang out with friends who smoke, and don't have any packs at home. Do you want to stop wasting your time on games? Delete all your gaming apps. Do you want to stop the compulsion of checking your phone every five minutes? Turn off all notifications, or turn on the "do not disturb" mode.

Creating good habits, on the other hand, is made easier by having plenty of reminders. One way I often recommend my clients implement this is to have a custom screenshot as their phone lock screen, with a message that reminds them of their resolution or target identity. Since we pick up our phone 50 to 100 times a day, this works as a constant reminder—until you get used to it, then you need to get a new wallpaper image.

Another way is to have an object, inspirational message, or image that reminds you of your long-term goals. Do you want to keep on track with your fitness goals? Buy an outfit that you want to fit into, and hang it on the wall of your room where you'll always see it; then, every time you see it, remember your goals and get to work! Do you want to drink more water? Have a water bottle in every corner of your home. Do you want to run every morning after coffee? Put your running shoes in front of your coffee machine. Do you want to replace watching TV by reading? Place your book on top of your remote control.

To break habits → Remove all reminders from your environment
To build habits → Add many reminders to your environment

Here are some examples of how I use this principle of *improving your environment* in my own life:

- I have no social media apps, games, or news apps on my phone
- My phone is on airplane mode from 9pm to 8am, basically every day
- I sleep with my phone five feet away from my bed, so I never snooze the alarm
- There are no cakes, donuts, pies, muffins, gum, or candies at home, ever
- My work environment, both physical and digital, is minimalistic and tidy

Making a good habit easy is also about setting yourself up with the needed tools, so that you can remove friction. Make choices in advance to have everything handy and make the behavior easy. Do you want to prepare your own meals every day, so you eat more healthily? Consider chopping the vegetables for the whole week on Sunday nights, so when it's time to cook for the day that activity is quicker and easier. Do you want to work on your pet project for an hour every morning? Have all the tools ready, so when the time comes all you need to do is to sit down and start.

Finally, in the beginning it is also advisable to have your daily schedule (morning and night routines) printed and pasted on several places in your home. Don't rely on your memory for it, and don't make it only digital. You want it to be there right in front of your eyes when you enter your room, or go to the bathroom, or go to the kitchen, or get to your car. For the same reason, you may also want to consider using a habit tracker on paper.

Make your environment a reflection of the person you want to become, and it will influence you to get there more quickly.

Exercise: What are the top five changes you will make to your environment today?

Share this concept:
MindfulSelfDiscipline.com/improve-your-environment

CHOOSE YOUR ACTION (*WHAT*)

After the cue comes your action. This is the habit you want to create. It is the action that, if done regularly, will help you meet your milestones and advance you toward your goals and aspirations.

In the previous chapter, we saw that the habit could be of three types: an *action habit* (e.g., read for thirty minutes every morning), a *replacement habit* (e.g., eat an apple instead of chips) or a *project habit* (a complex activity or routine with multiple steps). We also saw that your habit needs to be specific and, ideally, something you either enjoy or can learn to enjoy. The next step, now, is to attach your new goal-promoting habit to the cues you have selected in the previous section. It is also helpful that you start small, with what I call a "minimum action".

The ideal action is what you would like to perform. The minimum action is the very least that you will perform *no matter what*. It is what you have no excuse to skip (see the Never Zero concept, Chapter 31).

Ideal Action	Minimum Action
Write a thousand words	Write two hundred words
Run for an hour	Run for twenty minutes
Follow up with twenty prospects	Follow up with three prospects
Do the technical analysis on five positions	Do the technical analysis on one position
Meditate for half an hour	Meditate for five minutes

Ideal Action	Minimum Action
Practice my five best songs on the guitar	Practice my favorite song on the guitar
Take a ten-minute break every two hours	Take a five-minute break every two hours
Clean up the whole house	Put the dishes in the dishwasher
Do fifty pushups	Do five pushups

As you can see in all these examples, in both cases the action items are really specific. Also, in all cases, the commitment is to the action itself (e.g., run for an hour), not to the outcome (e.g., lose fifteen pounds). The difference between them is that the ideal action is where you want to take your habit to, while the minimum action is a starting point for you to get (and keep) your momentum.

Coming back to the idea of *effective habits*, what you want is a commitment that is **specific** and has a **minimum action** attached to it. You aim to do your ideal action every day, of course, but as long as you do at least the minimum action, that day was not wasted. You didn't break your commitment. You got a +1, and your habit chain is still intact. You can feel good!

The minimum action exists to make things easier for you. It allows you to keep your momentum no matter what. Professor Mihaly Csikszentmihalyi, known as one of the fathers of positive psychology, talks about the "activation energy of habits", which is how much effort or friction is required for you to perform that action. Having a minimum action where that activation cost is close to zero, and having an ideal action that grows as your commitment grows, are keys to sustaining habits.

In other words: in the beginning of building any new habit, start *really* small. That is why, in my *Limitless Life* meditation program, I guide the students to start with a three-minute meditation session; we then grow very gradually, and within five weeks everybody is meditating for fifteen minutes every single day. People who come in with greater ambitions—perhaps because they were already meditating thirty minutes per day, but only every once in a while—resist this approach in the beginning. And yet after a while they understand the value, as they also establish a solid daily discipline for meditation (something they didn't have before).

It's better to start small and grow gradually than to be too ambitious from day one and soon get frustrated. Make it easy on yourself in the beginning, so that you can get the habit going. In the first three to four weeks of building your new habit, your priority is to just *get it going* and not to be amazing at it. Only when the new habit is already solid should you begin to increase the requirements.

Use your drive and ambitions as a fuel for starting your habits, yes; but don't let them create impossible-to-sustain requirements that make you soon lose motivation and give up. When building new habits, often the most difficult thing is beating the initial inertia, and so your focus for the first couple of weeks should simply be to show up and perform the habit right after your cue. For that, remove all potential friction, making it as easy as possible.

Once you get to the point where you are consistently doing your ideal action and have not missed a day on your minimum action, then you can focus on making your ideal action longer or better, if needed. At this stage you could also increase the minimum commitment, but be very cautious with that—you don't want to get to a point where even the minimum action is something that makes you feel like skipping or procrastinating.

Your brain wants to save energy, and it loves automating behaviors for that purpose. If you do something every day, you are telling your brain, "Hey, I need to use this skill every day..." Then the brain says, "Okay, let me then turn that into a habit so you don't need to waste energy deciding what to do anymore." Every time you perform your chosen action after the cue, you are strengthening your habit and helping your brain save energy.

Share this concept:
MindfulSelfDiscipline.com/minimum-action

THE GOLDEN RULE

The *action* is the habit you want to create; the *cue* is your trigger, your reminder. We need a reminder because one of the main obstacles of self-discipline is forgetfulness. Until your chosen activity becomes an automatic habit, you will need to be actively reminded to do it. You cannot depend on your memory for this. You need an effective *cue* to remind you. If you have followed the steps in this chapter, by now you have an effective cue and know exactly what to do when you see it.

Whatever reminder works for you is okay. You can get creative with it, and also change the reminder over time if it ceases to be effective. There is only one rule you need to observe for reminders to work. It is so simple and commonsensical that it's even embarrassing to write. But common sense is not always common practice, so here we go:

Once you get the reminder, *do* the action.

The most amazing cue and the best reminder system in the world is useless if the moment you see/hear it you ignore it and instead say to yourself, "Great, I'll do this later" or "I'll get to it *soon*".

Know that once you get the reminder, you have only two options: do it and get a +1, or to ignore it and get a -1. So remember the golden rule: *once you get the reminder, do the action.*

Share this concept:
MindfulSelfDiscipline.com/the-golden-rule

GET STARTED

In the previous chapter, you chose which habits you need to build in order to advance your SMART goals, meet your milestones, and fulfill your Aspirations (Step 1). Then, in this chapter (Step 2), you chose the cue that will trigger your habit, the ideal and minimum action, and the changes that you need to make in your environment to make things easier. So now you know exactly what to do, when and how.

There is only one thing left. To actually do it. To get started. Don't postpone another day. You have all the elements you need to start taking consistent and purposeful action toward your goals.

Make your commitment right now. Start taking action today.

Your commitment needs to have a time frame. Even if you want to do your habit forever, you can't commit to "forever". Forever is a very long time, and as a result it doesn't help you to focus your energy and keep motivated. You need a time frame—let's say thirty days. You get started with your keystone habit, committing to a thirty-day period during which you will follow it daily no matter what (more about this in Chapter 31). At the end of that time you will have momentum, and then you can let go of time frames and aim for "forever" with less friction.

Once a habit is thus fully established, then you can go for a second habit. Once that is established, go for the next one, and so on, until your daily life has all the habits you need to live in harmony with your goals and values.

From this point on, it's all about following through with your action steps, staying focused on your purpose, and adapting as needed. This path, however, will not be without challenges—and if it were, it would not be worth pursuing, for it would bring no growth.

In the Awareness Pillar, you learned how to overcome two of the main obstacles to self-discipline: distractions and excuses. In the following chapters, we will address the other three obstacles to taking self-disciplined action: procrastination, doubt, and failure.

KEY POINTS

Introduction

- Habits are shortcuts to self-discipline; but not all actions can be automated.
- It may take a month to build a habit, but it will take you a lifetime to maintain it. Even well-established habits can vanish from one month to the next, especially if your environment or schedule changes.
- You need to continuously pay attention to your habits in order to maintain them.

Choose Your Cues

- A *cue* is a trigger in your environment that reminds you to do something you have decided to do (planned habit loops), or tempts you to do something you might not want to do (automatic habit loops), in order to experience an end reward.
- Using a cue for habit building is basically telling yourself that, "*When X happens, I will do Y*" or "*After X, I will Y*". This helps avoid decision fatigue.
- Choose a cue that is reliable and specific to the habit you want to create. If it happens every day at roughly the same time, that's even better.
- Having a cue doesn't mean that you will *feel like* performing the new behavior, but only that you are reminded; you will still need to apply some willpower.
- If your cue is no longer working, consider re-establishing it with a firmer intention, or else change the cue to something new and more effective.
- Harness the power of default: make bad habits as hard as possible by removing temptations (default to not doing) and make good habits as easy as possible by adding plenty of reminders (default to being reminded to do it).

- Remove friction in performing your habit by setting yourself up with the needed tools and making choices in advance to have everything you need handy.
- Have your schedule printed and pasted on several places in your home.
- Task #1: Choose the cues for your top three habits, and implement them.
- Task #2: Make five changes in your environment to make your habits easier.

Choose Your Action

- The ideal action is what you would like to perform. The minimum action is the very least that you will perform *no matter what*. It is what you have no excuse to skip, and will go Never Zero on. You aim to do your ideal action every day, of course, but as long as you do at least the minimum action, your commitment is still in place.
- In the beginning of building any new habit, start *really* small so you can beat the inertia. This reduces the activation energy of habits and makes it easier for you to build momentum.
- Task #3: Write down, in simple language, the minimum action and the ideal action for the first habit you want to create.

The Golden Rule

- Your cue is your reminder. You need it so you don't forget to do the habit.
- The best reminder system in the world is useless if you ignore it. So follow the golden rule: *once you get the reminder, do the action*. Every. Single. Time.

Implementation resources: to gain greater awareness of the cues that are leading you to bad habits, so you can change them, download the Workbook and make use of the *weekly self-awareness journal* (**MindfulSelfDiscipline.com/workbook**).

CHAPTER 27

ACTION STEP 3: DESIGN YOUR REWARDS

In order to create a habit, all you need are the first two elements we learned in the last chapter: cue and action. In order to maintain a habit, though, you will need to make sure you also have a third element: reward.

Your brain seeks rewards in the form of "feel good" chemicals. After the "survive and avoid pain" project, this is its main programming. It doesn't matter if the reward is a physical pleasure, emotional satisfaction, or psychological fulfillment—your brain is motivated to experience that reward, and this is what drives you to action.

Knowing this is valuable because it teaches us one of the main principles of habit building: have an immediate reward attached to your habit. Many of our long-term goals involve taking protracted action and experiencing the big reward only at the end (that is, if we are successful). This is the way it goes with some of our deeper aspirations, but unfortunately it's not how your brain works. Your brain needs to see some results right now, so the activity feels worthwhile. It needs to experience a reward *right after* you perform your activity. That is why "reward" is the third element of habit building, and key to reinforcing good behaviors.

Let's now talk about the different ways you can experience a reward from the habit you are trying to build. They are presented in order of preference: from the ideal case scenario (intrinsic rewards) to the last option if nothing else works (painful consequences).

INTRINSIC REWARDS (BEST OPTION)

So far in this book we have emphasized intrinsic rewards, which means finding the reward in the activity itself. This often comes automatically when you have a strong aspiration and your goals are aligned with your aspiration; or else it can be cultivated by using the Shift Your Perception technique (Chapter 19). To illustrate: if you aspire to always be healthy, fit, and full of energy, you will have a natural tendency to enjoy physical exercise and healthy eating; if not, you will be able to learn to enjoy these activities (because they are aligned with the life you want to live), by using the Shift Your Perception technique.

Intrinsic rewards happen when you either enjoy the activity itself (e.g., "I love eating salad"), or you enjoy how you feel after the activity (e.g., "I love how light my body feels after eating salad"), or you enjoy the emotional satisfaction of having done something meaningful for you (e.g., "I'm happy that I did something good for my health").

Intrinsic rewards are the best type of reward because they are the most natural. They are found within the activity itself. You are not going for a run because that's the condition you have set for yourself so that you can watch your favorite TV show, nor because you have made a bet and if you skip the run there would be painful consequences. You go for a run because you enjoy running, or you enjoy how you feel right after running, or at least you enjoy the psychological satisfaction of having taken a step toward your goal today.

These are the three pathways to intrinsic rewards. You just need to have one of them for it to work for you; but if you can combine two or all of them, the habit will be even stickier.

Intrinsic Reward Options

- Enjoy the activity itself
- Enjoy how you feel after the activity
- Enjoy having taken a step toward your goal

Don't worry if you don't naturally feel like this toward your goal-promoting activity. There are several ways you can train your brain to find that intrinsic reward.

You can learn to **enjoy the activity** by using the Shift Your Perception technique (Chapter 19). This technique has the power to make boring kale taste like a yummy snack, and the muscle burn in the gym feel like a burst of energy. It teaches you to enjoy the good in the bad, until there is no "bad" left. Adding variety to the activity can also help you enjoy it more (e.g., changing exercise sets in the gym, or not eating the same salad for lunch every day).

You can also learn to **enjoy the benefits of the activity** by becoming mindful of how you feel before and after it. Ask yourself, "How do I feel now in my body, mind, and emotions?" Do this before and after the activity, and pay attention to the positive shifts that happened. This may make you realize that meditation takes you from scattered and irritable to calm and centered, and that a thirty-minute run takes you from feelings of lethargy to feelings of aliveness and energy. As you become more in tune with your body, these types of natural rewards become easier to spot.

Finally, you learn to **enjoy the psychological satisfaction** of performing the goal-promoting activity by reconnecting to your future self (Chapter 18), magnifying your aspiration (Chapter 8) and developing gratitude toward yourself. After all, you've just done something great for yourself: you've taken a step toward your designed life! You have made progress, however small. Feel happy about that! Linger in that feeling. Celebrate it. Exaggerate it if needed. Make sure it registers.

Notice the progress you are making. Be glad that you are actively on the path to fulfilling your dream. When you feel that you are growing and making progress, there is a natural reward in the process. It becomes easier for you to remain motivated and on track, longing for that feeling of progress that comes from taking yet another step toward your aspiration. This is why the concept of minimum action is so important—it allows you to consistently experience small wins, and that is an effective intrinsic reward.

Whatever we pay attention to grows. Whatever we remove our attention from wanes. I call this *Law of Attention.* Make use of this law to enhance the reward of acting in harmony with your aspiration by dwelling on it longer.

Every time you assert your willpower and practice self-discipline, you get a natural boost of self-confidence. This makes you feel happier about yourself and about your life. Tune into these feelings, or deliberately evoke them. Then expand the experience by paying attention to them on purpose.

Exercise: Find a way to experience intrinsic rewards in your chosen behavior by using at least two of the modalities explained above.

Share this concept:

MindfulSelfDiscipline.com/intrinsic-rewards

EXTRINSIC REWARDS (IT WORKS)

While I truly believe that we can all learn to get intrinsic rewards from our habits, for the sake of completeness I need to cover, even if only *en passant*, the very popular methods of "hacking your habits" by adding extrinsic rewards.

But first, why are these methods more popular than the intrinsic ones? Because extrinsic rewards promise you a shortcut—and we live in a shortcut-obsessed society. They offer a *similar* benefit to the intrinsic rewards, but don't require the awareness and mindset work that the former does.

I say "similar benefits" because it involves tricking your brain. Instead of learning to love the salad, you are adding some dressing to mask the taste you dislike. Instead of learning to love running, you are adding music to make it bearable. Instead of enjoying the research for your thesis, you give yourself a reward so you look forward to finishing it. This is still effective, as it taps into the reward center of the brain and motivates you to take action. It works, and in some cases it might be the only option for you. It is just not as ideal as having intrinsic motivation (and it would be irresponsible of me not to mention that). It is much harder to remain on track with a habit or goal when you rely on an external reward, as compared to when you are intrinsically motivated to do that thing.

All right, let's now get to the practicalities of this approach. There are three main ways to use extrinsic rewards:

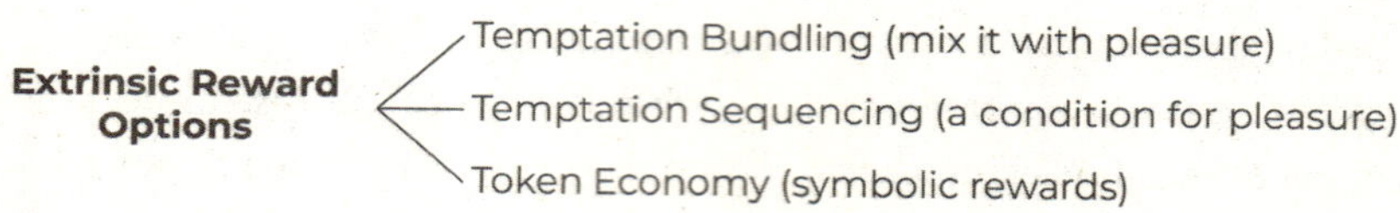

The **first approach** is known as *temptation bundling* and it involves mixing your chosen behavior with an activity you enjoy (something fun). This will allow you to experience some reward while performing your positive habit, even though it doesn't come from the core activity itself. It will make things easier for you by offsetting the pain of your effort with some pleasure or fun. It is proven to work. For example, there are studies showing that listening to music while exercising decreases the perception of effort by 10%.

The **second** is making your habit the condition for enjoying a given reward. This is known as "self-rewarding" in scientific literature, but I like to call it *temptation sequencing*, to relate it to the first method. The idea is that you select an activity or pleasure that you love and set it as a reward for performing your goal-promoting activity. The key for this to work is that you shouldn't be able to experience that particular reward in any other way—otherwise it defeats the purpose.

The basic formula is: "I will only _______(external reward) if I ________ (chosen habit)". It is an expression of the principle of *first aspiration, then pleasure*, covered in Chapter 22. Your "guilty pleasure" is your reward for having prioritized your long-term goals, and can be enjoyed without the guilt.

Desired Habit	External Reward	Formula
Wake up at 5am	Read my favorite book	"I'll only read my favorite book on the days I wake up at 5am"
Avoid sugar	Social Media	"I can only use social media on the days that I have no sugar"
Finish all household chores	Watch a movie	"I'll only watch a movie on the days that my home is fully clean"
Save X amount of dollars	Trip to Bali	"I will travel to Bali only after I've saved X amount of dollars."
Swim three times a week	Night out with friends	"I'll only allow myself to enjoy a night out with friends in the weeks I swam three times."
Sleep at 11pm	Play games	"I can't play games unless I've slept by 11pm the night before."

If the reward can be experienced immediately after the "boring habit", even better. That makes it easier for the brain to associate the two.

This second type of extrinsic reward, *temptation sequencing*, is better than trying to mix habit and pleasure in the same activity. One problem with it, though, is that you may become dependent, and unable to perform your habit without it. Another problem is that you may use it to justify indulging in unhealthy rewards. To avoid both of these problems, think of *temptation sequencing* as the training wheels of habit building, and choose a reward that will not severely detract from your goals.

Keep in mind that, for this to work, you will need to actually follow your own rules, and only enjoy the activity you love if the condition has been met. This does require some self-discipline. If you are a bit of a rebel, you might need some formal accountability, or else strong Commitment Devices, to make that work (see Chapter 22).

Finally, the **third** method of extrinsic rewards is probably the most harmless, and escapes the caveat I laid out in the beginning of this section. It is basically to give yourself a symbolic reward representing your progress—such as gold stars, points, poker chips, or whatever you like. This is known as *token economy* in psychology.

Then you create a list of experiences and things you will reward yourself with, once you accumulate a certain number of tokens. You don't allow yourself to do those things or experience those rewards in any other way, so that all your energy is focused on getting the tokens (by performing the habits) to "pay" for them. The rewards should be things that excite you, but don't detract from your goals. For example, it would make no sense to "reward" a week of sobriety by a night out in a pub.

Share this concept:
MindfulSelfDiscipline.com/extrinsic-rewards

PAINFUL CONSEQUENCES (LAST RESORT)

The first two types of rewards are like a type of carrot on a stick. When the carrot doesn't work, there's the stick. Here, what you seek is to avoid a painful experience, rather than to enjoy a pleasurable one. This is done by associating painful sensations, monetary loss, or shameful experiences to not performing your habit.

Breaking the commitment ⟶ pain, loss, or shame

In a study by the University of Pennsylvania, researchers examined which type of financial reward would be a better motivator to make people reach the goal of 7,000 steps per day. One group of people would receive money for every day that they reached the goal; another group would receive the whole price in advance and lose money each day they didn't reach the goal. After thirteen weeks, the result showed that the group that had received money upfront had performed much better.

This is known as *loss aversion*: we are more motivated by fear of losing something than by the desire of gaining that same thing.

For some people, or in some cases, the stick might be the only thing that works. Still, the problem with this strategy is that once the stick is gone, people almost always go back to their previous behavior. Studies have shown that when people lose weight using this approach, they regain all the weight lost once the threat of a punishment disappears. Therefore, this strategy might only be useful for short-term gains or tasks.

If you want to go forward with this approach and associate financial loss or shame to the undesired behavior, review the section on Commitment Contracts for tips (Chapter 22). On the other hand, if you want to use physical discomfort/pain as the stick, you can use a device called **Pavlok** to bring the future pain of the tempted (in)action into your awareness right now, and thus re-train your lizard brain.

Share this concept:
MindfulSelfDiscipline.com/painful-consequences

CHOOSING YOUR REWARDS

The best approach is to learn how to do the desired activity for its own sake—by learning to enjoy it, by becoming aware of its immediate benefits, or by relishing the psychological satisfaction of doing something that advances your goals and is aligned with who you want to be. This is the most sustainable long-term strategy for building habits.

In some cases, though, this is really not possible.

Dr. Dan Ariely, in his TEDx talk on self-control, narrates an incident from his life that illustrates an appropriate use of external rewards to motivate a difficult behavior. He needed to give himself three injections a week, for a year and a half, in order to save his liver from cirrhosis. The problem was that for the fifteen hours after each injection he experienced terrible side effects. He was only able to follow through by giving himself a reward: he would watch movies right after giving himself an injection. With that, he was able to endure the side effects of medication and saved his liver.

Sometimes intrinsic rewards may not be possible for you, like the example above. At other times, the action you want to take may be temporary (e.g., finish a research project) rather than a life-long habit or goal that needs to be sustained (e.g., meditate daily or "keep fit"). In these cases, try the extrinsic rewards of temptation bundling (acceptable), temptation sequencing (better), or token economy (best).

If all the carrots fail, then you can use the stick of painful consequences to keep yourself on track. However, at this point I would really encourage you to stop for a moment and reflect. If there is such level of resistance toward your goal-promoting habit or action, is this something that is truly in line with your aspiration and values? Are you pursuing the right goals?

KEY POINTS

- Reinforce your desired behaviors by having an immediate reward attached to your habit—it could be a physical pleasure, emotional satisfaction, or psychological fulfillment. Your brain loves rewards, especially when they come *right after* the behavior.

- Intrinsic rewards are the best type of rewards.
  - They are of three types: enjoy the activity itself (e.g., "I love salad"); enjoy how you feel after the activity (e.g., "I love how light my body feels after I eat a salad"); enjoy the emotional satisfaction of having done something meaningful or important (e.g., "I'm happy that I did something good for my health").
  - You can train yourself to experience intrinsic rewards by using positive reappraisal, mindfulness, or connecting the activities to benefits to your future self.

- Extrinsic rewards offer similar benefits to the intrinsic rewards and promise a more effortless shortcut. However, they may not be as sustainable in the long-term, as external rewards tend to wear off. They also don't help you to focus more deeply on the activity.
  - *Temptation Bundling* involves mixing your desired behavior with an activity you enjoy (something fun).
  - *Temptation Sequencing* (or self-rewarding) is to make your habit the condition for you to enjoy a given reward. Only allow yourself to enjoy that reward if the condition was met. The basic formula is: "*I will only (external reward) if I (desired habit)*".
  - *Token Economy* is giving yourself a symbolic reward representing your progress—such as gold stars, points, or poker chips. Use them to "purchase access" to desirable items/experiences.

- The third type of reward is actually avoiding pain. This should only be used if all others fail. You associate painful sensations, monetary loss, or shameful experiences with not performing your habit. This strategy is only useful for short-term gains or tasks.

Implementation resources: download the *Habit Mastery* checklist, as part of the Workbook that accompanies this book, at **MindfulSelfDiscipline.com/workbook**. There you will find a step-by-step checklist to implement the concepts of these last two chapters. And, for an up-to-date list of recommended tools for habit tracking and for implementing external rewards, go to **MindfulSelfDiscipline.com/tools**.

So now you have learned the three key elements to building habits: cue, action, reward. Here is a quick review of the last two chapters.

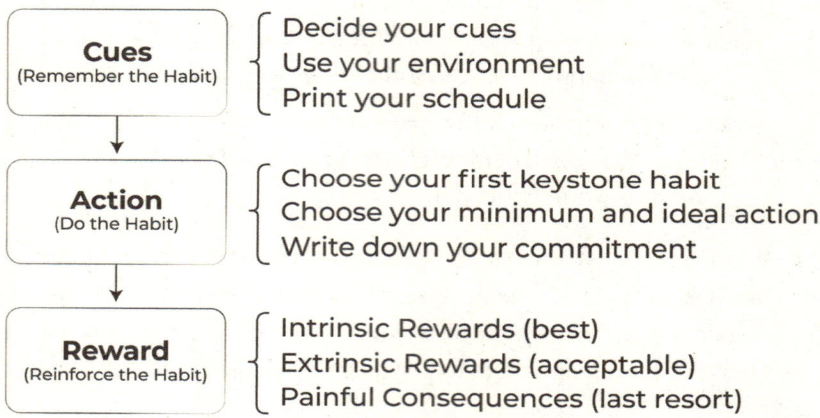

CHAPTER 28

OVERCOME PROCRASTINATION

With an effective *cue* (Chapter 26), you will remember to take action. Yet that doesn't mean that you will actually follow through with it. Sometimes you remember to take action, but for one reason or another, you avoid it. This is procrastination at play—it prevents you from taking action, delays your goals, and weakens your aspiration.

Why do we procrastinate? To avoid some form of pain—be it physical, mental, or emotional. It could be the pain of anxiety and fear—such as fear of failing, fear of loss, fear of being judged, or even fear of success (see Chapter 11). It could also be task aversion—such as when we are procrastinating because the activity is perceived to be meaningless, boring, or difficult.

Several books have been written on procrastination and its causes, but at the core here's all there is to it: we foresee pain, and our lizard brain kicks in to "save us" from it. Then we seek to soothe ourselves emotionally by engaging in an activity that provides a quick and easy shot of dopamine. Dopamine temporarily suppresses the experience of emotional distress, but this just makes the situation worse.

Procrastination's Vicious Cycle

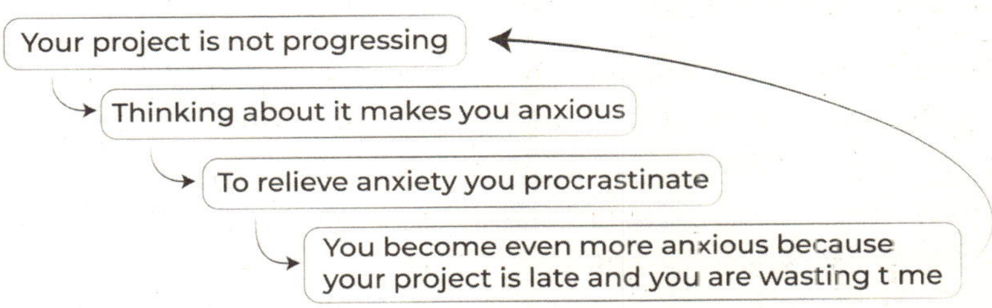

If procrastination is avoiding pain, then there are only three ways to really overcome it:

- Decrease the pain of action
- Increase the pain of inaction
- Embrace the pain and power through

All the different "tips and tricks" to overcome procrastination will typically fall into one of these buckets. If they don't, they are unlikely to address the core issue. For example, many blogs advise you to install apps that limit your access to certain time-wasting websites, as a way to prevent procrastination. Although this strategy can be very useful, the truth is that unless we address the underlying pain we are trying to avoid, removing one source of distraction will only be a temporary fix. We will always find a way to procrastinate with something else—our lizard brain is really good at that!

In Mindful Self-Discipline, the way we deal with procrastination is the same way we deal with most self-discipline challenges: by using a variant of the PAW Method (Chapter 17): Pause, Awareness, and Willpower. The first step is to **pause** for a moment, breathe, and slow things down. Then you become **aware** of the underlying pain that is making you procrastinate, by asking yourself: "What pain am I avoiding now?"

Find out what you are running away from. Be specific in your answer. Go deep and find the real cause—without it, it would be hard to overcome procrastination for good. Then, apply one of the following three willpower methods to shift your state, so that you can take action that is aligned with your goals, and get a +1.

Share this concept:
MindfulSelfDiscipline.com/procrastination

METHOD #1: DECREASE THE PAIN OF ACTION

If a certain activity is important for your goals and it's not in any way painful, you won't procrastinate. Therefore, in beating procrastination, the first thing you can try is to make the activity less painful. One way to do this is by learning to enjoy the activity itself—a concept we covered in the previous chapter. Another way to do this is to break down the task into Baby Steps—or what the social scientist and behavior expert B. J. Fogg calls "tiny habits".

Task or Habit	Baby Step
Meditate for thirty minutes every day	Meditate for three minutes
Write a 200-page book	Write 250 words per day
Stop eating junk food	Eliminate one junk food item per week
Declutter the basement	Get rid of five items every day
Do your taxes	Fill in the first field in the form
Go for a run	Put on your running clothes
Go to sleep at 10pm instead of midnight	Go to sleep every night at 11:45pm

Baby Steps is an extension of the concept of *minimum action* that we covered in Chapter 26. The difference is that *minimum action* is only about building habits; it is the minimalistic version of the habit you want to build. But Baby Steps is something we can apply not only for establishing habits (e.g. meditate, run, write), but also for routines, projects, and action steps that are not necessarily habitual—such as cleaning your garage or completing some boring research.

The philosophy is very simple: break down your task or habit as much as needed, until procrastination either disappears or becomes manageable. How much should you break it down? The rule of thumb is this: if your next step feels either difficult or confusing, it's still too big, and you need to break it down further.

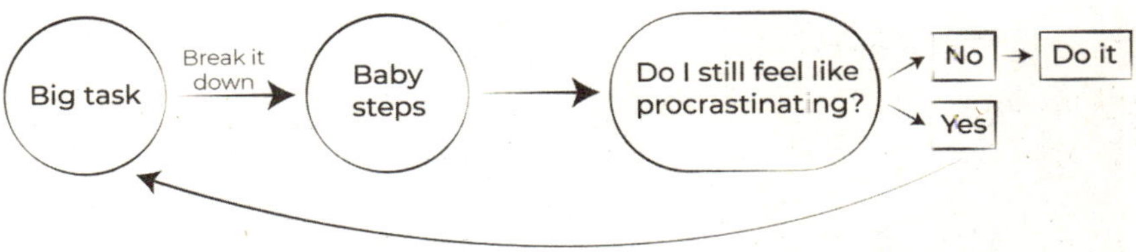

Breaking down your tasks like this removes the sense of overwhelm, and other types of pain associated with the activity itself. It gives you an easy way to take a step forward toward your goal. The step may not be big, but it is meaningful nonetheless, and gives you a small taste of success. Moving forward like this, one step after another, builds your sense of confidence and motivation, and creates momentum.

Building confidence with small wins is extremely important. As we saw in Chapter 4, if you believe that you have limited willpower, you will have less willpower at your disposal. Well, if you keep trying to do something that is above your current level of skill or motivation and keep failing, that will hurt your confidence and motivation. This, in turn, negatively affects the amount of willpower you have, which makes it even harder to progress past this current obstacle.

On the other hand, if you focus on getting small wins quickly, you will feel confident that you can make progress; you will know that you can succeed. With this confidence boost, your motivation and willpower also grow.

According to neuropsychologist Ian H. Robertson, author of *The Winner Effect*, the experiences of success and failure shape us deeply. In the wild, when an animal has won a few fights against weak opponents, he becomes much more likely to win future confrontations against stronger animals. That is because, with each smaller success there was an increase of testosterone and dopamine—which makes him more confident, focused, and stronger. The same happens for other species, including humans. So please don't spend all your motivation and energy on the first obstacle in front of you. Instead, break it down into Baby Steps, keep moving forward and building up your confidence and capacity over time.

This is what happens to your motivation if you start with big steps vs. Baby Steps:

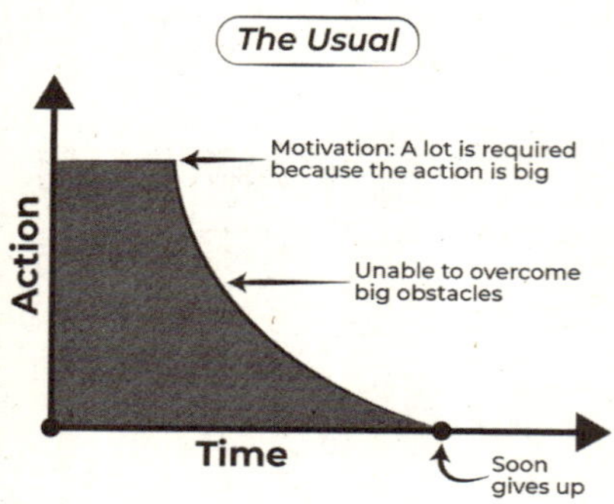

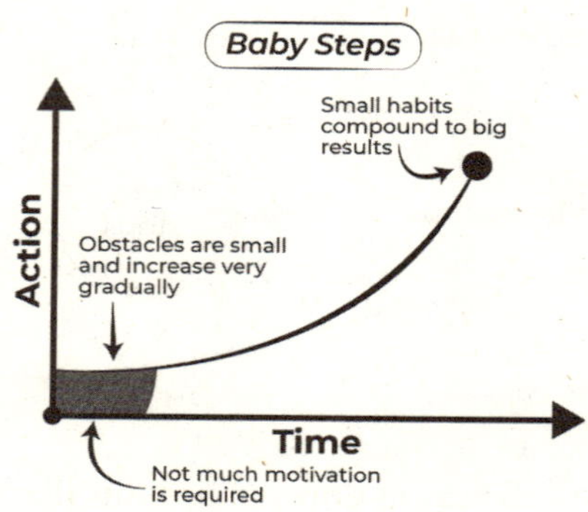

Using Baby Steps not only conserves your motivation, but as mentioned it also builds *momentum*. Newton's first law of motion states that an object at rest stays at rest, and an object in motion stays in motion unless acted upon by another force. The hardest part—with momentum and with life habits—is always getting started. Once you get the momentum working in your favor, it is much easier to keep yourself on track.

Therefore, all you should focus on in the beginning is simply getting started. Don't be idealistic, and don't be in a hurry. Make it as easy as possible to accomplish your goal, and to build your habits, by using Baby Steps.

You don't have to get it perfect, you just have to get it going.

JACK CANFIELD

Don't aim for perfect—aim for better than yesterday. Aim for 1% improvement every day. This compounds into huge results over time.

The next time you feel stuck or confused and want to procrastinate, instead break down the task ahead into smaller bits, until the next step is so clear and simple that there is no reason to postpone it or run away. What if you don't know what you should do next? Well, then figuring out the next step *is* the next step.

The Baby Steps you take every day quickly begin to compound into big results, and have effects for years in the future. It doesn't matter how small you start, so long as you are consistent, and keep growing. The sooner you beat the initial inertia and start compounding your positive habits, the better. Your future self will thank you for it.

Finally, a small caveat: if you are procrastinating to avoid a deeper psychological pain—such as shame or some form of fear—you may need to work through those emotions first, in one way or another. Taking Baby Steps might not be enough here. Instead, coaching, therapy, and other forms of personal growth work may be needed to support you moving forward.

Share this concept:
MindfulSelfDiscipline.com/baby-steps

METHOD #2: INCREASE THE PAIN OF INACTION

As we saw in the Awareness Pillar, every decision matters. Every action has consequences: it will either take you a step toward your goal (+1) or a step away from your goal (-1).

Moving away from your goal and your ideal self is painful—but we often don't notice that. In the chaos of daily life, with the amount of stuff going on in our minds, it's easy to forget our goals and values, and not see the costs of procrastinating.

Procrastinating on something important
is choosing to delay a better future.

JAMES CLEAR

If it were clear for you that procrastinating on writing that paper means you are taking a step toward being unemployable, unfulfilled, and irrelevant in your field—would you still procrastinate writing it? If it were clear for you that procrastinating on ending a toxic relationship meant that you are keeping yourself unavailable for something better for longer—would you still procrastinate ending it? If it were clear for you that procrastinating on cleaning your garage means spending more days feeling overwhelmed inside your own home—would you still procrastinate cleaning it?

If the pain is clear enough and *real* enough, you won't procrastinate.

Yes, thinking like this is painful. That's exactly the point—we want to make the pain of inaction greater than the pain of action, so you can move forward. When the pain of inaction becomes unbearable, you'll *have to* take action. (Hopefully, you'll be able to take action well before that.)

Here are some questions you can use to increase the pain of inaction:

- What pain am I falling into by avoiding this?
- What is this decision doing to my future self?
- What are the hidden costs of inaction?
- With this decision to procrastinate, am I training myself to succeed or to fail?

All of these questions point to the same conclusion: inaction is ultimately painful. Reflect on them deeply, until you can *feel* the consequences (and not only know them intellectually). You can also use the techniques of Shift Your Focus or Shift Your Perception (Chapters 18 and 19) to reconnect to your aspiration, to your future self and enhance the pain of inaction even more.

While Baby Steps is like clearing the path ahead so it's easy for you to move forward, Make Procrastination Painful is like pulling a slingshot: you are creating tension until it's almost unbearable. When that tension hits its maximum, it will propel you forward with great speed. At this point, procrastination won't be able to stop you anymore. Nothing will.

Share this concept:
MindfulSelfDiscipline.com/increase-the-pain-of-inaction

METHOD #3: EMBRACE THE PAIN

We often procrastinate because we hold on to the fantasy that we will *feel like* taking action when the right time comes. Then the moment comes and we still don't feel like doing that activity, so we end up procrastinating again. We do that to avoid the pain of action.

Overcoming procrastination, in this third method, is about your ability to act differently than you feel. It is about not running away from the pain but going toward it. You can do that either by pushing through forcefully or by using mindfulness to accept your pain and thus make it less painful. The latter method is the Mindful Self-Discipline way.

Refer to the Embrace Your Pain technique (Chapter 20) for more details on how to do this.

KEY POINTS

Procrastination is our brain avoiding pain and seeking comfort. It prevents us from taking important action and enjoying the benefits and the growth that would come from it. Mindful Self-Discipline is our brain learning to embrace meaningful pain. It is us outgrowing our reptilian nature.

On the other side of pain, there is greatness. On the other side of comfort, there is boredom. Knowing this, decide to move forward with your goal-promoting activities either by making them less painful, or by becoming aware of the costs of inaction, or by learning to mindfully embrace the pain.

- Procrastination happens when you remember to take action but yet avoid it in order to not feel some form of pain (physical, mental, or emotional). Solution: use one of the three methods to overcome procrastination.
- First, *decrease the pain of action* by breaking the task down into Baby Steps, until the next step is no longer confusing, painful, or overwhelming. Following this strategy builds confidence and momentum. Your small actions compound over time.
- Second, *increase the pain of inaction* by remembering your aspiration and using the questions provided. Here, it becomes painfully clear for you that procrastinating on taking action will ultimately lead you to a bigger pain—and so you move forward.
- Third, *embrace the pain* by accepting the pain and powering through it using either willpower or mindful acceptance.

Implementation resources: check out the step-by-step instructions for the Dissolve Procrastination meditation at **MindfulSelfDiscipline.com/meditations.**

CHAPTER 29

OVERCOME DOUBTS

When you doubt your power, you give power to your doubt.

HONORÉ DE BALZAC

The only limit to our realization of tomorrow will be our doubts of today. Let us move forward with strong and active faith.

FRANKLIN D. ROOSEVELT

Our doubts are traitors, and make us lose the good we oft might win, by fearing to attempt.

WILLIAM SHAKESPEARE

When you are 100% certain that something is right, you speak with confidence and authority. When you are 100% certain that something is possible, you focus on it and move forward with determination. When you are 100% certain that a particular technique will work, you practice it wholeheartedly until you achieve the results.

Certainty brings power and focus. It helps you persevere. It energizes you to keep taking action regardless of failures and setbacks. It magnetizes you and makes you charismatic.

Doubt does the opposite. Doubt is uncertainty. It pulls you back, slows you down, dissipates your energy, and may make you quit prematurely. You hesitate to move forward; and if you do, you are half-hearted. No meaningful goal can be achieved when you are half-hearted. We need the whole of you to step forward, please.

Don't ask yourself what the world needs. Ask yourself what makes you come alive, and go do that, because what the world needs is people who have come alive.

HOWARD THURMAN

According to willpower researcher Roy Baumeister, PhD, the state of uncertainty is a state of willpower depletion. When you are overwhelmed with doubts, you have less energy to move forward. Overcoming doubts, then, boosts your willpower by giving you some certainty, even if that certainty is later replaced by another one.

To Doubt or Not to Doubt

Doubt is a greater enemy nowadays than it was a few centuries ago, courtesy of the scientific revolution. In our modern life we overemphasize reason, linear thinking, and the analytical mind. Doubt and skepticism are considered badges of honor and signs of intelligence. In a way they are—but there are different types of intelligence.

The ability to doubt and question is the cornerstone of critical thinking. Without it, scientific enquiry is impossible. Putting assumptions to the test is what allows us to let go of biases and find the truth about things. The problem is that every virtue casts a shadow (see Chapter 38). If analysis, questioning, and skepticism are the only tools you have, and you use them for everything and in all areas of your life, then you are limiting yourself.

To constantly doubt your conclusions about the nature of things will push you forward; to constantly doubt your conclusions about your capacity won't.

For the purposes of self-discipline, there are three types of doubt that hold us back: doubts about ourselves, about the path, and about the goal. Professor Scott Geller, in his TEDx talk *The Psychology of Self-Motivation*, talks about the need for getting to the *three yeses*. "Yes, I can do this", "Yes, it will work", and "Yes, it is worth it". The three doubts are what prevent us from getting these three yeses.

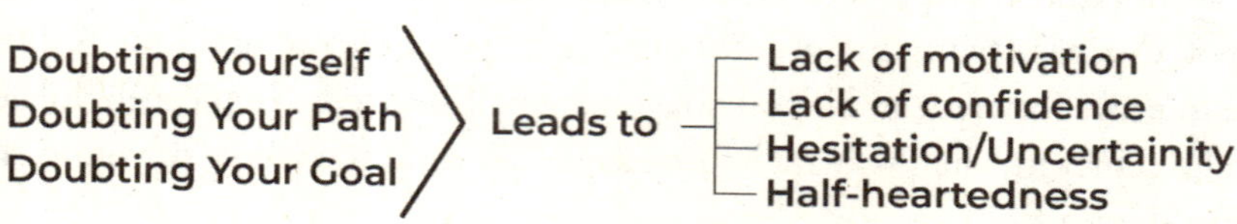

The first is doubting **yourself**—your capacity. This is questioning your abilities, assuming that you are not good enough and that you can't reach your goals. This type of thinking is like a virus in the mind; it is your mind defeating itself. You need to overcome it at whatever cost. (More about this in a moment.)

The second is doubting **your path**—your strategy. You may be certain about your capacity, but if you constantly keep doubting your methods and changing your strategy every week, you won't get anywhere. So spend time researching and figuring out the best way forward for you; get the best mentors, advice and systems that you can find. But once you do, have faith that it will work, and patience with the time it takes. Stay with it long enough before questioning its efficacy.

The third is doubting **your goal**—your purpose. When things move slower than you expected, and when challenges build up, you may have the feeling that you will never achieve your goal. You may feel that it's just too difficult for you. In order to protect yourself from such pain, you then lose interest in your goal ("Maybe this is not for me…") and go after another shiny object. You can overcome this with a strong aspiration, perseverance and self-belief (see Chapters 7-9, 13, and 21).

Doubt is great for understanding things, but bad for manifesting things. Doubt is a friend of knowledge, but an enemy of focus and creativity. It sharpens your analysis, but weakens your resolve, and dissipates your energy. The ability to doubt, thus, has a place in your life—but it's not something that you should use every time, in relation to everything. In keeping you disciplined, it's not helpful.

Exercise: Audit Your Doubts

Pause now for a moment. Take a deep breath, and ask yourself:

- How am I doubting my capacity?
- How am I doubting my chosen strategy?
- How am I doubting my purpose?

These questions assume that you *are* doubting—which is quite likely. Most of us will have some degree of doubt at least regarding one of these three.

Spend ten minutes going through this doubts-audit exercise. Scan your brain for all feelings of doubt in relation to yourself, your chosen path, and your goal. Write them down, one per line.

Share this concept: **MindfulSelfDiscipline.com/doubts**

WHY WE DOUBT

Doubt kills more dreams than failure ever will.

SUZY KASSEM

One of the reasons we doubt, as explained above, is because we are overrelying on our **analytical mind**. We are overplaying this virtue, and thus falling into its shadow side by trying to apply it to *everything* in our life. We have a great hammer and treat everything as a nail. The problem is that not everything is a nail.

Another cause for the virus of self-doubt is our **childhood conditioning**. Many of us had to grow up with an overcritical parent, a dominating sibling, or a bully at school. Or we were constantly compared to another kid who just seemed "better" at everything. This results in us being indoctrinated into believing that we are not good enough. Doubting ourselves, then, becomes second nature.

A third possible cause is a big **experience of failure**. Perhaps you had good self-confidence and high self-esteem, you did well in life, and then you fell and hit the ground *hard*. That can be a traumatizing experience, after which it becomes hard for you to bet on yourself again. You internalized not only the lesson from that failure, but a more defeatist self-image. There may now be a new voice inside of you, always asking you to play it safe. It is trying to protect you by keeping you away from perceived danger.

A fourth cause of doubting is **bad company**. The people we spend our time with influence us deeply. The people whose words we read (authors, bloggers, social media accounts) and listen to (friends, family, colleagues, podcasts) also influence us deeply. They impact the thoughts we have, the way we feel, and the decisions we make.

If you surround yourself with the wrong type of people, it becomes easier for you to doubt yourself, get distracted from your goals, and feel unmotivated. When you start something new in your life, some people will envy you and try to covertly hinder you. Others might be supposedly more "well-intentioned" and want to help you to "keep it real" so that you don't experience disappointment.

Finally, the three doubts may also be due to **lack of perspective**. We compare ourselves, and the results we are getting, with other people who look more capable or who got results more quickly. We compare our *process* with somebody else's *end result* and feel discouraged. Or we think that the difficulties we are facing right now will be there forever; that they are permanent and that we won't ever be able to overcome them. These are different ways of how we sometimes lose perspective.

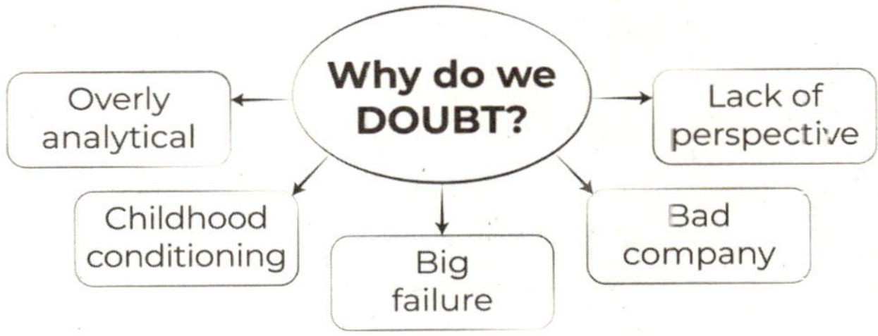

What are the causes behind your habit of self-doubt? Take a moment to reflect on that.

If the cause is bad company, the best way to overcome it is to find better company. Life is too short to be wasted with toxic people around you. Phase those people out of your life who only bring you down, and seek company with those who uplift you. Doing this is a service to yourself, to others, and to all people who are waiting for you to step forward and bring to life whatever you are creating. (See Chapter 35)

Should a seeker not find a companion who is better or equal, let him resolutely pursue a solitary course. In the path, there is no fellowship with the fool.

Buddha

Let's now discuss how you overcome the other four causes of doubt.

Share this concept:
MindfulSelfDiscipline.com/why-we-doubt

METHOD #1: THE *NOT NOW* TECHNIQUE

It's extremely difficult to win over doubt just by attempting to talk your way out of it. If self-doubt is a person, he is that stubborn skeptic who always has a "Yes, but…" objection to whatever you say. He can never be convinced. You need to take a break from it sometimes, so you can focus on moving forward.

There is a place for doubt, but it is not *every time* and *everywhere*. Healthy doubt is constructive and helps you see things from a new perspective; unhealthy doubt makes you uncertain and it paralyzes you. This is the shadow side of doubt, and it's a big obstacle to self-discipline.

A great way to overcome this shadow is to create a *doubt-free experiment*. You commit to a period of time during which no doubts are allowed. Every doubt is met with a simple response: "Not now". In this manner, fears, doubts, and anxieties are temporarily suspended. Without needing to figure out how to permanently overcome them, you already get the space you need to move forward! Only after that time ends are you allowed to question your skills and reevaluate your methods—and only if that is really needed.

This shift in mindset is extremely simple, yet effective. Keeping doubts at bay becomes easier, since it's "just an experiment", with a clear beginning and end. Doubts then don't need to fight their way into your mind, for they know that their time will come—it's just "not now".

During the doubt-free experiment, you focus wholeheartedly on the task at hand, with full conviction and enthusiasm. No doubts are allowed. Cultivate the feeling that you know *for sure* that you are on the right path, and that achieving your goal is just a matter of time. Trust that you are getting closer to your purpose with every step you take, even when it doesn't feel like it.

If needed, be delusionally optimistic, and fanatically dedicated—for that limited time. Then at the end you pause to reflect, learn, and start again with greater insight. Go on practicing like this for as long as you need. Eventually your doubts may give up and stop knocking at your door, knowing that nobody will open. Just as it happened for me.

Doubt your doubts before you doubt yourself.

LEWIS PUGH

Once you have started your doubt-free experiment, you snooze whatever doubts or fears come up to bother you. The Not Now technique is the snooze button in your brain. It is your capacity to use a skill that you are really good at (procrastination), on things that are actually worth procrastinating (doubts).

When doubts come, say "not now". Procrastinate on doubt. Procrastinate on fears, worries, and anxiety. Procrastinate on emotional dramas and distractions. For the chosen time period, focus all your energies on the task at hand, and press the snooze button on everything else. Act first, doubt later.

As for the length of the doubt-free experiment, it depends on your needs. It could be an hour every morning where you set aside your insecurity about your writing skills, and just write. It could be a thirty-day timeframe where you follow a certain diet and don't constantly step on the scale to see if the diet is working or not. It could be a year that you will dedicate to pursuing a new business idea without getting distracted with other "opportunities". Design your own doubt-free experiment, and then follow through wholeheartedly, snoozing all doubts and fears with the help of the Not Now technique.

What if the doubts come again? Repeat "not now" with a firm but calm inner voice. Do that as many times as needed, and eventually the mind will learn. You need to be in control, not your thoughts. Set boundaries for your thoughts. Claim back your power—this is the core message of meditation.

Not Now is an analysis-free zone. It's a much-needed vacation from your self-defeating mind. You will be surprised with how much you get done. You will tap into resources you didn't even know you had. There is tremendous power in this.

The Not Now technique is similar to the Procrastinate Distractions method (Chapter 22). As a matter of fact, you can also use the Not Now technique to overcome many of the enemies of self-discipline, such as distractions, excuses, fears, or any other limiting beliefs or emotional states.

This technique will not resolve any past emotional pains that might be behind it all, but it will prevent doubts and fears from spoiling your journey. Once you create this doubt-free space in your life, you are able to move forward with less friction, get the taste of small wins along the way, and prevent the overly-analytical mind from holding you back in analysis paralysis. With this, even if fears and doubts still exist in you, they cease to define you. They can't stop you anymore.

Share this concept: **MindfulSelfDiscipline.com/not-now-technique**

METHOD #2: REMOVE YOUR OPTIONS

In the ancient military manual, *The Art of War*, the Chinese strategist Sun Tzu advises (VII.36): "*When you surround an army, leave an outlet free. Do not press a desperate foe too hard.*" The idea behind this is that when people believe that there is no way out, they fight with all their might, tapping into a wealth of strength hitherto unknown.

We can apply the same strategy to our daily lives. When we have no option but to make a change, then we will work for that change wholeheartedly. When we *have to* succeed, we will. There is no room for doubts, so no doubts come.

If you *have* to earn an extra thousand dollars in the next two weeks to pay for the medication of your terminally-ill child, you will find a way to do it. You won't procrastinate, get distracted, or doubt yourself. You will focus and move forward with all your might.

In Buddhism there is a saying: "Meditate as if your head is on fire." When your head is on fire, you are not distracted. You don't have competing priorities. And you are most definitely not thinking about lunch.

On the other hand, when we have other options—a plan B, C, and D—it is harder to generate that intense type of energy. Since the consequences of failure are not as dreadful, it is easier to get distracted from the goal, make excuses, or not take action. When you know that you will fall on a comfortable cushion, you are not so focused on walking well. Part of you is indifferent.

Needless to say, this particular method is more extreme. It won't suit every type of person, nor every type of goal. Yet the core lesson applies to everyone: the more committed you are, the less you will doubt. So if everything else fails, remove all your options. This method will not fail you.

A determined person advances toward his goal like an arrow toward its target. Is that you? If no, why not?

Share this concept:

MindfulSelfDiscipline.com/remove-your-options

METHOD #3: GET PERSPECTIVE

Removing doubt is like removing a blindfold.

TIM FARGO

Self-doubt is just one out of many possible ways to look at things. It is a narrative—and a limiting one. The third method to overcome the three types of doubts is to *zoom out* and get some perspective.

One way to do this is to get **temporal perspective**, by remembering that *this too shall pass*. Whatever challenges you are going through will not last forever. Three months from now, you are unlikely to be dealing with the same obstacles; if not, three years from now you will definitely be in a different place, provided that you continue on the path and take action.

Always remember that "this too shall pass". Write this down somewhere where you can see it often. Tattoo it on your brain. Contemplate it in times of need.

A second way to have a perspective shift is to **adjust your expectations** regarding the length of the journey and the challenges that you'll encounter. We talked about this in Chapter 21, when covering the virtue of perseverance and one of its enemies: the false hope syndrome.

Let's imagine that your goal is to become great at singing (or any other skill, for that matter). You get the best teacher you can find and go to the classes with great enthusiasm. Then, after only two weeks of lessons, you feel disappointed that you are not progressing as quickly as expected. That is actually a normal experience, and not a reason to doubt. But if you start thinking that you don't have the voice for it (doubting yourself), or that this method of learning won't work (doubting the path), or that perhaps singing is not really for you or is not worth it (doubting your goal), you are likely to give up too soon. Instead, readjust your expectations regarding the process.

A third way to gain perspective is to **let go of unfair comparisons**. Comparison can bring doubts in your ability and in your path. The most common of these is comparing your *process* with somebody else's *result*. Imagine you're a beginner artist looking at someone's masterpiece and thinking, "I'll never be able to paint like that… maybe I'm not cut out for this." Or you are a tennis player and think, "I'm not progressing quickly enough… I'll never play like Sampras…" Is this a fair comparison?

Never compare your process with somebody else's end result. You don't need to be better than they are; you just need to be the best version of yourself.

Comparison is a hard-wired tendency of our minds. We may not be able to stop comparing, but we can learn to compare more wisely. If you need inspiration, compare yourself to those ahead of you, in things that are meaningful to you, without losing perspective of the path it takes to get there. If you need self-compassion and encouragement, compare yourself to the previous version of yourself, or to those behind, and feel how far you have come. But don't compare the beginning of your process with the end of someone else's.

Are you holding on to any disempowering comparisons? If so, it's time to replace them with more empowering ones. For that purpose, you can also use the method of shifting your self-talk (Chapter 12) and the method of poking holes in your negative thinking (Chapter 22).

In the beginning of this chapter you went through the doubts audit exercise, where you made a list of all the ways you are doubting yourself, your path, or your goal. Now spend a minute reviewing that list and deciding which technique you will use to overcome each doubt.

Share this concept:
MindfulSelfDiscipline.com/gaining-perspective

KEY POINTS

- Certainty brings power and focus. It helps you persevere. It energizes you to keep taking action regardless of failures and setbacks.
- Doubt pulls you back, slows you down, and dissipates your energy. You hesitate to move forward; and if you do, you are half-hearted. Doubt is sometimes a virtue but has its shadow side. If you try to apply it to every area of your life, you will struggle.
- The three types of doubts that you need to overcome in self-discipline are: doubting yourself (you question your capacity/worth), doubting your path (you are skeptical about your strategy and keep changing it), doubting your goal (you lose interest as a result of not making progress). The reason why we doubt could be over-reliance on the analytical mind, childhood conditioning, a big experience of failure, bad company, or lack of perspective.
- Method #1: *The Not Now Technique*. Commit to a period of time during which no doubts are allowed. Just focus on the task at hand, with full conviction and trust. Snooze all doubts, fears, and distractions by saying "not now" in your mind, as many times as needed, calmly and confidently.
- Method #2: *Remove Your Options*. When you have no option but to make a change, you will work for that change wholeheartedly. When you have other options, or the consequences of failure are not so dreadful, it will be harder to generate that intense type of energy. Remove your options so you become fully focused and committed. This method is extreme.
- Method #3: *Get Perspective*. Zoom out to see things more clearly. Get temporal perspective by remembering that whatever challenges you are facing are temporary ("this too shall pass"). Adjust your expectations regarding the length of the journey and the difficulties you'll encounter. Let go of unfair comparisons, such as comparing your process with somebody else's result.

CHAPTER 30

OVERCOME FAILURE

Fall down seven times, get up eight.

Japanese Proverb

To enter into a battle without a plan is the height of arrogance. Such generals should be put to death for they risk the lives of their warriors.

Sun Tzu

The mind game is that all pain eventually ends. And when you can understand that, it then becomes only a matter of enduring long enough.

David Goggins

The path toward your goal will likely be longer and harder than you expect. You will likely experience many false starts, doubts, loss of motivation, confusion, tiredness, competing priorities, distractions, unexpected results, failures, and delays. Knowing this is important, because when you expect challenges, you are ready for them; when you don't, you aren't.

Overcoming failure is about two different skills. The first skill is preparing for failure, so that it is less likely to happen, and if it does you can recover quickly. The second skill is learning how to fail gracefully, so that you don't fall into a pit of negative emotions such as shame, discouragement, self-loathing, or panic. Let's now learn how to develop these two skills.

HAVE A CONTINGENCY PLAN

If you expect that once you start your habit you will perform it without fail until you reach your goal, you're setting yourself up for disappointment. As a result, at the slightest deviation, you may start doubting yourself or fall into the *all-or-nothing* thinking (Chapter 23). If you expect that the path will be easy and smooth, you will fall into the trap of *false hope syndrome*, and that hurts your ability to persevere (Chapter 21). If you expect that your self-control skills are infallible, you fall into *restraint bias* (Chapter 38, balance your virtues), and will get a painful correction from reality.

The solution to all of this is to have a contingency plan and know exactly how you will respond to every type of challenge that may come up—inside of you or outside of you. Once you have prepared a contingency plan, you are not caught by surprise. You become more resilient to challenges, because now you know exactly how you will meet each of them. Failure becomes less likely because you are expecting challenges, and are ready for them. You have allocated more willpower for the journey.

This is a tool I use all the time with my coaching clients. If their goal is to exercise thirty minutes every morning, for example, I then guide them to create a contingency plan by asking them several questions. Here are some examples:

What will you do if...?	Contingency Plan
You don't wake up on time?	Do it in the evening after work
You feel extremely tired?	Take it easy, cut it in half, but do it nevertheless
You don't feel motivated?	I'm not expecting motivation; I'll do it regardless
You are traveling?	Plan my days accordingly so I have time to exercise
Your phone rings?	Leave it in airplane mode, or call back later
You forget?	Create alarms so I don't forget
Your equipment is broken?	Do an alternate set of exercises, but exercise!
It gets really difficult?	Remember that *this too shall pass*, and that the pain of exercising is better than the pain of poor health
You are offered the food you are trying to abstain from?	I will say "Thanks, but I don't eat X anymore" or "Thanks, but tonight I'll have a salad instead."

If you have never gone through a similar set of questions, when those challenges come up—and they will—you will be caught by surprise. You may not have the clarity of mind, time to figure things out, or the willpower needed to find and implement the solution there and then. The result? You skip that day and lose momentum. You break your commitment and get a -1.

As we saw in Chapter 22, Ulysses had a contingency plan. He knew the challenge he was up against. He knew what to expect of the Sirens. He knew his enemies, and he knew himself. That's why he had himself tied to the mast.

You too need a contingency plan.

> *If you know the enemy and know yourself, you need not fear the result of a hundred battles. If you know yourself but not the enemy, for every victory gained you will also suffer a defeat. If you know neither the enemy nor yourself, you will succumb in every battle.*
>
> **Sun Tzu**

Who are the enemies of your self-discipline? The usual suspects are: tiredness, busyness, excuses, procrastination, low motivation, distractions, failures, criticism from others, etc. Ignoring your enemies makes you unable to defend yourself. So here, too, awareness is key.

You need to expect bumps along the way. Expect it to be harder than it will. Know that there will be obstacles, and that you will meet resistance. Know your weaknesses, your excuses, your likely points of failure. Know what may trigger you to be your impulsive self. Know and expect all of this, but don't let it crush you—rather, have a contingency plan for how you will come out on top.

Exercise: Create Your Contingency Plan

The next step for you is to go through an obstacle audit and create your contingency plan. You will create simple "if/then" scenarios, also known as "implementation intentions".

1. Make a list of all the challenges, excuses, and obstacles that may tempt you to skip your habit or break your resolution. (*If______ happens,*)
2. Next to or below each item, write how you will respond. Specify the exact action you will take, or the exact self-talk you will use. (*I will_______.*)

3. Review this list at least once a week, until it is all internalized.
4. If needed, go through the POWER Visualization to program your brain to follow through with the plan (Chapter 23).

Going through this process allows you to make decisions in advance regarding how you will deal with temptations and challenges. When they show up, you know exactly how to address them. It will then take less willpower to remain on track with your goals. In a way, you have overcome failure before it happened.

What if things are actually much easier than you anticipated, and none of those challenges show up? Well, then you will be pleased with that surprise!

Share this concept:
MindfulSelfDiscipline.com/contingency-plan

FAIL GRACEFULLY

Everything that we have covered in this book so far is here to help you succeed in building habits and achieving your goals. It's all designed to help you prevent "failures". For example, we talked about focusing on the process and not obsessing about the results. We talked about starting really small (Baby Steps and Minimum Action), and growing gradually. We talked about the several ways you can overcome distraction, procrastination, excuses, forgetfulness, and self-doubt. We also learned how to create a contingency plan.

Yet, even if you have the best possible tools, and make a sincere effort to follow the principles in this book, you will still face setbacks and likely "fail" from time to time. When that happens, you can deal with this failure in a way that causes you emotional suffering and makes it harder for you to be disciplined, or you can deal with it with mindfulness and self-compassion—knowing that failure is only feedback, and that it's not the end of the world. Failure is not terminal, and it says nothing about who you are.

How do you deal with failure mindfully? You simply **acknowledge** what happened, **learn** from it, **forgive** yourself, and **take action** (recommit). Mindful Self-Discipline is about awareness, and, as we saw in Chapter 16, awareness is neutral and does not require shame or guilt.

If you forget your habit, end up procrastinating, or succumb to distractions—accept it and move on. If you tell yourself a lame excuse and believe it—learn from it and move on. If you had a bad week, full of relapses and poor decisions, and got more -1's than you can count—forgive yourself and move on.

Shaming Is Not Effective

Transforming yourself is not easy, because there is tremendous inertia holding you back. This inertia wants to keep things as they are; but you want to change them, so you need to be stronger than the inertia. Sometimes, though, the inertia will win—and how you choose to respond to these temporary "failures" will determine whether you will remain on track or not.

As we saw in the Awareness Pillar, when you shame yourself or go on a guilt trip, you are creating a state of emotional distress. You are creating (needless) suffering for yourself. And you know what we are really good at doing when we are suffering? Seeking quick relief. So adding shame, blame, or guilt to the mix only sets you up for further failure, because now you are in a state of emotional distress, and will seek relief through instant gratification and distractions—which offer you a feel-good experience for close to zero effort.

The conclusion is clear: the more you shame yourself for your failures, the more likely it is that you will give up, or at least to further stray away from your ideals. The same thing is true for other forms of negative self-talk, such as self-criticism, guilt, and feeling disappointed with yourself.

For most people, then, shaming is an ineffective strategy that just paralyzes them in fear of experiencing that emotional stress again. Yet this is not a universal rule. For some people, a healthy dose of self-criticism and fear of experiencing shame can be the fuel they need to move forward and do something they actually want to do.

How do you know which of these two you are? It's simple: just observe what happens when you shame yourself. Do you feel more driven and then go forward and take positive action? Great, then use that as a fuel, if you wish. But if instead you indulge and procrastinate even further, then practice being kind to yourself and failing gracefully, by using the ALFA Method.

The ALFA Method

The ALFA Method is a process of forgiving yourself and starting over—and it's a nice coincidence that it sounds just like "alpha", the first letter of the Greek alphabet and a symbol of the beginning of all things.

Here is how to do this method:

1. **Acknowledge**. Take ownership of what happened without beating yourself up. You do that by describing it in emotionally-neutral language. For example, instead of saying to yourself, "Ah, I messed up again", say "I chose to procrastinate, and now the project is late."
2. **Learn**. What can you learn about this situation, and about yourself? What triggered you to act this way? What will you change so this doesn't happen again?
3. **Forgive**. Remember that you are human, and don't beat yourself up. Release all narratives of self-criticism, shame, or blame. You made a mistake, and it's now in the past. Repair the damage if possible, but focus on being ready to move on.
4. **Act**. Start again. Remember the importance of your goals. Gently but resolutely recommit to your goals and habits. Get up as many times as you fall. (See Chapter 21)

In moments of discouragement, remember your aspiration and goals. **Your goal is more important than your failures.** Remember why you are doing all of this, why it really matters (Chapter 8), and know that everything else *shall pass*. If you need extra inspiration, read success stories of other people who did what you are attempting to do, and the failures they faced along the way.

Do whatever you need to do to move on from the self-pity stage, so you can once again be on track with living your designed life.

Share this concept:
MindfulSelfDiscipline.com/fail-gracefully

KEY POINTS

Theory

- Overcoming failure is about two different skills. The first skill is preparing for failure, so that it is less likely to happen, and if it does you can recover quickly (contingency plan). The second skill is learning how to fail gracefully, so that you don't fall into a pit of negative emotions such as shame, discouragement, self-loathing, and panic.

Contingency Plan

- Expect that the path toward your goal will be full of false starts, doubts, loss of motivation, confusion, tiredness, competing priorities, distractions, unexpected results, and delays. Be prepared for this by deciding beforehand how you will respond to each different type of challenge. This makes you more resilient.
- Formula: "If *this* (challenge), then *that* (response)."
- Task: Create your contingency plan. Review it weekly.

Fail Gracefully

- You will likely fail from time to time. When that happens, you can deal with it in a way that causes you emotional suffering and makes it harder for you to be disciplined, or you can deal with it with mindfulness and self-compassion.
- Shame is an ineffective response to failure because it creates a state of emotional distress, which pushes you to seek relief by indulging even further in procrastination and distractions.
- When you fail, practice the ALFA Method: Acknowledge and own what happened; Learn from it so that you can do better tomorrow; Forgive yourself and repair the damages; Act by recommitting and starting again.
- In moments of discouragement, remember your aspiration and goals. Your goal is more important than your failures. Remember

why you are doing all of this, why it really matters, and know that everything else *shall pass*. If you need extra inspiration, read success stories of other people who did what you are attempting to do, and who overcame similar challenges along the way.

Implementation resources: make use of the *Contingency Plan* template that is part of the Workbook (**MindfulSelfDiscipline.com/workbook**). Also, see instructions for the ALFA Method meditation at **MindfulSelfDiscipline.com/meditations**.

CHAPTER 31

COMMIT TO *NEVER ZERO*

You may have to fight a battle more than once to win it.

MARGARET THATCHER

You now have everything you need to start taking consistent and effective action toward fulfilling your aspirations. The next step is to now make a commitment to follow through with your plan and habits regardless of fluctuations of moods and motivation.

Motivation is important. It is often the initial spark that has set you on a journey. It is that emotional connection with your goal, the feeling of being pulled toward it, and energized to take action.

The problem is this: motivation is fleeting. It is a feeling—and, like all other feelings, it fluctuates. You can't rely on it because it comes and goes. Nobody feels motivated all the time. Self-discipline is, by definition, your ability to act *despite* motivation, despite what you are feeling or not feeling in the moment. Self-discipline is commitment.

COMMITMENT, NOT MOTIVATION

Motivation may get you started on the path, but it's only self-discipline that will help you see it through to the end. Motivation is the initial spark; self-discipline is continuously fanning the fire. Don't depend on motivation; instead, make a strong commitment.

If you rely on an inconsistent feeling (motivation) to take action, your action will also be inconsistent. It is like a sailor who only knows how to move forward when the wind is at his back—he won't go very far.

Therefore, don't expect motivation to precede action. Don't wait to feel motivated so you get started. Don't wait for it to "feel right". Act, regardless of motivation. Take a step forward in the direction of your goals every day, whether you feel like it or not. This is what makes the difference between regret and long-term success.

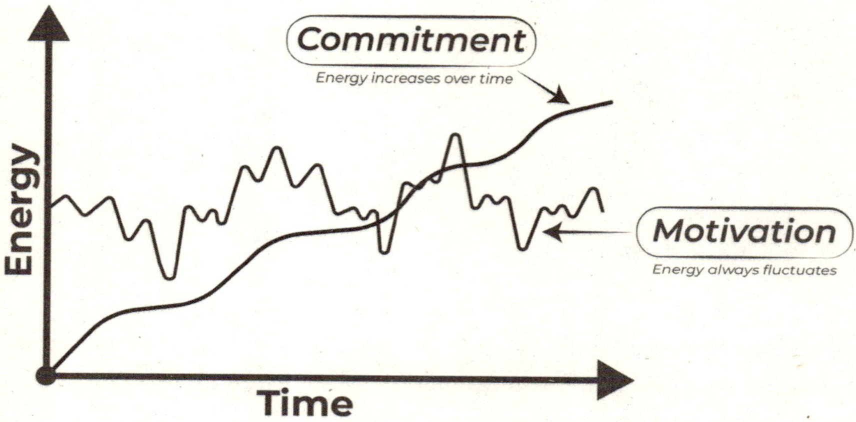

When the young comedian Brad Isaac asked Jerry Seinfeld for career advice, Seinfeld told him that he needed to write jokes every day. Not "every day that you feel inspired". Not "every day that you feel funny". Every day.

In the path toward your aspirations, you will face many setbacks, failures, and disappointments. You will, at times, doubt yourself and doubt the process. These are the defining moments in any journey; it's the time for you to prove what you are made of, and re-affirm your aspiration. Here, only commitment to your purpose can help you.

> *I have always felt that the mettle of a player is not how well he plays when he's playing well, but how well he scores and plays when he's playing poorly.*
>
> JACK NICKLAUS (PROFESSIONAL GOLFER)

There are different types of commitment. Some commitments should be non-negotiable—I call them *Never Zero* commitments. Others need to be a bit more flexible, so that there is not too much pressure in your daily life (which would lead to unnecessary stress). Just keep in mind that the more flexible your mindset is around your commitment, the more likely you are to find an excuse and skip it.

Share this concept:
MindfulSelfDiscipline.com/commitment-not-motivation

THE NEVER ZERO COMMITMENT

A commitment is *Never Zero* when it is uncompromising. Typically, it will also be a small commitment, and time-bound—especially in the beginning, when your self-discipline is not strong yet. In other words, you decide on the minimum acceptable version of your habit and commit to do it for a specific time period, *no matter what.*

Never Zero is taking full responsibility and control of your life. You decide what you will do, who you will become, and close the door to all possible excuses.

You create *Never Zero* commitments around the key habit(s) you need to cultivate to advance your goals. Here are some examples:

- I will meditate for at least five minutes every day
- For the next 100 days, I will write from 6am to 7am
- Until the end of this year, I won't go to sleep without showing appreciation to my partner
- I will study twenty minutes of Spanish every day until my trip to Spain
- I will not drink beer or eat sweets until the day after my marathon

You won't be able to make a *Never Zero* commitment around every habit. That would be unrealistic and too inflexible (see Chapter 3, on the need to balance self-discipline). Instead, just choose one or two keystone habits to practice *Never Zero* on, with a set start time and duration.

You may want to change many things in your life, but it is wiser to start with a single habit, and focus on it until it's solid before picking up another one. It's better to move forward steadily, even if slowly. Develop self-discipline by taking up one challenge at a time. **If you try to commit to everything, you commit to nothing**.

Once one of your habits is fully integrated, you can then add another one to the stack. For example, if you already have the habit of waking up at 6am and doing twenty minutes of meditation, then adding a third habit of doing twenty minutes of morning exercise is not as difficult. It just becomes "the thing that I do after meditation".

When you develop the skill of *Never Zero* in one area of your life, you can then apply it to other areas. With each habit added, self-discipline becomes easier—this is known as the "halo effect" in habit creation. Your brain now knows how to go through the process of resisting temptation, remaining focused, and prioritizing your long-term goals.

> *Australian researchers Megan Oaten and Ken Cheng have even found some evidence of a halo effect around habit creation. In their studies, students who successfully acquired one positive habit reported less stress; less impulsive spending; better dietary habits; decreased alcohol, tobacco, and caffeine consumption; fewer hours watching TV; and even fewer dirty dishes. Sustain the discipline long enough on one habit, and not only does it become easier, but so do other things as well. It is why those with the right habits seem to do better than others. They're doing the most important thing regularly and, as a result, everything else is easier.*
>
> EXCERPT FROM *THE ONE THING* BY GARY KELLER.

Let's now discuss each of the three elements of the *Never Zero* commitment: timely, small, and uncompromising.

A *Timely* Commitment

Making a *Never Zero* commitment is like turning a new page in the book of your life. It is a big deal, so it needs a proper start date. This helps build up expectation and focuses your energy.

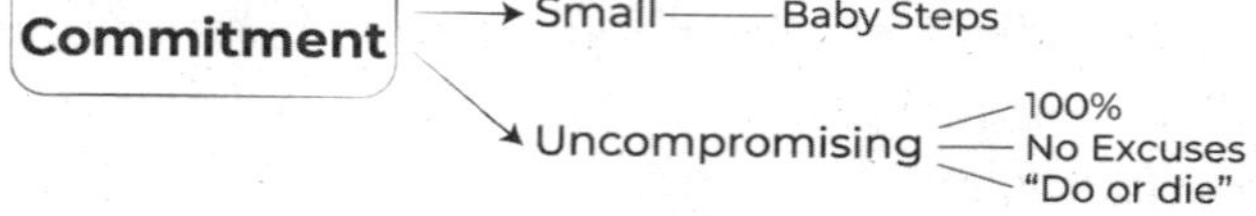

Decide on when you will start your commitment—it could be next Monday, or on your birthday, or tomorrow. Mark that date on your calendar. And if it is a bit far into the future, have a Post-it note somewhere, helping you constantly remember that a new beginning is approaching. Look forward to it!

You also need to decide on the length of your commitment: the number of days, weeks, or months that you will maintain it. Or it could be lifetime, if it's a commitment to a habit that is essential to who you want to become, or if it's a commitment to break an addiction, such as alcohol or smoking.

On March 21, 2000, I made my *Never Zero* commitment toward meditation. I told myself, after attending a workshop, that I would meditate at least five days a week for the rest of my life. That was my first attempt at *Never Zero,* and it worked for me. After a couple of years, I increased it to seven days a week, and I've been meditating daily ever since.

However, if you are a *Never Zero* newbie, it may not be a good idea to start with a lifetime commitment. Perhaps start with something smaller, such as "going sugar free for 50 days" or "face my social anxiety every day for three weeks". Choose whatever makes sense to you, and then stick to it *no matter what.* No excuses accepted.

During the chosen time, you have no option but to follow your commitment. Only after that timeframe can you then reevaluate what to do about it. You may want to go for another *Never Zero* sprint, tweak the time commitment (for more or for less), or make it a permanent part of your life.

A *Small* Commitment

A *Never Zero* commitment doesn't need to be small; but, in the beginning, I'd highly recommend that you make it so. Since the *Never Zero* commitment is immutable (for the chosen time period), it is better that you are not too ambitious with it in the beginning. Remember the Baby Steps concept and make it easier for yourself: start small. You can increase the difficulty later, after you have mastered the basics.

If you have never had the habit of regular physical exercise, don't commit that you will run two hours every day. This would simply create undue pressure, stress you out, and likely end in disappointment and frustration. Instead, start small. It doesn't matter how small the commitment is, so long as it's truly a *Never Zero* commitment. Staying with it *no matter what* is more important than starting big or progressing quickly.

Go as fast or as slow as you wish; play as hard or as gradually as you want. But when you make a decision, a commitment, a resolution—then follow it to the end as if it's a life-or-death situation.

An exception to this rule is if your *Never Zero* is a "not to do" commitment, such as to stop smoking or stop drinking alcohol. If that is your goal, and you are brave enough to accept a taste of hell for a couple of months, then you can go cold turkey. In these cases, going directly for complete abstinence may be easier than trying moderation and playing with fire.

An *Uncompromising* Commitment

During the timeframe of your commitment, there are NO acceptable excuses. The commitment is non-negotiable. You may tweak the amount of time you are committing to follow *Never Zero*, or the size and difficulty of your habit, but not its *uncompromising* nature. Otherwise, there is no point.

Once you start, you finish it. No matter what. In this sense, this method is an expression of the Remove Your Options technique (covered in Chapter 29).

Even in the presence of doubt, fear, or pain, **take action**. Even if you are confused or demotivated, take action. This is the meaning of "no matter what". It doesn't matter if you feel exhausted one day, or if you worked twenty-three hours that day. It doesn't matter if there is a death in the family, an economic crisis, a new pandemic, or the beginning of a Third World War. And it most certainly doesn't matter if you feel like doing it or not. That is the full meaning of "never" in *Never Zero.*

In Mindful Self-Discipline, a 100% commitment is easier than a 99% commitment—because it helps you avoid decision fatigue. When the rule is flexible (99%), you always need to consider if today is the day you should make that exception. But when the rule is uncompromising (100%), there is nothing for you to think about. You have already made your decision! Your mind is freed from the burden of weighing your options every time. This saves you energy and gives you peace of mind.

Never Zero is almost a *do or die* type of determination. This figure of speech may feel exaggerated, but this is how inner strength is forged. This strength of determination leads to self-respect, self-confidence, and self-love. And with that you can achieve *anything.*

It may feel scary to make a commitment like this, because it's powerful and unapologetic. You can feel how serious it is—and if it doesn't feel like that, it's either because your commitment is not uncompromising, or it is too small.

Take this fear and this feeling of gravity to be a good sign. You are moving out of your comfort zone. You are placing a big bet on yourself. Many good things will come out of it.

One of the meditation masters I most resonate with, Swami Vivekananda, used to say, "Believe in yourself and the world will be at your feet." You don't need to have any ambition for world domination to feel the power of that statement. He is not talking about regular self-confidence; he is talking about having *faith* in yourself and absolute trust in yourself. This is the kind of faith that moves mountains.

"Never Zero is the fuel of willpower"

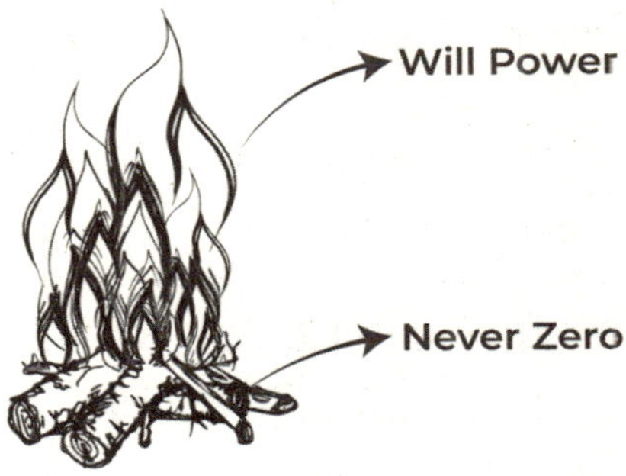

But how can you believe in yourself if you keep breaking your promises to yourself?

At the end of the day, self-discipline is much more than achieving your goals—that is just its training ground. Self-discipline, *mindful* self-discipline, is about developing this type of inner strength and power. Yes, with it you can achieve great things; but this, in itself, is already its own reward.

Don't let your personal fire die out through excuses, exceptions, and mood fluctuations. Let it be that, at least in one area of your life, for a small period of time, your willpower is absolute and knows no exceptions. Burn brighter.

Draw the line that you will not cross. And then don't cross it, *no matter what*. This is integrity. This is willpower. This is Mindful Self-Discipline.

Share this concept:
MindfulSelfDiscipline.com/never-zero

KEY POINTS

Motivation

- Motivation is important, but not enough. You need to rely on commitment, not motivation, because motivation is a feeling. It fluctuates.
- Don't expect it to "feel right". Act despite motivation.

Never Zero

- Create *Never Zero* commitments around your key habit(s), one at a time.
- A *Never Zero* commitment is timely, small, and uncompromising.
    - Timely: Decide a start date, and the length of the commitment. It could be lifetime if it's about an essential habit or if it's a commitment to break an addiction.
    - Small: Choose the minimum action, follow the Baby Steps concept, and stick to it no matter what. Don't be overly ambitious in the beginning.
    - Uncompromising: There are no acceptable excuses to skip. This may feel scary, because it's powerful and unapologetic.
- *Never Zero* commitments not only change your life, but they also build great self-confidence and willpower. This inner strength is its own reward.

You now know exactly what to do, how to do it, and why. So commit to take a step toward your goal *every day*. Do this now, before you read another page. This will change your life.

> "From this day onward, I commit to __________ every __________, no matter what."

Done?

CHAPTER 32

THE BIG PICTURE OF *ACTION*

In the Action Pillar, you started by designing an action plan for your aspirations. You created **milestones**, chose specific **habits**, and prepared all you needed to start your journey. You saw the need for regular **reviews** to make sure that you stay on track and that your strategy is still effective. (Step 1)

Then we went into the nitty-gritty of habit building, talking in depth about setting your **cue**, **action**, and **reward** (Steps 2 and 3). You learned how to choose effective cues, improve your environment so that your habits flow more easily, and have a minimum action that is your *no matter what* version of the habit. You saw that, for habit reinforcement, your brain needs to experience an immediate benefit as a reward for going through the effort, and that you can achieve that through intrinsic rewards (best type), extrinsic rewards (acceptable), or painful consequences (last resort).

In the Aspiration Pillar, we covered two obstacles of self-discipline: lack of motivation (no aspiration) and fear (self-sabotage). In the Awareness Pillar, you learned how to overcome three other obstacles of self-discipline: giving up, distractions, and excuses. Finally, in the Action Pillar, we covered the last three main obstacles: procrastination, doubts, and failures.

- Overcoming **procrastination** is about decreasing the pain of action via Baby Steps, increasing the pain of inaction through self-reflection, and learning to embrace the pain.
- Overcoming the three types of **doubts** requires you to either use the Not Now technique, use the Remove Your Options method, or to shift your perspective.

- Overcoming **failures** is about first preventing them by having a contingency plan; and, if not possible, failing gracefully with self-compassion, by using the ALFA Method.

The final chapter puts it all together, highlighting the need for commitment over motivation and inviting you to make a *Never Zero* commitment on your most important habit.

You now know what you want, and what to do next. You know how to overcome the different challenges that can come up on your path. You have learned the full framework of Mindful Self-Discipline. How will you use it to live your best life?

SELF-DISCIPLINE IN DAILY LIFE

CHAPTER 33

MINDFUL TIME MANAGEMENT

It is not enough to be busy… The question is:
what are we busy about?

Henry David Thoreau

Take care of the minutes, and the hours
will take care of themselves.

Lord Chesterfield

Time management is a misnomer;
the challenge is to manage ourselves.

Stephen Covey

The way you spend your time is the way you spend your life. So you need to manage it proactively in order to reflect your priorities and highest values. If you don't dedicate some of your *time* to your aspiration, it will never be actualized. It won't become real in the future—because you haven't made it real *right now*.

Mindful Self-Discipline is the art of spending your time in harmony with your highest goals and values. It's the art of living well and dying without regrets. For that purpose, developing awareness of how you spend your time is essential—that is the *mindful* element of time management.

If you have learned the first two pillars well, you have the foundation you need to manage your time well. Time prioritization and time awareness are the keys to *mindful time management*, and these two are expressions of the

Aspiration and Awareness pillars, respectively. They contain, in themselves, many of the classical principles of time management.

Mindful Time Management

- **Time Prioritization** (Aspiration Pillar)
  - Planning
  - Boundaries
- **Time Awareness** (Awareness Pillar)
  - Awareness
  - Focus

Take a moment now to ask yourself: How satisfied are you with the way you're currently spending your time? At the end of each day, as you look back and see how you've spent your life that day—are you happy with it? If you are, that's a fulfilling life; if not, it may build up to regret and frustration.

To make good use of your time, you need to be purposeful about it. That involves planning, setting boundaries, being more aware, and creating an environment for focus. In other words, creating structure (routine), and maintaining it. This is the theme of this chapter.

Time management is a big subject—one that has been the topic of many books. I will not attempt to address the whole topic here, but I will introduce some core principles, and then cover the overlaps between time management and awareness—what I call *mindful time management*. If you want more nitty-gritty details and a more elaborate time management system than what is presented in this chapter, I highly recommend you study David Allen's *Getting Things Done*.

Before we talk about the four core principles of *mindful time management*, however, a quick word on priorities.

CLARIFY YOUR PRIORITIES

Either you run the day, or the day runs you.

JIM ROHN

Work, family, self-care, health, friends, relationship, purpose, finances—we have a lot to juggle. The more roles you play in life, the more projects and commitments you embrace, the more goals you are pursuing at the same time—the harder it gets. Your time and energy are divided among so many things that you feel overwhelmed, and at times cannot give each thing the attention it deserves. It feels frustrating.

The first thing to do, then, is to simplify your life. In a way, to be more pragmatic, and don't assume that you can achieve everything at the same time. We all need to learn to respect our time and energy limits. To further explore this topic, I recommend you read *Essentialism* by Greg McKeown. It's one of my favorite self-development books.

If you want to create more space for your aspiration(s), you will need to give up certain things. As we covered in Chapter 13, you will need to make a sacrifice, letting go of things of lesser value for your aspirations—for example, letting go of spending an hour on social media every day so that you can instead dedicate that time to an activity that promotes your goal. If, as an experiment, you let go of half of your activities, you will discover a startling fact: the other half gets double the energy and attention. You will progress much more quickly in the half that remained—and also derive much more satisfaction from it.

This is time prioritization: you increase the amount of time and energy dedicated to activities that promote your goals and values, and diminish the time and energy you allocate to everything else—or perhaps even omit a bunch of activities altogether. You make these decisions using your core values and goals as a compass, as you learned in the Aspiration Pillar.

Regardless of how well you are able to follow the guideline of simplicity and sacrifice, you will *still* have to juggle a few different things in your life. Which means that you will need to master the four elements of mindful time management. The more complex your life is, the more you'll need these skills.

Share this concept:

MindfulSelfDiscipline.com/clarify-your-priorities

ELEMENT #1: PLANNING

Productivity is never an accident.
It is always the result of a commitment to excellence,
intelligent planning, and focused effort.

PAUL J. MEYER

If you don't plan your time,
someone else will help you waste it.

ZIG ZIGLAR

Planning how you will spend your time enables you to live more by design, and makes sure that all of the important things get covered every day. Not planning, on the other hand, means that you will live more reactively—you are much more likely to be distracted, fragment your attention across many (apparently) urgent tasks, be constantly interrupted, and feel more tired at the end of the day.

There are two types of time planning: fixed and flexible. In the fixed version, you plan once and rarely touch it—for example, your morning and night routines (Chapter 35). The rest of this section is about the other type, flexible planning, which changes from day to day.

To effectively plan how you will spend your time, you will need to dedicate a few minutes at the start of each day—or on the night before—to decide what are the most important things you need to do that day, how you will keep them a priority, and what you can do to make your day run more smoothly. Let's now dive into each of these three.

Reflection #1: What are my priorities today?

In living the self-disciplined life, your goals and aspirations will be your ongoing priorities—they will be present in your schedule every day, in one form or another. But there will likely also be other priorities in your life that will vary from day to day. Besides, within each area of your life, you will also have to prioritize among the various competing activities.

Here are three questions you can use to clarify your priorities every morning:

- *What will I do to advance my aspirations today?*
- *What are the three most important tasks I want to complete today?*
- *What task, if completed, will most contribute to my wellbeing?*

If you are currently working toward more than one aspiration, then choose (at least) one task for each. They don't need to be huge, but it is highly desirable that they are there in your day, seven days a week. It could be doing 10 minutes of reading, or making a phone call, or choosing to eat salad and skip the dessert. Don't let a day pass without you taking a step forward toward your aspirations.

As to the second question, there are different frameworks you can use to decide on your most important tasks. Stephen Covey, in his classic *The 7 Habits of Highly Effective People*, talks about the First Things First principle, and classifies activities into four quadrants based on their urgency and importance. Here is my reading of it:

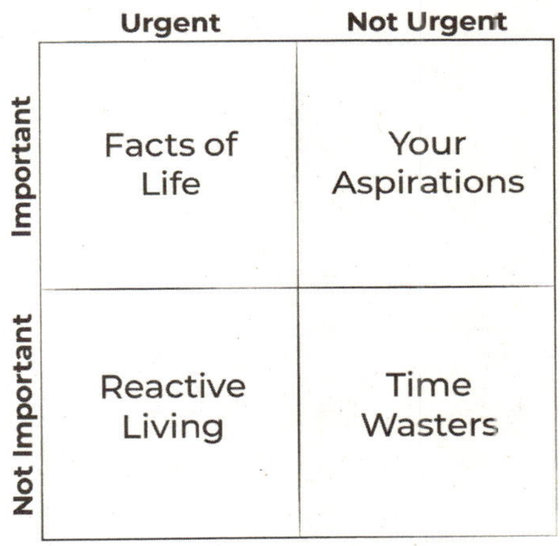

You might find it useful to apply this classification to your list of tasks and activities, in order to gain clarity. Your priorities for the day will almost always come from the first row.

Another way to answer this question is to apply the 80/20 rule, also known as the Pareto's Principle. This principle says that 80% of your results come from 20% of your activities. What you need to do, then, is identify what are those 20% of activities that bring the most results, and make them your priority. This works in all areas of life—work, relationships, hobbies, and even spirituality.

The third question is often not considered when people talk about priorities and time management. Since we are talking about *mindful* self-discipline, it makes sense that you also need to consider the impact that certain tasks, if not tackled, will have on your wellbeing. Perhaps a given task is not as important as others in your to-do list, nor as urgent, but it's a sticky thought in your mind that won't let you focus wholeheartedly on anything else until you complete that task. It might be a good idea to make it a priority today.

Reflection #2: How will I keep my priorities today?

After you decide *what* you need to prioritize, it's time to consider *how* you will do it. Here are the questions you can use for this purpose:

- *What will I need to skip, postpone, or delegate in order to focus on my priorities?*
- *What distractions and interruptions will likely happen, and how will I deal with them?*
- *How can I make sure that my priority tasks will get done?*

The first question helps you to decide what will *not* get done. Being clear on that means that you will feel less overwhelmed. This frees up headspace to focus on your chosen priorities for the day.

The second question is about anticipating challenges and deciding beforehand how you will tackle them if they arise. This is something most people don't consider, and it's the cause of much frustration. (See *Contingency Plan*, Chapter 30.)

For example, what happens if one of your tasks, which was supposed to take thirty minutes, takes two hours? What happens if you arrive late at work? What happens if you feel very tired and demotivated? What happens if somebody asks you for help with their own projects and priorities? Or if the person who was supposed to contribute didn't do their part? What will you do if you get constantly distracted or interrupted? You need to know how to respond to each possible challenge, otherwise the pressures of the moment may influence you to make a decision that you will later regret.

You might need to let other people know that you will be unavailable during certain times of the day. You might need to put your phone in airplane mode so there are no distractions. You might need to allocate more time to a particular activity or arrive at work earlier. You might need to decide to do the hardest things earlier in the day, when you have more mental energy available—a technique known as "eating the frog".

Eat a live frog first thing in the morning, and nothing worse will happen to you the rest of the day.

Mark Twain

Planning doesn't mean that things will happen according to your expectations; they very often will not. But it does skew reality in your favor and increases your chances of successfully completing your tasks.

The third question, "How can I make sure that my priority tasks will get done?" is all about budgeting your time, and then respecting the time slots you have allocated to each task. This could mean, for example, deciding that today you only have one hour to spend on email and admin tasks; once that hour is done, you stop and move on to something else—even if there are still pending emails waiting for you. For time budgeting, your calendar and alarm clocks are your best friends. Make use of them and respect their notifications (more about this in *Element #3: Awareness*).

By allocating a time budget to different activities and goals, you are making sure that all areas of your work and personal life get due attention, without taking time away from other priority tasks of your day.

In my night routine, spending two hours of quality time with my wife and daughter is a priority for me; but so is getting to sleep on time (otherwise my precious morning routine can get out of whack). That means that if we decide to watch a two-hour movie one hour into my family time, then one of two things will happen: either we will continue the other half tomorrow, or they will finish watching it that night without me. That is because I am aware of my time budgets, and getting to sleep on time is a priority for me.

Knowing and respecting your time slots will allow you to attend to all the different areas of your life, according to your priorities, while still feeling in control of your schedule.

Reflection #3: How can I make things run more smoothly today?

As you are planning for your day today, consider: is stress possibly booked into my day? If it is, you might want to find a way to remove it by making some simple changes.

The first one is by looking for a possible *clash of schedules*. Do you have overlapping meetings? Do you need to be in two places at the same time? Do you need to cram a one-hour meeting into forty minutes so you are not late for the next item on your list? Do you need to multitask three different activities just to stay on top of your schedule? If so, you are expecting too much from yourself, or you have underestimated the tasks—both of which result in frustration more often than not.

See if there is anything you can do to simplify things. That may involve rescheduling certain appointments, delegating tasks, postponing something, or deciding that some things are just not worth the effort. Knowing your priorities helps you decide what to keep and what to let go.

The second change you can make to help your day run smoother is to *schedule breaks and down time*. This means including space in your day for rest, pause, and self-care. If you struggle to do that because you are a type-A personality wanting to make the most use of every minute (welcome to the club!), then force yourself to go slower by scheduling in about 10-20% more time than you think each task will demand. Assume that things will take longer than you expect them to, so you include a buffer.

When you get a minute of down time here and there, you don't need to unlock your phone. It's okay to also just *be*. To just *breathe*. To just *do nothing*. Slowing down like this is an important part of Mindful Self-Discipline—it keeps your mind clear, replenishes your willpower and awareness, and helps you stay focused on what is most important.

The third change is to remove friction from your activities as much as possible, by streamlining your processes. Rory Vaden, in his TEDx talk *How to Multiply Your Time*, talks about "giving yourself the emotional permission to spend time on things today that will give you more time tomorrow".

This could mean spending an afternoon finding and migrating to a better calendar app, so that all the future work of scheduling appointments and checking for conflicts happens more smoothly. It could mean, to use Vaden's example, spending two hours to setup online payment for your bills so that you save a little bit of time every month when making payments. It could mean finding a better pair of running shoes, or a better meditation cushion, so that every minute of your effort in those activities is more pleasant and effective. It could even mean cleaning your office, changing where you eat, or getting a new nanny.

Removing friction and clutter is a more long-term strategy and doesn't often feel like a priority (it's not really important nor urgent). But it will make your life easier. It might even multiply your time or the output of your efforts.

Plan Your Time (Summary)

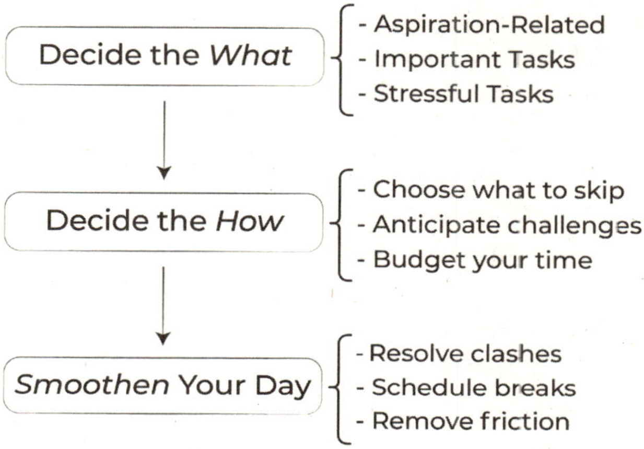

Share this concept:
MindfulSelfDiscipline.com/time-planning

ELEMENT #2: BOUNDARIES

Your time is limited, so don't waste it living someone else's life.

STEVE JOBS

You may create the best schedule in the world, but if you don't follow through, all you have is just a wish list. It is essential, then, that you protect your time from other people's demands, and this is what this second element is about. Unlike money, time is a non-renewable resource. It's the stuff life is made of!

Protecting your time requires observing the simple—and yet often challenging—discipline of saying *no*. Saying *no* to other people offloading their responsibilities onto you. Saying *no* to meaningless meetings and needless tasks. Saying *no* to answering a phone call during your exercise time, or checking emails while at a family dinner. Saying *no* even to some good things that come at the wrong time.

Every decision has a cost. Every decision matters. Every decision is either a +1 or a -1 in your life. Oftentimes, saying *yes* to a request is saying *no* to your aspiration. So don't be afraid to say *no*. Saying *no* keeps you in control; it allows you to live your best life, show up as your best self, and decide what things really matter to you.

If you can't say *no* to others, you can't be disciplined—because you are not in control of your time and energy. As a result, you can't be effective in your tasks, and you can't live a life of authenticity. You unconsciously relinquish your priorities and gravitate toward other people's. The end result is often regret for missed opportunities, frustration for lack of progress, and resentment for unreciprocated kindness.

Saying *no* is that important. So commit to learning this important skill. Practice saying *no* in a graceful yet assertive way. This often requires separating your decision from the relationship with the person asking for your time. You are saying no to the *request*, not the person. It is not a rejection of that person, but of a commitment.

The author of the book *Essentialism* recommends the following scripts for saying no:

- *"I'm afraid I don't have the bandwidth"*
- *"Sorry, I'm overcommitted at the moment"*
- *"I'm going to pass on this"*
- *"Not now, but maybe later"*
- *"I can't do X, but you might want to try Y"*
- (At work) "*Yes, I can make this a priority. Which of these other projects should I de-prioritize for that?*"

If you are bold, you can even try this: when a request comes your way, remain silent for several seconds. Almost always the other person then fills in the gap, giving you an easy way out: "I mean, just if you have nothing to do, if not it's okay, I know you're busy…"

Saying *no* is not selfish. In a society obsessed with fitting in, with people pleasing, saying *no* to other people's requests for your time—when not in line with your goals or values—is a great gift you give to others. Every time you say *no* like that, you give them permission to be equally focused and purposeful. You normalize freedom and personal space. You help create a culture of authenticity.

Share this concept:
MindfulSelfDiscipline.com/time-boundaries

ELEMENT #3: AWARENESS

This is the key to time management: to see the value of every moment.

MENACHEM MENDEL SCHNEERSON

In Element #2 you learned how to protect your time from other people's demands; now let's talk about how to protect your schedule from your own monkey-mind, with its forgetfulness and distractions. Almost everyone struggles with this to some extent. If you have ADD (Attention Deficit Disorder), you struggle with this even more.

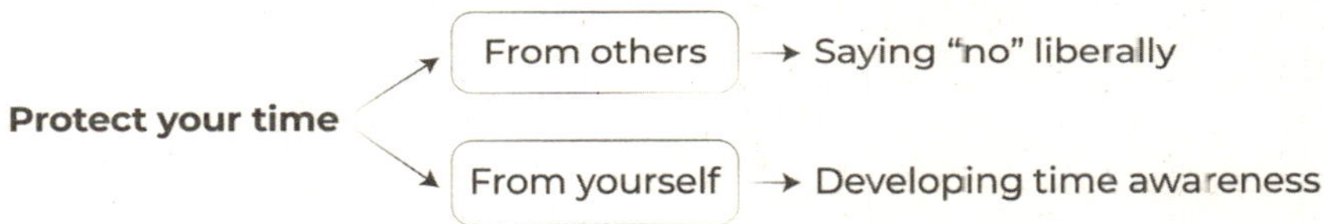

You can't follow your schedule if you forget your schedule, or if you get distracted with something else. So effective time management—*mindful* time management—requires constant time awareness. The way to practice this is to always *watch your time*; to pay attention to time, to be aware of time. And for this, you make your calendar and your watch your best allies: check them multiple times a day to make sure you stay on track.

For example, if you have scheduled a twenty-minute break in the middle of your afternoon, *watching your time* means that when you begin the break you *know* that you only have twenty minutes; you thus decide on how to spend your time during that break accordingly. It means that you are checking the time constantly, to make sure you don't go beyond the limits you have set for yourself; or you start a countdown timer at the beginning of your break. It means that you are aware that, after twenty minutes, you need to be doing something else.

Without this type of awareness, the monkey-mind will make a mess out of your schedule. It will say something like:

- I'll just *quickly* check my email and then get back to writing
- I'll snooze *just this time*
- I'll take a break for *ten minutes* and then resume my work
- I'll just finish this *five-minute* task, then I'll get ready for the gym

- I'll check Instagram for a *few minutes* and then I'll go to bed
- I'll just watch *one episode*
- I can take a few more minutes and I'm sure I'll still be there on time

When this happens, how likely is it for you to stick to your plan? If you are like most people, not very.

In the technique of Shift Your Focus (Chapter 18), we spoke about the need to realize the long-term costs of small decisions. Time awareness is a practical application of this. We all know that these apparently inconsequential decisions usually involve much longer time commitments than it seems. To be fully aware of the consequences of certain decisions, you need to become acutely aware of the time they will take.

Time Awareness

Many people talk about time management without talking about time awareness. However, self-discipline becomes really difficult without time awareness, and following a routine becomes a frustrating pursuit.

I've had several self-discipline clients who struggled to follow even a simple routine. After some time working together, they come to a point where they are consistently following a somewhat elaborate routine. One of these clients once told me, "It's like you have installed this program in my brain that helps me be constantly aware of time, thinking of my next steps and how to be ready for it." They had to track their activities against a fixed schedule that represented their priorities, and they knew that they would be asked about it in every session, as we zoomed in to what happened in the past week, day after day.

This is the power of developing time awareness. Without it, you simply can't follow a schedule. And if you can't follow a schedule, you can't guarantee that your priorities will be respected—and your aspirations, honored.

If you don't pay attention to how you spend your money, you'll run out of it, and live in debt. If you don't pay attention to how you spend your time, you'll also run out of it, and live in regret. You will need to pay it back sooner or later—often with interest in the form of the emotional pain of delayed projects, self-criticism, and overwhelm. You cannot endlessly borrow time against your future self with impunity.

Time awareness enables you to always be a step ahead. You are aware of what comes next on your schedule, and you know what you need to do to be ready for it. You are aware of what you are supposed to be doing right now, and how much time you have left in your current time slot. You don't go overboard. You don't start a two-hour movie an hour before your desired sleep time.

No, you don't need to live every minute of your life like this. That would not be balanced nor desirable. But, if you are like most people, chances are that you can greatly benefit from being a bit more purposeful about how you spend your time.

When you are mindful of how long each activity takes, and accept the natural limitations of time, then you are able to make better decisions about how to spend your day, and you will feel less overwhelmed.

Be aware of time. It's the stuff your life is made of.

Practical Considerations

Developing time awareness is about developing the habit to constantly check the time, consider the amount of time each activity might take, and be aware of what comes next on your schedule.

One thing you can do to help develop this habit is to put your schedule on a spreadsheet, and daily mark on it what you have done or not, and the time you started each activity. Then review it at the end of the day, and again at the end of the week. Notice the patterns. This will help you develop time awareness pretty quickly. It will also help you become better at estimating how long each activity takes.

I know, keeping track of time is boring. Perhaps even extremely boring—but important nevertheless. **What doesn't get measured doesn't get managed.** There is no time management without time awareness. And since time is life, not making good use of your time leads to the feeling of regret, of not actualizing your aspirations (which is the ultimate consequence of a lack of self-discipline).

Another thing that can help is when starting a break—or a type of activity that usually sucks your time—turn on a countdown timer on your phone for the desired amount of time you wish to allocate to this activity. Make sure that the volume is loud enough that it won't be ignored. You can also leave your phone several steps away from you, to prevent yourself from automatically snoozing the timer. That will help you break the pattern of mindlessly wasting time, and will give your rational brain the opportunity to kick in and remind you of your goals and schedule.

Share this concept: **MindfulSelfDiscipline.com/time-awareness**

ELEMENT #4: FOCUS

The successful warrior is the average man,
with laser-like focus.

BRUCE LEE

If you plan your time, protect your time, and monitor your time, you will then have a solid routine. You will show up on time to the tasks that you have chosen for yourself, and respect the boundaries of each time block. You will go through the motions, yet you may still not feel that you are making the best use of your time.

The final piece of the puzzle is about the quality and effectiveness of each of your activities. For you to get the most out of each activity, you need to be *focused*—which means doing one thing at a time, without constant interruptions and changes of direction. It means to be fully present and engaged in each activity, rather than just doing it mechanically. Don't let it just be an item in your to-do list that you are eager to tick off and move on. Make it count.

Being 100% present with what you are doing brings a whole new quality to your activity. You become more effective. You enter a state of flow more easily. You feel more connected with the activity, and more satisfied at the end.

The biggest enemy of our focus, in modern life, is arguably the internet. Or, rather, the *mindless* use of the internet. This happens when, instead of using our devices as tools that support our life, we use them as tools for distraction. Our devices then constantly pull us away from the task of the present moment by means of notifications, messages, sounds, and the luring temptation of a quick dopamine rush just a tap away.

Developing focus is one of the main benefits of having a regular meditation practice; and, just as in the meditation session, focusing means keeping your attention where you want it to be, for prolonged periods of time, and "snoozing" the distractions that come up. This is similar to the Not Now technique (Chapter 29).

Snooze Distraction

The key element to overcome the challenge of distraction is awareness. When you are focused and a distraction comes up, you have the option to indulge in it or not. Every time you indulge in it, you are training your mind to be scattered; every time you refrain from it, you are training your mind to be disciplined. The problem is that we are often unaware of these daily choices, and just mindlessly go from one shiny object to the next.

Let's illustrate this with an example. Suppose you are doing important research for a project, be it personal or work-related. Then one of the following things happens:

- Your phone dings and flashes with the notification of a new email—will you take a "quick peek" or will you remain focused?
- You get a phone call from a family member—will you pick it up for a quick chat or will you remain focused?
- You see an ad on your favorite search engine promoting the new-effortless-way-to-achieve-your-goal-for-only-one-dollar—will you click or will you remain focused?
- An interesting idea about an unrelated project pops up in your head—will you stop what you are doing and jump into that, or will you leave it for later and remain focused?
- You suddenly remember a delicious food item you have in the fridge—will you walk to the kitchen for a quick snack, or will you remain focused?

You *always* have the choice to remain focused and disciplined; but you are not always aware of it. And when you are not aware of it, you can't choose it.

Know that you have the power to *snooze* every distraction. You may not be able to do it every time—at least not yet—but having a clear intention to do so will help. A lot.

It also helps to make your physical and digital environment more focus-friendly by removing all possible distractions. This could mean cleaning up your desk, turning off phone notifications, working out in the basement of your home where there's no Wi-Fi, turning off the TV while talking to your partner, etc. You may have strong willpower to resist temptations but, if possible, it is often better to just not have them around, so you can save the cognitive cost of registering them just to then go and ignore them.

Practice Focused Work

A simple way to implement this concept of *snoozing distractions* is by working in short, focused batches of time—something that Francesco Cirillo in the late 1980s called "the Pomodoro technique". In his version of this method, you set a timer for twenty-five minutes, and for that period of time you work with absolute focus on a single task, without distractions and without multitasking. Then you take a five-minute break.

The Pomodoro technique is a great start if you struggle a lot with distraction. But please don't stop there. We are capable of much more than twenty-five minutes of undistracted work. There is no reason why you shouldn't be able to follow the same principle for one or two hours. You'll get there with practice.

In any case, the principle is the same: make a resolution to stick with one task until it's done. Then stick to it until it's done. In the meantime, snooze whatever distractions come. You can either commit to a specific task (e.g., "write a thousand words"), regardless of how long it takes, or commit to a time period (e.g., "write for an hour"), regardless of how much actually gets done. The latter is easier and more schedule-friendly. It is what I personally follow.

If you are going with the time commitment approach, decide how long you will spend fully focused on that single task, then turn on a countdown timer on your phone and work exclusively on that project until the timer goes off. Protect your time from all internal and external distractions and stick to your activity.

While the timer is running, do nothing except the task you have decided to focus on. It doesn't matter how small is the period of time you decided to start with—but only that you follow the *exclusive focus* rule with no exceptions. Be inflexible with all distractions and interruptions—this is the only way this is going to work. Of course, if there is a risk of something bad happening there and then if you don't act immediately, then you can make an exception; otherwise, no distractions or interruptions are allowed.

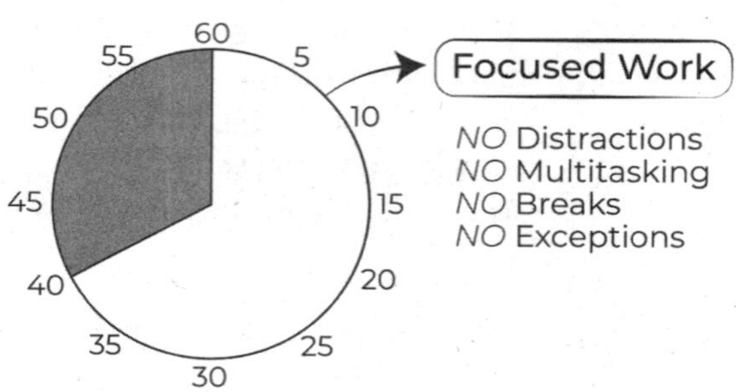

What happens to all the things that you've snoozed during your focused work time? It is important to allocate some time in your day to catch up with all those small tasks, ideally all at once. Bundle together all the small interruptions, all the one-minute things, all the fragmented attention activities and fake urgencies. Tackle it all in a fifteen- or thirty-minute slot of time, once or twice a day. This allows you to be unconcerned about those shallow tasks at all other times, and not let them interrupt your flow during your other activities.

In my own life, after two hours of focused writing work early in the morning, I go and tackle all the admin tasks and small errands—what author Cal Newport would call *shallow work*. After that I then close my Gmail tabs, and for the rest of the day I'm again free to do more focused work. If, during focused work, I get ideas about other projects or remember stuff I have to do, I get these out of my mind by writing them down, and then immediately get back to my focused work. This works really well for me, and you might want to try something similar.

Once you become proficient in the techniques of focused work and snoozing distractions, then you can try something that no self-discipline newbie should ever dare: to welcome interruptions selectively. This is playing with fire, of course. You can do this when you are confident in your ability to control yourself and quickly get re-focused; and save it for interruptions that are worth it.

I was actually not planning to include the above paragraph in this book, but as I was writing this section, I got interrupted by my wife who needed quick help with something. (Yes, ironically the interruption happens when I'm writing about working without interruptions!) I was able to attend to her and quickly come back to my train of thought. However, even with all my meditation training, I would not expect to be able to always do this with impunity. And there was still a cognitive cost to that switch.

Bottom line: stick to strict rules for your *focused work* periods of time as much as possible—especially in the beginning. Again, it is not possible, nor balanced, to attempt to do this for all your waking hours; but you will find it especially useful when you need to do work that requires a lot of cognitive power, or if you tend to be easily distracted.

Avoid Multitasking

With our modern technology and fast-paced lifestyle, it is so tempting to multitask—it is easy, often pleasant, and it feels as if we're making progress. It can feel like we are getting more things done and staying ahead of our schedule. So we quickly glance at our notifications while in a meeting, talk on the phone while we eat a sandwich, check Twitter while watching a movie, and keep our inbox open while going through that boring research.

In truth, however, multitasking is a myth.

> *When people think they're multitasking, they're actually just switching from one task to another very rapidly. And every time they do, there's a cognitive cost.*
>
> EARL MILLER (NEUROSCIENTIST)

One study from the University of London showed that multitasking while performing cognitive tasks represented a drop of ten points in IQ—the same as if you had skipped a full night of sleep. Ouch!

Multitasking makes you less effective, not more effective. It trains your brain to stay on the surface of things. It prevents you from going into a state of flow, which is where your best work can come forward. It prevents you from being fully present and picking up all the non-verbal cues of the person you are talking to. It prevents you from focusing on your muscles while you are doing a leg-press at the gym—which means that your muscles are less engaged, and you are also more prone to get injured.

Every time you multitask, you make it harder for yourself to focus. The only thing you get by multitasking is training your brain to be better at scattered, superficial work. Focused work, like meditation, requires exclusive attention to a single thing—and the willingness to let go of everything else, at least for the time being.

Share this concept:
MindfulSelfDiscipline.com/time-focus

KEY POINTS

Intro

- Your time is your life. If you don't dedicate some of your *time* to your aspiration, it will never be actualized. Mindful Self-Discipline is the art of spending your time in harmony with your highest goals and values.
- Making good use of your time involves planning it, protecting it, and creating an environment for focus.
- Your first task is to simplify your life so that you feel less overwhelmed and scattered across different roles and commitments. This will require you to let go of things of lesser value for the sake of your aspirations.

Element #1: Planning

- There is planning that you do once and rarely touch (your fixed schedules such as your morning routine), and there is planning that you do daily (your flexible schedule).
- For the flexible schedule, you will need to dedicate a few minutes at the start of each day—or the night before—to decide what are the most important things you need to do that day, how you will keep them a priority, and what you can do to make your day run more smoothly.
- The first reflection for planning your time is, "What are my priorities today?" Consider your aspirations, your three most important tasks, and what tasks, if completed, will most contribute to your wellbeing.
- The second reflection is, "How will I keep my priorities today?" Think about what will not get done, how to avoid distractions and interruptions, and budget your time so you make sure your priorities get covered.
- The third reflection is, "How can I make things run more smoothly today?" This involves resolving clashes of schedule ahead of time, scheduling breaks and downtime, and removing friction from your activities.

Element #2: Boundaries

- Protecting your time requires observing the very simple—and yet often challenging—discipline of saying *no*.
- Every decision has a cost. Every decision matters. Oftentimes, saying *yes* to a request is saying *no* to your aspiration. If you can't say *no*, you can't be disciplined. Saying *no* keeps you in control.
- Separate the decision from the relationship with the person making the request. Say *no* assertively but graciously (see examples).
- Saying *no* is not selfish. In a society obsessed with fitting in and with people pleasing, saying *no* to others' requests for your time—when not in line with your goals or values—is a great gift you give to them. Every time you say *no* like that, you give them permission to be equally focused and purposeful.

Element #3: Awareness

- You can't follow your schedule if you forget your schedule or get distracted with something else. Effective time management requires constant time awareness. The way to practice this is to always *watch your time*.
- Make your calendar and your watch your best friends; check them multiple times a day to see if you are on track.
- Time awareness allows you to be ahead of what comes next on your schedule and know what you need to do to be ready for it. You are aware of what you are supposed to be doing now, and how much time you have left in your current time slot. You don't go overboard. You don't start a two-hour movie an hour before your desired sleep time.
- Consider using time-logging spreadsheets and countdown timers to help you develop time awareness.

Element #4: Focus

- Improve the quality of your activities by avoiding distractions and being wholeheartedly present. Meditation practice helps with this.

- The biggest obstacle for most of us is the mindless use of the internet and our devices. This happens when our devices cease to be used as tools that enhance our life, and instead function as tools of distraction—pulling us away from the task of the present moment through notifications, messages, etc.
- The key element to overcome the challenge of distraction is awareness. When you are focused, and a distraction comes up, you have the option to engage in that distraction or not. Every time you indulge in the distraction, you are training your mind to be scattered; every time you refuse it, you are training your mind to be disciplined.
- Know that you have the power to *snooze* distraction. You *always* have the choice to remain focused. You may not be able to do it every time—at least not yet—but having a clear intention to do it will help. A lot.
- Work in short, focused batches of time, during which you remain absolutely focused on a single task, with no distractions or multitasking allowed. You can start by using the Pomodoro protocol for this.
- Bundle all trivial tasks, interruptions, and small errands to be dealt with together, once or twice a day. Ignore them when they come up at other times during the day, or make note of them for later.

Implementation resources: Check out my up-to-date list of recommended apps for enhancing time awareness and focused time, at **MindfulSelfDiscipline.com/tools.**

You can also print the one-page summary of this chapter from the Workbook (**MindfulSelfDiscipline.com/workbook**).

CHAPTER 34

THE MORNING ROUTINE

If you win the morning, you win the day.

TIM FERRIS

For the purpose of self-discipline, fixed schedules are preferred because they are easier to follow, and involve less decision fatigue. Yet you can't make your whole day into a fixed routine; that's too inflexible, and potentially even stressful. But you will be missing out on a lot if you don't make at least part of your day inflexibly focused on your highest priorities. My recommendation is this: have a fixed morning routine and night routine, and be flexible with everything else.

Regardless of the area of life that you want to grow in, developing a good morning routine and night routine is an excellent idea. The way you start and end your day matters a lot—getting this part right will help you develop self-discipline for everything else. Master the first and the last hours of your day, and you will be well on your way to a disciplined life. You will feel more in control of your time, your moods, and your life.

Here are the principles for an ideal morning routine:

- Fixed start time
- Fixed length
- Structured
- Focused
- Achievable

ELEMENT #1: FIXED START TIME

Morning routines thrive on consistent beginnings and are killed by irregular wake-up times. In order to start your morning routine always on time, you need to wake up always on time. This means *never* pressing the snooze button. (Easier said than done, right?)

The snooze button is the biggest enemy of your morning routine—avoid it at all costs. Every time you press it, you delay achieving your goals, and de-prioritize your aspiration. Every time you press it, you weaken your willpower, and make it harder for yourself to be disciplined. Don't do it.

Here is an effective tip for always getting up on time: leave your phone several steps away from your bed, with the volume set too loud to be ignored. This way you force yourself to get out of bed and move before you can turn the alarm off. Once you turn it off, there is only one simple rule you need to remember: "Go to the bathroom, not back to bed." Move forward, not backward.

For waking up always at the same time, you will also need to go to sleep always at the same time. Otherwise, if sleep-deprived, your morning routine will feel like a drag; and your day, unproductive. So, in a way, the most important thing about your morning routine is your night routine (we'll cover that soon).

If you still struggle with waking up early, even after implementing these two tips for at least a month, then consider making the first activity of your day something exciting or enjoyable. And set a rule that you can *only* do that activity at *that* time of the day; so if you skip it, it's gone! If you snooze, you lose.

The pleasurable activity could be reading a few pages of your favorite book, enjoying your favorite tea, or anything that you would be willing to "pay the price" of waking up early to experience. This is a form of *temptation sequencing* (see Chapter 27).

ELEMENT #2: FIXED LENGTH

The amount of time you have available for your morning routine depends on several factors—such as the time you need to officially start your workday (or take care of your kids), and how early you are willing to wake up. Ideally, set aside at least thirty minutes for your morning routine. The important thing here is to budget enough time for the habits and tasks that will push your aspirations forward in a meaningful way.

For me, the first five hours of my day always look the same—starting with a cold shower and some stretches, then a *long* session of meditation, affirmations, and then a long session of writing or research. It's my favorite part of the day, and I wouldn't miss it for anything! In fact, I wrote this book during my morning routine.

Of course, I didn't start out like this, and it will probably sound extreme for most people. You definitely don't need to be this ambitious about your morning routine. But if you can get the first hour or two of your mornings to always be fixed and focused on your key habits, you will live more aligned with your values, and will make consistent progress with your goals. You may find it helpful to actually book this time in your calendar. This is useful because it prevents other things being scheduled at that time and serves as a daily reminder.

ELEMENT #3: STRUCTURED

Your morning routine needs to be structured—otherwise it's not a routine, but a wish list of activities. To have a structured morning routine, use a "divide and conquer" approach: you get your available time and divide it into time blocks, then assign a block to each activity. You then stack your activities back-to-back so that each one naturally follows the previous one.

Your morning routine needs to include the most important habits related to the two or three most important areas of your life. Treat your morning routine as your daily checklist of the things you need to tick every day to make sure that you are moving forward in what matters most to you.

For example, if your morning routine is from 6:00am to 7:30am, and your main goals are career growth, health and wellbeing, a possible structure for your morning routine could be:

- 6:00 —> Wake up and go to bathroom
- 6:10 —> Meditate (20 minutes)
- 6:30 —> Career-related reading (30 minutes)
- 7:00 —> Exercise: treadmill/pushups/kettle bells (10 minutes)
- 7:10 —> Shower and breakfast
- 7:30 —> Finish

In order to follow this structure effectively, I strongly recommend that you create an alarm on your phone for each of these time blocks. This will help you to not overspend your time in any given time block, and follow the routine as planned. Some people also find it helpful to have multiple hard copies of the routine to paste at different places around their home. This can be useful for the first couple of weeks, until it becomes second nature for you.

Even if the rest of your day is incredibly busy and hectic, having a morning routine guarantees that you are at least following three simple disciplines every day that will advance your goals (in this case, meditation, reading, and exercise). The routine above is just an example. The structure, the activities, and the size of each time block will be unique for every person.

ELEMENT #4: FOCUSED

For the morning routine to be effective, it needs to be focused. This means creating a distraction-free environment and approaching each activity wholeheartedly. This is an expression of the mindful time management element of *Focus* (Chapter 33).

The most important thing for creating a distraction-free environment is to ~~minimize~~ eliminate interruptions, especially digital ones. In other words: stay offline. Sleep with your phone on airplane mode, and stay offline until you have finished your morning routine. If you are like most people, this little shift alone will change your life! Try it for a week and see what happens.

The other aspect is to actively focus wholeheartedly on each habit. As you are going through your morning routine, treat each activity as if it's *the most important thing in the world* for you. At that time, it is. When you are running, your priority is to run—there is nothing else in the world you need to be doing or thinking about at that time. When you read, just read. When you meditate, just meditate. When you eat, just eat.

Be wholeheartedly present with whatever you are doing. This is also a practice of awareness. Don't worry, there will be time for you to get to the other things you need to do—that is why you have planned your day, so that everything that is important gets its turn. Keep your morning routine sacred, and you will get a lot from it.

ELEMENT #5: ACHIEVABLE

You don't need to be a master of self-discipline to be able to follow an effective morning routine. And you don't need a perfect morning routine. The perfect routine is meaningless if you can't follow it. It's more important to have an okay plan that you can actually follow than a perfect one that you can't. So make sure that your morning routine is achievable.

As we've covered before, the key to making things achievable is starting small. If you think you can do forty minutes of exercise every morning, start with twenty. If you would love to fit in seven different things in your morning routine, start with three. If you like the idea of keeping your first three hours of the day fixed, start with one or two. Make it easy on yourself. Don't overstretch your motivation. Grow gradually.

This also means that your morning routine may be five or six days a week, instead of seven. For several years, I had a different morning routine for weekdays and weekends, and that worked well for me in that phase of my life.

Now you know the five elements/principles needed to create a powerful morning routine, and make sure that you start every day by working on your aspirations.

Principles for The Morning Routine

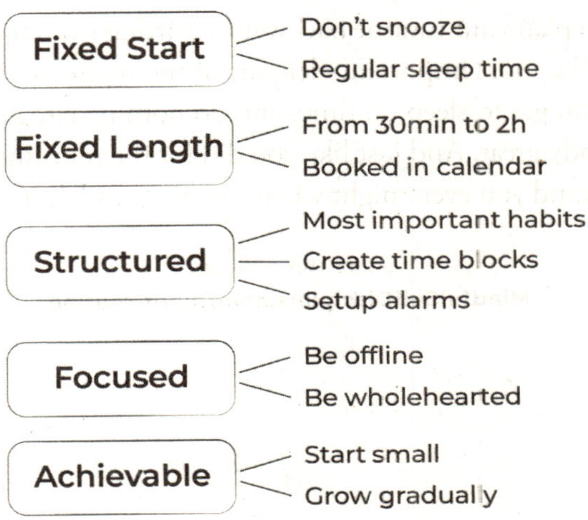

Share this concept:
MindfulSelfDiscipline.com/morning-routine

YOUR NIGHT ROUTINE

The night routine basically follows the same principles as the morning routine, but it has a slightly different purpose. While the morning routine is more focused on getting you ready for your day and checking the most important boxes in your life, the night routine is more about reviewing the day and winding down. It is also typically shorter than the morning routine.

Yes, there are people who are extremely disciplined and don't have a night routine. They work until the last minute before going to bed. This is also possible, and has its advantages, but it's not something I would generally recommend, given the theme of *balanced* self-discipline that we covered in Chapter 3.

Personally, at this phase in my life, my night routine is two and a half hours. The first two hours are family time, and the last half an hour is prepping for sleep, day review, and some affirmations or visualization. Within the family time slot, things are unstructured—I may be playing with my daughter, talking with my wife, watching a movie, or going for a walk. But family time itself always happens at the same time, and it is *focused* (I'm offline at that time).

For your night routine, decide what are the relaxation and winding down activities that make sense for you, the amount of time you wish to spend on them, and then plan your routine backwards, starting from the time you want to go to bed. The most important element of the night routine is your sleep time—if you can get to sleep on time, and do nothing else in your night routine, that's already great. And just like you did for the morning routine, set up an alarm to remind you every night when to start—and don't snooze it.

Share this concept:

MindfulSelfDiscipline.com/night-routine

KEY POINTS

- There are five core elements to a morning routine.
- The first one is that it has a *fixed start time*. Morning routines are killed by irregular wake up times. In order to start on time, you will need to always wake up on time. This means *never* pressing the snooze button, and having a regular sleep schedule.
- The second is having a *fixed length* (at least thirty minutes). Consider booking it on your calendar so it prevents other things being scheduled at that time and also serves as a daily reminder.
- The third element is *structure*. Divide your available time into time blocks, scheduled back to back, and assign one time block for each of your most important aspiration-related activities. Use alarms as reminders, and consider having a printed copy of your morning routine in each room of your home.
- The fourth element is *focus*. Have your phone in airplane mode so you are fully offline until you finish your morning routine. Be wholeheartedly focused on each habit, treating it as the most important thing in the world when you are performing it.
- Finally, your morning routine needs to be *achievable*. Initially, make it shorter than what you are able to do, so that it is easy to follow; then grow gradually. Consider having a different morning routine for weekends, or a day off from it.
- The night routine basically follows the same principles as the morning routine but has a slightly different purpose. While the morning routine is more focused on getting you ready for your day and checking the most important boxes in your life, the night routine is more about reviewing your day and winding down. It is also typically shorter than the morning routine. The most important element of the night routine is the time you go to sleep.

Implementation resources: print the one-page summary of this chapter from the Workbook (**MindfulSelfDiscipline.com/workbook**).

CHAPTER 35

SOCIAL INFLUENCES

Surround yourself with people who reflect who you want to be and how you want to feel. Energies are contagious.

RACHEL WOLCHIN

Show me your friends and I'll show you your future.

UNKNOWN AUTHOR

In the path, keep the company of those that are like you or higher. There is no place for the company of fools.

BUDDHA

When discussing the nature of willpower (Chapter 4), we saw that we cannot expect to not need to exercise willpower by just relying on the environment. Yet, as we covered, the environment is still very important. It is more difficult to exercise your willpower if you are sleep deprived, starving, or surrounded by the wrong influences. So while the right environment and life conditions cannot replace the need for self-discipline, they can make it easier or harder.

Let's now discuss four key changes that you can make in your lifestyle that can positively impact your self-discipline. This chapter focuses on the element that most directly affects your mindset and moods: the people in your life and your influencers. The next chapter will focus on the other three elements: sleep, food, and exercise.

REVIEW YOUR INFLUENCERS

We are profoundly influenced by the people we spend time with. Several studies in social sciences show how much we affect each other—consciously and unconsciously. There is a deeply-ingrained programming in our brain to conform with social standards, so that we can be accepted, fit in with society, and thus increase our likelihood of survival. For that purpose, we tend to adopt the same goals, preferences, biases, habits, and narratives as the people we associate ourselves with, because they are seen as the norm. This often comes at the cost of sacrificing our authenticity and personal values.

Knowing that there is this strong gravity toward becoming like the people you associate yourself with, it is wise to choose those people very carefully. It is not only your circle of close friends that we are talking about, but everyone that you spend time with, learn from, watch, and talk to. Everyone who is able to plant an idea in your mind or influence your moods in any way is your influencer.

There is research showing that if your friend becomes obese, your risk of becoming obese increases considerably; that if your friends or family members get a divorce, you're more likely to get divorced too; and that students will increase their GPA if they share rooms with high-performing students. (See references at the end of the book.)

If you spend time with people who are lazy, chronically distracted and addicted to social media, you will tend to feel (unconsciously) that this is normal and okay. If your partner doesn't believe in you, you will tend to experience self-doubt as well. If the news and movies you watch feel depressing, you will tend to feel depressed. If most of the information you consume is junk, your mind will be full of junk. If nobody on your team really cares about the project, you are unlikely to be an exception for very long.

On the other hand, if you spend time with people who are honest, you tend to become more honest. If most of your friends practice meditation and self-discipline, you will be influenced to do the same. If your partner encourages your dreams, you'll naturally feel more self-confident. If the blogs and books you read are uplifting, you will be uplifted. If your colleagues take great care of their health, you will feel the pull to do the same.

Here is the key take away: surround yourself with people, books, mentors, and ideas that uplift you. Choose influences that affirm the identity you are trying to build. Hang out with those who are on the same journey or, even better, have successfully completed it. Be around those who have the qualities you want to own—this is the easiest way to develop them (see Chapter 38).

This is the *only* self-discipline shortcut I know of.

Exercise: Review Your Influencers

Who are your influencers? This is an important question, because these people will naturally affect you with their beliefs, emotions, and goals. This is difficult to prevent, even if you are extremely conscious of it.

Take a moment to make an inventory of the influences currently operating in your life. List the ten people you spend the most time with. You may have direct contact with them (person to person), or indirect contact with them. Indirect contact includes the authors you read, websites you regularly visit, TV programs you watch, and social media accounts you follow—all of these people also influence your ideas, beliefs, and choices.

Then ask yourself, for each one of them: how is this person influencing me? Do I feel more empowered or more disempowered after engaging with them? Do they feed my good habits and qualities, or my bad habits and qualities? Do I feel energized or demotivated after engaging with them?

Once you know the influence each person has in your life, it's all about asking yourself: "Do I want more of this, or less of this?" Then decide to spend more time with those who empower you to be who you want to become, and cut out or diminish contact with those who just make you better at getting -1s.

The fact is that some people don't want you to succeed. Not necessarily because they are evil (although that could be the case). Maybe they just envy you. Maybe your progress highlights their feelings of inadequacy. Maybe they think *they* don't deserve to go after certain goals, and they feel triggered that you dare try to get those things yourself. Maybe they just don't believe that your goal is worthy, good, or possible. They may even appear selfless and concerned, trying to dissuade you from following your dreams so that you "don't get hurt".

Whatever may be the reason, know that spending time with these types of people will make your self-discipline journey harder. ~~Avoid them at all costs~~. Avoid them if you can. Life is too short for us to spend energy listening to haters, critics, naysayers, narcissists, and fools.

Seek the company of those who push you forward. Those who celebrate your success. Those who help you find a solution to every problem, rather than a problem to every solution.

Don't be afraid to cut ties with people who constantly drag you down or push you in the wrong direction. Doing that is not being arrogant and selfish. It is not about thinking "I'm better than you". It is about self-respect and setting boundaries. It is simply recognizing that your values and mindsets don't match. This way you respect your own time, energy, and goals—as well as theirs.

Again, it is worth remembering one of the tenets of Mindful Self-Discipline: *be balanced.* Exposing yourself to *intelligent* criticism from those who have your best interests at heart is healthy. Spending time with *virtuous* people who stretch you and widen your worldview is healthy. Caring for the wellbeing of those who deeply disagree with you is healthy. Listening to those who make you hate yourself is not. Being in the company of those who discourage your higher values is not. Putting up with negative influences that drag you down is not.

Share this concept:
MindfulSelfDiscipline.com/review-your-influencers

GET ACCOUNTABILITY

Accountability is considered by many to be the holy grail of habit-building and self-discipline. I do agree that it's a powerful tool that everyone can make use of, yet I choose to cover this topic toward the end of the book. Why? Because I want you to be self-reliant. I want you to be a light unto yourself and depend on nobody. To be someone *others* can depend on for motivation, inspiration, and support. To be an example of Mindful Self-Discipline in this *world of distractions.*

By all means, do make use of accountability. The only thing I emphasize is that you make it a *supplement* to your practice of the three pillars, and not a replacement for it.

There are three types or levels of accountability. Let's go through them from least to most intense.

Modes of Accountability
- Community
- Partner
- Coach

Community

The first type of accountability is community, which taps into the power of social expectations. It means joining a group of individuals with similar goals or habits. People who want to stop drinking join Alcoholic Anonymous; people who want to get fit may join a gym or sport club; people who want to create a business may join an online entrepreneur community; people who want to meditate join a community of meditators.

When you are part of a community where everybody around you is on the same journey and doing the same types of things, it becomes much easier to remain motivated and to keep your aspirations alive. Those in the community who have already achieved the goal show you what's possible; those who haven't yet achieved it show you that it's okay to fail (temporarily), that the process takes time, and that you need to persevere.

Accountability Partner

The second type of accountability is having an accountability partner. Ideally, this person would be on the same journey as you are, or at least trying to build similar habits. It is also essential that this person is honest with themselves and uncompromising in his/her feedback to you. His/her goal should not be to be nice, but to be effective.

To work with an accountability partner, you begin by establishing guidelines for the mode and frequency of communication, as well as expectations on how to communicate feedback. Here is an example of such a protocol, and how you would communicate it to your partner:

> My goal is to run outside for half an hour every day; if not, to at least do my minimum action of ten minutes on the treadmill. I want to practice *Never Zero* on this goal, so there are no acceptable excuses for skipping. Every night I will send you a message saying whether I did the exercise or not, and for how long. Please always reply, even if with just an emoji, so that I know you are there and expecting my check-in.
>
> If I don't check in, please message me and ask what happened. If I start giving you excuses, remind me of my aspiration and why it's so important for me.

Your partner would then share their expectations of you as his/her accountability partner. You decide on a start date and then get to work! If you want to take this type of accountability to the next level, you can also use habit contracts, also known as Commitment Devices (see Chapter 22).

Coach

The third form of accountability is having a coach or mentor. This is the most powerful form of accountability, for a couple of reasons. First, because a self-discipline coach is a *professional accountability partner* who knows how to both challenge you and support you in effective ways. Second, because coaching usually involves considerable financial investment, and this act of "sacrifice"—your *offering*—further strengthens your commitment to your goal. You are then much more likely to succeed. I see this happening all the time with my clients.

Ambitious people, or those who are already on top of their fields, often use the help of coaches to accelerate their process in multiple ways. Harvey McKay, who authored seven *New York Times* bestsellers, had twenty coaches—a speech coach, a writing coach, a humor coach, etc. A good coach serves as a mirror for you to see yourself clearly and stay true to your ideals; he will constantly point out the negative scripts you are running, and proactively help you course correct.

Take a moment to think about which of the three forms of accountability would suit you best, considering your personality and the nature of your goals. If you resonate with my way of thinking and are interested in accountability coaching, you can learn more about my work in the *Work with Me* section at the end of the book.

Share this concept:

MindfulSelfDiscipline.com/accountability

TO SAY OR NOT TO SAY

Should you talk about your goals, or should you keep them secret?

Some authors recommend telling the world about your goal: talking about it on social media, and telling your friends and family what you are trying to achieve. The rationale is that this is a form of public accountability: you know that you will be asked about it in the future, and it could feel a bit uncomfortable to say you have given up, or not made any progress.

While this can work, there are also strong reasons to keep your plans secret. Derek Sivers, in his TED Talk *Keep Your Goals to Yourself*, argues that telling people about your goal makes you less likely to achieve it. Why? Because it gives you a premature sense of completeness. There is good science to back this up.

When you have a goal, there are a number of difficult steps that you need to take until you achieve it; in fact, there is a whole process ahead of you. Normally, you won't be able to enjoy that final psychological satisfaction that you are seeking until you actually accomplish your goal. But when you share it with others, or visualize yourself already having that goal achieved, part of your brain already produces that sense of satisfaction. This, in turn, drains your fuel for moving forward.

Your brain seeks satisfaction. If it gets that by distracting itself with instant gratification (Chapter 22), or by imagining the end state, there will be little motivation left to go through the pains of the journey. Why should you work hard to have something you already have?

So, what is the right approach? Sivers suggests sharing the pain of the process ("I will train hard and run five times a week"), rather than the excitement of the end result ("I will run a marathon"). This seems to strike a balance between the two approaches, allowing you to benefit both from public accountability and from delaying the gratification of social acknowledgement.

Another way to think about it is this: keep your goals secret and get accountability via a single accountability partner or a coach. This is how I personally do it. I rarely (if ever) mention my goals in public; rather, I make strong resolutions to myself, work in silence, and talk about it when I have achieved it. This works for me; but you may need a different strategy.

Now that you know the pros and cons of each, you are better equipped to choose what's best for you.

Share this concept:

MindfulSelfDiscipline.com/to-say-or-not-to-say

KEY POINTS

- We are profoundly influenced by the people we spend time with—consciously and unconsciously. We tend to adopt the same goals, preferences, biases, habits and narratives as the people we associate ourselves with, because we see them as the norm.
- Surround yourself with people, books, mentors, and ideas that uplift you. Choose influences that affirm the identity you are trying to build. Hang around those who have the qualities you want to own.
- Go through the *Review Your Influencers* exercise where you list all the people, books, sites, groups, shows, etc., that feed you ideas. See how they are influencing you, and ask yourself if you want more of that or less of that.
- Some people don't want you to succeed. Avoid their company and input.
- Get one or more forms of accountability to support you in pursuing your goals, by using a group, accountability partner, or a coach.
- Sharing your goals publicly can give you accountability, but potentially demotivates you by giving you a premature sense of completeness and satisfaction. So either keep your goals secret—and get accountability more privately—or share only the *process* of working toward your goal, not the end result.

Implementation resources: get the *Review Your Influencers* template in the Workbook (**MindfulSelfDiscipline.com/workbook**) to follow the exercise more easily.

CHAPTER 36

SUPPORTIVE LIFESTYLE

Small disciplines repeated with consistency every day lead to great achievements gained slowly over time.

JOHN C. MAXWELL

Take care of your body. It's the only place you have to live.

JIM ROHN

Sleep, food, and physical movement are essential elements for our physical health, performance, and psychological well-being. Having enough of them, and in high quality, makes everything else easier in life. Just like having the right influences in your life, this doesn't replace the practice of the three pillars of Mindful Self-Discipline, but it can enhance them.

For the sake of self-discipline, of these three lifestyle elements, sleep is arguably the most important. So let's start with this one, and go a bit deeper with it.

SLEEP

With less than enough sleep, the quality of our day, decisions, relationships, and well-being all suffer. It is a single problem, but it has many consequences in different areas of our life. Many of us are thus living at a suboptimal level due to insufficient sleep—like a mobile phone constantly in the red, in desperate need of a full recharge.

There are plenty of studies showing that lack of sleep decreases motivation, mental clarity, and willpower. It shortens your attention span, decreases your memory, and makes it harder for you to focus. It impairs decision-making and increases the risk of several health conditions and mood disorders. Sleep deprivation is also proven to increase cravings for food and cigarettes.

According to a study by the University of New South Wales (Sydney, Australia), "moderate sleep deprivation produces impairments in cognitive and motor performance equivalent to legally prescribed levels of alcohol intoxication". When you are sleep deprived your cells are less capable of absorbing glucose, which is the main source of energy for your brain; this, in turn, makes you feel under-fueled, irritable, and impatient. Lack of sleep was found to lead to mild prefrontal dysfunction, a state where your brain struggles to regulate your emotions and to sustain attention in any task.

This is certain: if you are sleep deprived, self-discipline will be much harder. You will more likely give in to temptations, seek distractions, and not have the resilience to persevere through difficulties in your path. If you don't get enough hours of sleep, or if your sleep quality is poor, then this is an area you need to work on, in order to make self-discipline easier. It's harder to be *mindful* when you are sleep deprived.

Many books have been written on the topic of improving sleep quality; yet here we have only a few pages to cover this, so let us focus on the essentials. There are three core elements needed for improving the quantity and quality of your sleep: relaxation, environment, and routine.

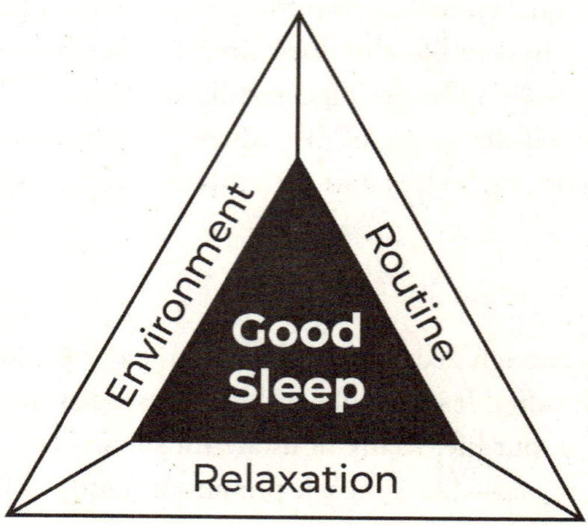

Sleep Element #1: Relaxation

Knowing how to relax is essential, because you cannot sleep well if your body is tense or if your mind is restless. So you need to learn how to relax your body and your mind before sleeping. Here is where meditation and other mind-body techniques are extremely useful.

Relaxing your body can be achieved through techniques such as yoga nidra meditation, alternate nostril breathing, and progressive muscle relaxation. For relaxing your mind, any style of meditation can be good, yet the following ones may be especially helpful: mantra meditation, inner silence, and trataka. Finally, the practices of gratitude journaling and brain dump can also help you get your mind in a relaxed state for better sleep.

Exploring these techniques one by one is beyond the scope of this book; but at least now you know their name and can seek to learn them on your own. There are also non-meditation activities that can help you relax before bed. Some examples are: listening to calming music, stretching, having aromatherapy with lavender oil, warming your hands and feet prior to sleep, and drinking certain types of tea (such as chamomile, valerian root, or passionflower).

The more you can relax your body and mind before bedtime, and the more you can manage your stress and anxiety throughout the day, the better your sleep will be.

Sleep Element #2: Environment

Your bedroom setup can help you fall asleep—and stay asleep—or it can be a hindrance. Here are some of the most important tips in creating a sleep-friendly environment:

- Make your room pitch dark
- Make your room temperature cool
- Make your room completely silent; if that is not possible, use ear plugs or white noise apps/soundtracks
- Don't work, watch TV, or use devices in your bedroom—associate being in your bedroom with rest
- Use a comfortable mattress, no more than nine or ten years old, ideally medium-firm

- Use a pillow that preserves the natural curvature of your neck (firmer is better); you can also try an orthopedic pillow
- Use a second pillow between or under your legs, for greater sleep comfort
- Avoid sleeping on your stomach; ideally sleep on your back or on your side
- Keep your pets out of your bedroom if they tend to wake you up in the middle of the night

Sleep Element #3: Routine

The third element for improving sleep is routine. This is about optimizing your activities and routine to improve your *circadian rhythm*.

The body likes consistency, and that is why it follows a circadian rhythm. This is the inner clock that tells the body when it's time to sleep, wake up, and eat. It affects our heart rate, body temperature, hormones and moods; it synchronizes our body with our environment, and it is at the center of many physiological systems in our body. The more stable and consistent your circadian rhythm is, the easier it will be for you to fall asleep, stay asleep, and wake up refreshed.

The most important factor in stabilizing your circadian rhythm is having **regular sleep and wake-up times**. This means going to sleep and waking up at roughly the same time every day—*even on the weekends!*

> *Nothing helps your circadian rhythms more than getting up and going to sleep at the same times every day.*
>
> Frank Lipman, M.D.

When you sleep and wake up at roughly the same time every day (even on the weekends), you help your body to have a healthier sleep pattern. Your body prepares to wake up one to two hours before you actually rise, and if it doesn't know when you should wake up, you'll have poor quality sleep. The same thing is true with getting to sleep: if your body doesn't know when you will sleep (because it's at a different time every day), it will not know when to prepare itself for it, so it will take longer to fall asleep.

The second important factor for stabilizing your circadian rhythm is

controlling your light exposure. The circadian rhythm is controlled mostly by light exposure. When we lived without electricity, our circadian rhythm was regular and stable: going to sleep and waking up with the sun. In our modern society, however, we often have dysregulated circadian rhythms due to exposure to artificial light and overstimulation at night.

As a result, your body gets confused about when it's time to sleep and when it's time to wake up. Your brain might be ready to shut down and go to sleep, but then you prevent it by staying up late, with lights on (from lamps or digital devices). Later, when you finally decide to fall asleep, you may have a hard time shutting down because you just told your brain some moments ago that "It's still daytime! Keep on working!".

For better sleep, you need to control light exposure in two ways: first, by avoiding blue light (produced by TVs, computers, tablets, and smartphones) an hour before bedtime; second, by getting some sunlight as soon as you wake up, and as much as possible during the day.

The third factor for good sleep is **avoiding overstimulation**. This includes no alcohol or caffeine six hours before sleep and avoiding physical exercise and heavy meals three hours before bed.

Sleep experts also recommend that it is wise to avoid the following an hour before sleep: smoking, heated discussions, mental stimulation, worrying, and drinking water. If you drink water or eat fruits an hour before bed, your sleep is likely to be interrupted by the need to visit the bathroom in the middle of the night.

Regular sleep and wake up times 7 days a week + Regulate light exposure (blue light and sun) + Avoid overstimulation before bed = Healthy Circadian Rhythm

NAPPING AND BREAKS

Having short naps during the day can be a good way to offset sleep debt and improve your wellbeing. They count as sleep and help replenish your mental energy for the rest of the day.

Just be mindful of the time you nap, so it doesn't interfere with your sleep routine. The general recommendation is to limit naps to the early afternoon and to not longer than thirty minutes.

On the other hand, keep in mind that the rest that your body and mind needs is not only achieved via sleep. Having breaks in your day, where you unplug completely and go for a walk, is also a way of getting rest and avoiding willpower fatigue. Likewise, going on a vacation, scheduling cheat days, or taking a break from a long project also count.

If you feel frustrated that you can't move forward; if you are overwhelmed, tired, or demotivated; if you feel your body and mind are not fully cooperating… don't give up. Have some rest. Sleep more tonight. Try again tomorrow.

Share this concept:
MindfulSelfDiscipline.com/quality-sleep

FOOD AND EXERCISE

The other two main variables in your lifestyle that can deeply affect your willpower and energy levels are food and physical movement. Eating well and exercising regularly are daily disciplines that make other disciplines easier. Yes, they do require some willpower, but keeping them going in your life also strengthens your willpower.

Personally, the food disciplines I follow are eating once a day (intermittent fasting), zero alcohol, no caffeine, and a vegetarian diet rich in fruits, plants, grains, and nuts. As for exercise, I do a mixture of martial arts and stretches for twenty to thirty minutes in the morning at home, at least four days a week. This work for me.

Having said that, these are not areas of expertise for me, so if you want to learn more you should look for specialized advice from experts in those topics. Here you will find just a couple of pointers as to the importance of these two elements, and what to look for.

Food

One of the key elements of diet, for the sake of cultivating willpower and self-discipline, is maintaining a stable level of blood glucose. This is done by eating food with a low glycemic index (the *what you eat approach*), or through intermittent fasting (the *when you eat approach*).

The glycemic index (GI) of a food item tells you how quickly that food is broken down into glucose, which then replenishes your system. The lower the GI, the more gradual the break-down process—meaning that there are no big spikes in glucose followed by rapid falls. With that, your energy and willpower become more stable and reliable.

Intermittent fasting is time-restricted eating. You get all your daily food intake in a small window of time and do a water-only fast for the rest of the day. The most common protocol is the 16:8, where you eat during an eight-hour window (e.g., from noon to 8pm) and fast for the other sixteen hours. Another common protocol is the 20:4, also known as OMAD (one meal a day), which is what I follow. Just like with eating a low glycemic diet, intermittent fasting also has the effect of stabilizing your blood sugar levels, since you are no longer getting spikes and falls every three hours.

Exercise

What is the importance of physical exercise for self-discipline?

It trains your willpower. It reduces fatigue, and in doing that it improves your self-control (which is negatively affected by fatigue). Exercise also increases the supply of oxygen and glucose to the brain and is known to increases the volume of the prefrontal cortex (which, as we saw, is the part of the brain responsible for self-discipline). Research shows that just a few months of regular exercise can already significantly improve your self-control and willpower—and that this translates to positive changes in emotional control and financial decisions as well.

Kelly McGonigal, PhD, in her book *The Willpower Instinct*, explains that regular exercise not only reduces temptation, but also relieves stress, and it's as powerful an antidepressant as Prozac. Physical exercise—like meditation—makes your brain bigger and faster; it increases your baseline heart rate variability, and has also been shown to improve your sleep.

Eating a healthy diet and exercising regularly will not automatically make you a master of self-discipline, but these habits will improve your willpower baseline and thus multiply the fruits of your efforts.

Share this concept:

MindfulSelfDiscipline.com/food-and-exercise

KEY POINTS

Good Sleep + Healthy Eating + Regular Exercise = Self-discipline gets easier

Sleep

- Lack of sleep leads to poorer decisions, more mood swings, decreased mental clarity, and weaker willpower. To make self-discipline easier, make sure you get enough quality sleep every night, or nap during the day to complement your sleep.
- There are three core elements to be mindful of for having great sleep: relaxation, environment, and routine.
- *Relaxation* involves using specific meditation techniques, as well as some calming activities, to bring your body and mind to a calm and tension-free state before sleep.
- *Environment* involves setting up your bedroom to help you fall asleep and stay asleep. The most important elements are having a pitch dark and fully silent room, not using devices in the bedroom, and having a good mattress and pillows.
- *Routine* is about optimizing your activities and schedule to improve your circadian rhythm. The most important things for this purpose are having regular sleep and wake up times, controlling light exposure, and avoiding overstimulation in the hours before sleep.

Food and Exercise

- Eating well and exercising regularly are daily disciplines that make other disciplines easier.
- Eating in a way that maintains a stable level of glucose in your blood is good for your willpower. You can achieve this by eating food with a low glycemic index, or through intermittent fasting.
- Regular physical exercise reduces fatigue, increases the supply of

oxygen and glucose to the brain, increases the volume of the pre-frontal cortex, and thus makes your willpower and self-control stronger.

Implementation resources: see a list of helpful sleep apps on **MindfulSelfDiscipline.com/tools**. Or, for a more thorough solution, check out my *Deep Sleep* course, which is part of the *Limitless Life* meditation program (**MindfulSelf-Discipline.com/limitless-life**).

GOING DEEPER

CHAPTER 37

MEDITATION: THE SELF-DISCIPLINE GYM

By effort and mindfulness, discipline and self-mastery,
let the wise one make for himself an island
which no flood can overwhelm.

Buddha

True freedom is impossible without a mind made free by discipline.

Mortimer J. Adler

Rule your mind or it will rule you.

Horace

Meditation is one of the best ways to train *awareness*. And awareness is at the core of Mindful Self-Discipline—because discipline starts in the mind. It starts with how you think and how you manage your emotions.

Meditation also trains your *willpower*—and this is something most people don't realize. In meditation you don't just sit and passively watch your mind; you also actively control your attention. You choose where you want to place your attention (e.g., your breathing or a mantra), make an effort to keep it there, and bring it back whenever it wanders into thoughts. That micro-exercise of self-control happens dozens of times whenever you sit to meditate, and it is thus great training for willpower.

Awareness (to *see*) and willpower (to *act*) are the two ingredients of Mindful Self-Discipline. Therefore, the more you practice meditation, the more you are able to practice self-discipline, because it trains them both. Meditation is the ultimate self-discipline gym.

Yes, you can find some extremely disciplined people who never had a formal meditation practice. How is that possible? They have taken another path and trained their awareness through relentless self-reflection and self-observation. Or they overcompensated lack of awareness through forcefulness and by sticking to supportive environments. They are, however, often unable to translate that self-discipline to other environments or areas of life.

Meditation is an easier path to self-discipline. It is less forceful and more direct. And it also brings with it several scientifically-proven benefits to your health, relationships, and wellbeing. When your physical and mental health improve as a result of regular meditation practice, your ability to be disciplined also improves. So meditation helps self-discipline both directly (by enhancing awareness and willpower) and also indirectly (by contributing to better health, mood, and energy levels).

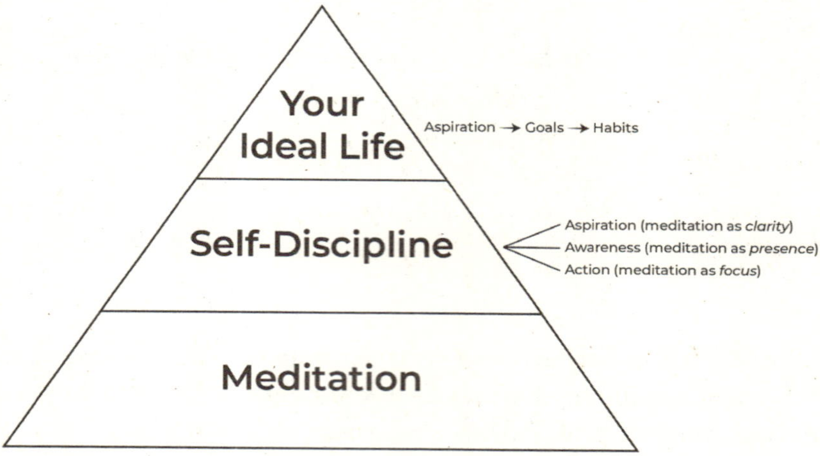

In the Awareness Pillar you learned a very simple meditation exercise (Chapter 16). Now we will dive deeper into the topic, so you understand better what meditation is, its benefits for self-discipline, and how to deepen your practice with the *Three Pillars of Meditation*. While a comprehensive presentation of the topic is beyond the scope of this book, the next few pages will equip you with the concepts you need to understand what you are doing, and know how to move forward from here.

Share this concept:
MindfulSelfDiscipline.com/the-self-discipline-gym

MEDITATION 101

Let's start by going through some of the basics such as what meditation is, and the different types of techniques.

Meditation is a mental exercise that involves *relaxation*, *awareness*, and *focus*. Meditation is to the mind what physical exercise is to the body. The practice is usually done individually, in a still, seated position, and with eyes closed—meditation thus often involves bodily *stillness*. But there are also ways to do walking meditation, and to integrate mindfulness into other activities (we could call this "dynamic stillness").

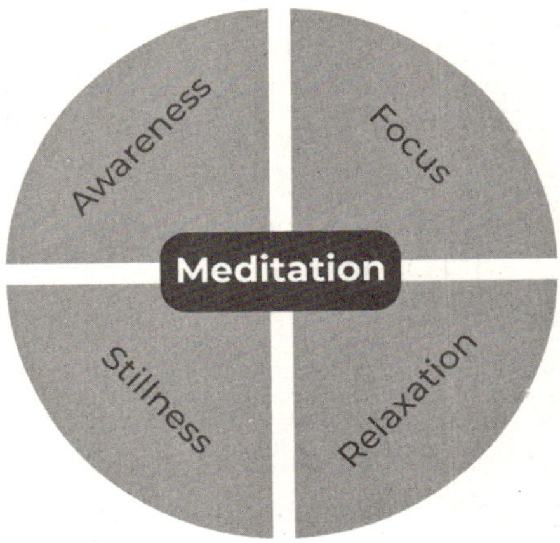

Meditation has similarities to other contemplative practices—such as affirmations, self-hypnosis, prayer, contemplation, and breathing exercises—but it is not the same thing.

Meditation originated in India, a very long time ago. The oldest documented evidence of the practice is from wall arts in the Indian subcontinent, from approximately 5,000 to 3,500 BCE, showing people seated in meditative postures with half-closed eyes. The oldest written mention of meditation is from 1,500 BCE in the Vedas. In the following centuries, all over the world, most of the spiritual and philosophical traditions of mankind developed their own forms of meditation.

The English word "meditate" actually means to think deeply about something. However, when Eastern contemplative practices were imported to Western culture, this is the term that was used to define them, for lack of a better word. Nowadays, meditation refers more to the exercise of focusing your attention than that of reflecting deeply.

For practicing meditation, you don't need to be religious, hold any special beliefs, or sit in an exotic, difficult pose. Meditation is not a selfish indulgence, nor an invitation to run away from life—quite the contrary, it is an essential practice to keep yourself healthy, sane, and well. Finally, meditation is for everybody, not only for calm people or for monks who can "empty their minds". You don't need to be a calm person in order to meditate, just like you don't need to be strong in order to go to the gym.

The Different Types of Meditation

There are hundreds of different styles of meditation. In general terms, however, we can classify them all into four categories, according to way we use our mind in the practice.

The first one is *concentration meditation* (known as "focused attention" in the scientific literature). This is the most commonly known and practiced style of meditation. You focus all of your attention on a single object, moment after moment—the attention is narrow and deep. The object chosen for the practice could be almost anything. The most commonly used ones are a physical sensation (breath), a sound (mantra), a feeling (e.g., loving-kindness meditation), a part of your body (e.g., *chakra* meditation), an image (visualization) or a physical object that you gaze upon (e.g., a candle flame).

The second more common type is *observation meditation* (known as "open monitoring" in the scientific literature). Here the attention is not focused on any particular object but monitors the panorama of the present-moment experience. You observe the different sensory inputs (sounds you hear, sensations in the body, etc.), and/or what is going on inside your mind (thoughts, feelings, memories, etc.). The attention is wide and shallow. Mindfulness, inner silence, and some styles of vipassana fall into this category.

The third category of meditation styles is *relaxation meditation.* In this type of practice, the goal is not necessarily to train your attention, but to arrive at a deep state of rest and relaxation. Yoga nidra and body scan are the most well-known techniques in this category.

Finally, there are meditation techniques that are *pure being* practices. Here you are not focusing nor observing, but just dropping everything and simply *being.* These are typically more advanced practices, not directly relevant to developing self-discipline. Styles that come here are the Chinese *zuowang*, the Buddhist meditations of *zazen* and *dzogchen*, and the nondual practice of self-enquiry.

For the sake of developing self-discipline, the meditation styles of concentration are the most important ones, and they develop both willpower and awareness. Relaxation meditation and observation meditation can also play a role in developing awareness and dissipating negative emotional states that would otherwise lead to unwanted indulgences.

Share this concept:
MindfulSelfDiscipline.com/meditation-101

MEDITATION AND PASSIVITY

Sometimes, goal-oriented individuals have a sense of aversion or disdain toward meditation practice. They feel that meditation is just about living in the moment, chilling out, and being happy with whatever you have here and now. They fear that meditation may make them slow, apathetic, or passive. They worry that meditation may rob them of their fuel to pursue their goals.

Obviously, my experience is that that is not the case—otherwise it would make no sense to talk about *mindful* self-discipline. Self-discipline is all about achieving goals and aspirations; and meditation, in this framework, is at the service of that. Of course, meditation will give you much more than just boosting your ability to achieve your goals; but it will *also* serve you in this, and very well.

Some people who practice meditation do become more passive in their lives; they lose the motivation to achieve their goals because they feel peaceful and happy here and now. (Shame on them, right?) Their inner drive cools down.

That is not what happened for me, and it is not what happens for my students. This is *not* how I teach meditation—especially within the context of Mindful Self-Discipline. In my many years as a meditation practitioner and teacher, I've noticed that the passivity that can come from meditation, for some people, is due to one of two things: (a) wrong choice of technique, or (b) an overemphasis on letting go.

Let's start with the first element. In some styles of meditation, the qualities of passivity and acceptance are more emphasized, directly or indirectly. This is not a criticism. There are no bad styles of meditation; but the goals, philosophy, and effects differ from practice to practice. So it's important to choose a style that suits your needs and personality (more about this in the section below). As general advice, for the purpose of using meditation to make you more disciplined and effective in life, focus on concentration-based meditations. Your motivation will be safe, and likely even augmented.

> **Concentration meditation** enhances your willpower and discernment, while also training your awareness. You have a goal to remain focused—for example, on counting your breaths. That requires some energy and motivation. To make that happen, you will need to constantly be monitoring your mind, checking, "Am I focused on the breath or am I distracted?" That requires awareness and discernment.

> **Observation meditation**, on the other hand, while also powerful in developing awareness, can lead to a state where you just see all things equally, and don't feel pulled to move in any particular direction anymore. That is, in a way, one of the aims of the practice. Rather than focusing your mind on a specific goal or object, you are keeping it open and receiving whatever inputs come from within or without.

Motivation and focus are about feeling powerfully moved by one ideal—not about seeing all things equally. Letting go of cravings and difficult emotions, on the other hand, is more about diminishing impulsivity and watering down the emotional charge of certain triggers for you. So, as a general rule of thumb, we can say that concentration meditation is better for focus and motivation, and observation meditation is better for impulse control and processing negative emotions.

Concentration meditation is more active; it is like fire. Observation meditation is more passive; it is like water. Both are wonderful practices, and have their value. As covered in Chapter 3, you need a balance of both fire and water in your life, and that balance can also change over time.

What about the other two types of meditation? **Relaxation meditation** is also passive, but doesn't tend to kill your motivation; rather, it replenishes you and dissipates emotional tension that could otherwise push you toward seeking emotional relief through instant gratification. **Pure Being** meditation is more spiritual by nature; it takes you to a place beyond all goals and efforts, and there is a chance that you will love it so much that you won't want to pursue anything else.

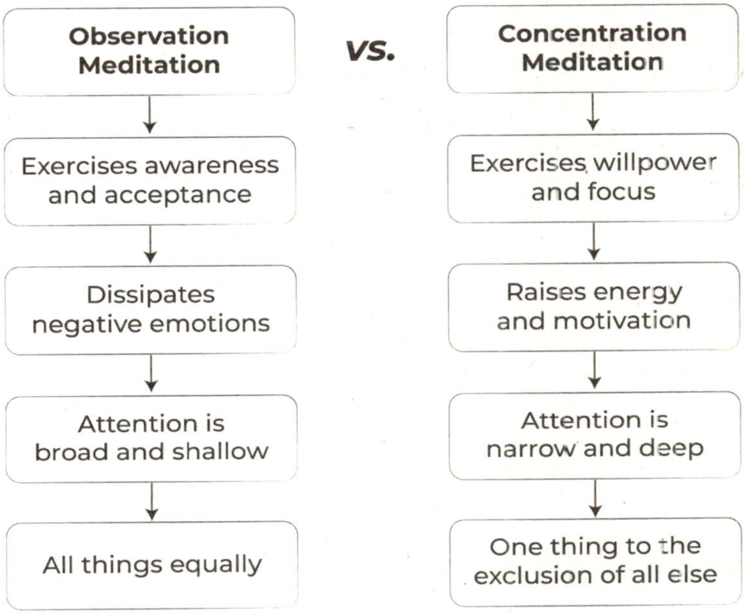

I don't mean to discourage you from practicing *observation* types of meditation or *pure being* types of meditation. If you already practice these styles, and enjoy it, by all means continue. But if your intention is to feel more motivated to achieve your goals, make sure to include some concentration meditation to the mix.

The second reason why meditation may have the risk of creating passivity and diminishing motivation, for some people, is connected to the spiritual philosophies that may come together with meditation. Depending on how you learn meditation—what teacher/group you go to—there may be too much emphasis on the *letting go* and *contentment* aspects of meditation. Thinking about the future is discouraged; you have to only be present, always. In other words, too much water, not enough fire. This could be the result of some of the monastic origins of that particular style of meditation (and their world-denying tendencies), or of the escapist intentions of certain practitioners.

Whatever style of meditation you practice, though, one thing can happen: your goals will evolve. The awareness that comes from the practice may make you realize that you were seeking the wrong things; that you were not on the best path. Knowing this is valuable—ideally you would want to know that you were climbing the wrong ladder before going all the way to the top. This realization then opens space for deeper and truer goals to emerge from within you—goals that, once achieved, will *truly* make you happy.

In summary, some of the ways people teach meditation out there may make you passive and less motivated. That is *not* the way meditation is taught in this book. In my personal practice and in my teaching, meditation is not just about peace, but about *empowered* peace. Meditation has to be useful not only for you to *love what you get* (acceptance), but also for you to *get what you love* (empowerment).

This is the balanced way of practicing meditation when you live *in the world*. This is the way of Mindful Self-Discipline.

Share this concept:
MindfulSelfDiscipline.com/meditation-and-passivity

MEDITATION BENEFITS FOR SELF-DISCIPLINE

All of humanity's problems stem from
man's inability to sit quietly in a room alone.

BLAISE PASCAL

If Pascal said that in the seventeenth century, imagine what he would say today, when most people can't spend one minute alone without unlocking their phone and scrolling through something. Indeed, a study from University of Virginia found that many people would rather be electrically shocked than left alone with their thoughts. No wonder, then, that some people have an aversion to meditation!

Meditation is a way to "sit quietly in a room alone" in a very purposeful way. I'm not sure I agree with Pascal that meditation will solve all of humanity's problems, but one thing I know: it will help you solve your self-discipline problems.

There are more than 4,000 scientific studies showing the benefits of meditation for physical health, mental performance, relationships, and emotional well-being. In this chapter, we will only briefly cover the ways that meditation boosts your self-discipline. (You can check the scientific references for these at the end of the book).

Meditation improves your **memory**. In our modern life our brain's "working memory" is usually full. We have too much input coming from all sources.

Too much information. When our brain is thus busy, it is hard to keep in mind our goals and aspirations, our commitments and resolutions. There is no space left, so we forget them. And as a result, we don't make the best decisions. We don't consistently act based on our long-term goals, because they are not top of mind. By improving your memory, meditation also helps you be more on track with your goals.

Meditation improves your **moods**, decreases stress, and increases your **baseline happiness**. It does this, among other things, by decreasing the size of the amygdala, which is the part of the brain responsible for stress, anxiety, fear, and anger. As we saw in Chapters 21 and 28, the main reason why we procrastinate and the main reason why we don't persevere in our goals are both the same: we want to avoid experiencing some form of mental or emotional pain. If you experience less emotional pain, or if you know how to embrace it when it comes, you won't need to procrastinate.

Meditation creates a greater sense of **wellbeing**; it makes you more content and happy with yourself—with that, it also increases your capacity for experiencing discomfort without feeling overwhelmed. This works as an effective buffer against life's challenges, making us more resilient and capable of going through difficulties without procrastinating or needing to distract ourselves.

Meditation also gives you the ability to pause more in your life, to be less distracted, to "zoom out" and get clarity. It creates more space inside of you—space for your goals and aspirations. It allows you to master your mind and master your life. Let's now unpack these benefits.

Meditation Gives You the *Pause* Superpower

Meditation trains you to **pause**, which then allows you zoom out and see things more clearly. This is one of the key benefits of meditation for self-discipline.

During meditation we practice slowing things down, observing our mind, and pausing whenever we get entangled in our thoughts, memories, or feelings. This ability to pause and *zoom out* is one of the superpowers gained through meditation, and it helps you with self-discipline big time. How? Whenever you are facing distractions or temptations in your daily life, you then have the ability to pause and zoom out—rather than act on impulse and then regret your decisions.

Rather than fighting with your impulses—which taxes the brain—meditation teaches you to be aware of them, accept them, and still remain in control. This not only saves you energy but is also more effective. It shows you that there is a difference between experiencing an impulse and acting on it. When that space between you and your impulse is present, by virtue of your meditation practice, then you have freedom to act on it or not—you are in control. As a result, you can stay on track with your goals and good habits without needing to shame yourself or use forceful repression.

The fact that you crave sugar does not mean that you have to go and grab a pot of ice cream right now; the fact that a cold shower is uncomfortable doesn't mean you can't do it; the fact that your research project is boring doesn't mean you have to procrastinate it; the fact that you are tired doesn't mean you can't go for your run; the fact that you've failed doesn't mean you need to give up. The impulse or emotion is one thing; the action is something else. Your ability to pause gives you the space between the two. This space is the space of your freedom.

Whether your impulses and emotions are weak or strong, you can always claim back your power and exercise your freedom. It almost doesn't matter how strong the craving is, so long as there is the space of pausing and the objective distance it brings. Pausing allows you to live by design, not by default. This is what Mindful Self-Discipline is about.

If you can't pause and see, you can't apply any of the techniques from this book—or from any other personal development book for that matter. It all starts with pausing and being aware. Because nothing can be done when you are living in automatic mode, unconscious, in the reptilian brain. In that state you are just reacting to the environment, and your future will be a repetition of your past.

Meditation helps you disconnect the emotion/impulse from the action. It turns out that this is more effective for managing cravings than forceful willpower. Indeed, there are scientific studies showing that mindfulness-based eating programs have a much longer-term effect than trying to change your diet without using mindfulness. Mindfulness training has been shown to help you to limit the amount of unhealthy food you eat, alcohol you drink, and cigarettes you smoke. It also helps you increase the amount of physical exercise you do. These habit changes created by mindfulness are also proven to last longer than if you try to change habits without including mindfulness.

Meditation Creates Space

Meditation helps you to slow down. It allows you to have fewer thoughts, and more space inside yourself. This is essential for self-discipline because if your mind is constantly busy with a multitude of needless thoughts, it will be very difficult for you to be aware of your goals. If you are not aware of your goals, it will be unlikely that you will make decisions that are in harmony with them.

As we saw above, meditation improves your memory—both the long-term and the short-term memory. Improving long-term memory is good for learning; but it's the improvement of short-term memory that we are most interested in, for the sake of boosting your self-discipline. Scott H. Young, in his mega article *The Complete Guide to Self-Control*, explains this phenomenon well:

> "For a self-control conflict to happen, you need to be acutely aware of your long-term goals at the same moment as you decide whether to indulge or not. In other words, you need to actively think about your goal to be healthy when you're faced with a dessert. If you can't do that, then you'll indulge by default, without even knowing that there was a conflict in the first place (unless you've formed a different habit).
>
> (...) To be able to keep your goals in your mind, you must have sufficient available working memory capacity. Working memory is your mental bandwidth—it holds together information about the present so that you can weigh different options and make decisions. The problem with working memory is that its capacity is limited. It fills up very quickly—it can hold only 4-7 items (letters, words, numbers, etc.) at the same time."

In other words: when our mind is constantly busy, we don't keep up with our commitments, resolutions, values, and goals. There is not enough space in the mind for that. Meditation helps you to improve this situation by broadening your working memory.

Meditation not only creates mental space, but also emotional space. For similar reasons to the phenomenon described above, when you are overwhelmed with stress or other difficult emotions, it is hard to remain disciplined. By working as a natural mood booster and giving you a healthy and effective means to process difficult emotions, meditation enhances the willpower you have at your disposal in your daily life.

Meditation Helps You Change Your Story

Self-discipline is about making better decisions in our lives—decisions that are more in line with our long-term goals and aspirations. For that we need to look into the stories we tell ourselves, because they inform our mindsets, our beliefs, and the way we feel about things.

If you can change the stories you tell yourself, you can change anything in your life. As I like to say in my programs, *master your mind, master your life*. Other authors have expressed it perhaps more eloquently:

Your soul takes on the color of your thoughts.

MARCUS AURELIUS

If you change the way you look at things, the things you look at change.

DR. WAYNE DYER

The stories you tell yourself form your identity. They are your repeated and unquestioned thought patterns about who you are, what the world is like, and how things work. The most important thing to realize here is that they are not truths; they are *habits*. They were *learned*. You absorbed them from people around you.

This is important to realize, because these stories can be empowering or disempowering. They can be positive or negative, pleasant or unpleasant, helpful or unhelpful. Thought patterns such as "I can't do this", "I'm not good enough", "If I fail it will be a disaster", are disempowering and can hold you back from your goals. The good news is that you have the power to change them.

Your thoughts are not truths; they are opinions. They are habits. As you practice meditation this becomes clear—not as a concept, but as an *experience*. This, for me, is one of the greatest gifts of meditation practice.

Since your self-talk, beliefs, and mindsets are just habits, then they can be changed. They can be unlearned. How do you break a bad habit? By not doing it anymore, and by replacing it with a better habit. It's the same with habits of thought—you unlearn them by not paying attention to the old ways of thinking (letting go), and replacing them with healthier and more useful ways of thinking (focusing).

Here again is the value of meditation on your journey of self-discipline. Meditation teaches you how to let go, and how to focus, by teaching you how to control your attention. The voices inside of you that you stop paying attention to will weaken and eventually disappear; the voices that you pay attention to will strengthen and come to life. I call this *The Law of Attention*. Attention gives life to whatever it touches.

What are you *paying attention into existence* in your life?

When the voice of fear comes up, saying, "Don't do that... you will fail, and it will be horrible", you have a choice. You can listen to it, believe it, and follow it by not taking action. Or you can ignore it, let it be there in a corner, and take action anyway. You can even deliberately bring up the voice of courage in you and feed it with your attention.

You may not be able to control the voices that come up, nor the stories they tell—but you can choose what you do with them. Meditation helps you recognize these voices, their origins and the effects they have on your life. It gives you the power to decide which voice will get the mic, and for how long. With that power, living a life of purpose and wellbeing becomes easier.

We need to have a deep look inside our mind, and change whatever patterns are holding us back. Why? Because often the mind is the boss—we do what our mind tells us to do. Meditation helps you become the boss of your mind; or, at the very least, a caring friend that it will listen to and sincerely try to help.

How much easier will it be for you to achieve your goals if you can stop listening to the narratives that hold you back, and be moved by empowering self-talk instead? Meditation enables you to do that.

Meditation Optimizes Your Brain

As we saw in Chapter 1, self-discipline, willpower, and self-awareness are expressions of the most evolved part of our brain—the prefrontal cortex. The prefrontal cortex is the seat of rational thought and conscious decisions; it is the part of the brain responsible for working memory, impulse control, ignoring distractions, and cognitive flexibility.

On the other hand, what often prevents us from acting in harmony with our better knowledge are our impulses and emotions, which come from the reptilian brain. When you are stressed, angry, or anxious, your prefrontal cortex goes offline, and you then operate from the reptilian brain. Self-discipline is not possible from this point.

Several studies show that meditation practice increases gray matter in the prefrontal cortex and diminishes amygdala activation (see references at the end of the book). How much meditation is needed for that? Some researchers found that a total of just three hours of meditation practice led to improved attention and self-control. After eleven hours, researchers could see those changes translated in the subjects' brain structures.

The value of meditation for self-discipline, then, becomes obvious: it makes it easier by working on both sides of the equation. It enhances self-awareness and willpower (stronger prefrontal cortex) and downregulates the stress response (smaller amygdala). That is why meditation and awareness are the central themes of my approach to self-discipline. Meditation is the gym of self-discipline.

Share this concept:
MindfulSelfDiscipline.com/meditation-benefits-for-self-discipline

THE THREE PILLARS OF MEDITATION

Just like there are three pillars of self-discipline, there are also three pillars for meditation. They are the key areas that you need to focus on in order to have a meditation practice that is pleasant and effective. If you have those three pillars in your life, your practice will flourish and you will experience the benefits. But if you don't—if even one of them is missing—then the benefits you get will be limited.

The three pillars of meditation are Habit, Technique, and Transformation. In short, you need to practice meditation *daily*, with the optimal *technique* and approach, and then apply the skills you got from meditation to *transform* your daily life.

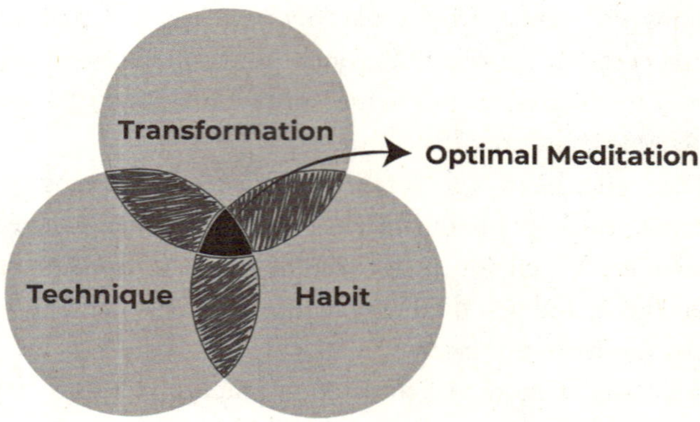

Habit

Meditation is not like physical exercise, where you can get away with practicing only two or three times a week. It's actually the sort of thing that you need to do *daily*—just like eating, sleeping, showering, and brushing your teeth. It's in *that* category of activities.

Why? Because you are exposed to stress on a daily basis. Because your mind may be bogging you down with negative thoughts and stories on a daily basis. Because your ego is working on a daily basis. Because impulses are there distracting you on a daily basis. So you need to meditate on a daily basis too. Otherwise, it will be very difficult to reverse negative patterns of thoughts and emotions. Thoughts are spinning in your head non-stop, and anxiety doesn't go on vacation.

What happens if you meditate only once a week? There is no doubt that you will experience some benefits. Right after the meditation, you will likely feel more calm, centered, and focused. You may immediately feel more clear and present. But that won't last—because once a week is not enough for you to get real momentum in the practice. It will not be transformational for you.

Suppose you want to boil some water. You need to leave your kettle on the heat for five minutes, so the water will boil. But instead you leave it on for two minutes, then turn it off, and come back to it the following week to turn it on for more two minutes... You may do that for all the weeks of your life, but the water will never boil because, in the following week, the water doesn't continue from the temperature it was at the end of your previous two minutes; rather, it has now completely cooled down to the baseline, so you are starting from room temperature again.

In a way, meditation practice is like that. And that is why it's essential to practice it every day—even if for only five or ten minutes. If you do that, you will have some continuity in your practice, and it will grow. A daily habit is what makes the difference between having a practice that *feels good when you do it* and one that will actually transform you and your daily life.

Building a daily habit of meditation is all about self-discipline and following some simple habit principles. This book gives you all the tools you need for that. Here is a quick overview of the key principles of building a daily meditation habit:

1. Set up your habit—choose the time, place, and tools for your practice
2. Setup a reminder—it could be an alarm, calendar or an object
3. Start small—three to five minutes a day
4. Follow *Never Zero*—see Chapter 31

5. Grow gradually—add one minute per week
6. Renew your commitment—re-affirm your intention after each session
7. Be patient—keep your expectations low and don't over-evaluate
8. Remain non-judgmental—no self-criticism, shame, or blame
9. Enjoy the process—make meditation its own reward
10. Be prepared—know the obstacles and excuses you may meet (contingency plan)

Technique

The second pillar is to practice meditation with the right technique and right approach.

The right technique doesn't mean that there is one style of meditation that is superior to all others, and that you should only practice that one. That is narrow-mindedness and dogmatism—unfortunately the type of thing that we see in some meditation groups/teachers out there. Right technique means the style that is most optimal *for you*, at this moment in your life. As mentioned above, there are hundreds of styles of meditation, and each of them has a different focus, process, and benefits.

When most people think of meditation techniques, what comes to mind is either watching their breath, or repeating a mantra. Those techniques are great, and they do work for some people—but not for everyone. Maybe those practices even work okay for you, but until you experiment with a variety of styles, you can't know if there is a more effective technique out there for you.

The good news is that meditation is an incredibly vast and flexible practice. There is a great variety of methods developed by different contemplative traditions over more than 3,000 years. They were developed not because the monks were bored, but because different people have different needs and temperaments.

Some techniques:

- may make you feel too passive, while others may energize you
- make you feel more centered, while others make you feel more spaced-out or detached
- will lift your energy (good for those with depression), while others will ground your energy (good for those with anxiety)

- are more suited to improve work performance and concentration; others may be better for exploring the spiritual side of meditation
- are easier for people who are more visual by nature, while others are better for people who are predominantly auditory or kinesthetic

There is no "one size fits all" in meditation; yet that is the way it is often taught. Most teachers and courses teach you only a couple of techniques. In fact, it is safe to say that there are as many meditation techniques as there are different types of sports and diets. Now imagine the problem if everyone was only taught either basketball or running… Or if everyone was given the same type of food, regardless of their preferences, health conditions, and allergies!

While most meditation techniques share a great number of common benefits, there is still a big difference between practicing a technique that *works for you* and practicing a technique that is *optimal* for you. Just like there is a big difference between an okay job and your ideal job, or an okay house and your ideal house.

It is beyond the scope of this book to explore the main styles of meditation and how to choose the ideal practice for you. Besides, a book is the not the best way to go about this process—ideally you would want to use guided meditations or be mentored systematically by a teacher knowledgeable in the different styles of meditation. Of course, you can also do this by yourself by doing your own research.

In any case, the bottom line here is that there are many different styles of meditation, and discovering the right one for you matters *a lot.* Meditation is something we will ideally practice for the rest of our lives, so isn't it worth it to spend some time in the beginning, making sure we have the best technique for us? Therefore, don't skip this step. Experiment with different techniques and philosophies for some time, and see what resonates and moves the needle for you the most.

Transformation

The third pillar is *transformation* or *integration*: applying the meditation skills to daily life. Meditation is not only what you do while sitting on a cushion for a few minutes every morning—it needs to be applied into your daily life. When that happens, the benefits multiply, and you experience the real goal of the practice: self-transformation.

The key message of the *transformation* pillar is that your daily life is an extension of your meditation, and your meditation is the foundation of your daily life. You need them both.

It is true that if you practice meditation daily, with the right technique for you, that over time some things will automatically begin to change. The way you see the world, the way you see yourself, how you react to people around you—all will change. But this process can be greatly accelerated if you do it *on purpose*. And this is what the third pillar is about: applying the insights and qualities that you experience in meditation to the rest of your life. It's taking meditation beyond the cushion.

In your meditation sessions you develop important skills, such as:

- Pausing
- Self-awareness
- Focus
- Willpower
- Calming down
- Zooming out
- Letting go of unhelpful thoughts
- Managing emotional states
- Self-acceptance

What is the most important skill of meditation that you want to integrate into your daily life? And how are you going to do it? You need to remember it constantly, and make use of it. That requires self-discipline.

This whole book is, in a way, an unfolding of the *transformation* pillar of meditation. It brings together all the skills listed above into daily exercises that you can use to live better, transform yourself, and achieve your goals. The application of meditation skills informs all chapters of this book—which is why I call it Mindful Self-Discipline.

Share this concept:

MindfulSelfDiscipline.com/the-three-pillars-of-meditation

KEY POINTS

Intro

- Meditation is one of the best ways to train *awareness*, and awareness is at the core of Mindful Self-Discipline. Because discipline starts in the mind: with how you think and how you manage your emotions.
- Meditation also trains willpower, which is the second core ingredient of self-discipline.

Meditation 101

- Meditation is a mental exercise that involves *relaxation*, *awareness*, and *focus*. Meditation is to the mind what physical exercise is to the body.
- There are hundreds of different styles of meditation, but they can all be classified into four big categories.
    - Concentration meditation: focus all your attention on a single object.
    - Observation meditation: monitor the panorama of the present-moment inputs.
    - Relaxation meditation: release physical, mental, and emotional tensions.
    - Pure being meditation: let go of everything and just be.
- Meditation does not require any specific belief or ritual. You don't need to sit in a difficult cross-legged posture (it's enough to keep your back straight and unsupported). It is not selfish, nor is it escaping from life. Having a calm mind is a result of the practice, not a requirement to begin.

Meditation and Passivity

- If you just practice *observation meditation* or *pure being meditation*, there is a risk that you may feel more passive and lose some of your drive. Therefore, either focus more on *concentration meditation* or at least include that as part of the mix.

- Concentration meditation is more active; it is like fire. Observation meditation is more passive; it is like water. You need a balance of both fire and water in your life.
- As a general rule of thumb, concentration meditation is better for focus and motivation, and observation meditation is better for impulse control and processing negative emotions.
- Meditation is not just about peace, but about *empowered* peace. Meditation has to be useful not only for you to *love what you get* (acceptance), but also for you to *get what you love* (empowerment). This is the balanced way of practicing meditation when you live *in the world*, and it is the emphasis of this book.

Meditation Benefits for Self-Discipline

- Meditation improves your memory, which allows you to keep your goals in mind when making decisions in your day to day.
- Meditation improves your moods, decreases stress, and increases your baseline happiness—this makes you more resilient against negative emotions, procrastination, and giving up.
- Meditation trains you to pause, which then allows you to zoom out and see things more clearly. If you can't pause and see, you can't apply any of the techniques from this book—or from any other personal development book for that matter. Nothing can be done when you are living in automatic mode, unconscious, in the reptilian brain. In that state you are just reacting to your environment.
- Pausing also allows you to overcome your impulses through awareness and acceptance, rather than by fighting them. You disconnect the emotion/impulse from the action. When that space between you and your impulse is present, by virtue of your meditation practice, then you have freedom to act on it or not—you are in control.
- Meditation helps you to slow down. It allows you to have fewer thoughts, and more space inside yourself. This is essential for self-discipline, because if your mind is constantly busy with a multitude of needless thoughts, it will be very difficult for you to keep your rules, resolutions, values, and goals. They are not top of mind.

- Meditation helps you take control of your attention, which then allows you to choose which voices and thoughts inside of you become stronger, and which ones become weaker. This enables you to change the stories you tell yourself—and with that you can change your life. You can let go of the negative and disempowering stories, and focus on the positive and empowering ones.
- Meditation optimizes your brain for self-discipline by enhancing self-awareness and willpower (stronger prefrontal cortex) and downregulating the stress response (smaller amygdala).

The Three Pillars of Meditation

- *Habit* is practicing meditation daily, no matter what. This is essential for you to fully benefit from the practice. The daily habit is what makes a difference between having a practice that feels good when you do it, and one that will actually transform you.
- *Technique* is finding the style of meditation that is optimal for you. Different techniques lead to different experiences and benefits; each is better suited for a different type of person and goal. You need to experiment with different techniques in a systematic way, ideally with some support, to help you find the best one for you.
- *Transformation* is applying the meditation skills to daily life—such as pausing, awareness, willpower, focus, and letting go. Your daily life is an extension of your meditation, and your meditation is the foundation of your daily life. You need them both. This whole book is, in a way, an expression of the *transformation* pillar.

Implementation Resources: this chapter was just a brief overview of meditation. If you want to go deeper, you can read my book on the topic (*Practical Meditation*) or join my step-by-step online meditation program, *Limitless Life* (**MindfulSelfDiscipline.com/limitless-life**).

CHAPTER 38

VIRTUES: YOUR SUPERPOWERS

What are virtues, and what do they have to do with self-discipline? In Chapter 1, we saw that Mindful Self-Discipline has both an external and an internal aspect. The external aspect is about building habits, following a routine, and moving forward toward your goals. The internal aspect is about self-mastery and self-transformation. The topic of virtues is related to the internal aspect of self-discipline.

Virtues are positive character traits that are considered a foundation for living well, and a key ingredient to greatness. They are your psychological assets, your personal strengths, your "superpowers". We are talking about things such as courage, patience, trust, kindness, confidence, focus, serenity, determination, resilience, integrity, etc. They are more important than goals, for they are transferable skills that you can apply in any journey you find yourself on.

Each virtue is a shield to protect us from difficulty, trouble, and suffering. Each virtue is a special sort of "power" that enables us to experience a level of well-being that we wouldn't be able to access otherwise. Indeed, the word "virtue" comes from the latin *virtus*, meaning force, worth, or power.

Virtues have been valued by wise people of all cultures since ancient times. The Greek philosophers, Persian Sufis, Indian yogis, Roman emperors, Buddhist monks and Shamanic leaders all had their list of valued virtues and their means of developing them.

We've already covered some virtues, such as ownership (responsibility), perseverance, and sacrifice. And, as we saw in Chapter 1, Mindful Self-Discipline already contains many virtues in itself. Simply by following the three pillars and strengthening your self-discipline, you will already be developing several virtues. On the other hand, you can also deliberately use self-discipline to accelerate this process and develop the virtues you need for your life. This is the purpose of this chapter.

VIRTUES ARE NARRATIVES

Every virtue is a way to see the world, feel the world, and navigate the world. Behind every virtue there is a narrative that enables it—a type of self-talk, belief, or mindset. Virtues express, in action, your narratives about yourself and the world.

For example, the narrative of "I care about people and want to do good" powers the virtue of kindness. The narrative of "I will remain calm and centered no matter what happens" powers the virtue of equanimity. The narrative of "I'm scared, but I'm going to do this because it's important to me" powers the virtue of courage.

Our narratives are the way we talk to ourselves, inside our minds. They matter a lot, for our life is made of the stories we tell ourselves. These stories can create virtues, or they can create difficulties. These stories forge our character and, with it, our destiny.

Yet most people pay no attention to their narratives. They make no effort to develop empowering narratives, and they just continue repeating and believing the same disempowering old stories as if they were absolute truths. If that is you, in one degree or another, then please don't worry. This chapter will give you practical tools to develop more empowering narratives in your life, and the virtues that come with them.

Where do our narratives come from? We've picked up most of them from our parents, friends, TV, and society as we were growing up. Others were developed along the way. Regardless of their origin, they can all be changed. The stories you are telling yourself are *habits*, not immutable laws. They are *beliefs*, not absolute truths. That means that if they are either untrue or unhelpful, you can replace them with better narratives, with virtue-creating narratives.

How do you develop a new narrative or self-talk? The same way that you developed the original ones: through belief and repetition. You choose to adopt a new narrative, and then persistently practice it until it becomes your new default. It's the PAW Method all over again: you slow down automatic thinking (pause), notice the old habitual story coming up again (awareness), and shift to the new one (willpower).

Now let's look at two universal methods of developing virtues.

Share this concept:
MindfulSelfDiscipline.com/virtues-are-narratives

TECHNIQUE #1: KINDLE THE VIRTUE

Every virtue has a "footprint" in your body, mind, and heart. Virtues are subjectively experienced as bodily sensations, emotions, and a narrative or self-talk. For example, *perseverance* for you might be associated with a bodily sensation of firmness or solidity in your spine, or maybe a sense of gathering your energy, or maybe even a sense of heat and readiness in your muscles. The narrative behind perseverance could be something like, "This is important to me. I won't give up. I will see this project to completion, no matter what!" The emotional experience behind it could be a feeling of hope, optimism, or confidence—a sense of aliveness in your chest.

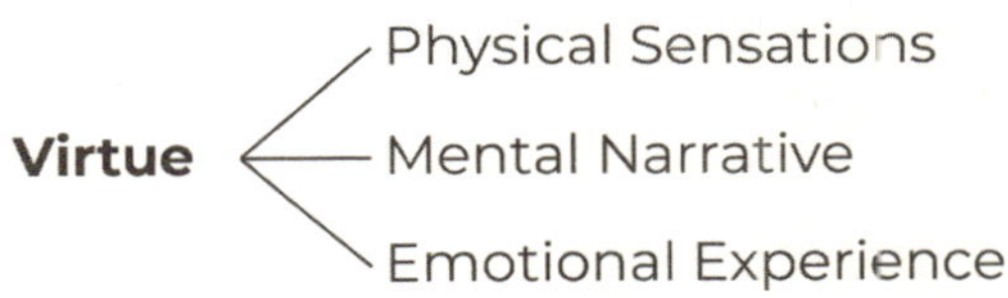

Whenever a virtue is present in you, you can find these three elements. The interesting thing is that by deliberately recreating those three "handles", you can kindle that virtue inside of you. The process goes both ways.

So the next time that you are experiencing a certain virtue or a positive emotional state, take a moment to look for the footprints of that state in your body, mind, and heart. These are the three handles you can use to re-create that state whenever you need it. They might be different things for different people, and it does require some practice and self-awareness to notice them.

The Process

The first universal method for developing any virtue is a meditation technique of kindling the virtue inside your mind, and then enhancing it by focusing on it. This is the methodology used by the well-known and well-researched loving-kindness meditation in Buddhism. It can be used in relation to any feeling or virtue.

How do you re-recreate the virtuous state by using the three handles? You go into a state of relaxation, then kindle the virtue by using your memory or imagination, and then enhance it by focusing on it.

The first step is **relaxation**. You go into a state of deep relaxation and mental calmness by using your favorite meditation technique. You could use a body scan, mindfulness of sensations, breath awareness, mantras—whatever suits you (see Chapter 37).

The second step is **kindling**. You re-create the bodily sensations, emotional experiences, and narratives associated with that virtue. You do this by vividly remembering a time in your past when you experienced that virtue, and then paying attention to the three handles. If you haven't experienced this virtue before, then you can instead imagine how it feels to experience it. In any case, let your remembrance/imagination be vivid, detailed, and real, so that you *actually experience* those sensations and that emotional state here and now.

The third step is **enhancing.** This means to feed the virtue inside of you by focusing all your attention on it, moment after moment, via the three handles. The virtue itself becomes the object of your meditation. The more attention you give it, the deeper the neuropathways you will be creating in your brain regarding that mode of being. You can also create an affirmation and repeat it mentally, to enhance the experience.

The more you use this technique, the easier it will be for you to tap into that virtue in your daily life simply by remembering one or all of the three handles.

Share this concept:
MindfulSelfDiscipline.com/kindle-the-virtue

TECHNIQUE #2: ABSORB THE VIRTUE

By three methods we may learn wisdom:
First, by reflection, which is the noblest;
second, by imitation, which is the easiest;
and third, by experience, which is the bitterest.

CONFUCIUS

Another way of developing any virtue is to find it in others, and then adopt that mode of being. You look for a person who has that virtue highly developed—perhaps the role models you chose in Chapter 7—and then you "absorb" it from him or her.

The simplest way to do this is to spend time with people who have the virtue you wish to develop. They could be friends, family members, colleagues, mentors, or even experts that you connect with online. This is absorbing the virtue by *association* (covered in Chapter 34).

A more powerful way to do this is to go through a protocol of connecting your consciousness to the consciousness of that person. This is absorbing the virtue by *identification*.

Here are the simplified steps for this:

- **Step 1:** Go into a state of deep relaxation and mental calmness through whichever meditation technique you wish to use.
- **Step 2:** Visualize or imagine your role model standing right in front of you, as best as you can. Feel their presence.
- **Step 3:** Think of the quality that you wish to absorb from her/him. Contemplate all the ways that person expresses that quality. Contemplate the self-talk behind it, the feelings that fuel it, and the physical sensations associated with it. Get the full picture of the experience.
- **Step 4:** While still imagining your role model and contemplating that quality, begin paying attention to your breath. With every inhalation, have the attitude that you are absorbing that quality yourself; with every exhalation, you spread that quality throughout your body.
- **Step 5:** Forget your separate identity for a few moments and *become* that quality. It can almost feel like you become that other person—you feel what they feel, think as they think, act as they act, and see the world as they see it.
- **Step 6:** Pay close attention to the footprints of that quality inside of you. Take a "mental snapshot" of how it feels in your body, in your emotions, and in your mind. This way, you'll be able to re-create it more easily. This concludes the meditation.
- **Step 7:** As you go about your day, tap into that quality or virtue by remembering the mental snapshot, and recreating those thoughts, feelings, and sensations inside of you. Act as if that is already you. Keep doubts at bay, and just do it.

Practice this technique for ten minutes every morning for twenty-one days and notice the difference. After that, you can try another virtue, or keep the practice as a permanent part of your morning routine.

Kindling: 1 Deep Relaxation > 2 Visualize Role Model > 3 Contemplate Quality

Absorbing: 4 Inhale the Quality > 5 Become it > 6 Remember it > 7 Act on it

This technique does require some imagination, open-mindedness, and concentration to make it happen. The more skeptical, linear, and overly analytical you are, the harder it will be to pull this one off. You need the ability to let go of your identity for a short period of time, and believe your thoughts into reality. You need to "become" somebody else, so that you can see life through their eyes, and "download their superpowers".

This method can be used to develop any skill or quality you need, and it can be used with any type of "target". It doesn't matter whether you are visualizing a real person you know, an expert in your field, a mythical figure, or a movie character. You could absorb the virtues of James Bond, Katniss Everdeen, Apollo, or Yoda.

When I was a teenager at school, I completed sucked at soccer—which is a very bad idea when you live in Brazil. I had no coordination to run with a ball, and no control over where I wanted the ball to go. I seemed to be much better at kicking the other players' shins than actually hitting the ball (later on I figured out I'm good at martial arts, not team sports).

One day in physical education class at school, when the soccer game was about to start, I decided to try something radically different. Instead of staying at the back, hoping the ball would not come my way, I went to the center and asked the team captain to pass me the ball as soon as the game starts. "Are you sure?" he asked, making a face I will never forget. "Yes, just pass me the ball." "All right. This will be hilarious…" he said.

At that point, I had convinced myself that I was a professional soccer player, full of skill and coordination. I imagined that I had been kind of "possessed" by that quality, if you will, and that I was no longer myself. I held that mental picture in my mind with full faith. There was no place for doubts.

When the referee blew the whistle, the captain passed me the ball, and watched, astonished, as I ran with it toward the goalkeeper, and scored a goal in under ten seconds. I ran (with the ball!) like an arrow toward its target. The impression I had is that all members of the opposite team just opened space for me, bewildered.

Later on, I successfully repeated this experiment while playing handball, bowling, and also in social skills. (Needless to say, it has also failed multiple times, because this also needs patience and perseverance—things I can't be proud of possessing in my teenage years.)

As the years passed, I realized that the trick I had "discovered" was nothing new or original. As far as I could research, this method was first developed as a spiritual technique in India and Tibet. Their goal was for the practitioner to achieve a type of mystical connection with the contemplated deity, and thus "download" the wisdom, virtues, and powers of that deity into himself/herself. In the past century, several modern-day self-help authors have adapted this technique (or discovered it through other means) and given it fancy names.

It is hard to explain why this works without going into metaphysical theories. Perhaps the closest we can get to it here is by talking about the phenomenon of *quantum entanglement*: when two particles have been "entangled", the state of one particle affects the state of the other particle, regardless of their distance in space and time. Einstein called it "spooky action at a distance". Or maybe it's connected to the way mirror neurons work. In any case, on a very pragmatic level, it doesn't matter why this method works, but only that it does.

Give it a fair go and see what happens for you. And "fair go" doesn't mean to try it half-heartedly for five minutes while you're waiting for a bus or laying down in a hammock, doing it once and then giving up. It means practicing it daily for a couple of weeks before you draw any conclusions.

Your mind is programmable, and your identity is not as fixed as you imagine. A great actress fully internalizes her character—feeling, thinking, and breathing as the character—and as a result she can act in such a way as to *make us believe*, because she has first believed it herself. You too have the ability to internalize the virtues of your role models and dare to *act as them* whenever the situation calls for it.

Life is like a movie, and you can choose the role you want to play. You don't need to play the role that you were given. So, who will you choose to be?

Share this concept:
MindfulSelfDiscipline.com/absorb-the-virtue

BALANCE YOUR VIRTUES

Virtues are amazing psychological assets that we can have, and every effort to develop them pays rich dividends. Yet, it is also true that every virtue casts a shadow. Our greatest strengths, when not balanced, are often the source of our greatest weaknesses.

Every virtue is a tool, and we need different tools for different jobs. To use a well-known metaphor: if all you have is a hammer, you will treat everything as a nail. The problem is that not everything is a nail. Therefore, you need to develop yourself holistically, and pay special attention to developing virtues that are opposite to the ones you already have. I call this principle *balancing your virtues*.

Here are some examples of virtues and opposing virtues.

The virtue of **ownership** is taking responsibility for everything in your life and focusing on what you can control. When you overplay this virtue and don't balance it with the opposite virtue (letting go), then you become too hard on yourself, and end up taking responsibility for things that you are not really responsible for.

The virtue of **self-belief** is having complete trust and faith in yourself, and being confident that you can achieve anything you set your mind to. When you overplay this virtue and don't balance it with the opposite virtue (humility), you may tend to become arrogant, defensive, conceited, and reckless.

The virtue of **perseverance** is not giving up; it is continuing on your path despite challenges. When you overplay this virtue and don't balance it with the opposite virtue (acceptance), you can stay far too long on a path that is no longer meaningful for you, or with a strategy that doesn't really work anymore. You may become too stubborn, inflexible, and even blind to new input.

The virtue of **sacrifice** is making an offering and letting go of something you value in the present for the purpose of getting a greater reward in the future. When you overplay this virtue and don't balance it with the opposite virtue (healthy enjoyment), you tend to be too future-focused, feel that you are not good enough, and have indulgence guilt. (See Chapter 3 for more details on balancing self-discipline.)

This applies to all virtues. You need to balance kindness with boundaries, motivation with patience, consistency with adaptability, optimism with prudence, idealism with pragmatism. Each pair of opposing virtues gets balanced in a different way, and it's not possible to cover them all here. The point of balance also varies from person to person, depending on your personality, lifestyle, and goals. Keep this concept of opposing virtues as a general principle for yourself, and the *how* of it will emerge little by little in your life, as you strive to live with greater awareness.

Share this concept:

MindfulSelfDiscipline.com/balance-your-virtues

Balancing Self-Belief

Before closing this chapter, it is worth spending some time discussing in greater detail one of these pairs, which is more relevant to the topic of discipline: the self-belief vs. humility pair. When this is properly balanced, you have *wise confidence*, and can practice Mindful Self-Discipline.

In Chapter 12, we covered how not having enough self-belief or self-confidence can make self-discipline very difficult. You may wonder how too much self-belief can be a problem. Well, when you are overly confident you tend to be blind about your biases and shortcomings. You ignore certain feedback and possibilities, and when reality hits in a way you don't expect you may then end up feeling discouraged and abandoning your pursuit.

Let's have a closer look at a couple of examples of this "overconfidence bias".

The first is called the **Dunning-Kruger effect**. According to the Wikipedia entry on this topic, "the Dunning–Kruger effect is a cognitive bias in which people with low ability at a task overestimate their ability. (…) Without the self-awareness of metacognition, people cannot objectively evaluate their competence or incompetence."

When you have such inflated self-confidence, you end up expecting extraordinary results. For example:

- You put all your money into a questionable investment opportunity because you *know* it *has to* go up in value.
- You believe that your book will become a *New York Times* bestseller and that everybody will be excited about it, even though nobody has ever heard of you and you don't do any marketing.
- You think that by following your new diet you will have lost thirty pounds in three weeks.
- You are convinced that you are such a great partner that there is no way your significant other would ever leave you.
- You procrastinate working on that important project of yours because you are certain that you can finish it up in a week.

We all know what often happens when we engage in this type of thinking. When reality doesn't confirm our expectations, we fall into the pit of confusion and self-doubt.

The second one is known as Restraint Bias, which is believing that you have greater control over your cravings and impulses than you actually have. It is basically the Dunning-Kruger effect applied to your self-control skills. Others call this the empathy gap effect, which is the fact that while you are in a "cold state" (calm and rational) you don't appreciate the power that impulses will have on you when you get to a "hot state".

With overconfidence in your self-control abilities, you indulge today, because you believe that you will be able to restrain yourself tomorrow; you try some drugs because you are confident that you won't get addicted; you tell yourself that you will "just check social media for five minutes", or that you will "just eat one small piece of chocolate". If you have experienced any variant of these, then you know what restraint bias feels like.

Scientific studies show that people with greater restraint bias actually end up indulging more in the temptations. This is a perfect example of how unbalanced self-belief can hurt your self-discipline.

This is how the virtue of self-belief can cast a shadow. In order to have self-belief without getting trapped by its shadows, you need to develop self-awareness—the ability to see yourself clearly, past your biases. With this comes the opposite virtue, humility. You then are *wisely* confident, and not foolishly so. This is the way of Mindful Self-Discipline.

Share this concept:
MindfulSelfDiscipline.com/unbalanced-self-confidence

Balance is the Goal

Every virtue is a tool and an asset. Virtues give you more well-being, allow you to live better, and empower you to actualize yourself. But when they are unbalanced, you may at times fall into their dark sides and, with that, experience suffering and limitation.

Balancing your virtues with Mindful Self-Discipline is, at the end of the day, about three things:

Do what is ultimately good for you.
Stop causing suffering to yourself.
Make the world a better place.

These seemingly simple ideas are the summary of thousands of hours of reflection and spiritual practice for me. They speak volumes, but I'll leave it at that. Keep them in mind as a compass for your decisions, and year after year you will see them unfold deeper layers of meaning in your life.

KEY POINTS

Virtues (Theory)

- Our virtues are our psychological assets. Even if we fail in our goals, if we have developed virtues and grown along the way, it was all worth it. Personal growth is the ultimate purpose of pursuing any goal.
- Every virtue is a way to see the world and navigate the world.
- Behind every virtue there is a narrative that enables it—a type of self-talk, belief, or mindset. Your narratives are a *habit*, not an immutable law. You can change them through repetition and belief.

Technique #1: Kindle the Virtue

- Find the three handles of your chosen virtue: physical sensations, emotional experience, and mental narrative.
- Use the three-step process outlined above to kindle and enhance that virtue inside of you. Then begin to tap into it multiple times during your day.

Technique #2: Absorb the Virtue

- Look for a person who has your desired virtue highly developed—perhaps the role models you choose. It doesn't matter if you know them or not.
- Absorb their virtue either by association (spend time in their company), or by identification (follow the seven-step process outlined above).

Balance Your Virtues

- Every virtue casts a shadow. Our greatest strengths, when not balanced, are often the source of our greatest weaknesses.
- Balance ownership with letting go, self-belief with humility, perseverance with acceptance, and sacrifice with enjoyment.

- If you don't balance self-belief and self-confidence, you will fall into the Dunning-Kruger effect, and/or the restraint bias and empathy gap effect. As a result, you will overestimate your self-control abilities, get disappointed and confused, and stray even more from your goal. Escape these shadows by developing self-awareness and humility.

Implementation resources: checkout the printable meditation instructions for both the techniques taught in this chapter at **MindfulSelfDiscipline.com/meditations.**

CHAPTER 39

SPIRITUALITY: THE DEEPER LAYER

A disciplined mind leads to happiness,
an undisciplined mind leads to suffering.

DALAI LAMA

Look at consciousness as a function of matter and you have science.
Look at matter as the product of consciousness and you have spirituality.

NISARGADATTA MAHARAJ

That aim in life is highest which requires
the highest and finest discipline.

HENRY DAVID THOREAU

You obviously don't need to be spiritual in order to be disciplined. You don't need to be spiritual even to practice *mindful* self-discipline—for that, meditation and awareness are enough. But can spirituality help self-discipline? Yes, tremendously.

Both spirituality and self-discipline share a similar journey: taking you from the reptilian brain to the evolved brain, from the animal to the human, from reactive to conscious. They both aim to elevate you above your impulses and negative emotions, and truly master yourself.

If you are open to spirituality, this chapter can add an extra layer of depth, meaning and strength to your practice of self-discipline. And if you are not, feel free to skip it. At this point of the book, you have already learned plenty of effective tools for your journey.

What is Spirituality?

It is challenging to define spirituality in a way that encompasses all its manifestations and makes everyone happy, yet we need a definition so that we can be somewhat on the same page. Here is my working concept:

> Spirituality is a worldview and a way of living based on the intuition that there is more to life than what meets the senses, more to the universe than just purposeless mechanics, more to consciousness than electrical impulses in the brain, and more to our existence than the body and its needs.
>
> Spirituality embraces this mystery and seeks to explore it. It often involves the belief in a higher form of intelligence or Consciousness as the source of the universe, as well as life after death and the existence of subtler levels of reality. It is an answer to the deep human thirst for meaning, peace, connection, and truth. It incorporates the transcendental aspect of human existence, the depth of our being, and gives context to transcendental experiences.

Spirituality is not the same as religion. Religion is one of the manifestations of spirituality, but you can also be *spiritual but not religious*. For the purposes of this chapter, it doesn't matter what form of spirituality you practice—but only that you have awareness of the non-material aspect of life, and willingness to explore it.

There is a lot of scientific research showing the mental health benefits of a spiritual practice. Recent studies have reported positive outcomes of a spiritual worldview and practice for the purposes of treating depression, anxiety, PTSD, schizophrenia, and trauma, as well as for patients coping with illnesses such as cancer. More of such research is bound to come, as the scientific inquiry on meditation deepens. For the purpose of this book, we will just focus on how spirituality can support your self-discipline, and how self-discipline can support your spirituality. Let's begin with the former.

Share this concept:
MindfulSelfDiscipline.com/spirituality

SPIRITUALITY FOR SELF-DISCIPLINE

When we sit down day after day and keep grinding, something mysterious starts to happen. A process is set into motion by which, inevitably and infallibly, heaven comes to our aid. Unseen forces enlist in our cause; serendipity reinforces our purpose.

STEVEN PRESSFIELD

Spirituality almost always brings with it strong values such as integrity, compassion, patience, forgiveness, self-control, determination, awareness, and morality. It requires honest self-reflection. It asks you to develop certain virtues and do certain practices regularly. All of that, of course, requires self-discipline. Indeed, the word discipline and the word *disciple* have the same root—discipline is what is required for growth and learning.

If you follow a spiritual path seriously, you are already very familiar with the practice of self-discipline, and you have the added advantage of having the inspiration of your peers, mentors, community, mystical experiences, and sacred texts to keep you on this path.

Spirituality also brings greater peace of mind, calms down your impulses, and makes you more resilient. It gives you a stronger sense of self-worth, because you see yourself as something greater than your body and personality—some call it Self, Awareness, Spirit, Soul, or Buddha Mind. It also gives you greater ability to forgive yourself for your mistakes, and practice self-compassion, because you see your failures as just small hiccups along the endless journey of personal expansion/purification/transcendence. Your vision is broad.

The Power of Faith

As we saw throughout the book, self-discipline requires the virtues of *self-belief*, *perseverance*, and *sacrifice* (Chapters 12 and 13). All of these are naturally developed when you have strong faith in something, because faith allows you to bypass doubt completely. Faith is not a conclusion—it is a *decision*, an emotion, or an experience. It is not the end-result of analytical thinking—it is trans-rational. It belongs more to the realm of feeling than that of reason. And it is not the exclusive domain of religion.

You have to trust in something—your gut, destiny, life, karma, whatever.

STEVE JOBS

When Tony Robbins was asked what was the core belief that has been most helpful in his life, he replied: "That life is happening *for* you, not to you." The same message is echoed by many other voices in the personal development world, under different forms. And it is a *belief*, an act of faith. It is something that you cannot prove true or false, but it is definitely helpful and empowering.

If you believe that you are a soul or spirit, then you will naturally believe that there is great wisdom and power within you; that means you will be able to tap into that in times of need, and persevere. If you believe in God, you can tap into that unlimited power through prayer. If you believe in the existence of supportive non-material entities, you can ask for their help, and feel the hope and peace of mind that comes from knowing that you don't need to go through this alone. If you believe in an intelligent and compassionate universe you may, like Tony Robbins, have the resilience and resourcefulness of knowing that all happens for your greater benefit.

I have no mission of convincing you of any particular faith. It has to come from within you, in the form of something that just *feels* true, good, and meaningful. Faith is taking as truth something that cannot be scientifically proven or dismissed, but upon which a good life can be built. It is something that makes life better.

The most important decision we make is whether we believe we live in a friendly or hostile universe.

ALBERT EINSTEIN

We live better when we have trust in a higher intelligence, and in the inherent goodness of the universe. Faith is the thread that can be used to organize the chaos of life, the unknown, and make sense of it. One day you might need to replace that thread—but until then, it will have served you well.

Faith is picking out, from the sea of unknowables, the one hypothesis that makes it all come alive for you; that makes it all worth it for you. Then you choose to see the world through those lenses, navigate uncertainty with that map, and experience the benefits—until you find something better. This is not irrational; it is trans-rational. It is not foolish; it is wise. It is not narrow-minded; it is empowering.

At the very least, you need to develop strong faith in yourself. Unwavering faith in yourself. So you stand like a mountain that no wind can move; so you be a light unto yourself. This is also spirituality. As one of my favorite meditation masters, Swami Vivekananda, says, "You cannot believe in God until you believe in yourself".

Long-Term Outlook

Self-discipline is the art of prioritizing long-term goals. This is another area in which spirituality empowers self-discipline, because its outlook on life is *really* long-term.

If you seriously follow a spiritual path, you will tend to be more disciplined. Spirituality involves long-term thinking. Spiritual people consider the consequences of their choices not only for a few years from now (what is typically considered "long-term") but also for their future life/lives. Whether it is under the context of the Judgment Day (in Abrahamic religions) or of karma (in Eastern religions), the idea is that what you say and do here and now matters a lot, and for a long time. As a result, you tend to pay more attention. You tend to live more mindfully, and make more thoughtful decisions. This broader outlook facilitates the practice of Shift Your Focus (Chapter 18).

Another benefit of having this longer timescale for your life is that you tend to worry less about the small stuff. You gain more inner space and a broader perspective. As a personal example, I believe in the theory of reincarnation, and I cannot tell you how many times this broader timescale has helped me get perspective on the problems and difficulties I was facing. Every challenge and worry looks incredibly small from that 100,000-foot view. From that point of view, there is no need to be anxious or to fear.

When you have a long-term perspective, and yet understand the value of every moment, then it is much easier to get up every time you fall.

Stronger Sense of Purpose

Many spiritual philosophies emphasize having a strong sense of purpose. They teach that we are here to grow and contribute, each of us with our own gifts, perspectives, and uniqueness. There is a sense of *duty* toward who we can be and what we can give—a sense of *I must do this*. We read in the Bible that:

> *To those who use well what they are given, even more will be given, and they will have an abundance. But from those who do nothing, even what little they have will be taken away.*
>
> MATTHEW 25:14-30

Hindu spirituality also echoes this idea through the concept of dharma—which are your "duties" in life. Our duties and roles in life are considered to be sacred. They are seen as the way we express ourselves and polish our soul. And they are seen as the way that the higher consciousness expresses itself through us. They are what we were born to do.

I sit at the core of all beings and pull the strings
of their heart according to their destiny.

BHAGAVAD GITA

When we cultivate this stronger sense of purpose and duty, there is a natural force within that pushes us to make the best use of our time and life. Charged with this spirit, it becomes much easier to stay focused on what matters, to overcome procrastination, and to persevere on the path of our calling. Without this larger context, our goals may often feel forced, selfish, or even meaningless.

Earlier in this book, we saw that self-discipline is the power to achieve your goals and live your values. It does not judge whether your goals are good for you or not; it simply helps you accomplish them. Picking the right goals and values is the domain of wisdom, not discipline.

As you cultivate your spirituality, through both practices and contemplation, your wisdom will grow. Your intuition will awaken. You will get in touch with something deeper inside yourself; something beyond the ego and its needs. With this new wisdom and depth, you'll be able to choose better goals for yourself. Goals that are more authentic—and thus more compelling. Goals that you will naturally want to be more disciplined in.

If you have discipline without wisdom, you may end up at the top of a ladder that you didn't really need to climb. If you have wisdom without discipline, you will know the right ladder to climb but won't go past the first few rungs. To live fully, you need both wisdom and discipline.

Share this concept:
MindfulSelfDiscipline.com/spirituality-for-self-discipline

SELF-DISCIPLINE FOR SPIRITUALITY

Ask me not where I live and what I like to eat.
Ask me what I am living for and
what I think is keeping me from living fully for that.

THOMAS MERTON

We saw how spirituality can help enhance self-discipline. Now let's look at how self-discipline can enhance spirituality.

Well, spirituality is a *discipline*. Actually, true spirituality is the hardest of all disciplines, because it involves disciplining your thoughts, emotions, intentions, and actions all the time. While the discipline needed to achieve other goals in life is often a part-time pursuit, the discipline to grow and awaken spiritually is full-time.

In ancient times, self-discipline and spirituality were actually not two different things. Self-discipline was the cornerstone of morality, which was one of the main functions of religion as a force that organized society and promoted goodness. At that time, self-discipline was a given; today, it is considered by many as an optional bonus. Ah, how much we have yet to learn from the ancients!

There are many different spiritual paths and traditions. And all of them—except the ones that have been made up in the last century—require self-discipline as an essential ingredient for self-transformation. Whether you are practicing fasting, mindfulness, silence, meditation, prayer, study, simplicity, self-reflection, asceticism, or service, you will need self-discipline. And you will need even more of it to practice ongoing self-awareness and self-purification.

All spiritual practices require effort, and they stretch your limits. Through the friction of your will, these practices kindle and grow your inner fire. They generate a force known as *tapas* in the Yoga tradition, which as we saw is a type of "inner heat". This heat will make your body, mind, and heart malleable—allowing you to mold them as you desire. This heat will also be available for you to use to achieve all sorts of things in your life.

Goal Achievement as a Spiritual Path

At the surface, it might seem that self-discipline is all about getting what you want in life—more health, money, skill, recognition, knowledge, influence, "success". At its core, however, Mindful Self-Discipline is about deep personal growth and self-transformation. It is about cultivating your personal power and overcoming your limitations.

Your goals are just a reason for you to go through this process. They are like carrots that encourage you to move forward, and keep you engaged with life. And they are much better than the alternative: apathy and stagnation.

A goal is not always meant to be reached.
It often serves simply as something to aim at.

Bruce Lee

Your goals are life calling you to move forward, so you can outgrow your current desires and be ready for higher desires. On this path you will get what you want, of course! (That is probably why you bought this book.) But, after a while, you will begin to notice that the fulfillment you experience after achieving a goal soon normalizes, and then opens the way for something bigger.

Once you achieve your goals, you'll outgrow them. This is the journey of Mindful Self-Discipline: from goal to goal, you grow as a human being. From goal to goal, you go from outer to inner, from external values to more internal values.

A point will come where your interest naturally turns toward spirituality and service, in one form or another. When that happens, the self-discipline you have developed to achieve your so-called worldly goals will be extremely valuable for you. You will see that your goals and desires have served as a training ground for self-discipline, and prepared you for a bigger journey.

A New Spirituality

Joseph Campell said "follow your bliss". The spiritual masters say: in pursuit of a higher bliss, let go of the smaller bliss. This letting go doesn't need to be forceful. It doesn't need to feel like self-denial. Just as a child eventually loses interest in playing with children's toys, without needing to force him/herself to abandon them, we can also organically outgrow our goals and needs by fulfilling them wisely. This is more organic, and gentler to yourself.

Spirituality has traditionally been associated with self-denial, rejection of the body, and renunciation of worldly ambitions. That is the old way of spirituality: you were expected to abandon your material goals rather than strive to fulfill them. You were expected to be desireless, rather than moved by desire. You were expected to let go, rather than go after.

In my life I strived to follow that path for many years, and learned much from it. But I've noticed that this approach is for very few people. Indeed, if you are not a monk, that type of spirituality will not suit you fully. A part of you will always remain disconnected from it. You may even feel guilty, divided, numbed, or not good enough.

The world needs a new type of spirituality. A spirituality that is more integrated, engaged, empowering, and active. A spirituality that fulfils your needs, rather than ask you to efface them. A spirituality that empowers you to better achieve your worldly goals, and that uses this journey as a path to something higher. A spirituality in which you outgrow your (healthy) desires by fulfilling them wisely.

Mindful Self-Discipline allows you to do that. It empowers both material goals and spiritual aspirations. That is the spirit of this book.

Share this concept:
MindfulSelfDiscipline.com/self-discipline-for-spirituality

THE JOURNEY OF A LIFETIME

On several occasions, my wife—who probably knows me better than anybody else—has expressed her astonishment at how I persevere with things, and stick with my chosen disciplines even if I am not getting the expected results for *years*. Well, dear reader, now that we are approaching the end of this book, I can tell you a little secret: faith is my secret weapon. It supercharges my self-discipline.

I'm spiritual, but not religious. Over the years, what I believe in has changed. My faith has changed—but not the strength I derive from it. And I have never ceased believing in myself, even when doing so felt silly or irrational. This has served me tremendously.

At the end of the day, I don't think I have any special talents, really. I am just incredibly stubborn. I refuse to give in. I refuse to be defined by my impulses. I refuse to allow what is easy but shallow to distract me from what is difficult but deep. I refuse to be held back by my environment and upbringing. I refuse to shy away from pain and effort. I refuse to doubt myself, even if the whole world does.

This self-discipline thing got me somewhere. So I have faith it will serve you too.

Have faith in the process. Have faith in yourself. And have faith in something higher, too. Stay with it, and don't be in a hurry. This is the journey of a lifetime.

NEXT STEPS

CHAPTER 40

IMPLEMENTATION CHECKLIST

How do you put all of these concepts and exercises into practice in your daily life? This section is meant to give you a starting point.

YOUR SELF-DISCIPLINE SETUP

Begin by going through the exercises in Steps 1 to 3 of the Aspiration Pillar (Chapters 7, 8, 9)—this will help you have an aspiration that is clear, strong, and also translated into actionable goals. Then create milestones and specific habits for each of these goals, so that you have an action plan and you know exactly what you need to do to move forward, without feeling overwhelmed (Chapter 25). These are all things that you set up once and then review *quarterly*.

Once you have clarity about your aspiration, goals, milestones, and habits, it's time to design your daily life in a way that will allow you to effectively build those habits and make progress toward your goals. You do that first by choosing the best cue for each habit, the ideal and minimum action, and the rewards that will help you remain on track; you then take steps to improve your environment, and create a contingency plan so you avoid "failures" (Chapters 26, 27, and 30). After that, you create a morning routine that includes your most important habits (Chapter 34). You might find the need to review and fine-tune this second group of tasks *weekly*, until you find what works best for you.

Depending on where you are in your life, you may at this point decide that you need a hard dopamine reset, and plan your first Monk Week (Chapter 22).

This whole initial *self-discipline setup* can take anywhere between two hours to a whole day. When you are finished, you will be ready to take action in a way that is effective, purposeful, and consistent. Consolidate it by making a *Never Zero* commitment (Chapter 31), and then get started.

YOUR FOCUS TECHNIQUE

Having gotten so far into this book, you now likely have a much clearer idea about what are the biggest obstacles that you need to overcome in order to live a more self-disciplined life, and what are the virtues that will help you get there. It's time now to choose which obstacle you will focus on first, and then start practicing the concepts and techniques in that particular chapter of the book.

Below is a list of self-discipline challenges and where to go to learn the tools for dealing with them. Refer also to the *Index of Practices* section at the end of the book for a more complete list of tools.

- Lack of motivation (Chapters 7-10, 13, 31, 35)
- Inner conflict (Chapter 11)
- Lack of self-belief (Chapter 12)
- Victim mindset (Chapter 12)
- Lack of commitment (Chapter 13)
- Fears and anxiety (Chapter 20)
- Giving up (Chapter 21)
- Distractions (Chapter 22)
- Excuses (Chapter 23)
- Forgetfulness (Chapter 27)
- Procrastination (Chapter 28)
- Doubts (Chapter 29)
- Failures (Chapter 30)

You only need to focus on the chapters that address the challenges that you actually have. And, even then, you don't need to do all the exercises. As soon as you find something that works for you, focus on that technique for your daily practice, until you get results. I call this your Focus Technique.

Your Focus Technique can change over time. For example, perhaps right now you are struggling with fear or anxiety, and so you decide to focus on the Embrace Your Pain technique (Chapter 20). Then, after a couple of months, you may realize that fear and anxiety don't hold you back so much anymore, but you find yourself procrastinating a lot, and so your Focus Technique changes to Baby Steps (Chapter 28).

I suggest you work on one obstacle or virtue at a time, focusing on it for a full month before moving on to another one. You *could* practice two at a time, but for many people that leads to too much strain on their willpower, a sense of overwhelm, and then frustration for lack of progress. It's better to start small and be consistent. Remember, self-discipline is the journey of a lifetime.

Together with meditation, integration (PAW), and journaling, your Focus Technique forms the core of your self-discipline daily practice.

YOUR DAILY PRACTICE

Once you do your initial setup and you're aware of what your biggest challenges are, it's all about maintaining a daily practice that keeps you on track with your goals and values. Here is a template for you to try.

Morning

As part of your daily morning routine, practice at least ten minutes of meditation (Chapter 37). You can learn more about it in my first book, *Practical Meditation*, or by joining the *Limitless Life* program, or by following any guided meditation from any teacher you trust.

After your meditation practice, you then take a couple of minutes to do the **Three Rs**:

- **Remember**. Remember your aspirations and review the main self-discipline technique that you are focusing on, so that they are more top of mind.
- **Recommit**. Think of your SMART goals and chosen habits, and recommit to following them. Keep doing this every day until it becomes second nature.
- **Resolve.** Set an intention for your day today. Your intention is a goal for your practice of awareness—something for you to pay attention to during the day, and constantly come back to.

Day

Throughout the day, practice the PAW Method and one of the three main willpower techniques (Chapters 17-20). Get into the habit of pausing more before every decision, becoming aware of the +1 and -1 options, and then using your willpower to shift your state, so that you can live more in harmony with your goals.

Enhance *pausing* by including one-minute mini-meditations, three times a day. Enhance *awareness* through tracking your actions as +1 or -1.

Evening

At the end of the day, go through the three-question journaling method described in Chapter 16. This only takes two to five minutes, and it helps you develop gratitude, awareness, and intention.

These daily practices don't take a lot of your time, yet they pay rich dividends. They allow you to be more self-disciplined with your life, time, and energy. Every day that you follow these practices is a day when you have taken a firm step toward your ideal self.

FINE-TUNING

If you do your initial self-discipline setup and follow the daily practices above (including your Focus Technique), you are well on your way.

At this point, you may want to make sure that you are set for practicing self-discipline in a sustainable way, without burning out or missing out on other aspects of life (Chapter 3). You can also fine-tune your lifestyle choices to make sure that you are making things easier for yourself by having good nutrition and enough sleep (Chapter 36), by keeping good influences in your life (Chapter 35), and by organizing your day in a way that manages your energy well and prevents decision fatigue (Chapter 4). Finally, you can learn to use self-discipline to better manage your time (Chapter 33), and to develop the virtues you need to be the person you want to be (Chapter 38).

As an aid to implement all of this in your life in an effective way, you can download the free Workbook (**MindfulSelfDiscipline.com/workbook**) and consider subscribing to the app (**MindfulSelfDiscipline.com/app**).

EPILOGUE

With life no matter what you do you are all in. This is going to kill you.
You might as well play the most magnificent game you can.
Do you have anything better to do?

Jordan Petersen

The height of a man's success is gauged by his self-mastery;
the depth of his failure by his self-abandonment.

Leonardo da Vinci

Mindful Self-Discipline is about self-mastery. It is the art of living in harmony with your highest goals and values. Now you know how to do it, and why it matters. You have learned the tools that enable you to achieve your goals more quickly and smoothly, to live well, and to fulfill the vision you have for yourself, in a balanced way.

You've learned how to finish what you start. How to set meaningful goals, prioritize them, and stay on track with important habits in your life. You've learned how to overcome obstacles—such as distractions, procrastination, excuses, low motivation, self-doubt, and fear—by using powerful awareness and and mindset tools.

Self-discipline is a form of personal power. It's the power to accomplish the goals you set for yourself, and get things done. The power to master your impulses rather than be their slave. The power to become who you want to be.

Use it wisely.

This power comes with practice, and it is worth every effort. Because the disciplined life leads to growth and fulfillment; the undisciplined life leads to stagnation and regrets. Regrets about the time wasted, the dreams not chased, the potential not actualized. The pain of self-discipline is the price for self-actualization.

A Quick Recap

In the first part of this book, you've learned what self-discipline is, how it works in your brain, and the benefits of developing this skill. We covered the need to be balanced with our disciplines, so we live well and don't burn out. We then discussed the essential role of willpower, and how to develop it.

In the second part, we covered the Aspiration Pillar. You learned how to find your deepest aspirations in life, magnify them, create specific goals out of them, and prioritize them in your daily life. You saw how to deal with self-sabotage, and also how to adopt three powerful virtues that allow you to live your aspirations more fully: ownership, self-belief, and sacrifice.

The third part of the book was about the Awareness Pillar, which is the heart of Mindful Self-Discipline. Awareness is a quality developed through daily meditation and self-reflection, and applied in daily life with the help of the PAW Method. You learned three different ways to use willpower to shift your state, so you are able to make decisions that advance your goals rather than take you away from them. We also learned techniques to help you develop the virtue of perseverance, and overcome the obstacles of distractions and excuses along the way.

In the fourth part of this book, we covered the last pillar of self-discipline, Action. We started with designing your action plan by creating milestones for your goals and going through the nitty-gritty of setting up effective habits that will move you forward. Then we learned specific techniques for overcoming procrastination, self-doubt, and failure. You also learned how to improve your environment so that self-discipline is easier. We closed with a golden key by talking about the *Never Zero* commitment.

In the final part of the book, you learned principles of mindful time management and specific guidelines for building effective morning routines and night routines. You saw the importance of choosing your influences carefully, getting enough sleep, eating healthy, and exercising. You learned about the importance of virtues as a practice of the internal aspect of self-discipline, and how to develop them. We then covered the topic of spirituality as an optional layer that can add greater strength and meaning to your self-discipline, as well as grow with it.

The purpose of this book is to be the ultimate self-discipline manual. As a result, we've covered many concepts and practices. A final reminder, at this point, is this: don't overwhelm yourself. It's not possible for you to practice all of this at once—not even desirable. Please don't try. Instead, select two or three practices that most appeal to you, and begin with those. Once they become second nature, you can then add new practices.

Even if you implement well just one technique from this book, your self-discipline will already improve. So take it easy on yourself. Consistency is the most important thing.

From the bow of self-discipline, shooting forward like an arrow flying toward its target, success will eventually be yours. It's just a matter of time. Do not doubt it.

What It's All About

Self-discipline is the foundation of a good life. It can enhance your health, improve your wellbeing, increase your income, deepen your relationships, and fulfill your dreams. It can help you master any skill, art, or trade. It can make you a better human, and pave the way to spiritual awakening (if that is your thing).

Self-discipline helps you not only to check off your goals, but also to grow as person, develop virtues, and live better.

Some say that self-discipline is the father of all virtues. It makes sense, because every virtue is a *discipline*. Every virtue is a commitment that needs to be kept. But if self-discipline is the father of all virtues, self-awareness is the mother. In Mindful Self-Discipline, they are united. Without them, very little is possible. With them, the sky is the limit.

At the end of the day, the ultimate reward of Mindful Self-Discipline is not that you will achieve your goals. Of course, that will happen too, in due time—and it's great. Achieving your goals is, most likely, why you bought this book. In the bigger picture of life, though, the joy that you will experience achieving your goals will be temporary, and your new achievements will soon become your new normal. So what's beyond that?

The ultimate reward of self-discipline is the person you will become. You will be proud of yourself. You will feel happier and engaged. Your life will be deeper, your mind wider, and your possibilities… greater.

This growth, this change, is worth your every effort.

It's Your Turn

You have a choice now.

You can think "Great, I've learned a lot!" and then close this book and start a new one tomorrow, hoping that, somehow, just reading these pages was enough for self-discipline to automatically appear in your life.

Or you can REALLY take action based on what you have learned—again and again. You can highlight, summarize, review, and seriously think about it. You can clarify your goals, create your daily routines, and go *Never Zero*. You can download the workbook and do the exercises. You can choose the two techniques you will begin applying in your daily life right now. You can add reminders on your phone, paste some notes around your home, and create a calendar event to continuously come back to this book and integrate more of its principles.

What is more valuable: to read 100 self-help books, or read one and apply it 100 times? These two different choices lead to two different future versions of yourself. Which one will it be for you?

Reading this book can be the beginning of a new life. A big reset. A line in the sand. If I did my work well, it will be. And if I didn't—then I've failed you.

Life is short. The task ahead of you is difficult. Do not waste time. Do not hesitate. Do not postpone. Trying to escape your meaningful tasks will leave you void of meaning, and regretful.

Begin now. Take a step forward, wholeheartedly. Keep yourself on track no matter what.

A new life is possible. A new YOU is possible.

Go and live an amazing life! Be true to your higher self.

WORK WITH ME

In this book you have learned a lot of principles and practical exercises that you can apply in your life to become more disciplined. I have not held anything back. All the information about self-discipline that I could put in a book is here for you—this is the *complete system* of Mindful Self-Discipline.

If you feel that you have all you need, I am happy for you and wish you success! You can skip this page.

On the other hand, at this point you might feel that you want to go deeper, or at least to accelerate this process. Perhaps you want to know which of the *dozens* of exercises in this book you should focus on, and how to go about it. Perhaps you need some support customizing this system for your personality and needs, or you want help optimizing your daily routine. Perhaps you feel stuck somewhere and know that having some mentorship will help you move forward quicker and save you a lot of trials and errors. Perhaps you are playing small, or held back by certain limiting beliefs and fears. Finally, there may be an inner conflict that you just cannot figure out—a part of yourself that is holding you back and sabotaging the journey—and you need help resolving.

There is a level of transformation and support that can never happen through a book, however complete. Having the knowledge is one thing; effectively implementing it in your life is something else altogether.

You can have the best set of videos for exercising at home or for improving your public-speaking skills—but still, having a personal trainer or a speaking coach will take you to the next level. He will hold you accountable every step of the way and inspire you to be better. He will give you personalized feedback and tips that apply only to you. He will show you shortcuts that can only be shown face to face. You will be much more committed to the process, and thus much more likely to succeed. You will have clarity about what to do, and the confidence that you are on the right path. You will be guided and supported.

The same thing is true for learning self-discipline: having a coach will help you take it to the next level. So here is my invitation for you: if you want to accelerate your journey toward your goals (or make it smoother), and you are ready to invest in yourself, then contact me for self-discipline coaching at **MindfulSelfDiscipline.com/coaching**. If we work together, you are *bound* to succeed—whatever your goal or aspiration. My success rates with self-discipline clients are very high.

The book is for everyone. The coaching isn't. It requires you to be coachable, moved by an inspiring goal, and ready to commit more deeply by making a substantial investment in yourself. If this is you, let's talk.

THE APP

If you want to really change your life with the techniques of this book, you will have to implement them *daily*. For that, you will need to *remember* them daily, and have a frictionless way to practice them in times of need.

With this goal in mind, I've created a mobile app to help you take what you've learned to the next level, and to make sure that you *actually follow* the exercises in the book, so you can get the transformation that you seek.

The **Mindful Self-Discipline app** contains more than a hundred practical summaries of all the main concepts in the book, and also several interactive tools to help you implement the Awareness Pillar more easily. It gives you access to:

- More than 20 exclusive guided meditations for self-discipline
- The step-by-step PAW Method
- Interactive breathing exercises
- The *Life Tracker*, for easily tracking your +1s and -1s
- Graphs showing your progress in your goals and habits
- A reward engine, which uses the *token economy* principle to keep you motivated
- The three-question daily journal (gratitude, awareness, intention)
- Reminders for meditation, tracking, PAW, journaling, and reviews
- Member-only Q&As with me

The guided meditations include the techniques of ROAR, ALFA, Power Visualization, and also meditations for finding your purpose, grounding, increasing focus, shifting negative self-talk, developing virtues, sleeping better, and overcoming procrastination—among others.

Look at this app as an ongoing training program for self-discipline and self-awareness. Its goal is to help you live a life of greater purpose and fulfillment. It exists to make self-discipline easier for you.

Learn more about it here:
MindfulSelfDiscipline.com/app

May you find it useful in your journey.

THE MOVEMENT

Mindful Self-Discipline needs to be more than a book. It needs to be a *movement*—in your life and in society. Because self-discipline makes things better. It makes humans better.

All the inventions and facilities we enjoy are the fruit of someone's self-discipline. All the culture, art, science, and technology is the fruit of the self-discipline of a few individuals. Self-discipline creates personal fulfillment and also legacy.

Self-discipline changes lives. And it can also change the world.

What can you do to be part of this bigger movement? Cultivate Mindful Self-Discipline in your life, of course! But let this go beyond you. Share the inspiration. Help spread the ideas in this book to those around you.

If you got anything of value from this book—any exercise, quote, or idea—then please gift a copy to someone you care about (or lend them yours). Ask them to read it and practice it. Talk about it. The more the people around you are disciplined, the easier it will be for you to be disciplined too; this is the power of company and accountability.

Spread the word.

The self-disciplined shall inherit the earth—let it be good people like you and the ones you trust. Thank you!

INDEX OF PRACTICES

Here are the main techniques, methods, and exercises taught in this book. Use this table as a quick practical reference, as well as to mark which ones to focus on.

SORTED ALPHABETICALLY

Method, Tool, Exercise	Chapter
Intrinsic Rewards	27
Journaling	16
Keystone Habits	26
Kindle the Virtue	36
Letting Go of False Hope	21
Letting Go of Perfectionism	21
Make Your Offering	13
Meditation	37
Minimum Action	26
Morning and Night Routines	34
Never Zero Commitment	31
PAW Method	17
Plan Your Time	33
POWER Visualization	23
Procrastinate Distraction	22
Protect Your Time	33
Regular Reviews	25
Remove Your Options	29
Shift Your Self-Talk	12
Shift Your Focus	18
Shift Your Perception	19
SMART Goals	9
Snooze Distractions	33
Soul-Longing Meditation	7
The "Not Now" Technique	29
The ALFA Method	30
The Deeper Why	7
The Monk Week	22
The Red-Pill Test	11
The Triple Commitment	10
Voluntary Discomfort	13
Watch Your Time	33
Willpower Challenge	4
Yoga Nidra for Aspirations	8
Your Core Values	7

SORTED BY OBSTACLE

In the table below you will find most of the tools covered, ordered by purpose. Many of the tools in this book can be used for more than one purpose; and there is also a lot of overlap between the different obstacles to self-discipline.

The first section contains the wildcard tools, which can be used to deal with any of the obstacles. Things like having a strong aspiration, and the three practices of awareness (meditation, journaling, PAW Method), power the whole Mindful Self-Discipline framework, and are not limited to any specific challenge. As to the *contingency plan*, it is something that you do to prepare yourself to deal with all challenges.

The one or two of the most powerful tools for each obstacle will have a star (*) next to them.

Obstacle	Methods You Can Use	Chapter
Any Obstacle	Aspiration Pillar (Steps 1-4)	6-10
	Make Your Offering	13
	Meditation	37, 16
	Journaling	16
	PAW Method	17
	Contingency Plan	30
Procrastination	Accountability	35
	Baby Steps *	28
	Commitment Devices	22
	Embrace Your Pain (ROAR) *	20
	Rewards	28
	Increase the Pain of Inaction *	28
	Letting Go of Perfectionism	21
	Minimum Action	26
	Never Zero Commitment *	31
	Remove Your Options	29
	Shift Your Focus	18
	Shift Your Perception	19
	The Monk Week	22
	POWER Visualization	23
	Virtue Development	38

Obstacle	Methods You Can Use	Chapter
Low Motivation	Never Zero Commitment	31
	Minimum Action *	26
	Virtue Development	38
	Rewards *	27
Excuses	Never Zero Commitment	31
	Habit Building	26
	Commitment Devices	22
	Remove Your Options	29
	The "Not Now" Technique	29
	Challenge Your Excuses *	23
	POWER Visualization *	23
	Accountability *	35
	Baby Steps	28
	Shift Your Focus	18
Forgetfulness	Accountability	35
	Habit Cues *	26
Doubts	Review Your Influencers	35
	Get Perspective	29
	Remove Your Options	29
	The "Not Now" Technique *	29
	Challenge Your Excuses	23
	Letting Go of False Hope	21
	Letting Go of Perfectionism	21
	Baby Steps *	28
	Focus on Success	12
	Get Inspired	12
	Shift Your Self-Talk *	12
	POWER Visualization	23
	Willpower Challenge	4
	Virtue Development	38

NOTES AND REFERENCES

Here you will find the scientific references, sources, and notes for several of the studies quotes in the book.

1. What is Self-Discipline?

- June P. Tangney, Roy F. Baumeister, and Angie Luzio Boone, "High Self-Control Predicts Good Adjustment, Less Pathology, Better Grades, and Interpersonal Success," *Journal of Personality* 72, no. 2 (April 2004): 271–324, https://doi.org/10.1111/j.0022-3506.2004.00263.x.
- June P. Tangney, Roy F. Baumeister, and Angie Luzio Boone, "High Self-Control Predicts Good Adjustment, Less Pathology, Better Grades, and Interpersonal Success," *Journal of Personality* 72, no. 2 (April 2004): 271–324, https://doi.org/10.1111/j.0022-3506.2004.00263.x.
- Wilhelm Hofmann et al., "Dieting and the Self-Control of Eating in Everyday Environments: An Experience Sampling Study," *British Journal of Health Psychology* 19, no. 3 (June 10, 2013): 523–39, https://doi.org/10.1111/bjhp.12053.
- Marja Ilona Kinnunen et al., "Self-Control Is Associated with Physical Activity and Fitness among Young Males," *Behavioral Medicine (Washington, D.C.)* 38, no. 3 (2012): 83–89, https://doi.org/10.1080/08964289.2012.693975.
- Larissa Barber, Matthew J. Grawitch, and David C. Munz, "Are Better Sleepers More Engaged Workers? A Self-Regulatory Approach to Sleep Hygiene and Work Engagement," *Stress and Health* 29, no. 4 (October 2012): n/a-n/a, https://doi.org/10.1002/smi.2468.
- Thomas A Wills et al., "Behavioral and Emotional Self-Control: Relations to Substance Use in Samples of Middle and High School Students," *Psychology of Addictive Behaviors : Journal of the Society of Psychologists in Addictive Behaviors* 20, no. 3 (2006): 265–78, https://doi.org/10.1037/0893-164X.20.3.265.
- A. L. Duckworth and M. E.P. Seligman, "Self-Discipline Outdoes IQ in Predicting Academic Performance of Adolescents," *Psychological Science* 16, no. 12 (December 1, 2005): 939–44, https://doi.org/10.1111/j.1467-9280.2005.01641.x.
- Eli J. Finkel and W. Keith Campbell, "Self-Control and Accommodation in Close Relationships: An Interdependence Analysis," *Journal of Personality and Social Psychology* 81, no. 2 (2001): 263–77, https://doi.org/10.1037//0022-3514.81.2.263.
- Camilla Strömbäck et al., "Does Self-Control Predict Financial Behavior and Financial Well-Being?" *Journal of Behavioral and Experimental Finance* 14 (June 2017): 30–38, https://doi.org/10.1016/j.jbef.2017.04.002.
- Denise, Marieke Adriaanse, and Kentaro Fujita, *The Routledge International Handbook of Self-Control in Health and Well-Being : Concepts, Theories, and Central Issues* (Abingdon, Oxon; New York, Ny: Routledge, 2018).

2. The Benefits of Self-Discipline

- A. L. Duckworth and M. E.P. Seligman, "Self-Discipline Outdoes IQ in Predicting Academic Performance of Adolescents," *Psychological Science* 16, no. 12 (December 1, 2005): 939–44, https://doi.org/10.1111/j.1467-9280.2005.01641.x.
- Norman Anderson et al., "Stress in America: Our Health at Risk - 2011 Survey Reveals Mental Health of Young Adults as Most at Risk," https://www.apa.org/, January 11, 2012, https://www.apa.org/news/press/releases/stress/2011/final-2011.pdf.
- Alex Bertrams, Roy F. Baumeister, and Chris Englert, "Higher Self-Control Capacity Predicts Lower Anxiety-Impaired Cognition during Math Examinations," *Frontiers in Psychology* 7 (March 31, 2016), https://doi.org/10.3389/fpsyg.2016.00485.
- Wilhelm Hofmann et al., "Yes, But Are They Happy? Effects of Trait Self-Control on Affective Well-Being and Life Satisfaction," *Journal of Personality* 82, no. 4 (August 8, 2013): 265–77, https://doi.org/10.1111/jopy.12050.
- Shahram Heshmat, "How Self-Control Can Help You Live a Healthier Life," *Psychology Today*, July 28, 2016, https://www.psychologytoday.com/us/blog/science-choice/201607/how-self-control-can-help-you-live-healthier-life.

3. Dangers and Misconceptions

- Wilhelm Hofmann et al., "Yes, But Are They Happy? Effects of Trait Self-Control on Affective Well-Being and Life Satisfaction," *Journal of Personality* 82, no. 4 (August 8, 2013): 265–77, https://doi.org/10.1111/jopy.12050.
- Maia Szalavitz, "Self-Disciplined People Are Happier (and Not as Deprived as You Think)," *Time*, June 24, 2013, https://healthland.time.com/2013/06/24/self-disciplined-people-are-happier-and-not-as-deprived-as-you-think/.
- Ran Kivetz and Itamar Simonson, "Self-Control for the Righteous: Toward a Theory of Precommitment to Indulgence," *Journal of Consumer Research* 29, no. 2 (September 2002): 199–217, https://doi.org/10.1086/341571.
- Daniel S. Hamermesh and Elena Stancanelli, "Long Workweeks and Strange Hours," *ILR Review* 68, no. 5 (June 19, 2015): 1007–18, https://doi.org/10.1177/0019793915592375.
- Ran Kivetz and Anat Keinan, "Repenting Hyperopia: An Analysis of Self-Control Regrets," *Journal of Consumer Research* 33, no. 2 (September 2006): 273–82, https://doi.org/10.1086/506308.
- Denise, Marieke Adriaanse, and Kentaro Fujita, *The Routledge International Handbook of Self-Control in Health and Well-Being : Concepts, Theories, and Central Issues* (Abingdon, Oxon; New York, Ny: Routledge, 2018).
- Anat Keinan and Ran Kivetz, "Productivity Orientation and the Consumption of Collectable Experiences," *Journal of Consumer Research* 37, no. 6 (April 1, 2011): 935–50, https://doi.org/10.1086/657163.

4. Willpower, Habits and Environment

- Maia Szalavitz, "Decision Fatigue Saps Willpower—If We Let It," *Time*, August 11, 2011.
- S. Danziger, J. Levav, and L. Avnaim-Pesso, "Extraneous Factors in Judicial Decisions," *Proceedings of the National Academy of Sciences* 108, no. 17 (April 11, 2011): 6889–92, https://doi.org/10.1073/pnas.1018033108.
- Maia Szalavitz, "Mind over Mind? Decision Fatigue Saps Willpower—If We Let It," *Time*, August 23, 2011, https://healthland.time.com/2011/08/23/mind-over-mind-decision-fatigue-may-deplete-our-willpower-but-only-if-we-let-it/#ixzz1WRGB2Bya.

- Roy F. Baumeister, *Self-Regulation and Self-Control: Selected Works of Roy Baumeister* (Abingdon, Oxon; New York, Ny: Routledge, 2018).
- D. C. Molden, C. M. Hui, and A. A. Scholer, "Chapter 20 - Understanding Self-Regulation Failure: A Motivated Effort-Allocation Account," ed. Edward R. Hirt, Joshua J. Clarkson, and Lile Jia, ScienceDirect (San Diego: Academic Press, January 1, 2016), https://www.sciencedirect.com/science/article/pii/B9780128018507000202.
- Maarten A.S. Boksem, Theo F. Meijman, and Monicque M. Lorist, "Mental Fatigue, Motivation and Action Monitoring," *Biological Psychology* 72, no. 2 (May 2006): 123–32, https://doi.org/10.1016/j.biopsycho.2005.08.007.
- Denise, Marieke Adriaanse, and Kentaro Fujita, *The Routledge International Handbook of Self-Control in Health and Well-Being : Concepts, Theories, and Central Issues* (Abingdon, Oxon; New York, Ny: Routledge, 2018).
- Benjamin C. Ampel, Mark Muraven, and Ewan C. McNay, "Mental Work Requires Physical Energy: Self-Control Is Neither Exception nor Exceptional," *Frontiers in Psychology* 9 (July 5, 2018), https://doi.org/10.3389/fpsyg.2018.01005.
- Peng Qi et al., "Neural Mechanisms of Mental Fatigue Revisited: New Insights from the Brain Connectome," *Engineering* 5, no. 2 (April 2019): 276–86, https://doi.org/10.1016/j.eng.2018.11.025.
- Amitai Shenhav et al., "Toward a Rational and Mechanistic Account of Mental Effort," *Annual Review of Neuroscience* 40, no. 1 (July 25, 2017): 99–124, https://doi.org/10.1146/annurev-neuro-072116-031526.
- Benjamin Y. Hayden, "Why Has Evolution Not Selected for Perfect Self-Control?," *Philosophical Transactions of the Royal Society B: Biological Sciences* 374, no. 1766 (December 31, 2018) 20180139, https://doi.org/10.1098/rstb.2018.0139.
- Roy F Baumeister, *Self-Regulation and Self-Control : Selected Works of Roy Baumeister* (Abingdon, Oxon; New York, Ny: Routledge, 2018).
- Walter Mischel, "The Marshmallow Test : Understanding Self-Control and How to Master It" (London Corgi Books, 2015).
- Katharina Bernecker and Veronika Job, "Beliefs About Willpower Moderate The Effect of Previous Day Demands on Next Day's Expectations" ResearchGate (Frontiers, October 14, 2015), https://www.researchgate.net/profile/Katharina_Bernecker2/publication/282856846_Beliefs_About_Willpower_Moderate_The_Effect_of_Previous_Day_Demands_on_Next_Day.
- Walter Mischel, Ebbe B. Ebbesen, and Antonette Raskoff Zeiss, "Cognitive and Attentional Mechanisms in Delay of Gratification." *Journal of Personality and Social Psychology* 21, no. 2 (1972): 204–18, https://doi.org/10.1037/h0032198.

6. The What and the Why

- https://www.facebook.com/BlueZones, "How Finding Your Purpose Can Improve Your Health and Life," Blue Zones, August 22, 2011, https://www.bluezones.com/2011/08/the-right-outlook-how-finding-your-purpose-can-improve-your-life/.
- B. L. Fredrickson et al., "A Functional Genomic Perspective on Human Well-Being," *Proceedings of the National Academy of Sciences* 110, no. 33 (July 29, 2013): 13684–89, https://doi.org/10.1073/pnas.1305419110.
- Alan Mozes, "A Sense of Purpose May Help Your Heart," medicalxpress.com, March 6, 2015, https://medicalxpress.com/news/2015-03-purpose-heart.html.
- Megumi Koizumi et al., "Effect of Having a Sense of Purpose in Life on the Risk of Death from Cardiovascular Diseases," *Journal of Epidemiology* 18, no. 5 (2008): 191–96, https://doi.org/10.2188/jea.je2007388.

- Gallup, Inc. and Healthways, "State of Global Well-Being. Results of the Gallup-Healthways Global Well-Being Index," http://info.healthways.com/, 2013, http://info.healthways.com/hs-fs/hub/162029/file-1634508606-pdf/WBI2013/Gallup-Healthways_State_of_Global_Well-Being_vFINAL.pdf?t=1428689269171.
- "The Many Benefits of Caring for Others," *Caregiver Stress*, May 31, 2017, https://www.caregiver-stress.com/stress-management/daughters-in-the-workplace/benefits-of-caring-for-others-canada/.
- W. M. Phillips, "Purpose in Life, Depression, and Locus of Control," *Journal of Clinical Psychology* 36, no. 3 (July 1, 1980): 661–667, https://doi.org/10.1002/1097-4679(198007)36:3<661::AID-JCLP2270360309>3.0.CO;2-G.
- Clifton B. Parker, "Stanford Psychologist Explores How Meaningfulness Cultivates Well-Being over Time," Stanford University, October 22, 2014, https://news.stanford.edu/news/2014/october/aaker-happy-choices-10-22-2014.html.
- Patricia A. Boyle et al., "Effect of a Purpose in Life on Risk of Incident Alzheimer Disease and Mild Cognitive Impairment in Community-Dwelling Older Persons," *Archives of General Psychiatry* 67, no. 3 (March 1, 2010): 304, https://doi.org/10.1001/archgenpsychiatry.2009.208.
- Marina Milyavskaya et al., "Saying 'No' to Temptation: Want-to Motivation Improves Self-Regulation by Reducing Temptation Rather than by Increasing Self-Control," *Journal of Personality and Social Psychology* 109, no. 4 (2015): 677–93, https://doi.org/10.1037/pspp0000045.

14. Be True to Who You Are

- Denise de Ridder, Marieke Adriaanse, and Kentaro Fujita, *The Routledge International Handbook of Self-Control in Health and Well-Being : Concepts, Theories, and Central Issues* (Abingdon, Oxon; New York, Ny: Routledge, 2018).
- Chang-Yuan Lee et al., "Past Actions as Self-Signals: How Acting in a Self-Interested Way Influences Environmental Decision Making," ed. Claus Lamm, *PLOS ONE* 11, no. 7 (July 22, 2016): e0158456, https://doi.org/10.1371/journal.pone.0158456.
- Ravi Dhar and Klaus Wertenbroch, "Self-Signaling and the Costs and Benefits of Temptation in Consumer Choice," *Journal of Marketing Research* 49, no. 1 (February 2012): 15–25, https://doi.org/10.1509/jmr.10.0490.

16. The Why and How of Awareness

- Daniel M Wegner et al., "Ironic Processes of Mental Control," *Psychological Review* 101, no. 1 (2004): 34–52, http://www2.psych.ubc.ca/~schaller/Psyc590Readings/Wegner1994.pdf.
- Ryan J. Giuliano and Nicole Y.Y. Wicha, "Why the White Bear Is Still There: Electrophysiological Evidence for Ironic Semantic Activation during Thought Suppression," *Brain Research* 1316 (February 2010): 62–74, https://doi.org/10.1016/j.brainres.2009.12.041.
- Donal E Carlston, *The Oxford Handbook of Social Cognition* (Oxford ; New York: Oxford University Press, 2014).
- James A.K. Erskine, "Resistance Can Be Futile: Investigating Behavioural Rebound," *Appetite* 50, no. 2–3 (March 2008): 415–21, https://doi.org/10.1016/j.appet.2007.09.006.
- James A.K. Erskine, George J. Georgiou, and Lia Kvavilashvili, "I Suppress, Therefore I Smoke," *Psychological Science* 21, no. 9 (July 26, 2010): 1225–30, https://doi.org/10.1177/0956797610378687.
- Nicolette Siep et al., "Fighting Food Temptations: The Modulating Effects of Short-Term Cognitive Reappraisal, Suppression and up-Regulation on Mesocorticolimbic Activity Related to Appetitive Motivation," *NeuroImage* 60, no. 1 (March 1, 2012): 213–220, https://doi.org/10.1016/j.neuroimage.2011.12.067.

- Sarah Bowen et al., "The Role of Thought Suppression in the Relationship between Mindfulness Meditation and Alcohol Use," *Addictive Behaviors* 32, no. 10 (October 2007): 2324–28 https://doi.org/10.1016/j.addbeh.2007.01.025.
- S Yokum and E Stice, "Cognitive Regulation of Food Craving: Effects of Three Cognitive Reappraisal Strategies on Neural Response to Palatable Foods," *International Journal of Obesity* 37, no. 12 (April 9, 2013): 1565–70, https://doi.org/10.1038/ijo.2013.39.
- Daniel M Wegner et al., "Paradoxical Effects of Thought Suppression," 2004, http://www.communicationcache.com/uploads/1/0/8/8/10887248/paradoxical_effects_of_thought_suppression.pdf.

17. The PAW Method

- M. Wallaert, A. Ward, and T. Mann, "Reducing Smoking Among Distracted Individuals: A Preliminary Investigation," *Nicotine & Tobacco Research* 16, no. 10 (August 6, 2014): 1399–1403, https://doi.org/10.1093/ntr/ntu117.
- Eric Robinson et al., "Eating Attentively: A Systematic Review and Meta-Analysis of the Effect of Food Intake Memory and Awareness on Eating," *The American Journal of Clinical Nutrition* 97, no. 4 (February 27, 2013): 728–42, https://doi.org/10.3945/ajcn.112.045245.
- Stacey Long et al., "Effects of Distraction and Focused Attention on Actual and Perceived Food Intake in Females with Non-Clinical Eating Psychopathology," *Appetite* 56, no. 2 (April 2011): 350–56, https://doi.org/10.1016/j.appet.2010.12.018.
- Suzanne Higgs and Morgan Woodward, "Television Watching during Lunch Increases Afternoon Snack Intake of Young Women," *Appetite* 52, no. 1 (February 2009): 39–43, https://doi.org/10.1016/j.appet.2008.07.007.
- Dolly Mittal et al., "Snacking While Watching TV Impairs Food Recall and Promotes Food Intake on a Later TV Free Test Meal," *Applied Cognitive Psychology* 25, no. 6 (December 5, 2010): 871–77, https://doi.org/10.1002/acp.1760.
- Rose E Oldham-Cooper et al., "Playing a Computer Game during Lunch Affects Fullness, Memory for Lunch, and Later Snack Intake," *The American Journal of Clinical Nutrition* 93, no. 2 (December 8, 2010): 308–13, https://doi.org/10.3945/ajcn.110.004580.

18. Technique #1: Shift Your Focus

- Kristian Ove R. Myrseth and Ayelet Fishbach, "Self-Control," *Current Directions in Psychological Science* 18, no. 4 (August 2009): 247–52, https://doi.org/10.1111/j.1467-8721.2009.01645.x.
- Elizabeth C Webb and Suzanne B Shu, "Is Broad Bracketing Always Better? How Broad Decision Framing Leads to More Optimal Preferences over Repeated Gambles," *Judgment and Decision Making* 12, no. 4 (2017): 382–96, https://go.gale.com/ps/anonymous?id=GALE%7CA505130881&sid=googleScholar&v=2.1&it=r&linkaccess=abs&issn=19302975&p=AONE&sw=w.
- Lisa K. Libby, Eric M. Shaeffer, and Richard P. Eibach, "Seeing Meaning in Action: A Bidirectional Link between Visual Perspective and Action Identification Level," *Journal of Experimental Psychology: General* 138, no. 4 (2009): 503–16, https://doi.org/10.1037/a0016795.
- Judson Brewer, "Judson Brewer - No Willpower Required: Hacking the Brain for Habit Change - YouTube," www.youtube.com, 2020, https://youtu.be/nFuVUZFm9AI
- James Clear, *Atomic Habits*, 2017.
- Oliver J. Sheldon and Ayelet Fishbach, "Anticipating and Resisting the Temptation to Behave Unethically," *Personality and Social Psychology Bulletin* 41, no. 7 (May 22, 2015): 962–75, https://doi.org/10.1177/0146167215586196.

- Oleg Urminsky, "The Role of Psychological Connectedness to the Future Self in Decisions Over Time," *Current Directions in Psychological Science* 26, no. 1 (February 2017): 34–39, https://doi.org/10.1177/0963721416668810.
- Camilla Strömbäck et al., "Does Self-Control Predict Financial Behavior and Financial Well-Being?" *Journal of Behavioral and Experimental Finance* 14 (June 2017): 30–38, https://doi.org/10.1016/j.jbef.2017.04.002.
- Elliot T. Berkman et al., "Self-Control as Value-Based Choice," *Current Directions in Psychological Science* 26, no. 5 (2017): 422–428, https://doi.org/10.1177/0963721417704394.
- Kaitlyn M. Werner and Marina Milyavskaya, "Motivation and Self-regulation: The Role of Want-to Motivation in the Processes Underlying Self-regulation and Self-control," *Social and Personality Psychology Compass*, December 11, 2018, e12425, https://doi.org/10.1111/spc3.12425.
- Mark Muraven, Marylène Gagné, and Heather Rosman, "Helpful Self-Control: Autonomy Support, Vitality, and Depletion," *Journal of Experimental Social Psychology* 44, no. 3 (May 2008): 573–85, https://doi.org/10.1016/j.jesp.2007.10.008.
- Marina Milyavskaya et al., "Saying 'No' to Temptation: Want-to Motivation Improves Self-Regulation by Reducing Temptation Rather than by Increasing Self-Control," *Journal of Personality and Social Psychology* 109, no. 4 (2015): 677–93, https://doi.org/10.1037/pspp0000045.

19. Technique #2: Shift Your Perception

- Kosuke Motoki and Motoaki Sugiura, "Disgust, Sadness, and Appraisal: Disgusted Consumers Dislike Food More Than Sad Ones," *Frontiers in Psychology* 9 (February 6, 2018), https://doi.org/10.3389/fpsyg.2018.00076.
- Hedy Kober et al., "Regulation of Craving by Cognitive Strategies in Cigarette Smokers," *Drug and Alcohol Dependence* 106, no. 1 (January 2010): 52–55, https://doi.org/10.1016/j.drugalcdep.2009.07.017.
- Nicole R. Giuliani, Rebecca D. Calcott, and Elliot T. Berkman, "Piece of Cake. Cognitive Reappraisal of Food Craving," *Appetite* 64 (May 2013): 56–61, https://doi.org/10.1016/j.appet.2012.12.020.
- Shane W. Reader, Richard B. Lopez, and Bryan T. Denny, "Cognitive Reappraisal of Low-Calorie Food Predicts Real-World Craving and Consumption of High- and Low-Calorie Foods in Daily Life," *Appetite* 131 (December 2018): 44–52, https://doi.org/10.1016/j.appet.2018.08.036.
- S Yokum and E Stice, "Cognitive Regulation of Food Craving: Effects of Three Cognitive Reappraisal Strategies on Neural Response to Palatable Foods," *International Journal of Obesity* 37, no. 12 (April 9, 2013): 1565–70, https://doi.org/10.1038/ijo.2013.39.

22. Awareness Overcomes Distraction

- Plató and W R M Lamb, *Laches Protagoras ; Mano ; Euthydemus* (London William Heinemann, 1924).
- TEDxTalks, "The Pleasure Trap: Douglas Lisle at TEDxFremont - YouTube," www.youtube.com, n.d., https://youtu.be/jX2btaDOBK8.
- Anthony G. Phillips, Giada Vacca, and Soyon Ahn, "A Top-down Perspective on Dopamine, Motivation and Memory," *Pharmacology Biochemistry and Behavior* 90, no. 2 (August 1, 2008): 236–249, https://doi.org/10.1016/j.pbb.2007.10.014.
- Nicole Y.L. Oei et al., "Acute Stress-Induced Cortisol Elevations Mediate Reward System Activity during Subconscious Processing of Sexual Stimuli," *Psychoneuroendocrinology* 39 (January 2014): 111–20, https://doi.org/10.1016/j.psyneuen.2013.10.005.

- Rajita Sinha, "How Does Stress Increase Risk of Drug Abuse and Relapse?" *Psychopharmacology* 158, no. 4 (December 1, 2001): 343–59, https://doi.org/10.1007/s002130100917.
- Arie W Kruglanski et al., "A Theory of Goal Systems," ResearchGate (Elsevier, December 31, 2002), https://www.researchgate.net/publication/242082665_A_theory_of_goal_systems.
- Wilhelm Hofmann, Hiroki Kotabe, and Maike Luhmann, "The Spoiled Pleasure of Giving in to Temptation," *Motivation and Emotion* 37, no. 4 (April 7, 2013): 733–42, https://doi.org/10.1007/s11031-013-9355-4.
- Kaitlin Woolley and Ayelet Fishbach, "For the Fun of It: Harnessing Immediate Rewards to Increase Persistence in Long-Term Goals," *Journal of Consumer Research* 42, no. 6 (January 5, 2016): 952–66, https://doi.org/10.1093/jcr/ucv098.
- Denise, Marieke Adriaanse, and Kentaro Fujita, *The Routledge International Handbook of Self-Control in Health and Well-Being : Concepts, Theories, and Central Issues* (Abingdon, Oxon; New York, Ny: Routledge, 2018).
- Wilhelm Hofmann et al., "Yes, But Are They Happy? Effects of Trait Self-Control on Affective Well-Being and Life Satisfaction," *Journal of Personality* 82, no. 4 (August 8, 2013): 265–77, https://doi.org/10.1111/jopy.12050.
- Brad J Schoenfeld et al., "Evidence-Based Personal Training Attentional Focus for Maximizing Muscle Development: The Mind-Muscle Connection," n.d., https://bretcontreras.com/wp-content/uploads/Attentional-Focus-for-Maximizing-Muscle-Development-The-Mind-Muscle-Connection.pdf.

27. Reward Yourself

- Extrinsic Rewards:
  - Avinash E Thakare, Ranjeeta Mehrotra, and Ayushi Singh, "Effect of Music Tempo on Exercise Performance and Heart Rate among Young Adults," *International Journal of Physiology, Pathophysiology and Pharmacology* 9, no. 2 (2017): 35–39, https://www.ncbi.nlm.nih.gov/pmc/articles/PMC5435671/.
  - Emma M. Brown et al., "Do Self-Incentives and Self-Rewards Change Behavior? A Systematic Review and Meta-Analysis," *Behavior Therapy* 49, no. 1 (January 2018): 113–23, https://doi.org/10.1016/j.beth.2017.09.004.
  - Katherine L. Milkman, Julia A. Minson, and Kevin G. M. Volpp, "Holding the Hunger Games Hostage at the Gym: An Evaluation of Temptation Bundling," *Management Science* 60, no. 2 (2014): 283–99, https://doi.org/10.1287/mnsc.2013.1784.
  - Denise, Marieke Adriaanse, and Kentaro Fujita, *The Routledge International Handbook of Self-Control in Health and Well-Being : Concepts, Theories, and Central Issues* (Abingdon, Oxon; New York, Ny: Routledge, 2018).
  - TEDx Talks, "Self Control: Dan Ariely at TEDxDuke," You*Tube*, April 18, 2011, https://youtu.be/PPQhj6ktYSo.
- Painful Consequences
  - Mitesh S. Patel et al., "Framing Financial Incentives to Increase Physical Activity Among Overweight and Obese Adults," *Annals of Internal Medicine* 164, no. 6 (February 16, 2016): 385, https://doi.org/10.7326/m15-1635.
  - Xavier Giné, Dean Karlan, and Jonathan Zinman, "Put Your Money Where Your Butt Is: A Commitment Contract for Smoking Cessation," *American Economic Journal: Applied Economics* 2, no. 4 (October 2010): 213–35, https://doi.org/10.1257/app.2.4.213.
  - Heather Royer, Mark Stehr, and Justin Sydnor, "Incentives, Commitments, and Habit

Formation in Exercise: Evidence from a Field Experiment with Workers at a Fortune-500 Company," *American Economic Journal: Applied Economics* 7, no. 3 (July 2015): 51–84, https://doi.org/10.1257/app.20130327.

» Leslie K. John et al., "Financial Incentives for Extended Weight Loss: A Randomized, Controlled Trial," *Journal of General Internal Medicine* 26, no. 6 (January 20, 2011): 621–26, https://doi.org/10.1007/s11606-010-1628-y.

35. People in Your Life

- Shawn Achor, "The Happiness Advantage The Seven Principles of Positive Psychology That Fuel Success and Performance at Work," accessed January 7, 2021, http://ebsp.s3.amazonaws.com/pdf/happinessadvantagen_s.pdf.
- Joelle Elicker, Alison O'Malley, and Paul Levy, "(PDF) Employee Lateness Behavior: The Role of Lateness Climate and Individual Lateness Attitude," *ResearchGate*, October 8, 2008, https://www.researchgate.net/publication/232846898_Employee_Lateness_Behavior_The_Role_of_Lateness_Climate_and_Individual_Lateness_Attitude.
- Lena Hensvik and Peter Nilsson, "Businesses, Buddies and Babies: Social Ties and Fertility at Work," June 30, 2010, https://www.econstor.eu/bitstream/10419/45767/1/635426633.pdf.
- Rose McDermott, James Fowler, and Nicholas Christakis, "Breaking Up Is Hard to Do, Unless Everyone Else Is Doing It Too: Social Network Effects on Divorce in a Longitudinal Sample," *Social Forces; a Scientific Medium of Social Study and Interpretation* 92, no. 2 (December 1, 2013): 491–519, https://www.ncbi.nlm.nih.gov/pmc/articles/PMC3990282.
- Nicholas A. Christakis and James H. Fowler, "The Spread of Obesity in a Large Social Network over 32 Years," *New England Journal of Medicine* 357, no. 4 (July 26, 2007): 370–79, https://doi.org/10.1056/nejmsa066082.
- Ladd Wheeler, "Kurt Lewin," Social and Personality Psychology Compass 2, no. 4 (July 2008): 1638–50, https://doi.org/10.1111/j.1751-9004.2008.00131.x.

36. Supportive Lifestyle

- Sleep
  » A M Williamson and A M Feyer, "Moderate Sleep Deprivation Produces Impairments in Cognitive and Motor Performance Equivalent to Legally Prescribed Levels of Alcohol Intoxication," *Occupational and Environmental Medicine* 57, no. 10 (2000): 649–55, https://doi.org/10.1136/oem.57.10.649.

  » Sanne Nauts and Floor Kroese, "The Role of Self-Control in Sleep Behavior," https://www.researchgate.net/profile/Sanne_Nauts/publication/305208390_Self-control_in_Sleep_Behavior/links/5784adfa08ae37d3af6d8503.pdf, 2017.

  » T. W. Boonstra et al., "Effects of Sleep Deprivation on Neural Functioning: An Integrative Review," *Cellular and Molecular Life Sciences* 64, no. 7–8 (March 8, 2007): 934–46, https://doi.org/10.1007/s00018-007-6457-8.

  » Stephanie M. Greer, Andrea N. Goldstein, and Matthew P. Walker, "The Impact of Sleep Deprivation on Food Desire in the Human Brain," *Nature Communications* 4, no. 1 (August 6, 2013), https://doi.org/10.1038/ncomms3259.

  » Georgina Heath et al., "The Effect of Sleep Restriction on Snacking Behaviour during a Week of Simulated Shiftwork," *Accident Analysis & Prevention* 45 (March 1, 2012): 62–67, https://doi.org/10.1016/j.aap.2011.09.028.

  » Jennifer R. Goldschmied et al., "Napping to Modulate Frustration and Impulsivity: A Pilot

Study," *Personality and Individual Differences* 86 (November 2015): 164–67, https://doi.org/10.1016/j.paid.2015.06.013.

- Exercise
  - » J.J. Clarkson et al., "Perceived Mental Fatigue and Self-Control," *Self-Regulation and Ego Control*, 2016, 185–202, https://doi.org/10.1016/b978-0-12-801850-7.00010-x.
  - » Cassandra J. Lowe, Dimitar Kolev, and Peter A. Hall, "An Exploration of Exercise-Induced Cognitive Enhancement and Transfer Effects to Dietary Self-Control," *Brain and Cognition* 110 (December 2016): 102–11, https://doi.org/10.1016/j.bandc 2016.04.008.
  - » Matthew M Robinson, Val J Lowe, and K Sreekumaran Nair, "Increased Brain Glucose Uptake After 12 Weeks of Aerobic High-Intensity Interval Training in Young and Older Adults," *The Journal of Clinical Endocrinology & Metabolism* 103, no. 1 (October 25, 2017): 221–27, https://doi.org/10.1210/jc.2017-01571.
  - » Kirk I Erickson, Charles H Hillman, and Arthur F Kramer, "Physical Activity, Brain, and Cognition," *Current Opinion in Behavioral Sciences* 4 (August 2015): 27–32, https://doi.org/10.1016/j.cobeha.2015.01.005.

37. Meditation: The Self-Discipline Gym

- Fariss Samarrai, "Doing Something Is Better Than Doing Nothing for Most People, Study Shows," *UVA Today*, July 3, 2014, https://news.virginia.edu/content/doing-something-better-doing-nothing-most-people-study-shows.
- Y.-Y. Tang et al., "Short-Term Meditation Training Improves Attention and Self-Regulation," *Proceedings of the National Academy of Sciences* 104, no. 43 (October 11, 2007): 17152–56, https://doi.org/10.1073/pnas.0707678104.
- Yi-Yuan Tang et al., "Central and Autonomic Nervous System Interaction Is Altered by Short-Term Meditation," *Proceedings of the National Academy of Sciences of the United States of America* 106, no. 22 (June 2, 2009): 8865–8870, https://doi.org/10.1073/pnas.0904031106.
- Adrienne A. Taren, J. David Creswell, and Peter J. Gianaros, "Dispositional Mindfulness Co-Varies with Smaller Amygdala and Caudate Volumes in Community Adults," ed. Allan Siegel, *PLoS ONE* 8, no. 5 (May 22, 2013): e64574, https://doi.org/10.1371/journal.pone.0064574.
- Marieke K. van Vugt and Amishi P. Jha, "Investigating the Impact of Mindfulness Meditation Training on Working Memory: A Mathematical Modeling Approach," *Cognitive, Affective, & Behavioral Neuroscience* 11, no. 3 (July 6, 2011): 344–53, https://doi.org/10.3758/s13415-011-0048-8.
- Repression is not good
  - » Yan Wang, Lixia Yang, and Yan Wang, "Suppression (but Not Reappraisal) Impairs Subsequent Error Detection: An ERP Study of Emotion Regulation's Resource-Depleting Effect," ed. Ingmar HA. Franken, *PLoS ONE* 9, no. 4 (April 28, 2014): e96339, https://doi.org/10.1371/journal.pone.0096339.
  - » Kaitlyn M. Werner and Marina Milyavskaya, "Motivation and Self-regulation: The Role of Want-to Motivation in the Processes Underlying Self-regulation and Self-control," *Social and Personality Psychology Compass*, December 11, 2018, e12425, https://doi.org/10.1111/spc3.12425.
  - » Marleen Gillebaart and Denise T. D. de Ridder, "Effortless Self-Control: A Novel Perspective on Response Conflict Strategies in Trait Self-Control," *Social and Personality Psychology Compass* 9, no. 2 (February 2015): 88–99, https://doi.org/10.1111/spc3.12160.
  - » Denise De Ridder and Marleen Gillebaart, "Lessons Learned from Trait Self-Control in Well-Being: Making the Case for Routines and Initiation as Important Components of Trait

Self-Control," *Health Psychology Review* 11, no. 1 (December 12, 2016): 89–99, https://doi.org/10.1080/17437199.2016.1266275.

» Marina Milyavskaya et al., "Saying 'No' to Temptation: Want-to Motivation Improves Self-Regulation by Reducing Temptation Rather than by Increasing Self-Control.," *Journal of Personality and Social Psychology* 109, no. 4 (2015): 677–93, https://doi.org/10.1037/pspp0000045.

» Daniel M. Wegner et al., "Paradoxical Effects of Thought Suppression.," *Journal of Personality and Social Psychology* 53, no. 1 (1987): 5–13, https://doi.org/10.1037//0022-3514.53.1.5.

- Mindfulness is better for managing cravings

» Ashley E. Mason et al., "Effects of a Mindfulness-Based Intervention on Mindful Eating, Sweets Consumption, and Fasting Glucose Levels in Obese Adults: Data from the SHINE Randomized Controlled Trial," *Journal of Behavioral Medicine* 39, no. 2 (April 1, 2016): 201–213, https://doi.org/10.1007/s10865-015-9692-8.

» Ruth A Baer et al., "Using Self-Report Assessment Methods to Explore Facets of Mindfulness," *Assessment* 13, no. 1 (2006): 27–45, https://doi.org/10.1177/1073191105283504.

» Sunjeev K. Kamboj et al., "Ultra-Brief Mindfulness Training Reduces Alcohol Consumption in At-Risk Drinkers: A Randomized Double-Blind Active-Controlled Experiment," *International Journal of Neuropsychopharmacology* 20, no. 11 (November 1, 2017): 936–947, https://doi.org/10.1093/ijnp/pyx064.

» Jacob D. Meyer et al., "Benefits of 8-Wk Mindfulness-Based Stress Reduction or Aerobic Training on Seasonal Declines in Physical Activity," *Medicine & Science in Sports & Exercise* 50, no. 9 (September 2018): 1850–58, https://doi.org/10.1249/mss.0000000000001636.

» Evelien Van De Veer, Erica Van Herpen, and Hans C. M. Van Trijp, "Body and Mind: Mindfulness Helps Consumers to Compensate for Prior Food Intake by Enhancing the Responsiveness to Physiological Cues," *Journal of Consumer Research* 42, no. 5 (November 17, 2015): 783–803, https://doi.org/10.1093/jcr/ucv058.

» Ashley E. Mason et al., "Reduced Reward-Driven Eating Accounts for the Impact of a Mindfulness-Based Diet and Exercise Intervention on Weight Loss: Data from the SHINE Randomized Controlled Trial," *Appetite* 100 (May 2016): 86–93, https://doi.org/10.1016/j.appet.2016.02.009.

» Ruth A Baer et al., "Using Self-Report Assessment Methods to Explore Facets of Mindfulness," *Assessment* 13, no. 1 (2006): 27–45, https://doi.org/10.1177/1073191105283504.

» Eric Robinson et al., "Eating Attentively: A Systematic Review and Meta-Analysis of the Effect of Food Intake Memory and Awareness on Eating," *The American Journal of Clinical Nutrition* 97, no. 4 (February 27, 2013): 728–42, https://doi.org/10.3945/ajcn.112.045245.

» Stacey Long et al., "Effects of Distraction and Focused Attention on Actual and Perceived Food Intake in Females with Non-Clinical Eating Psychopathology," *Appetite* 56, no. 2 (April 2011): 350–56, https://doi.org/10.1016/j.appet.2010.12.018.

» Suzanne Higgs and Morgan Woodward, "Television Watching during Lunch Increases Afternoon Snack Intake of Young Women," *Appetite* 52, no. 1 (February 2009): 39–43, https://doi.org/10.1016/j.appet.2008.07.007.

» Dolly Mittal et al., "Snacking While Watching TV Impairs Food Recall and Promotes Food Intake on a Later TV Free Test Meal," *Applied Cognitive Psychology* 25, no. 6 (December 5, 2010): 871–77, https://doi.org/10.1002/acp.1760.

» Rose E Oldham-Cooper et al., "Playing a Computer Game during Lunch Affects Fullness, Memory for Lunch, and Later Snack Intake," *The American Journal of Clinical Nutrition* 93, no. 2 (December 8, 2010): 308–13, https://doi.org/10.3945/ajcn.110.004580.

38. Virtues: Your Superpowers

- Loran F. Nordgren, Frenk van Harreveld, and Joop van der Pligt, "The Restraint Bias: How the Illusion of Self-Restraint Promotes Impulsive Behavior," *Psychological Science* 20, no. 12 (December 1, 2009): 1523–1528, https://doi.org/10.1111/j.1467-9280.2009.02468.x.
- Stan Clark, "The Restraint Bias: How Much Self Control Do You Really Have?," https://woodgundyadvisors.cibc.com, n.d., https://woodgundyadvisors.cibc.com/documents/525322/661211/The+Restraint+Bias+How+much+control+do+you+really+have.pdf/8148d938-c990-4154-97cd-efa5240e99b7.
- Loran Nordgren, "Beware the Siren's Song," *Kellogg Insight*, August 3, 2009, https://insight.kellogg.northwestern.edu/article/beware_the_sirens_song.

39. Spirituality: The Deeper Layer

- Julianne Ross, Gerard Kennedy, and Francis Macnab, "The Effectiveness of Spiritual/ Religious Interventions in Psychotherapy and Counselling: A Review of the Recent Literature," 2015, https://www.pacfa.org.au/wp-content/uploads/2012/10/Spiritual-and-Religious-Therapy-Literature-Review.pdf.
- Mehdi Akbari and Sayed Morteza Hossaini, "The Relationship of Spiritual Health with Quality of Life, Mental Health, and Burnout: The Mediating Role of Emotional Regulation," *Iranian Journal of Psychiatry* 13, no. 1 (January 1, 2018): 22–31, https://pubmed.ncbi.nlm.nih.gov/29892314/.
- B. R. Whitehead and C. S. Bergeman, "Coping with Daily Stress: Differential Role of Spiritual Experience on Daily Positive and Negative Affect," *The Journals of Gerontology Series B: Psychological Sciences and Social Sciences* 67, no. 4 (December 22, 2011): 456–59, https://doi.org/10.1093/geronb/gbr136.
- Lydia K. Manning, "Spirituality as a Lived Experience: Exploring the Essence of Spirituality for Women in Late Life," *The International Journal of Aging and Human Development* 75, no. 2 (September 2012): 95–113, https://doi.org/10.2190/ag.75.2.a.
- Brendan T McMahon and Herbert C. Biggs, "Examining Spirituality and Intrinsic Religious Orientation as a Means of Coping with Exam Anxiety," *Vulnerable Groups & Inclusion* 3, no. 1 (January 2012): 14918, https://doi.org/10.3402/vgi.v3i0.14918.
- Kirk A. Johnson, "Prayer: A Helpful Aid in Recovery from Depression," *Journal of Religion and Health* 57, no. 6 (January 30, 2018): 2290–2300, https://doi.org/10.1007/s10943-018-0564-8.
- Amy B. Wachholtz and Usha Sambamthoori, "National Trends in Prayer Use as a Coping Mechanism for Depression: Changes from 2002 to 2007," *Journal of Religion and Health* 52, no. 4 (October 6, 2012): 1356–68, https://doi.org/10.1007/s10943-012-9649-y.
- Abraham Verghese, "Spirituality and Mental Health," *Indian Journal of Psychiatry* 50, no. 4 (2008): 233, https://doi.org/10.4103/0019-5545.44742.